IRON WILL

IRON WILL

*Brunel's Battle to Become the
Greatest Engineer of the Victorian Age*

Toby Strauss

Matador
9 Priory Business Park,
Wistow Road, Kibworth Beauchamp,
Leicestershire. LE8 0RX
Tel: 0116 279 2299
Email: books@troubador.co.uk
Web: www.troubador.co.uk/matador
Twitter: @matadorbooks

ISBN 978 1838594 695

British Library Cataloguing in Publication Data.
A catalogue record for this book is available from the British Library.

Printed and bound in Great Britain by 4edge Limited
Typeset in 11pt Adobe Caslon Pro by Troubador Publishing Ltd, Leicester, UK

Matador is an imprint of Troubador Publishing Ltd

First of all, my thanks go to Isambard Kingdom Brunel for leading the most extraordinary life. In today's complicated, technologically-driven world, polymath engineers like him don't have a role. Experts and specialists rule the day. The more I delved into his life, the more I wanted to base a novel around it. I hope I've done it justice and you enjoy reading about him.

I also want to thank my family: Cressida, Josh, Ella and Ollie, who allowed me the space and time (and in the case of Ollie, lack of timely walks), to bring this to fruition.

Chapter 1

_____

1834

I laid down my quill and blew softly into my hands. God, it was cold. Too cold to concentrate on the columns of figures in front of me, let alone put pen to paper at the speed the chief clerk, Mr Purley, demanded. A sparse figure, he sat bent over his tall writing desk, his porridge-coloured scalp showing through his thinning grey hair. Behind him was hidden a little coal fire, its flickering flames too weak to do more than warm his back, the rest of us wrapped up against the winter chill seeping in from the edges of the room.

I looked down at my brown woollen mitts, lovingly knitted by my mother but old and tired now, frayed from the constant rub against parchment. How I would have liked to take a few sheets of the paper from my desk and roll them into long, thin sausages to seal the window frames.

The door opened and in scurried Ollie, one of the messengers, his worn sandals clacking like castanets on the wooden floorboards. As he sped past me on his way to sit on the edge of the raised

1

platform at Mr Purley's feet, he paused by my desk and whispered, 'Brunel's raising merry hell on the shop floor. He says they haven't got the dimensions of his beams right but the foreman says he's trying to cover up his own mistake.'

I hadn't had any direct dealings with the Brunels, but everyone knew they were difficult. There were often problems in bringing the father's complex designs to life and it fell to Maudslay to keep the peace. At least the father was civil; from what I had heard, the son was just difficult.

Rapid footsteps sounded in the corridor outside and then I heard an angry voice.

'Why can't your men do what they are asked? The drawings were clear enough.'

A few minutes later the bell above the door clanged. Mr Purley nodded to Ollie crouched down beside him, to go and fetch the message. He came back seconds later and whispered into Mr Purley's ear. Mr Purley beckoned me over.

'Mr Maudslay wants you in his office immediately, Bennett. Run along.'

I knew better than to ask why. Mr Purley had always treated me well, but he wouldn't take kindly to me questioning the summons. Slowly, I hauled myself up the stairs to Mr Maudslay's office, my stomach churning as I tried to work out what I might have done wrong.

As I entered the room, I saw the younger Brunel standing beside the desk, rather short and dressed in the dark frock coat, grey worsted trousers, waistcoat and cravat of an English gentleman. He looked as if he took care over what he wore and was, to my eyes at least, stylishly turned out. He stared at me intently as I hovered inside the door wondering what error I might have made. I was so anxious that I couldn't think clearly. Even so, I was pretty sure I hadn't recently dealt with any paperwork with respect to the Brunels.

'Bennett, I would like to introduce you to Mr Brunel. He is keen to secure your services,' said Mr Maudslay. I was stunned, conscious that my mouth hung open as I struggled to find a polite way to ask how he knew who I was. Seeing my confusion, Maudslay swiftly continued, 'That is to say, he needs to bolster the staff in his office and I thought of you.'

Brunel stayed silent, watching me, an amused glint in his eye. He was clearly someone who could quickly leave his anger behind. A good few inches shorter than Maudslay, he was strong featured, with piercing brown eyes below his bushy dark eyebrows. He looked to be in his late twenties, only three or four years older than me, but held himself with far more authority than I could ever muster. When he finally spoke, his voice was steady and clear. Notwithstanding his young age, I could tell he was accustomed to deference.

'You seem surprised. Mr Maudslay told me how you came to work here and I was intrigued.'

I wondered how much of my story Maudslay had shared with him. I felt as a slave must feel, my attributes and qualities being discussed as if I had no feelings or wishes of my own. Perhaps recognising this, Maudslay intervened.

'I have told Mr Brunel that, if you are willing, I could spare you for a few months to help him get his office organised.'

I struggled to speak as I tried to conjure up a polite way to say no. It had been a big leap to join Maudslay's, causing endless ructions at home. I had no desire to work for Brunel, and I wasn't keen to go upsetting any more apple carts with my parents either. Sensing my discomfort, Maudslay asked me to wait outside.

I stood in the corridor, my back against the wall, as if I was waiting outside the headmaster's study. I could see I had handled things badly but I had been taken by surprise. I knew turning down my employer's request wouldn't end well but I was content where I was. I loved what the company did and there was plenty more for me to learn. What's more, who in their right mind would want to work for Brunel? I stared at the door, feeling miserable.

Moments later, it swung open and Brunel emerged. He stopped beside me and sniffed the air.

'Lovely aroma, isn't it?'

Despite my anxiety, I smiled and nodded. I knew instantly what he meant. The smell drifting up from the worked metal in the machine shop was sweet and pungent, like the oil warming in the pan at home before dinner was set cooking. It was one of the things that had attracted me to work at Maudslay's in the first place.

'You know, I never tire of coming here,' he continued. 'It's extraordinary to watch the automated machines carry on their work without need of interference from their minders. Sometimes I imagine those machines with legs, marching unstoppably across the country, causing havoc as they trim everything in their path.'

He laughed a little self-consciously, and suddenly looked more like the young and enthusiastic twenty-something that he and I both were. Keen to get past the awkward moment, I quickly replied, 'The machines are extraordinary, sir, but what I really admire is the skill of the master craftsman at work – filing a bearing until it fits perfectly. It might take half an hour or so of careful labour and concentrated effort to get it just right, but as one of them told me: "If I've done my job properly, it'll last for years."'

He gave me a friendly look and patted me on the shoulder as he headed off down the corridor.

'Don't worry, working for me won't be as bad as you might think.'

'Not at all, sir,' I stammered as I watched him walk away.

I was knocked off balance by this warm exchange; I'd expected him to be as terse as he was reputed to be. I turned to see Maudslay standing in the doorway.

'Come back in, Bennett.'

I followed him in and he shut the door and leant against it, looking tired. He stared at me for a moment before speaking.

'I know that my request has come as somewhat of a surprise, but I need to assist Mr Brunel. He and his father are long-standing customers of this firm.'

'But I am happy here, and things are very busy at the moment.'

'I know, I know, but we will manage, don't worry. I need your help and understanding on this, Bennett. You will still be dealing with your colleagues here, and it would be a great opportunity for you.'

Walking home that evening, I was so deep in thought about how I might avoid working for Brunel that I had no recollection of the journey, and it took me by surprise when I reached the corner of my street. I immediately felt that comforting sense of homecoming as I spied the familiar sight of large tin baths, basins and buckets hanging outside my parents' shop. We stocked all the usual household items: mops, scrubbing brushes and scourers; commonly used ironmongery, such as nuts, bolts, washers and nails; tools, paint, cooking utensils and pans – everything anyone might ever need around the house. As a youngster, I dreamt that I lived in Aladdin's cave. I used to secretly rub the oil lamps in the hope that a genie might appear.

My father was serving a customer. It sounded as if we didn't have what she wanted. I could see gaps on the shelves where stock was running low. I knew the shop was struggling, although my father and I carefully avoided talking about it. At least my wages from Maudslay's should be helping to keep things afloat.

We exchanged the briefest of nods as I walked through to the kitchen and scullery at the back of the shop. I had time for a quick wash and freshen up before supper was served. Meal times were quiet affairs nowadays, the only sounds the rattle of spoon against plate and the occasional slurp as we sat and ate with little to say. Things hadn't been the same since I had taken the job at Maudslay's.

It was only at the end of the meal, as we sat around the kitchen table with our cups of tea and my mother making small talk about what had been happening in the neighbourhood that day – the old family tradition of lingering at the table preserved – that I began to relax. Perhaps that was why I spoke without thinking.

'Mr Maudslay called me into his office today.'

My father looked up sharply.

'Why was that?'

My mother sighed. She looked tired, weary even, her hair grey and scraped back from her wan face. I knew she had been greatly affected by the schism between her only son and her husband. I regretted that I had spoken, but it was too late now. I tried to keep my voice even and calm.

'He asked me if I would go and work for Mr Brunel for a while. I told him I wasn't keen. I am happy at Maudslay's and I have heard tell that the Brunels can be very demanding.'

'Wouldn't it be safer to do what your employer wants, whatever you might think?'

There was an uncomfortable silence. My mother, anxious to avoid an argument, offered more tea. I muttered 'no thanks' while my father said nothing, but stared at me, waiting. The silence dragged on and I felt compelled to answer.

'But I like working at Maudslay's. I have no desire to make a change.'

I looked down to avoid my father's gaze.

'I can't hear you, Joseph. You're mumbling,' he replied, putting down his cup and leaning across the table.

I raised my head and made an effort to push the words out clearly, one by one.

'I was saying that I like working at Maudslay's.'

My father looked at me quizzically, as if he were trying to solve one of the puzzle games we used to do together when I was small. I took a deep breath and explained my real concern.

'At the moment, I have Mr Purley to call upon if I am unsure of what to do. Mr Brunel will be a tough taskmaster and I don't think I yet have enough experience to provide him with satisfactory service.'

I spoke quietly, wishing my father hadn't forced me to admit the truth.

'Why don't you tell Mr Maudslay that?' he replied, leaning back.

'I don't think it will make any difference. He doesn't want to hear about my concerns. He just wants to help out an important client.'

But I was also in his debt. I thought back to my first visit to Maudslay's, a little over five years ago now. Once he realised I was fascinated by all things to do with engineering and the man-made wonders of the modern world, Mr Maudslay had asked one of the apprentices to show me around. His name was Tom, and he had an open and friendly face.

It was nothing like the factories I had visited before, where men worked at firepits or over moulds, hammering metal into shape, or were seated at wooden workbenches working smaller items by hand, as their parents and grandparents had done before them. They would turn out all manner of things that we stocked in the shop – spades, nails, hammers, wire, knives, metal plates and bowls. Maudslay's was different. Instead of being tucked away down an alley and entered through a narrow door in a tumbledown wall, the approach was through imposing iron gates that led into a paved courtyard in front of the factory itself, which had large doors left open to catch the afternoon breeze. Above the doors was a round window throwing light into the large factory beyond. Inside, it was amazingly bright and airy. I was astonished to see there were no pillars supporting the roof. I looked up to see that it was constructed from a ridged grey material I had never seen before but which I now know to be corrugated iron. It was thin but strong enough to span the entire width of the factory and pierced with skylights which added yet more light to the interior.

Men stood at machines painted a uniform grey and laid out in rows down both sides of the central gangway. In the distance I could hear heavy pounding, but all around me was the high-pitched sound of scraping and cutting. It was more like a weaving loft than a metal works, nothing like the hammering and forging I was used to from my father's suppliers,

We were standing close to one of the lathes. I watched a sharp blade slowly chisel a ribbon of metal away from the object being worked, like the peel of an apple being stripped away in one long spiral, the aromatic smell of hot metal filling the air. Cupping his hand around my ear to avoid shouting, Tom explained that Maudslay's had invented a means by which the machine moved the cutting blade along the piece being worked without human intervention.

'Tom, it's so strange to see the machines carry out their tasks unaided; it's as if they have a mind of their own,' I said.

'You're right, it's ingenious, isn't it? All sorts of things have come out of this factory,' said Tom proudly. 'We ... well, they – it was before my time – manufactured the machinery they use down at Portsmouth to make the pulleys for the rigging on navy ships. Did you know that they need 130,000 a year and it used to take over a hundred men to make them by hand? Now, with Maudslay's machines, just ten men can make them all.'

Every sailing ship that crowded the wharfs and jetties along the Thames was festooned with pulleys, which were used to manage everything from the raising of sails to the turning of the rudder. It was hard to imagine how ten men could produce so many, even with the aid of machines.

'That's incredible. I'd never really thought before about how much effort must go into making them,' I replied.

'Maudslay's specialise in those things that others can't do. Let me show you something.'

He took me to the back of the factory where, on a polished mahogany table placed against the wall, was an enormous nut and bolt, its threads gleaming in the light from the window above.

'It's five feet in length and two inches in diameter. The nut is twelve inches long and contains six hundred threads, all cut precisely by machine to match the bolt. Maudslay made it to show what his new processes are capable of.'

'That's remarkable,' I gasped.

I had seen workmen laboriously cutting small nuts and bolts by hand. It was almost inconceivable to think of a machine making such a large component so accurately.

As we walked back through the ranks of machines, each carefully tended by one or two workers, I was struck by how precisely it was all laid out. It was like my mother's sewing box, everything in its rightful place.

'What are they working on now?' I asked.

'We are mainly making steam engines. Almost all of the smaller engines in use around the country are constructed here. We build them for the navy, too.'

We stopped by a different machine which was twice my height. On it sat a large lump of metal, a chisel moving rhythmically up and down, removing a little of the surface on each downward stroke.

'This is the main block for one of the steam engines. Its sides are being cut and shaped by this milling machine so it will fit seamlessly to the rest of the components. We'll go to the foundry now and you can see where we cast the block itself.'

We crossed the yard to a second building where grey smoke was pouring from a tall brick chimney. The foundry was more like some of the factories I was used to – dark and noisy and built on a vast scale. In one corner a furnace glowed bright red, belching out fumes and throwing off sparks as molten metal flowed into moulds before being bashed and melded into shape. The noise reverberated through my body and the soles of my shoes buzzed in time to the thuds of huge hammers working the metal. The metal fizzed and spat as it cooled, its smell acrid, like burnt food or houses on fire.

Tom took me back to the gate and bade me farewell. I stood on the pavement, feeling as if I had been ejected from some magic kingdom, destined to remain forever outside staring at the wondrous sights within. I sighed and walked briskly away.

The visit haunted me over the days that followed, the shop seeming dull and dark by comparison. It would have been easier to put my tour out of my mind, but I couldn't. As I carried out my daily chores, I relived the sights, sounds and smells of that extraordinary place.

A week later, just before supper, there was a loud knocking. I rushed through to the front to find Mr Maudslay standing outside the shop. I was alarmed. What was he doing here?

'Hello Joseph,' he said quietly. 'I can see you are surprised to see me. You told Tom a little about your family shop and it wasn't difficult to track you down.'

'I see, sir,' I said, nodding as if I understood. Of course, I did now understand *how* Mr Maudslay had known where to find me, but I still had no idea *why* he had come. Had I done anything wrong? I racked my brains. Had I forgotten something?

'Thank you again for allowing me to look around the factory. I loved it. The work you are doing there is wonderful!' I blurted out, in the absence of anything more useful to say.

He smiled kindly at me.

'Thank you. Tom told me how much you enjoyed your visit.'

He paused before continuing.

'I don't know if he told you, but we are always on the lookout for promising new apprentices. It was a tradition my father started and I want to carry it on.'

'No, he didn't,' I stammered.

'Well, would you be interested, young man?'

I couldn't believe what I was hearing. A surge of excitement filled with me warmth, only to be replaced with a cold lump in the pit of my stomach when I thought about how my parents would react to the proposal.

'I would, sir, but my parents – my father in particular – may be less keen.'

'Let's go and ask them, shall we?'

Wishing I was somewhere else, I showed Mr Maudslay through into the back parlour. My parents were sitting in their usual places in the old armchairs on either side of the fire, my father reading a book and my mother working at one of her never-ending cross-stitches. They both jumped to their feet, my mother brushing her hands down the sides of her apron, my father dropping his pipe into the ashtray beside him and holding out his hand. They looked at me, waiting to hear what this well-dressed stranger might want at this hour of the evening. I realised that I was going to have to make some introductions.

'Father, this is Mr Maudslay. Mr Maudslay, Mr Bennett.'

I trailed to a halt, unsure what to say next. Luckily Maudslay took over the conversation.

'Mr Bennett, Mrs Bennett, delighted to make your acquaintance. I met your son the other day when he passed by my factory and I had one of my apprentices show him around.'

'Oh yes?' said my father, looking bewildered.

'One of the advantages of having been in business for many years is that you get to be a good judge of character. I am sure it's the same for you with your shop. I may only have met your son briefly, but I would like to offer him an apprenticeship, a clerical job in the office. As long as he stays five years, I will fund it.'

I was astonished. Everyone knew that apprentices – or rather their parents – were expected to pay for an opportunity like this.

'But he has a job here at the shop,' my father said, continuing to look nonplussed.

I looked from one to the other, sure the opportunity was about to vanish before my eyes.

'I know this is all a bit of a surprise. Why don't you take a few days to talk it over with Joseph and then we can speak again.'

I quickly moved to see him out, thanking him again for coming to see us.

'Don't worry,' he said as he left. 'I expect that your father will come round once he's had a chance to think about it.'

It was all very well for him to say that, I thought, as he got up into his gig, his driver waiting patiently outside. He didn't have to stay and deal with my father. I watched until he disappeared around the corner, then slowly made my way back into the shop.

My father jumped up as soon as I came back into the parlour. 'What was all that about?'

It was hard to know where to begin. I tried to explain: 'I went to see the factory because I had read about a lock that couldn't be picked. Someone told me he had made it, but it turned out it was his father.'

My father shook his head and looked at me with incomprehension.

'I have no idea what you mean or why he turned up on our doorstep and offered you a job.'

I took a deep breath and described how I had come to visit the factory.

'I am as surprised by the offer of a job as you are, Father,' I finished. 'I didn't ask for one, but I must admit it sounds exciting. The work they do is incredible.'

He stooped over the fireplace and lightly tapped his pipe against the brickwork to free the spent tobacco. When he straightened up, I was shocked by the cold look he gave me.

'Your place is here, Joseph. We've got the shop to run. It's a family business. We need your help and this is your future. Who knows what might happen if you join Maudslay's? They could go bust and you'd be out on your ear in months.'

'But father,' I said, trying but failing to keep my voice calm. My hands trembled and my voice matched it. I had never sought to defy my father before. 'I really want to do this. There is an engineering revolution going on and Maudslay's are at the heart of it. Steam engines and new materials and methods will change the world. It will make life easier for everyone and bring new prosperity and new jobs.'

I surprised myself by banging the table to emphasise my point. I believed what I was saying with all the surety that a young adult deploys in support of their beliefs. I could have been reading from one of the pamphlets promoting some new scheme that I read so avidly.

'That's enough,' said my father curtly. 'We won't talk of this anymore.'

I stormed upstairs and threw myself on my bed. I realised I was crying and hated my father for it. We had a close relationship and this was the first time we had fallen out over anything more serious than a broken dish or a failure to help my mother with the chores.

It was perhaps fifteen minutes later when I heard the creak of a floorboard outside my room. I assumed it would be my mother coming to comfort me, but it was my father. He spoke quietly from the doorway.

'I don't agree with it, but I can see it's what you want and I won't stand in your way.' He took a couple of steps into the room, leant over, clumsily patted me on the shoulder and turned and left.

Despite that brief moment of tenderness, the atmosphere in our house from then on was very different. I now felt more like a lodger than part of the family. My father and I were excessively courteous to each other, asking politely how our respective days had been.

That was five years ago, but the memory was still raw. My father brought me back to the present when he stood up, took down his pipe from the shelf to the side of the fireplace and gently tamped the tobacco down ready to light it.

'I am sure you don't want to hear this, Joseph, but you wanted to be part of the "brave new world", as you called it. You've made your bed and now you are going to have to lie in it. You are going to have to do what your employer wants.'

I stared at him miserably, wondering how much his advice was coloured by his disappointment that I hadn't chosen to stay working with him. He leant down and lit a taper from the fire, held it over the pipe and sucked hard. His face was stern, but grew indistinct as a cloud of smoke enveloped him.

'If you don't want to put Mr Maudslay in the same position as I was, you will have to do it.'

My eyes stung and I felt tears well up. Cross with myself for showing weakness, I got to my feet and faced him.

'I know I upset you, Father, in wanting to take the job at Maudslay's in the first place, but it's not fair of you to bring that up now. I let you down then but this isn't the same thing at all. I am worried I won't do the job properly and Mr Maudslay will regret having put me forward.'

My father sighed and shook his head.

'It's about time you grew up and shouldered your responsibilities.'

I was annoyed that I had shared my dilemma. All it had done was reopen old wounds. I stood up.

'This conversation isn't really getting us anywhere,' I said stiffly. 'I'll say goodnight.'

I stomped upstairs, leaving my mother shaking her head sadly as she slowly picked up the teacups and took them over to the sink.

I lay on my bed, angry with myself. How could I have allowed myself to get into a disagreement with my father so easily? He had let me do what I wanted, to leave the shop and join Maudslay's. I knew how much I owed him. Why do your parents always bring out the worst in you?

Two days later, I received a short note summoning me to Brunel's office on the ground floor of his home on Parliament Street, near Westminster Abbey and close to St James's Park. I arrived early so walked down Downing Street, crossed to the park and took the winding path around the lake. It was a clear, crisp winter's morning and the sun was shining brightly. The scent of damp grass filled the air as the dew was lifted by the start of a new day.

Ladies and gentlemen of leisure were strolling past the newly flowering crocuses and chatting about the happenings of the night before, the gossip of the day or their plans for the next. It wasn't a world I was familiar with, but I was made up in my Sunday best of top hat, dark frock coat and trousers. So, while I felt awkward, my garb fitted in with my surroundings and any glances that came my way slid easily past me and on to other more interesting vistas.

I walked around the lake, oblivious to the gardeners' carefully crafted flowerbeds and borders. Thoughts swirled around in my head. I was happy with my job... I didn't want to work for Brunel ... what would Maudslay say – or do – if I said no? I could go back to working in the shop but the thought weighed me down, as if dark clouds had suddenly filled the sky. I sighed deeply. Did I really have any option but to accept the job?

I checked my pocket watch frequently, aware of Mr Maudslay's parting words about the importance of his relationship with the Brunels, and not wishing to be late. When it was a few minutes to the interview, still no further ahead in my search for the best way forward, I made my way back to Parliament Street, walked up the tiled steps and rang the doorbell of the handsome four-storey Georgian house. The footman took me through the hallway, past the gleaming mahogany bannister that spiralled up into the upper reaches of the house, and knocked on a door on the right, gesturing for me to enter.

'Ah yes, the young man from Maudslay's! I'll be with you in a few moments,' Brunel called out from behind his desk.

He waved me towards the window seat that spanned the far end of the room. I carefully moved a pile of papers out of the way, sat down and studied the room as he stayed at his desk finishing off some paperwork. The office was fitted out within what would once have been the drawing room. The lower parts of the walls were lined with dark wood panelling, reminding me of the barbers' shops I used to peer into as a boy. The sun shone strongly through the windows, dust sparkling in the shafts of light reflecting off the wood. Lining one wall were row upon row of narrow drawers, which I assumed held plans for Brunel's various projects. Above the drawers were pigeon-holes, and sandwiched in between, a wooden counter ran the length of the room.

The pigeon-holes were full of documents and papers. Drawings were scattered on the counter and on Brunel's desk, all suggesting to me the need for clerical assistance. Given the height of the many piles of paper, I imagined a lot of time was spent in this room searching for lost documents. Above the pigeon-holes were mounted marble busts of famous engineers of the age: Telford, Stephenson and Brunel's father, Marc. On the opposite wall were bookshelves built on both sides of the fireplace, filled with an eclectic mix of titles: many on engineering and mathematics, but I also spied classical literature, plays and poetry. In the centre of the room was Brunel's imposing leather-topped desk, and further along a pair of smaller plain wooden desks, presumably for his clerks.

His manner was serious and he exuded energy and vigour as he worked his way through a stack of papers, the room filled with the scratching of his pen and his quiet but intense muttering as he annotated them or boldly struck through a section. I felt increasingly nervous. On his desk was one of those little brass bells you often see in shops; thumping the top causes the bell to ping to call the shopkeeper from the back of the store. Brunel used it to summon the footman each time he had finished a missive. Compared with the calm and ordered progress I was used to under Mr Purley, it seemed there wasn't a minute to lose before Brunel's instructions must be acted upon. My sense of unease was steadily growing, sweat trickling down my back inside my heavy formal clothes.

After ten minutes or so, I would think – I didn't look at my pocket watch for fear of appearing rude – Brunel called me across to a simple wooden chair on the other side of his desk. He took a moment to study me carefully and I made sure to hold his gaze, while trying to avoid appearing impertinent.

'I still have some letters to finish, but I have kept you waiting long enough. Why don't you start by telling me about your background and what makes you want to come and work for me.'

He picked up his pen and started to write. After a few moments, he looked up and with a touch of impatience waved for me to begin. It was disconcerting to be invited to speak while he continued to work at his correspondence. Despite my misgivings, I had assumed I would be greeted as a saviour, whereas instead I found myself justifying my presence.

'I am sorry, sir. I was under the impression that you were in need of someone to help with the increase in work.'

'I am, I am,' said Brunel, without raising his head or ceasing to write. 'But I need people who share my vision and commitment.'

He paused, his pen suspended in mid-air.

'It was good of Maudslay to put you forward,' he said, looking me in the eye, 'but I won't take on anyone that hasn't decided for themselves they want to work with me.' He pinged his bell once more and as the footman arrived he stood up and ushered me towards the door. 'Go away and have a think about it. If you are interested, come back and see me on Friday.'

Seconds later, I found myself standing outside the house, wondering what I was going to say to Maudslay. I took a deep breath and decided a rapid walk to the Lambeth factory would be the best way to calm my nerves and clear my head. I reached the landing steps to find a queue waiting to cross the river. As I looked out over the water, I realised all I could do was tell him the truth.

The river stank today.

'A slow tide always makes the river smell,' said an old fellow in a tattered coat standing in front of me, glancing anxiously at the rickety cage at his feet where a pair of scrawny hens were peeking out through twigs knotted together with twine. A clump of fat and gristle from the tanneries floated past, awash in a tangle of dead fish and meat scrapings from the market up-river. I held a handkerchief to my nose and scrambled aboard the wherry. The two boatmen pulled hard at the oars as we set off towards the other bank.

The factory was a short distance from the landing. As soon as I arrived back, I asked to see Mr Maudslay.

'How did it go?' he asked, beaming expectantly.

I explained what had happened. He frowned, looking out the window at the grey clouds overhead.

'I thought I made it clear to you that it was in the company's interests that you took this role.' He sighed, and turning back to me said, 'Typical of Brunel. Why does everything have to be so difficult with that man? You need to go back to see him and persuade him that you can think of nothing more appealing than to work for him. And a word of advice: you are going to have to mean it.'

He waved me away, leaving me to curse the vagaries of employers as I headed back to my desk.

It was later that day that Purley came over to my desk.

'Bennett, I hear you might be going to work for Brunel. If you want to understand a bit more about him and his father, it's worth a visit to the Thames Tunnel over at Rotherhithe. It was a baptism of fire for young Brunel,' he said.

I had read about the tunnel. London was the biggest port in the world, but downstream from London Bridge there was no way of crossing the river except by boat. Marc Brunel, Isambard's father, had invented a tunnelling shield, which was built by Maudslay's. It was designed to enable a tunnel to be dug through the soft clay on which London was built. However, the work had been bedevilled by slow progress and regular floods; when half-completed yet another flood had caused serious damage and the end of the tunnel had been bricked up. Now its only purpose was to provide an excursion under the river for sightseers.

That evening, still wishing I could think of a way to avoid Brunel's employ, I reluctantly made my way to the octagonal building that had been erected alongside the access shaft. After paying my penny due, I entered a small rotunda with a glazed dome and a blue and white marble mosaic floor; weaving my way through stands selling gifts, pamphlets and refreshments, I reached an opening in the far wall, which led to a large chamber.

I descended a few steps to a viewing platform and could now see down to the circular base of the shaft. Organ music reverberated around the chamber, as if we were in church. The walls of the shaft were finished in stucco and hung with paintings illustrating the efforts that had brought the project to this stage: men working at the tunnel face, steam engines pumping, dignitaries smiling as they gathered to celebrate the optimism of the start. On the far side of the chamber, I could make out the entrance to the tunnel. Lit by shadowy flickering candles its brickwork glowed in shades of amber, like an ancient Persian rug caught in the firelight.

I resumed my downward journey and eventually reached the bottom of the shaft some eighty feet below the entrance. Once again there were all sorts of sideshows aimed at relieving visitors of their money: Egyptian clairvoyants, jugglers and dancing monkeys to name a few. The cacophony of their cries as they promoted their offerings and the chatting of the crowds echoing around the

walls of the chamber made me faintly nauseous. Although the
entertainment did not appeal to my sensibilities, I could see why
the attraction was so popular with Londoners and tourists alike. It
was nothing if not atmospheric. It was like a fairground brought to
life beneath the ground.

The tunnel consisted of two glorious arches, each containing
a roadway fourteen feet wide and twenty-two high, with a three-
feet-wide pedestrian pathway to the side. The smell was of brick
and burning candles. A breeze blew gently through and the air
seemed neither damp nor fetid despite all I had read about the
floods and the constant fear of water that the tunnellers had faced.
As I made my way into the tunnel, every twenty yards or so were
arches joining the two roadways, and within each of these were
little gift shops offering all manner of curios and souvenirs.

Tapestries and purple velvet hangings decorated the walls, as
you might see in a painting of a medieval castle, while a steadily
moving throng crowded the avenues. It was as if they were taking
an early evening promenade through one of the new shopping
arcades in the most fashionable parts of London, pausing at each
of the stalls to admire the goods on offer. Most were staffed by
pretty young ladies seeking to catch the visitor's eye and entice
them into buying something.

As I approached the end of the tunnel, I saw a large mirror covering
the wall in front of me, reflecting the light and creating an illusion
of endless corridors populated by the same set of shadowy figures
heading down tunnels to nowhere. I found a small alcove, thankfully
bereft of any stalls, or indeed people, and paused to contemplate what
it must have taken to build this grand passageway under the river.
All I had read suggested it had been a heroic endeavour: Brunel and
his father pushing on against all odds, men losing their lives as they
desperately sought to hold back the river's waters.

I looked up at the ceiling, spanned by a wide arch, its red
bricks squeezed tightly together in rows that disappeared off

down the tunnel like a well-drilled army marching in formation. I had a vision of the bricks bursting inward, the force of the water sending the horrified sightseers flying, all desperate to get out as the structure collapsed around us. I leant against the wall, feeling a little dizzy. I took a deep breath, then another, forcing myself to calm down. Of course it was all secure now. I was being ridiculous.

I made my way out, walking slowly, keen to restore my sense of equanimity. I stopped in front of one of the paintings, noting the look of pride in the eyes of the men as they posed in front of their handiwork. That could be me, bringing a whole new project to life, making a difference to people's lives, admired for what I'd achieved.

As I gazed at the picture, I suddenly saw things differently. The likes of Brunel were creating a future where people and goods would be able to travel speedily and easily around the country. He had just been appointed chief engineer on the proposed Great Western Railway, which would run from Bristol to London, changing society in ways I didn't yet understand. From all I had read, I sensed that Brunel was at the centre of this, whereas Maudslay was only a supporting actor, providing the tools and equipment. I ran back up the stairs, wondering what had happened to the sense of adventure that had led to me joining Maudslay's. Maybe it was time to take a different path. Perhaps my destiny should and would be to help Brunel bring his vision to life.

I reached the open air and walked to the river's edge. As I looked across to the other bank, I thought about the tunnel below me, reaching out under the grey waters. What a remarkable effort, and how sad was its altered purpose, like an old Shakespearean theatre converted to musical hall entertainment. I smiled at the thought that perhaps I could play some small part in ensuring that a similar fate didn't befall the railway.

Chapter 2

A week later I returned to Parliament Street. This time, Brunel immediately put down his pen and instructed me to take the seat in front of his desk.

'You asked why I would want to work for you, Mr Brunel,' I said without preamble as I sat down.

'Indeed I did young man,' he said, smiling.

'In all honesty, I didn't. The day Mr Maudslay called me to his office, I was taken by surprise. I was flattered, of course, but I wasn't sure what was required and it was presented as somewhat of a fait accompli.'

'I understood that was the case,' replied Brunel. 'That's why I wasn't comfortable taking you on.'

'Since then I have had a chance to think about it. I still don't know exactly what the job will entail, but I do know that Maudslay's provide the spades but aren't digging up the gold.'

He looked at me with interest.

I knew I wasn't explaining myself well and felt nervous, realising now how much I actually wanted this job. I tried again.

'I've been very happy at Maudslay's, but I have come to understand that the excitement and satisfaction I experience there doesn't come from building machine parts alone. It comes from working directly with those who are taking the risks and bringing it all to fruition – people like you, the engineering pioneers.'

I paused for breath, aware that I had lost my composure and was almost babbling as I sought to persuade him.

'Hmm, I will think about—'

'Sir, I don't know if Mr Maudslay told you about how I came to work for him?' I interrupted, knowing this was likely going to be my only opportunity to make an impression. I was striving to get my voice under control.

Brunel frowned, but asked me to continue.

'I had read in one of those new mechanics magazines about a special lock called the Bramah, after its inventor Joseph Bramah. You might have heard of it?'

Brunel nodded brusquely. He didn't suffer fools gladly, but he looked like I had just treated him as one.

'Yes, it's an extraordinary piece of work. Finely made.'

I blushed. Brunel had probably been given a tour of the lock's intricate mechanisms by its designer, whereas I had only been able to gaze at it through the shop window. Its bronze face had glowed in the light of the candles lit to brighten up the shopfront as the evening drew in. The workings were partly obscured by a velvet cloth, I suppose to avoid people seeing the secrets of its construction. A complicated key hung on hooks below it. *Two hundred guineas to the man that can pick this lock, many have tried and none have succeeded* proclaimed a sign in front of the display. I had yearned to hold it my hands and examine the mechanism. I could see that each component was meticulously crafted. How many hours and what machinery could produce such finely worked parts?

'I went to see it in Bramah's shop window on Denmark Street,' I said. 'I was overwhelmed, to be honest. I couldn't understand how anyone could produce anything so perfectly made. A runner told me that although Mr Bramah had designed it Mr Maudslay was the only craftsman good enough to actually make it.'

'In fact, it was Mr Maudslay's father,' replied Brunel, his voice warmer now.

'Yes, sir. I found that out when I made a point of passing by the Maudslay factory a few days later. I got caught by the gatekeeper wandering back and forth trying to get a glimpse of what was going on inside. Then Mr Maudslay arrived. I was lucky that he chose to take an interest in me rather than calling the peelers – the gatekeeper certainly wanted to.'

Brunel pulled out his watch and glanced at it.

I rushed on.

'The reason I mention all that, sir, is that I have been fascinated by all things to do with engineering since I was a small boy growing up in an ironmonger's shop. What I was trying to say just now is that I have only recently come to understand that the real excitement lies with people like you. You set the standards, you decide what will get built.'

Brunel looked thoughtfully at me for a few moments. I thought he might still say 'no' but I stopped myself from arguing my case further. I knew it would begin to sound desperate.

'Alright,' he said. 'You've made your case. I am willing to give it a go.'

I exhaled deeply, not realising that I had been holding my breath awaiting his answer.

'You won't regret it, sir.' I said, struggling to avoid grinning like an idiot as I digested the news.

However, he hadn't finished. He held up his hand to pause my thanks.

'I have one more, rather unusual, condition. As you can see, I have a huge amount to do to bring the new railway to life, and I intend to take on more projects. My team will have no time for a life outside work. If you join me, it will be on the understanding that you will devote yourself entirely to my service. In particular, there would be no time for the distractions of a wife and family.'

I stared at him. On the one hand it didn't seem a high price to pay, as I didn't know any women, apart from my mother and a few of the shop's customers. I had little in the way of savings and could see no prospect of acquiring a wife. But, on the other hand, it was such an odd request. Presumably it meant that I would have no life at all while working for Brunel. Would he be as unreasonable with his employees as he was with his suppliers, as I had seen at Maudslay's? I had to make a decision. I knew that Brunel's patience was short and I had no desire to return to face Mr Maudslay after being sent packing again. Who knew, he might also send me on my way. I nodded my assent.

I went straight home and slipped through the back door into our simple kitchen where my mother was standing in front of the range preparing the evening meal. She turned, her smile lighting up her face. As I whispered my news she frowned slightly.

'Let me tell Father,' she said in a low voice. 'I know he was advocating you take the job, but it would be nice to avoid the possibility of stirring up another scene like the other night.'

She turned back to her cooking but called quietly over her shoulder, 'Congratulations, though, my dear.'

'I'm not sure congratulations are in order,' I said. 'I am still worried that I won't be good enough for him.'

'But they chose to ask you to do it, Joseph,' she replied. 'That's a vote of confidence, isn't it?'

A week later I packed my few possessions away and bid my farewells at Maudslay's. As I walked out of the works for the last time, I stopped at the gate and looked back. I vividly remembered my first visit; the same smell of worked metal and warm oil filled the air. The hostility of our first encounter long gone, the old gatekeeper and I clasped hands as we wished each other well.

Despite my show of enthusiasm in front of Brunel, I now felt sick, as if it was all a ghastly mistake. It was the same feeling I had had when I had joined Maudslay's when I was just eighteen years old – a fear of the unknown. As I crossed the street and made my way home, my pencils, quills, ink and drawing instruments in my satchel, I felt as if I had been cut adrift with no easy route back to shore.

The next day I arrived at my new workplace promptly at seven-thirty. The house was bigger than I had imagined from my brief glimpses on my previous visits and Brunel was waiting to show me around and introduce me to his domestic staff. We began by descending to the basement. It was dark and smoky and I was fascinated by the network of small rooms, each with a different purpose: the pantry for storing meat, the kitchen with a newfangled gas stove for cooking, the wine cellar, the servants' hall complete with a dining table five times larger than the one at home, and rooms for the butler and housekeeper.

At the shop, my mother and father got by with a little part-time help. Brunel had a butler, a housekeeper, two footmen, two maids, and a cook and her assistant. He told me he would soon have twenty or even twenty-five people working to bring the GWR to life. Even so, it seemed incredibly extravagant when, for now, there was just Brunel and a handful of his staff to cater for.

On the first floor, the rooms had been stripped of furniture, and desks lined the walls, the elaborately decorated coving and cornicing looking somewhat out of place.

'This floor and downstairs is where the real work's done,' Brunel said. 'Up above is just my bedroom and the servants' quarters.'

There were ten desks, of which four were occupied. He pointed at the first two.

'These are my senior engineering assistants.'

Before Brunel had a chance to introduce him, a man perhaps ten years older than me jumped up and bounced out from behind his desk.

'I'm John Hammond,' he said, shaking my hand vigorously. 'Welcome to the mad-house!'

'Bennett. Joseph Bennett,' I replied, smiling gratefully into his twinkling eyes. They looked full of mischief and I wondered what he got up to when not at work.

'And over here is William Gravatt,' said Brunel.

William got up carefully and shook my hand. He spoke slowly and a little ponderously as he introduced himself and I found myself slowing my own speech in return.

Back in his office, Brunel pointed me to one of the clerk's desks that I had seen on my previous visits and left me to it. For a few minutes I sat reeling from the grandeur of the house and Brunel's expansive domestic arrangements but soon decided I must start work and that I should begin with what Purley had recommended, which was to familiarise myself with Brunel's workload by creating a list of all the projects underway.

I was completely engrossed in the task when, at twelve o'clock, he surprised me by pinging his bell.

'Come along!' he called as he sprang up from behind his desk. 'Lunchtime!'

I dutifully followed him into the dining room, even though I would have felt more comfortable with the sandwich hidden in my satchel beneath my desk. At Maudslay's we clerks ate a simple lunch of a sandwich or a pasty, or occasionally wandered outside to one of the street vendors for a tasty snack of fried fish or penny pies. Here it looked like we were to be waited upon by the footmen and butler.

Brunel took the chair at the head of the table, telling me to sit to his left. We were joined by Hammond and Gravatt and two of their deputies. As I took my seat, I looked around the room. Large oil paintings hung on the walls, which seemed to depict scenes from the theatre. A white marble fireplace dominated the room with an ornate gilt mirror set above it. The bay window provided a panoramic view of the street outside and across to the park opposite. I could hear the clip clop of horses passing by below, and I could see people strolling along the path by the lake, just as they had the day I had first come here.

A large grandfather clock stood tall and dark in the corner. The table was set with an array of glassware and linen. Most alarming was the wide variety of silver cutlery arranged in front of me. There were four pieces to each side, with more set out across the top. What could they all be for? In what order should I use them? As each course was served, I watched to see which items my fellow diners picked out. I had never before tipped a soup bowl away from me, but that's what I did as I carefully aped the habits of my new colleagues.

'So, Hammond, how are things progressing?' Brunel asked.

'The team are doing a good job pulling together the specifications for the works at Slough. Of course, we will be stymied at the London end until the route is finalised.'

Even though it was my first day, I understood what they were discussing. Brunel had already told me that Hammond and his team were managing the preparatory work on the eastern end of the railway from Swindon into London.

'Are you seeing much interest from contractors?' he continued, swallowing his soup at a pace that was rapidly draining his bowl.

'Yes, absolutely. From old established firms and some new to railway work.'

'Excellent, excellent!'

He turned to look at me.

'Eat up, Bennett. We haven't got all day.'

'Yes sir,' I replied, indicating to the footman he could take my part-finished bowl. Every time I had tried to sup faster, I had found myself making loud slurping noises. I didn't fancy having the whole table listen to me finish.

'Hammond, do you want to go to a play tonight?' Brunel asked. 'Everyone is talking about the one at the Strand called *Rifleshot*. Have you heard of it?'

It was a surprise to me that Brunel could find time for the theatre. I would have thought he'd have been too tied up with his professional life to enjoy such a pastime. However, I was pleased my guess about the subject of the paintings might be correct. The closest I had been to a theatrical performance was watching the comedy sketches at the local music hall. I kept my head down, dreading that I might be asked if I would like to join them, or even worse, what my favourite play might be. I had thought I'd be out of my depth working for Brunel, and that's exactly how I felt.

'I saw a review in *The Times* the other day. Is it the one that has a group of Red Indians enacting a sacrifice?' replied Hammond.

'Yes, that's the one. Although I don't think they end up sacrificing anyone, at least not on stage!' laughed Brunel.

The meal seemed to last an age as I desperately sought to avoid embarrassment. I assumed we were reaching the end as I picked up the last of the cutlery in front of me. I began to congratulate myself on having emerged from the ordeal unscathed when I caught sight of the butler, Bourton. He was standing behind Brunel and I realised that he had been watching me for a while. He was tall and gaunt, with sunken cheeks and pasty white skin that made you wonder whether he might be harbouring some deeply held sickness. He stood tall and erect, his clothing so starched, formal and meticulously arranged that it appeared as if it were holding him up rather than the other way around. I heard later that he had arrived here from a much grander house, and that the other servants often gossiped about what had led him to take such a step down in circumstances. A smile played across his lips and I saw he had been smirking at my difficulties. I looked down as I felt myself starting to redden. I wondered what he would be saying about me to the other servants.

As I made my way from the dining room, Hammond caught my elbow and steered me into a quiet corner of the hall.

'Don't worry about Bourton. I saw his face. He is a snob. Brunel isn't.' He paused and chuckled before continuing, 'Well, maybe at times he can be, but he values the quality of your work above all else. Focus on your job and don't worry about all this.' He waved at the elegant plasterwork around us.

I nodded gratefully, but on each of the following days we followed the same lunchtime routine and I cannot say that I relaxed very much. As the menu changed, each new dish seemed to require its own particular method of consumption.

A few days later, around mid-morning, I realised that everyone else was out and I would be the only person present in the office at lunchtime. I called Bourton in and suggested to save effort I had my meal downstairs.

'It would also be more sociable than eating up here on my own,' I said.

'Oh no, sir. The servants wouldn't like it.'

I frowned. 'You know, Bourton, I've only just been elevated to this position; I was brought up in a shop. I would be happy to dine with you and the rest of the servants.'

He took a deep breath and I would say that he drew himself up to be even taller, but given how ramrod straight he already was, it must have been a figment of my imagination.

'I am sorry, sir, but they just wouldn't feel comfortable with you being there. Each of us has our own position to maintain,' he concluded with a smile that didn't reach his eyes. He bowed his head slightly and backed out of the room.

Lunch that day was a gloomy affair. I slowly munched my way through the courses, the steady funereal tick of the grandfather clock marking the slow passage of time. I wished I could break with protocol and fetch a book from the office to peruse while eating, but I didn't want to risk enduring the disapproving look I would get from Bourton that would undoubtedly linger with me well past lunch. I couldn't believe that I had allowed him to overrule me. How would I ever be capable of doing this job? I thought miserably.

The footmen came and went, bringing a single tray and plate each time. All the while Bourton stood behind me, gesturing discreetly when my plate should be cleared and the next course fetched. It was ludicrous. I realised it was a ritual that dowagers and other wealthy singletons up and down the land must suffer day after day.

'I will take lunch out today,' I said to Bourton the next time I knew I would be dining alone.

I found myself drifting aimlessly around the park and along the river, using up time that I could ill afford, with work clogging up my desk. The gentry, office workers and nursemaids with prams strolled slowly along or sat on park benches chatting, enjoying a brief interlude in their day. I felt strangely solitary as the lunchtime crowds pushed past me, hurrying from one place to another, as if I were the only one who was single but purposeless, a lone duck looking around for a companion, bobbing in the stream of people.

It did give me time to think, though. Brunel's office was chaotic. I spent many hours searching through stacks of documents, looking for papers he had requested, while he burst in and out at various times of the day, dropping yet more papers on my desk. When that was filled to overflowing, he left them on the spare clerk's desk alongside mine – still unused, as I had not yet had time to hire a junior. When he was working, he brooked no interruption or noise, so I was forced into quietly leafing through the stacks, trying to find what he had asked for.

I worked on, suffering from raging headaches, the tension of this disordered life causing me palpitations. At times I felt so trapped by my circumstances that I couldn't breathe. I couldn't go back to Maudslay's and had nowhere else to turn. I could hardly leave after a few weeks in the job. Returning to work in the family shop seemed the only choice. It was contemplating this that finally steeled me to have a conversation with Brunel. I rehearsed it in my mind: 'Sir, I can't continue like this.' Too aggressive. 'Perhaps we could spend a little time reviewing how we work together?' Too wishy washy.

It was mid-March, three weeks after I had begun working for him and on a day when he seemed calmer and less preoccupied than usual, that I coughed, then stammered, 'Mr Brunel, sir. I wonder if you have a moment?'

He looked up at me.

'Yes?' he replied in a tone that made it clear that he had little time for niceties and I had better get to the point.

I swallowed, and trying not to mumble – which I knew from experience would cause him to bark, 'Speak up, man!' – began.

'Sir, I believe that there are better ways we could organise the office.'

'What did you have in mind?'

It was said in a neutral tone, but nevertheless I had to clear my throat twice before I could respond.

'I think it would be best if for a week or so I devoted myself to indexing all of the papers in the office… It would mean that I wouldn't be able to deal with anything else during that time,' I added nervously.

He nodded. 'Of course. I understand. Do what you think's best. That's why I employed you.'

He looked back down to the papers he was studying and I scurried back to my desk, still sweating but relieved and excited. I reflected that we are so often our own worst enemies. I had been waiting for the right moment to seek his permission, while Brunel assumed I would just get on and establish the office patterns that even he recognised were required. That was indeed why he had employed me.

'Sir, there was one other matter I wanted to raise with you,' I said, emboldened by our exchange.

'Yes?' he replied, looking up wearily.

'When I am the only one present in the office, it seems wasteful to take my dinner upstairs. I think it would be easier to eat with the servants.'

'I am not sure that would be entirely appropriate.'

'At home, sir, I have my meals with my parents at the kitchen table. It would make me feel more comfortable.'

He had been working on a drawing but stopped, laid down his pencil and looked me directly in the eye.

'Bennett, a word of advice. I have learned in life that how you are perceived and who you are eventually become the same thing.'

I held his gaze but felt my face redden.

'I am not sure I understand, sir.'

'I am young and yet I have been entrusted with this immense responsibility. Why is that, do you think?'

I knew that Brunel was very young to have been given the responsibilities he had, but I had not given much thought as to why, or what had enabled this to happen.

'I don't know, sir,' I said, rather lamely, wishing I had never raised the issue of my dining arrangements in the first place.

'It's because I know how to act the part. People need to think you already are the person you want to be.'

I nodded. I understood the point he was making, even though it wasn't how I had succeeded in my career, such as it was. It was on my way home, thinking that I couldn't bear another solitary dining session but with Brunel's words echoing in my head, that I came up with a better option. There was a part I could act. I could play the role of a member of Brunel's team too busy for a mundane matter like lunch.

I summoned Bourton the following day, when I knew I would be facing yet another solitary lunchtime, and told him I would have a plate of cold cuts at my desk.

'Are you quite sure, sir? Mr Brunel and other gentlemen I have been accustomed to serving always take time for a proper lunch, however busy they are.'

'Well, in my case I am afraid that I just have too much to do.'

I returned busily to my work and waved him away. Inside I was seething, wishing I had the courage to confront him. How could someone who was so supposedly devoted to service presume to tell me what to do in such a supercilious manner?

The day after, I was immersed in the mammoth task of bringing order to the office. There were piles of papers everywhere as I steadily worked my way through indexing and filing the huge quantity of reports, drawings and plans Brunel had already amassed in his short time as an engineer in his own right, independent of his father. I worked steadily, methodically moving the papers about the room and filing them alphabetically or by project, while all the time seeking not to disturb Brunel as he huffed and puffed at his desk, clearly struggling with a problem that was frustrating him. He pinged his bell and called Hammond in and then he stood with him, poring over a large rectangle of parchment laid out on the long waist-high counter that ran the length of the room.

'It's difficult, isn't it?' he grunted. 'Still, I like a tricky little problem to sort out.'

Hammond tapped his pencil on his teeth.

'Perhaps we could shift the line of the railway further south. If we went north, we would have to cut into the hill and it would be a lot more work.'

'Yes, but going south will mean building embankments to bring the level up. I knew this would be a problem when I surveyed the line, I thought a solution would become obvious, but clearly not.'

Brunel started to hum some sort of ditty – I wasn't sure what it was, probably from one of his favourite musicals. Then he opened his notebook, rested his forearm on it, and started to draw with long, sweeping strokes.

I guessed what they were discussing. Hammond had been working on this section of the line for days, and had told me that he was facing a dilemma. There was a canal that ran through the area and which had taken the best route, leaving him with no easy option for the railway. Worse, there was a well-used lane that crossed the canal, right where they had been hoping to run the railway.

I was intrigued and stayed close, glancing over every now and then to see what solution Brunel had dreamt up. Layers of canal, rail and road rapidly took shape, expertly brought to life by clean pencil lines and a little shading. The road and rail bridges crossed each other at different angles, the canal running beneath it all, the whole edifice like a topsy-turvy wedding cake. It was an extraordinary feat of the imagination.

Hammond nodded appreciatively.

'I see what you have in mind. Ingenious. It'll be a devil to build, though.'

Brunel smiled.

'It will just need accurate measurements on site. I can help with that. It's nice to get my hands dirty with the detail from time to time.'

The new maid came in to stoke the fire. Hammond had told me that for days the household had been alive with talk about this new arrival, saying that she must be of peasant stock, perhaps because of her olive skin. But all anyone actually knew, Hammond said, was that she was French, called Hortense, and a relative of the Breguet family, the famous watchmakers.

Brunel had laid down precise requirements for how often his office fire should be made up and how much coal should be added depending on the weather. He liked the temperature in the office to be just so. Hortense curtsied briefly, moved around to the fireplace and picked up the coal scuttle, hefting it into position. It was shaped like a jug, with a chute at the top rather than a spout, the kind you have to shake gently when tilted past the horizontal to get the coal to tumble slowly out, rather than in large, clattering clumps.

She had it tipped way too far over, as if she were stoking a ship's boiler or locomotive hungry for yet more coal, and with a rumbling crash it discharged its contents on the fire. As the smoke and coal dust cleared, we remained frozen, like a group of actors in a tableau, fine specks of soot falling on the papers and plans stacked in neat piles around the room.

I think she muttered '*merde*' but it may have been something else. It was hard to be sure. Brunel launched himself out of his chair and pointed at the door.

'Get out of here, you numbskull!' he roared. 'How can we work when imbeciles like you are spreading muck everywhere?'

She fled from the room and I jumped up and followed her, shutting the door behind me. I caught up with her in the corridor.

'Hold on, wait a moment. Look, don't worry. His bark is worse than his bite. Practise with the scuttle when he isn't in the room so it doesn't happen again, and it will all be forgotten.'

She turned to me, her flushed cheeks emphasising her darker complexion; her skin glowed, smooth like a polished gemstone. A curl of silky soft black hair poked out from under her simple white lace bonnet. She wiped away a tear, smudging her face with coal dust in the process. She bobbed her thanks, turned away and hurried back down to the servants' quarters.

I looked after her, wondering what on earth had possessed me to follow her out. I had seen Brunel's look of surprise as I leapt up. I suddenly felt anxious – would he consider that I had taken the side of the staff against him? Taking a deep breath, I turned the door knob and gently opened the door. I made my way quietly back to my desk. Brunel looked up.

'They need to learn, you know. No point pussyfooting around. People benefit from clear direction.'

I wondered if he believed what he was saying, or just wasn't able to admit that he had over-reacted. Was I in the presence of an inspirational genius or a bully – or both? I didn't reply, but busied myself with my work.

As Brunel bent back to the document in front of him, the only sound in the room the scratching of his pen on paper, I couldn't shake off the image of the dark-haired, dark-eyed beauty that had just strayed into my life.

Chapter 3

I t was one of those crisp spring mornings that makes you feel winter is finally ending and summer is just around the corner. The mist lifted slowly from the rolling fields. It was cold but tranquil, frost clinging to the tops of the grass like white hairs on the head of an ageing mythical giant. We had set out on horseback early in the morning while the world was still monochrome in the half-light between night and the rising of the sun at dawn.

Brunel and I had stayed overnight in Basingstoke, a pretty market town. As we had drawn close on the express coach service the previous evening, one of our fellow passengers had remarked that he was never sure whether to inhale deeply or to hold his breath. Brunel had ignored the comment but I had told him I agreed. The pungent, sickly smell of fermenting hops was overwhelming. The town was known for its breweries and it was difficult to know whether to embrace the aroma or try to hold it at a distance.

This morning, though, the air was fresh and sharp. Ice crackled under our horses' hooves as we made our way west, along the lanes and out of the town. Smoke rose gently out of the chimneys of the last few houses at the edge of town, spiralling upwards like a twisted plait of hair. As the tang of burning wood hit the back of my throat, I had a sudden yearning to be back inside, in front of a warm fire eating a hearty breakfast. But as we crested the next hill, the remains of the frost glistening and sparkling in the early morning sunshine and the cold air clearing away the after-effects of the beer the landlady had pressed upon us the night before, I began to relish the day.

We dismounted and unloaded the theodolite, carefully removing it from its wooden box and setting it up on a smooth patch of grass. I thought back to the moment Brunel announced we were to complete a full survey of the alternative southern route proposed for the GWR, the Great Western Railway. It seemed a lifetime ago that I had started work in his office, but it was only a few weeks. The parliamentary committee was about to begin taking evidence in preparation for the proposed bill for the new railway. Anyone other than Brunel would simply have studied a few maps to determine how a route to Bristol via Basingstoke might compare to his plan for the railroad to go via Reading and Chippenham, but when Charles Russell, MP for Reading, said that the alternative route being promoted by the London and Southampton Railway was a serious contender, Brunel wanted to see for himself how the two routes compared.

He had been nervous the day Russell called round. He was distracted all morning, leaping from his office chair when the doorbell rang, and striding out to meet Russell as soon as the footman opened the door. He showed him into the drawing room, asking me to stay and take notes. He invited his guest to sit, offered him refreshment and then took time to light up one of his cigars. I hadn't known him long but had already noticed that he used this technique to give himself breathing space to settle into a situation. They took the two armchairs that faced each other in the bay window, and from my chair to the side of them I could see that Brunel – usually a bundle of energy and rapid-fire decision-making – was striving to adopt a more statesmanlike air. As he puffed on his cigar, he began to explain the pains he had taken to survey the route.

'I believe it's only by having taken the trouble to examine each element of the topography in detail that we can be certain that we can build it in the timescales and to the cost that we have listed in our prospectus. I have been preparing a thorough—'

'I am sure you have,' Russell interrupted somewhat condescendingly. He was a large man with a commanding presence and was clearly used to holding court while others listened. 'Of course, the committee will need convincing about the practicality of your plans and that the funds raised are sufficient.'

Brunel looked taken aback at being interrupted. When people disagreed with him, he would growl out his views, face set like a bulldog, unwilling to entertain a different perspective. On this occasion, though, he held himself in check, took a deep breath and indicated that his visitor should continue.

'Parliament doesn't like having to order the compulsory purchase of land. We need to be ready to describe our efforts to appease or reduce the impact on the landowners along the route.'

I was becoming increasingly irritated by Russell's manner, but I sought to maintain an impassive façade, like Brunel aware that it was important to retain him as an ally.

'However,' he said, finally getting to the point, 'the critical issue is the competing proposal for a line via Basingstoke. I have taken soundings with a number of my parliamentary colleagues and the idea of using a branch of the London and Southampton line to get to Bristol from Basingstoke is attractive to them.'

'But that will lead to delays while they complete the mainline to Southampton. And, assuming a branch to Bristol is eventually built, it will be a much slower route than the one I am proposing,'

Brunel responded rather sharply. He was looking more and more frustrated.

Russell drummed his fingers on the arm of the chair, his face set in a frown, and I worried that the obvious clash of wills might mean that Brunel's attempts at diplomacy would quickly go to waste.

'I know all that,' he said, 'but you need to find a way to prove it to the committee. They may well judge the delay as less important than the advantages to be gained by reducing the impact of the new railways on landowners by using part of an existing route. You need to make more of the benefits of your proposal versus theirs.'

Brunel opened his mouth to speak, but Russell carried on, eyes slightly closed as he concentrated on what he was saying. He ticked off the points he wanted to make one by one on his chubby fingers.

'Firstly, you need to show how the two different routes compare in terms of the time it will take to get from London to Bristol; secondly, you need to explain the relative effect on local landowners; thirdly, you need to set out which towns would receive a train service in each case that wouldn't otherwise; finally, you need to say by when each of the routes would likely be completed.'

I marvelled at his large gold signet ring, squeezed between folds of flesh on his little finger as he marked his final point.

All of this was already clear to Brunel, but again showing admirable restraint he merely thanked his guest for his time and suggested they meet again once he had prepared answers to the very useful questions that the MP had raised. After bidding him farewell, Brunel and I returned to the office to discuss what we should do next. He leant forward with his elbows on the desk and rubbed his face with his hands.

'My God, that man was tedious but he does know his stuff,' he sighed. 'Given what he said, I think we have no choice but to plot a southern route so we can compare the two.'

'I should be able to obtain maps for that part of the country by tomorrow,' I replied.

Brunel leapt up and strode over to the fireplace. He leant against the mantelpiece and shook a cigar free from the brown leather case that he always carried. He pulled out his metal cutter from a trouser pocket as he rolled the cigar between his fingers and sniffed it gently, like a bloodhound testing the air, then he inserted it into the cutter and carefully clipped the end. Lastly, he took a long taper and held it to the fire for a few moments before bringing it to the tip of the cigar and drawing deeply.

He blew out a cloud of smoke, looking thoughtfully at one of the busts resting on the pigeon-holes.

'I might not like the bugger much, but he's nothing if not thorough. What would Telford do in these circumstances, I wonder.'

Thomas Telford was a famous engineer, renowned for the care with which he had built new roads and bridges spanning the country. I also knew from Hammond that Brunel and Telford had fallen out a few years before over the design for a new suspension bridge in Bristol. I started to say something. I can't remember what, but Brunel held his hand out to quieten me as he took a puff on his cigar, stroking his chin, deep in thought.

'I know what he would do,' he said at last. 'He would go out and survey the route so he could talk with the authority of first-hand experience.'

'But,' I said, without pausing to consider whether I would be better advised to keep my thoughts to myself, 'we have so much other preparatory work to do.'

'We'll take it with us. And in any event I know our route like the back of my hand. We will leave this evening.'

He headed back to his desk and shooed me away towards mine. I spent the rest of the day frantically pulling together all the papers and documents we might need to continue our preparations while we were away. In the mid-afternoon, I made my way to William Faden's shop in Charing Cross. There was a risk he wouldn't have the maps we needed, but a visit to the headquarters of the Ordnance Survey at the Tower of London was always a lengthy business; they might be good at producing maps, but there was often a considerable wait to be served. Brunel had made it clear he was catching the early evening coach, whether or not I had returned in time to join him. I dreaded having to find him in the open countryside, edgy with impatience, unable to do much without my assistance. Luckily, Faden's had the maps I needed.

I crossed the Strand to the Golden Cross Inn to find Brunel striding up and down waiting for me, the horses already hitched up. When he saw me, he threw his cigar to one side and bustled me into the coach. As we made our way out of London, he had already spread the first map across his knees, its edges spilling out either side. He ignored the disgruntled looks from the other passengers as he scribbled furiously, working out what the best course for a railway would be.

That evening, over roast pigeon and the local stout, Brunel talked me through how we would work together to map out the route.

'We don't have time for a proper survey, so you will travel to the furthest point we can see that looks like it could provide a reasonable passage for a railway. I will measure the elevation and then we will repeat the whole process again.'

So that was what had brought us to this grassy hillside in the Hampshire countryside on a fine frosty March morning. Brunel deftly assembled the wooden tripod and screwed the theodolite on top. He had explained to me how it worked the previous evening.

'I will first set up the tripod and adjust it using a spirit level to ensure it's perfectly horizontal. You hold up the measuring stick at the place we have agreed. I will train the telescope on it and read off the elevation from the side of the instrument.'

As instructed, I left Brunel and rode along a winding track towards the horizon. The ground was softening now, small white clouds scudding across the sky as the wind started to pick up. A few farm workers were out in the fields alongside the path, and I tipped my hat as they looked up, nodding briefly in return before bending back down to their toil.

We made good progress, Brunel rejoining me each time he had taken a reading. I then rode ahead to the next measurement point while he was busy setting up the tripod at the last. By three o'clock we were well on our way to Salisbury. Even as a novice, I could see that the route we were mapping out would need to weave its way through undulating landscape and was going to be far from ideal.

I was scanning the horizon while waiting for Brunel to rejoin me, thinking how pleasant a pastime this was compared to sitting in the office, when I saw a line of men making their way towards me across the fields. They were soon upon me. The group was led by a man on a horse, silhouetted against the afternoon sun.

'This is my land,' he shouted as soon as he was close enough to be heard. 'What are you doing here?'

My horse whinnied and I glanced over to make sure he was securely tied. It was hard to make out the features of the man who had called out. He was high above me with the sun behind him, his face hidden in the shade of his black top hat. I could see that he was dressed in a thick dark coat and heavy breeches with the only patch of colour two rows of large ivory buttons down the front of his waistcoat. Ranged behind him were three of his labourers carrying shovels and pickaxes. They were looking at me as if they would prefer chasing me off the land to building fences, digging ditches or whatever else they were out here to do.

'I asked what you are doing here?' he repeated in the tone of someone who was accustomed to being obeyed.

I stood rooted to the spot, not sure what I should say. I knew landowners had taken matters into their own hands when finding surveyors out on their land, but at least these had no dogs with them, although the man did have a long whip coiled in his hand. As he scowled at me, he let the end fall to the ground ready for use. The labourers stood beside him, leaning on their tools, eyes flicking back and forth between me and their master as they waited to see if there was sport to be had. I trembled as I realised we were in the middle of nowhere. There was no place to run or hide, no friend or help for miles.

We were still staring at each other when our attention was diverted by the thundering of hooves as Brunel arrived and drew his horse to a halt. He had seen the men and I suppose had sensed trouble.

'Good afternoon,' he said, removing his hat. 'Can I be of assistance?'

'I was asking your man here what the devil you are doing on my land, sir.'

The man's horse took a step backwards from Brunel's, forcing him to bend forward and calm it, stroking its neck with his gloved hand.

'I apologise if we are mistaken,' said Brunel, reaching behind him and pulling out the roll of maps from his saddlebag, 'but according to the map this is a bridlepath and there is a long-established right of way along it.'

'That's as maybe,' said the man, leaning forward, his hand placed on the front of the saddle for balance, 'but that's intended for local folk going about their lawful business, not people like you. Judging by your equipment, you are surveying for a road or railway and I don't want either of those crossing my land.'

His horse shifted under him again and he tugged sharply on the reins.

'You people are always talking about progress. Bringing prosperity to our towns and villages. We don't need any of that around here. Things are fine as they are.'

'You are right,' Brunel said with an open smile, seeking to exercise his considerable charm. 'We are surveying for a railway from London to Bristol, but only to show that this route is inferior to the one we are proposing further north.'

'I have heard all sorts of stories to justify coming and surveying my land and I am not interested. I want you off my land,' he barked, almost like a dog, making me jump.

He looked down at his men and pointed beyond us: 'See them back to the main road.'

Brunel's efforts to charm him aren't going to work, I thought anxiously.

As they started to shuffle forward, Brunel surprised them by dismounting. They hesitated.

'You have my word that I am telling you the truth. Hold my horse please, Bennett.' He turned back to the man in the top hat.

'Let me show you my credentials and demonstrate to you the verity of what I have been saying. My name is Isambard Brunel. May I ask yours?'

The man paused, then his manners got the better of him.

'My name, sir, is Samuel Peters,' he said, but he stayed on his horse, frowning down at Brunel.

Brunel ignored him for a moment, took the blanket fastened at the rear of the saddle and spread it on the ground. He unrolled the map I had purchased from Faden's and asked Peters to join him. Sighing deeply, Peters got down from his horse and handed the reins to one of the labourers. He stood watching while, on his knees at the edge of the blanket, Brunel extolled the virtues of his proposed northern route, pointing out the flat lands running alongside the Thames before cutting through the hills to Bath.

Peters stood with his hands on his waist, looking unimpressed or perhaps simply unable to read a map. Then Brunel gestured towards the rolling hills around us.

'This is a beautiful part of the world, but not good for a railway. That's what we are proving by carrying out a more detailed survey.'

He opened his notebook to show the tables of elevation. As he pointed to features on the map, Peters couldn't help but be drawn in, dropping to his knees to examine it, the two kneeling side by side like a pair of schoolboys playing marbles. Brunel sketched an imaginary railway with a serpentine sweep of his arm.

'You can see that the contours would require the railway to follow this valley. The bends would have to be tight as the track swept back towards us to go around this hill and on to the other side.'

'I see, I see. As you go further west, the Bradford-on-Avon valley will be even worse, from what you say. It's steep-sided, winding and narrow.'

I watched as Brunel's boyish enthusiasm infected the landowner. He couldn't stop himself absorbing some of Brunel's passion. The two of them were still studying the maps as long shadows started to creep across the fields. Brunel rocked back on his heels and started to make his excuses so we could reach Salisbury before dark. Peters wouldn't hear of it. The transformation that Brunel had wrought was extraordinary. Over the course of an hour Peters had shifted from aggressive landowner to welcoming host.

'You must stay with me,' he insisted. 'I can write letters of introduction to other landowners further along the route to make things easier for you.'

Brunel accepted, and we proceeded to Mr Peters' comfortable house with the two of them talking as if they were long-lost friends, their horses swaying along beside each other. The labourers followed behind, perhaps disappointed not to have seen a fracas, but their chatter indicating that they were happy to be on their way home.

The letters of introduction made our job much easier. We didn't need to skulk about, seeking to avoid being accosted. We rode directly up to each estate along the way and presented our credentials. We made good time, a few days later finishing in Bath where the northern and southern routes came together.

Back in the office, we worked long days in the run-up to the first meeting of the parliamentary committee which would make the final decision on the route of the GWR. On the last evening, as Hortense came in to light the candles, Brunel looked up from the drawings and notes we had spread across the desk in his office, yawned and stretched.

'Joseph, I don't think there is any more that we can do. Let me buy you a drink.'

He suggested we go to his club. It was not far away, in St James's, so we walked. As we left the room, Hortense raised her eyebrows and gave me a brief smile, as if to say 'Aren't you the lucky one, suddenly in the master's good books.'

The streets were still busy with street hawkers, beggars and cabs calling for fares. A small child, lurking in the shadows of a narrow alley leading off the main street, held out his hand and called for alms. I don't know what it was about the child that caught my eye. Maybe it was because it was hard to tell if it was a boy or a girl, with long blond hair curling out haphazardly from underneath a battered flat cap, or perhaps because he had a lost look about him, as if he hadn't been there long. Brunel was striding ahead but I paused and asked him (I could see now it was a boy, with an unwashed but winsome face not yet pock-marked by disease) how he came to be on the streets.

I expected a long tale of woe, of misfortunes befalling him and his family, but he simply said, 'Father took to the booze'.

I didn't need more than this shorthand summary to capture an image of the inevitable consequences: falling behind on the rent, turned out on the streets, placed in a workhouse, the cruelty that follows, and finishing with a child preferring to run away and take his chances in the city than be straitjacketed into an adulthood breaking stones, unpicking old ropes for ships' caulking or making up hessian sacks. I stood there for a few moments, reflecting on how easily a comfortable, or at least unsurprising, life could be turned upside down. Brunel had stopped a few yards up the road and called after me to hurry up. I gave the child a small coin and headed after him.

Despite its grand portico, Brunel's club was one of the enlightened in that it admitted guests from a broader section of society, provided they could be considered as middle class, and more importantly were well mannered and turned out. When we arrived, I caught the occasional appraising glance in my direction. Perhaps I was being overly sensitive, but I suppose that my attire – although clean and neat – marked me out as being of a lower social standing than those in the room. We were all dressed in dark suits, some with cravats and some bow ties, but I was painfully conscious of how inferior the quality and cut of my cloth was to those around me.

I straddled a world between that of the new and prosperous professional classes and the modest background of my parents. The divide between the upper- and lower-middle classes seemed as great as that between the entire middle class and the aristocracy. Families like ours always seemed to be teetering on the edge of a drop into the circumstances of our poorest customers. My parents were always worrying that a bad run of business could see us evicted from our shop and forced to scratch a living on the streets. It was true that Marc Brunel had once spent a short time in a debtors' prison, but he'd had powerful friends to help him. The Duke of Wellington in particular believed that the nation had a moral duty to repay him for his various inventions to improve the effectiveness of the army and navy – from inventing new ways to make boots to automating the production of wooden pulley blocks. At no point would those friends have allowed the Brunel family to lapse into penury, whereas my family had no such influential and wealthy connections to protect them. I felt at any moment I might be exposed as a fraud, attempting to pass myself off as a gentleman; whatever insecurities Brunel might have, he looked more comfortable than I in playing the part.

I rarely drank alcohol but as I sipped from a glass of sherry in a round-backed armchair in the club's smoking room I began to relax; the dark panelled walls combined with the quiet murmurings from the club members dotted around the room were all rather soothing. We chatted about the past few weeks as if we were old friends, Brunel regaling me with his version of the meeting with Peters.

'When I saw the four of them on the horizon, I thought we were in for trouble. It reminded me of when I surveyed the original GWR route and we were chased off some land east of Bath by the landowner with his dogs. I had to go back that night and do the survey as best I could by moonlight with a lantern.' Brunel grinned at the memory and then lifted his hand to acknowledge an acquaintance before he continued, 'My assistant had to hold up the lantern so that I could measure the elevation to the measuring stick. He was terrified that the locals would see the light and shook so much that he couldn't keep it still. It bobbed about like a firefly in the evening twilight – took us ages to get accurate readings.'

'I was very glad to see you arrive,' I said.

'I came as soon as I saw them. I didn't fancy another night out with the lanterns. You didn't look too happy. And that gun he had tucked in his saddle was worrying me.'

Luckily, I hadn't seen the gun until Peters dismounted. Brunel seemed to enjoy taking risks, and while I could laugh about it now, it hadn't seemed so funny then.

He ordered us each another sherry from a passing waiter and then asked me who I was talking to in the alley on the way to the club. I relayed my encounter with the boy.

'What struck you especially about it, given child beggars are so commonplace?' he asked, with a perplexed expression.

'I don't know. There was an air of vulnerability – I suppose he hadn't been on the streets long.'

'We can't help them all, though, can we?' Brunel blew out the smoke from his customary pull at his cigar. 'What we can do is to create the economic conditions and new enterprises that allow such families and their children to prosper.'

Perhaps it was the sherry or the convivial atmosphere of the warm smoky room that made me respond as I did. If I had been more on my guard, I would have chosen my words with greater care.

'Of course an improvement in the country's prosperity will eventually help the thousands living in dire straits, but I don't think that means that charity has no place in the meantime,' I replied.

There was no answer, only a chill in the air. I knew immediately that I had taken too much for granted in my relationship with my employer. In the awkward silence that followed, I made a show of pulling out my pocket watch and studying the time.

'I will be off now, if I may, sir. I want to be in early to make sure everything is ready for tomorrow.'

As Brunel got up to see me out, a thickset, pugnacious-looking fellow stopped by his chair and grasped his elbow. Brunel gently removed his hand from his arm, shook his hand and introduced us.

'Bennett, this is Mr Hudson, a major investor in the northern railways and in the GWR. Mr Hudson, this is my new assistant, Bennett.'

Although Hudson spoke quietly, his voice carried well enough for me to hear what was said, his broad northern accent betraying his humble origins. He was about five and a half feet tall, and appeared to have little in the way of a neck, his lack of stature the result of the direct attachment of his bullet-shaped head to his body. He wasn't the kind of person I would associate with the club.

'I hear that you are intending to use a broad gauge for your railway. At seven feet across, yours will be nearly two and a half feet wider than the one we have settled on with Stephenson and Locke. Think of the expense of all those bigger bridges and embankments. Never mind that we will need different locomotives and rolling stock. It's madness!'

'That is a matter still under consideration,' Brunel replied calmly. 'However, using something that came out of a coal pit doesn't, on the face of it, seem the most obvious choice.'

Hudson jabbed a pudgy finger at him.

'We need to create a national network that allows people to travel anywhere they want simply and easily. That means one ticket covering their entire journey, and one gauge so that a single train can complete the whole trip.'

'Most people will just be going from A to B with the GWR,' replied Brunel. 'We haven't got the patchwork of different operators you have up north. If we do decide to build to a different gauge, there will only be a requirement to change between networks at a couple of stations; at these we will construct transfer facilities to shift passengers and goods between trains quickly and easily. Now, if you will excuse me, I need to see my guest from the club.'

He started moving towards the door, but Hudson called after us.

'Have you spoken to your father about this? He seems to have a better understanding of what's in the national interest.'

Brunel stopped and spun around, his body tense and his eyes narrow. For a moment I thought he would strike the man.

'My father has nothing to do with the GWR,' he spat.

Faced with Brunel's anger, Hudson took a step back, but soon rallied.

'I can see that you have no intention of using the standard gauge unless forced to. Have no doubt that I will make sure that you do.'

Brunel stared at him, and then spoke slowly, his voice icy cold.

'Bullying your way around might work up north but it doesn't down here. Now, if you will excuse me, I don't wish to keep my guest waiting any longer.'

Brunel and I walked away together. As we reached the entrance, he drew me to one side.

'That man's a menace,' he said quietly. 'He's been trying to consolidate the northern rail companies into one network, which I can understand; there are multiple lines running all over the place, not as we are planning down south at all. I'm worried, though. He has a lot of influence, both in Parliament and with the GWR shareholders.'

He paused, looking uncharacteristically unsure about what he was about to say next. He surprised me by changing the subject.

'Bennett, my father is hoping to get the funding to complete the Thames Tunnel at a meeting the day after tomorrow. Would you like to come along? He could do with some moral support.'

I had met Brunel senior only briefly, but he struck me as a decent sort of fellow, keen to do the right thing. I said that of course I would be happy to come and support him.

I took my leave and walked the first part of the route home to get some fresh air. As I passed the alleyway, I looked to see if the boy was still lurking. It was dark but he was nowhere to be seen and I walked on feeling oddly melancholy. The forces ranged against us seemed ominous, like clouds gathering before a storm. I wondered whether my new employment was going to be short-lived. I suddenly realised that I desperately wanted it to continue. Even though I had only been involved for a few weeks, I wanted to bring this damn line into being as much as Brunel, Hammond and the others.

I found an omnibus in Parliament Square and headed home.

Chapter 4

The night before the tunnel meeting, Hammond and I sat in the Old Star, a cosy little pub on the edge of St James's Park. I had only been once or twice but it had become a favourite. Not too noisy but busy enough to have character. Hammond was one of Brunel's most trusted engineering assistants. He was a bluff, no-nonsense kind of chap and although I hadn't known him long I had already noticed that his relationship with Brunel was different from anyone else's in the office. He would tease Brunel and make him smile, whereas with anyone else he might take offence. I knew he had been involved with the tunnel and told him about the visit I had made before I joined.

'I had mixed feelings, to be honest,' I said as we settled into a corner of the public bar with pint pots of London Porter. 'It's an extraordinary achievement and a beautiful and atmospheric place, but it's sad to see it unfinished. You feel like you are starting on an exciting journey but then you don't end up anywhere, like an underground seaside pier.'

Hammond grunted. 'You're right. I have avoided visiting since it was open to the public. I don't want to see how that hard work and sacrifice has been transformed into an amusement arcade.'

I took a sip of my beer and asked what had led to him working with the Brunels.

'I started as a volunteer working for Brunel's father, Marc,' he said. 'It was hard to get a job when I came out of the army. Eventually they decided I was useful enough to pay me, but when the work was suspended following the floods we were all laid off.'

'How long ago was that?'

'It was five or six years ago, I can't remember exactly. I did various odd jobs until Brunel got in contact a few months ago when he was appointed consulting engineer on the GWR.'

'Why did you want to work on the tunnel? It must have been quite a sacrifice to work for no money.'

'I just loved the idea,' he said with a sigh. 'I was young, wasn't sure what to do with my life, and it sounded exciting and a bit dangerous – like the army but without the endless parades and hanging around waiting for something to happen.'

As the light began to fade and the evening drew in, he told me a little about the history.

'A few years before the Brunels were involved, a team of Cornish miners managed to dig a small shaft three-quarters of the way across the river before the timber props started to give way. They had to scramble hundreds of feet back to the tunnel mouth. I've been down there when the waters start flooding in.' He shook his head as if to chase away the memories. 'It's terrifying. They were very lucky not to have drowned.'

After a moment's reflection, staring at the shadows of the workers heading home past the pub window, he declared: 'Anyway, after that nobody did anything about it until Marc Brunel came up with his tunnelling shield idea.' Taking a sip from his drink, he continued, 'The early stages went well. Marc came up with a brilliant idea for the access shafts. He designed a fifty-feet-wide iron ring made up in sections. We set it out on the ground and bolted it together, and within days bricklayers had built a circular wall on top of it to a height of about forty feet.' He drew the ring out on the pub table with his finger. 'The labourers dug out the ground below and the brick rotunda slowly sank into the ground. People came from all over London to see this huge cylinder disappearing into the earth. It was like watching one of those new gasometers slowly descending into the ground.'

The log fire crackled as I leant in to listen. He described how they had cut an opening in the brick cylinder at the bottom of the shaft to start digging under the river. They had carefully dug out a little of the clay at a time, with the rest supported by planks. The planks were held in place by the frames of the tunnelling shield. The bricklayers had followed close behind, building arches to support the roof and walls of the tunnel as the shield was moved forward using screw jacks.

'It was exciting,' said Hammond, his eyes brightening at the memory. 'We managed to move the shield forward a few feet every day and within a month the tunnel was forty feet under the river, lined with brick and lit with lanterns. It looked like it was going to be straightforward with Marc's tunnelling shield working exactly as designed, but then the clay seam ran out. It wasn't as thick as we had been led to believe by the geologists, and we started to encounter gravel and, even worse, sewage and all sorts of revolting muck that had been dumped in the river over the years.'

He sat back in his chair, sighing deeply.

'It became almost impossible to work or even stay down there for any length of time. Water... well, not really water... a disgusting smelly slurry... was running in streams from all around the shield. We were soaked all the time. But the stench was far worse. It was that smell you get from walking in mud alongside a stagnant pond, or when your foot slips into an open drain. You know that brief intense cesspit smell? Well, it was like that all the time. You never got used to it. And every now and then, even with the safety lamps, the methane gas would light and send flames shooting across the tunnel face. Everyone had scarfs tied around their heads and noses, like Bedouins in a sandstorm.'

It was hard to imagine what it must have been like. I thought about those times I had been forced to visit the most unsanitary of public toilets, that almost overpowering need to gag, to get out of there. Being forced to go back day after day was unimaginable.

'How on earth did you manage to get the workers to keep going back in?'

He shrugged. 'They needed the money. But when Marc's first on-site engineer, Riley, became ill – he died not long after – those that weren't off sick started drinking and often turned up late, or not at all. The press were having a field day, drawing caricatures of Marc looking hopelessly at the tunnel face with a small pickaxe in his hand, workers lying on the floor, bottles in their hands. We had the company directors turning up at the offices at all hours demanding to know what he was going to do to get things back on course.'

I was distracted by two men pushing in through the door laughing. They dropped their bags on a table near us and called loudly for drinks. Turning back to Hammond, I asked, 'Is that when his son got involved?'

'That's right. He and Marc had been working together on experiments with a machine they called a Gaz engine but they couldn't get it to work. Marc had been trying to keep him away from the tunnel because of the conditions, but Brunel was desperate to help his father and eventually Marc agreed he could. I guess Marc was pretty desperate by then, too.'

Hammond's glass was empty and it was my turn to get a round in. The pub was getting busier and I stood impatiently at the bar waiting to be served. Eventually I returned to the table, set the beers down and asked Hammond to continue. He took a quick sip and then picked up the thread of the story.

'We started to make good progress. It was fun having Brunel around. He was full of energy and lifted our spirits. He pitched in alongside the workers, manhandling the boards, adjusting the screw jacks and ramming clay into weak spots. Even though he was filthy from the day's work, he slept many nights in a cot just back from the face so that he was on hand to help. We were feeling more confident about things, when one afternoon in mid-August the face of the tunnel started to collapse.'

Hammond paused, took another sip of his beer, wiped his lips with the back of his hand and continued, 'I was petrified. It all happened so fast. The soil had become more and more waterlogged during the shift, the mud weeping over the sides of the spades as the workers dug away at the face. A little after six in the evening, the usual trickles of water started to build into small streams, then within minutes torrents of slimy muck were streaming down the tunnel. Brunel and two other men tried to staunch the flow by wedging wooden boards in place using the frames of the tunnelling shield, but they couldn't keep up as the water dragged with it what was left of the firmer soil, opening up even bigger gaps. All I could see were foaming geysers spilling out everywhere, like waves crashing on a beach, melting the sand and drowning the men in spray.'

I tried to imagine the men desperately trying to save themselves from being buried under the spewing grey fountains.

'God, it sounds awful.'

'It was,' said Hammond grimacing. 'Most of the workers ran back along the tunnel to the safety of the ramps up the access shaft. Brunel and two of the tunnellers stayed and tried to stem the flood. It was madness. They didn't have a hope. As the water pressure built, the frames and the scaffolding behind began to twist and break up. The pumps couldn't cope and the water was past their knees. I turned and ran, screaming for them to do the same. I only just made it out.'

He paused for a moment.

'You know, I was nearer to death that day than on any I served in the army.'

'What about Brunel? How did he manage to survive?'

Hammond shook his head and smiled ruefully as he recalled Brunel's narrow escape. 'Brunel realised it was too late to follow us so instead he led his men through a small opening into the other half of the tunnel where the water was rising more slowly. Just as we were giving up hope, they emerged. We cheered them to the rafters. Until then I hadn't realised how much I had come to admire him. He is a fighter. He keeps on going come what may and he wasn't going to leave that tunnel without his men.'

'That's quite a story,' I said. 'He's an extraordinary character. Maybe that brush with death is why he is so driven now?'

'Maybe, but I would say he has always been like that.'

'Was it then that the tunnel was closed up?'

'No,' he replied laughing. 'You should know that the Brunels wouldn't give up that easily. First, we borrowed a diving bell from the East India Docks. I don't know if you've seen one?'

I shook my head.

'Hard to describe, actually,' he said, setting his glass down and drawing a shape in the air with his hands. 'I suppose you could say that it looked like a giant thimble, about ten feet wide at the mouth and fifteen feet high.

'We took it out on a barge and moored it in the middle of the river. Myself, Brunel and a chap called Pinkerley clambered inside as it swayed a few feet off the deck, held up by a rope from a crane on the barge. We had to crawl underneath and then sit on a wooden platform fixed around the inside rim, holding tightly to metal grab-handles. The men told us to make sure we were evenly spaced to stop the bell leaning over as it went into the water, otherwise it would fill up. I can tell you we shuffled around pretty quickly as they winched it up over the side of the barge and began lowering it.'

'Weren't you scared?' I interrupted. 'It sounds alarming.'

'I have to confess I didn't enjoy it much,' he said, giving a wry smile at the memory. 'I can't swim, and even inside we could hear the rope creaking as the men slowly released the turns on the winch to let the bell down into the water. Although we had waited until low tide when the river was as its quietest, the eddies were pushing the bell around and water was slopping inside. The riverbed was about thirty feet down and as the rope paid out the bell groaned at the build-up of water pressure. Brunel was grinning, looking like he was enjoying every moment, while Pinkerley looked like I felt – white-faced and nervous, holding tightly with both hands.

'As we neared the bottom, the breach in the tunnel roof appeared out of the gloom. There was a huge crater where the riverbed had been sucked into the hole, the grey twisted frames of the tunnelling shield poking out like the remains of a shipwreck at the bottom of the ocean. The bell came to a halt above the shield. Brunel was first up from his seat. He stepped down gingerly onto the frames, the diving bell rocking gently. Although it felt more like a baby's cradle under the light touch of a parent than anything else, I was still holding on tightly to the handles, my knuckles white. I was very aware that we were at the bottom of the river rather than tucked up in a nursery!'

'Do you mean to say that you can actually walk about under one of those bells?' I exclaimed. It seemed extraordinary that someone could wander around on the riverbed without wearing a clunky diving suit.

'Yes, you can. It did look strange, though. It was like he was paddling about shin deep on a beach rather than at the bottom of the river. With one hand holding on to the seat to steady himself, he used his other to reach down and feel how bad the damage was.

I don't know whether it was Brunel's first time down in a bell but he certainly made it look like he had done it before.'

Hammond went on to describe how they used a speaking tube connecting them to the surface to direct the barge to move slowly around on its mooring cables, allowing them to explore each part of the rupture. Pinkerley's job was to carefully note down and sketch the damage at each location.

'Pinkerley was leaning over to get a good look at one of the frames when he over-balanced and fell off his seat. He grabbed at the handholds, then the seat, but it was wet and slippery. With a big splash, he fell between the frames and headfirst into the water. As he emerged spluttering, Brunel reacted instinctively and held out his leg, yelling for him to grab it. Pinkerley took hold of his ankle, and the two of us clutching his jacket hauled him back up.'

'Crikey! Could he swim?'

'No. I don't know whether he learned after that episode! He certainly didn't go down in the bell again.'

Hammond finished his beer and told me that he needed to go. We pushed open the pub door to find darkness had fallen completely, the streets quiet now with only a few people heading for home, eyes down.

'I'll finish the story another time if it doesn't all get aired at the meeting,' he said. 'It should be interesting tomorrow. Lots of people lost money on the tunnel.'

The next morning when I got to work, I found that day's newspaper on my desk with the front page headline 'Work on troubled tunnel to restart'. The article continued, 'Mr Marc Brunel tells us he is anxious to restart the tunnel works. Some argue that he is a misguided and foolhardy businessman who, having once been declared bankrupt, has needlessly squandered investors' funds on unrealistic projects like the Thames Tunnel and his infamous Gaz engine experiments. But many others see him as a hugely talented engineer and war hero to whom we all owe a debt of gratitude.

'Although he didn't fight himself, he aided the war effort by designing machinery to make wooden pulley blocks for the navy's sailing ships. The work of two hundred skilled craftsmen was replaced by sixty semi-skilled workers using a series of specialist machines designed by Mr Brunel. And we are told by his supporters that, if that wasn't enough, a shortage of army boots led to him designing machinery to make them much more efficiently too. However, this may count for little when Mr Brunel today faces angry investors who have lost most, if not all, the money they subscribed to the Thames Tunnel project.

'When asked if his son Isambard would be reappointed as chief engineer, Brunel senior explained that unfortunately he would be fully occupied with his GWR railway.'

I walked to the meeting with Hammond and William Gravatt. While Hammond had been welcoming and friendly, I found Gravatt prickly. He had also worked with the Brunels on the tunnel and had been elected a member of the Institute of Civil Engineers at a very young age. He was proud of his qualifications and I would guess found working under another engineer, particularly one as inexperienced as Brunel junior, irksome. He had barely acknowledged my presence when I had originally joined, merely nodding his head and turning back to his work, muttering something about being late with his calculations.

Hammond was about to continue the story of how they had filled in the hole after Pinkerley's adventures in the diving bell, when Gravatt interrupted, speaking sourly: 'If they had done what I suggested, we wouldn't have had all the problems we then suffered from.'

'William, you know that it would have cost too much, but let's not go over old ground,' Hammond replied.

'If we had excavated in front of the tunnel and laid bags of clay pre-emptively, as I proposed at the time, it would have proven cheaper in the end,' persisted Gravatt, kicking a loose stone angrily out of his way.

'You are probably right,' sighed Hammond, 'but the investors would never have agreed to it. That's politics for you. Sometimes you have to take the long way round.'

'I'm an engineer, not a politician,' responded Gravatt testily.

'I know, I know,' laughed Hammond. 'But unfortunately we engineers would never get the money to build anything if it weren't for the politicians.' He turned to me and said, 'That's one thing with Brunel. When he puts his mind to it, he can be both.'

I could see that the rest of the story would have to wait for another day as we reached the hall where the meeting was due to take place. The press loitered outside, trying to get quotable comments from the arrivals, but we brushed past them. Double doors opened into a high-ceilinged room circled by a gallery. I was glad to see there was no one up there. I imagined, given Hammond's comments, that they might perhaps have been ready to throw rotten fruit to demonstrate their displeasure, as if at the theatre watching one of Shakespeare's bawdy tales.

We took our seats as the chairman called the room to order, made some introductory remarks concerning the reason for the meeting (to approve a loan from the Treasury to complete the tunnel in the absence of an appetite for further investment from shareholders) and opened up for questions. They came thick and fast.

'You have wasted all the money we have already given you, why should we trust you now?'

I don't know who the speaker was, but he had lost money financing the Thames Tunnel and wanted to know how he was going get it back. He was the first of a series of disgruntled investors waiting to have their say.

We were sitting in rows facing the company directors who were sheltering behind a long baize-covered table on a raised platform. Marc got slowly to his feet.

'I understand that you are angry but I do think that it was made clear from the outset that a project as transformational as this was by its nature risky. We now have the financial means to complete the works and to achieve some return on your investment.'

Marc was a short, round-faced man, dignified but bent with age, seeming to bear on his shoulders the weight of Thames silt that he had been seeking to drive a tunnel through for the last ten years. He paused for thought before he spoke and when he did so made his points in a mild-mannered but firm and logical manner.

Members of the public stood up one after the other to criticise the way their money had been invested, and by implication Marc himself, and clearly thought he hadn't been doing the right thing for them. An elderly vicar in a crumpled off-white linen suit took his turn.

'I invested because I believed you when you said that you had conducted appropriate geological surveys and as a result understood exactly what you would be dealing with and had designed your patented tunnelling shield specifically for those geological conditions,' he said, his voice quivering with indignation.

'We did commission extensive geological surveys which suggested a much thicker band of clay than we have encountered. Unfortunately these things aren't exact and you can only know for sure when you start tunnelling,' Marc replied.

The vicar responded with a lengthy speech. I began to make notes but laid down my pencil when I realised he was strong on rhetoric but short on any useful facts or perspectives. He was clearly a man used to public speaking. As he spoke, he glanced around and seemed mostly interested in the impact he was having on the rest of the audience. He was spritely despite his age and I guessed that the small investment he had made in the tunnel was repaying itself many times over in congregations willing or obliged to listen to his sermonising.

Brunel was a few rows forward of us, sitting alone. I could see that he was sketching in a notebook – I would guess working away at a GWR engineering problem – while the proceedings rumbled on. Although short in stature like his father, he seemed to stand out from the crowd. He radiated a restless energy even with his head down hard at work. He reminded me of a small bird pecking at scraps, concentrating on the job in hand but always alert and ready to fly off to deal with a new challenge.

Despite the press caricatures and finger pointing, I thought the Brunels' endeavour to tunnel under the Thames was heroic. The conditions Hammond had described sounded horrific. Although he hadn't had time to tell me the full story, I knew that Brunel had been badly injured in the final collapse that had led to the closure of the tunnel and that Marc had spent the intervening years working tirelessly to raise the money to finish the works.

The person who was next up spoke hesitantly, hunched over slightly as if to reduce the surface area available for verbal or any other form of assault. His tale was an abject one. He had been employed at Marc's wellington-boot factory before the business went bust when orders from the army dried up after the war. Although he had lost his job and was now doing what labouring work he could find, he believed in Marc and had invested his life's savings in the tunnel. As he spoke, he couldn't bring himself to blame Marc even as he asked if there was any real prospect of a return from his shares.

'I only ask,' he said, 'so that I can know if I will be able to look after my family once I am too old to labour.'

Marc looked shocked and humbled.

'My dear fellow, what can I say other than I too have sunk my life's work and savings into this project? What I perhaps can offer you is work on the tunnel when we recommence shortly. It's hard, dirty work but if you come and see me after the meeting, we can look at the jobs that might suit your skills.'

His companion, presumably his wife, patted his arm as he slowly sat down. He turned to her and smiled, a glimmer of hope in his tired eyes.

A butcher whose shop was near the tunnel entrance was next.

'You persuaded me to invest because of the increase in trade that I would see pass my door once the tunnel was open. Granted, I have had some trade from the company to feed the workmen, but that's hardly the same thing as the assurances you gave me about the business that would result from creating a major new crossing point on the Thames.'

Perhaps unwisely, at this point my employer intervened. Brunel paused, seemed to reflect for a moment and then rose, putting his sketch pad on his chair behind him. He cleared his throat loudly and once he had the audience's attention started to speak.

'I understand your frustrations, but the government is financing the completion of the work because we need a new crossing point downstream at Rotherhithe as much as we have ever done. We learned a lot digging out the first sections, and with a new improved shield I am confident that the team will make better progress with the remainder.'

I was struck by how confidently my new employer came across. He set out his point of view calmly, slowly and clearly and with the expectation that it would be treated with due weight. Nevertheless, I say that he might have been unwise to intervene because his comments sparked a storm of questions about his suitability for the role when he was appointed chief engineer by his father, given how little experience he had at the time, and how that lack of experience might have helped cause the original problems and overruns. Charges of nepotism flew around the room.

'I chose my son because he was the best option available,' said Marc. 'He had the right experience and education, and as importantly, he had experienced the conditions in the tunnel and understood the difficulties he would encounter day-to-day.'

'But did you interview anyone else or advertise the role more widely?' a man at the back of the room called out. 'If you didn't, how do you know he was the best candidate?'

A murmur of 'Hear, hear,' rippled through the audience.

'The previous chief engineer had been taken gravely ill,' Marc replied in a calm and steady voice, like a teacher patiently dealing with a class of unruly pupils. 'We needed to act quickly and with the full support of your board decided that appointing Isambard was the best option.'

'It's still nepotism!' the man rejoined.

'I don't agree,' the elder Brunel responded angrily. 'The decision has been vindicated by the effort and sacrifice Isambard made in the performance of his duties. He made himself ill and almost drowned in the last collapse, such was his commitment to the project and to realising the plans of the company. I don't see how his performance can be faulted in any way.'

He had finished speaking and took his seat, peering out at the audience, his face set firm, like a judge, as if daring anyone to challenge what he had said. His son smiled lightly in line with the praise lavished upon him, but his eyes were scanning the room as his father spoke. I wondered what was going through his mind. Here was his father defending him to the last, but perhaps like most young men – myself included – all he wanted to do was to outgrow the parental shadow.

His words had done the trick. The mutterings in the audience subsided and the meeting soon came to a close with the loan approved, in the absence of any alternatives. Like seagulls flocking around a tasty morsel, Marc was surrounded by investors not yet prepared to give up on the injustices they felt they had suffered.

Brunel quickly headed towards a rear door, hoping to slip away unnoticed. Hammond indicated that we should follow suit, and making our way through those standing in small groups near the doors, hurried after him. Brunel had almost reached the door when a man grabbed his elbow.

'Hold on. Not so fast!'

He was of average height and well built, but now sported a large belly and looked out of shape, like a retired rugby player or boxer whose toned muscle has turned to fat. He was wheezing, trying to catch his breath after rushing to apprehend Brunel before he could leave.

'You had a part in the debacle, too. You should be answering to the likes of me rather than sloping off.'

'Take your hands off me, Lowther,' snarled Brunel, as we stood behind him, unsure of what to do.

The man let go his arm, but continued to block Brunel's route to the exit.

'While you have been winning new commissions for your fancy bridge in Bristol and your grand new railway, I have been struggling under the debts I took on to finance purchase of the shares. It was you and your father that persuaded me that the future is in engineering rather than farming.'

'Get out of my way,' said Brunel, pushing past him. As he reached the door, he paused and turned back. 'As I recall, you were keen to take the shares at the time. I can't abide people who look to blame others for their own decisions. Good day.'

And with that he swept out, forcing us to scamper after him as his accuser stared balefully after us. In answer to my whispered question, Hammond quietly told me that Lowther was a landowner from up north who had just been elected as Member of Parliament for York.

Brunel marched along the pavement, his cane tapping in time with his rapid walk. He grumbled, almost as if to remind himself of how affronted he should act.

'They lost money but so did I. Have they no idea how much effort and sacrifice the whole project has entailed?'

It was only as we reached Whitehall that he slowed his anger-fuelled pace.

'How quickly they turn on you,' he said shaking his head ruefully. 'That man Lowther was begging us to allow him to buy more shares just a few years ago. He's got a stake in the GWR too. What's he going to say when that faces its inevitable problems? Can't they see that achieving great things isn't always straightforward?'

Maybe Lowther should have known what he was getting into, but I had been moved by the other stories I had heard during the meeting. It might be true that the tunnel was a heroic endeavour, but I wondered whether acknowledging that had to be at odds with feeling at least some compassion for the people affected by its tribulations. They weren't all wealthy shareholders.

Chapter 5

1835

We walked past the charred remains of the Houses of Parliament. A policeman stood guard at one end, his job now to protect the ruin from looting, rather than the members from angry mobs. Abandoned and forlorn, fractured beams lay amongst the stone foundations while discussions rumbled on over what a replacement should look like and how much should be spent. It was strange to think of the centre of the British Empire having been burnt down, an accidental fire doing what Guy Fawkes had failed to achieve.

In the meantime, parliamentary business carried on wherever room could be found. We entered an old red-brick building just behind Westminster Abbey. A porter at the entrance took our names and guided us to a meeting room in the basement. The narrow corridor smelt of damp, bringing back a sharp memory of me and a couple of friends scavenging on the foreshore of the Thames. 'I've found gold,' yelled Charlie. Pete grabbed the small chunk of metal Charlie was holding up and scratched off the last of the gold paint.

Pete and I were overcome with laughter. Charlie headed back to the river's edge to resume searching for his El Dorado.

As we turned the corner, I was alarmed to see Hudson and Lowther, lurking like highwayman waiting to accost the mail coach. Standing beside them was a third man whom I recognised as the wonderfully named Dr Dionysius Lardner. A large, corpulent man with his long red hair scraped tightly back to keep its wildness in check, Lardner had written a series of articles to explain steam technology to the general public that had proven wildly popular. I would never admit it to Brunel, but I had read them avidly. He was now in the process of producing an encyclopaedia of all matters scientific and philosophical and had engaged various writers to produce sections or treatises for it. Where he couldn't find someone or they missed deadlines, he was said to be writing the missing parts himself. His lectures and the publication in instalments of his encyclopaedia had led to him being seen as an expert on all manner of scientific topics. I was dismayed to see him in the company of Lowther and Hudson. Brunel's fears seemed well-founded, after all. It didn't bode well to see Hudson already assembling the forces to take us on.

Brunel tried to continue past them but Hudson held out his arm barring the way. Brunel had little option but to stop. After our encounter at the club, Brunel had told me a little about Hudson. His parents had died at a young age and he had been brought up by his brothers and apprenticed to a draper's in York, aged fifteen. There followed a dizzying rise in his fortunes. He married the owner's daughter and became a partner. A few years later he came into a substantial inheritance from his elderly uncle, reportedly by staying close by his bedside in his final years. He had carved out a position for himself as a man of substance in the city of York, and was the prime mover behind efforts to bring railways across the north of England into a coherent network. Lowther and he looked to be natural brothers in arms.

'We suggest you reconsider the matter of the broad gauge before the proceedings begin. You don't want all of us ranged against you, believe you me,' he started.

'Look,' said Brunel. 'Nothing has been decided about the broad gauge. These meetings are mostly about the route.'

'You've always been a law unto yourself, Brunel,' replied Hudson. 'You managed to get Harrison fired as joint surveyor so that you could do what you liked with the route. I... we... aren't going to let you do the same for the gauge. For once you will do what the board of directors want or face the consequences.'

Lowther spoke next, his voice calmer and smoother than in my first encounter with him. I noted that he was adjusting rapidly to his new role as an MP.

'My dear Brunel, it would be so much easier if we could all work together on this – avoid another disaster like the Thames Tunnel, don't you think?'

I gasped inwardly. He might have moderated his voice, but he had still delivered a barb that was likely to enrage Brunel.

'Do as you will. As I said, no decision has been made. Now, if you will excuse me, I have a hearing to attend,' replied Brunel icily as he brushed past the pair.

I followed quietly behind, leaving Lowther and Hudson with their heads locked conspiratorially together with Lardner, like a three-headed mythical beast lurking in the shadows. I was a natural seeker of compromise but even I could see there would be no meeting of minds with them for as long as Brunel stuck to his broad gauge guns.

We passed through an arched door into a long low-ceilinged chamber with a vaulted ceiling. Candles had been lit to supplement the weak winter light filtering in from the small leaded windows near the top of the walls.

George Burke, the GWR's lawyer, bustled over to welcome Brunel as soon as we arrived. He was a larger-than-life character, reaching out to embrace Brunel as an old friend. To my surprise he returned the hug, slapping him on the back and then after a few moments introducing me.

'George, meet my new assistant, Joseph. Joseph and I have been out surveying together. It reminded me of old times.'

'I don't miss being woken up by the bell for those early morning starts,' replied Burke, laughing.

He turned to me and shook my hand, saying, 'While we were preparing the Bill for the GWR, Brunel and I travelled together to negotiate with some of the landowners. Brunel used to live opposite me and after I was late once he rigged up a bell.'

Creases formed at the corners of his eyes as he smiled at the memory.

Brunel snorted. 'It was attached to a cord that I strung up across the street, so when it was time to get up I gave it a yank at my end and it started the bell jangling right by his bed. Burke was never late again.'

I smiled, imagining the scene. Typical of Brunel, I thought. I warmed to Burke also. It wasn't often that one of Brunel's circle chose to speak to me as an equal.

The chattering groups around the room broke up and took their seats as the committee members filed in and sat behind the tables placed across the end of the room. I was perturbed to see Lowther make his way to the front and join them. Had Hudson already populated the committee with his supporters? I pondered dismally. We had thought ourselves fortunate that Charles Russell had been appointed chair, but he had made it clear that he would need to remain impartial. Things were not looking good.

The committee met daily, each session more enervating than the last, as the opposing side set out their stall: landowners concerned not to have a railway forcibly crossing their land, Eton school worried that the railway would allow their pupils to visit the fleshpots of London more easily (this caused a brief outbreak of merriment in the audience), the government lawyer – Serjeant Merewether – asking endlessly nitpicking questions of Brunel. His purpose seemed solely to find fault with Brunel's proposals. He was like a boa constrictor, wrapping his words around a topic and slowly squeezing the life out of it.

It was two weeks later when Lardner was called as an expert witness to discuss the proposed tunnel through the hill at Box between Chippenham and Bath. When complete, at one and three quarter miles this would be the longest tunnel in the world, driven through a steep hillside of solid rock. It was the one section of the route where Brunel had been forced to use a steeper incline than elsewhere on the track.

I sat up in my seat as Lardner waddled to the front and eased his stocky body into the witness chair which had so often been occupied by Brunel. He was dressed in a fine yellow silk jacket over the top of a heavily brocaded waistcoat. As he made his way past me, I caught a whiff of a strong pomade; the aroma and his attire reminded me of one of the characters from Hogarth's paintings of The Rake's Progress. I had heard talk that Lardner had a colourful private life and was in the midst of a divorce from his estranged Irish wife.

Brunel sat in the front row, with me just behind. He puffed constantly on his cigar while Lardner spoke, muttering to himself at regular intervals.

'I have a number of concerns about the proposed tunnel,' he began, pausing dramatically to survey his audience before continuing. 'The speed of the trains may cause people to pass out, and due to the steep incline within the tunnel, if there is a failure of the brakes the train may reach a velocity whereby it runs out of control and crashes, with fatal consequences. If I may direct the attention of the esteemed members of the committee to the illustrations I have prepared…'

He heaved himself out of his chair and made his way over to the drawings he had pinned on boards at the side of the room.

'I have made various calculations and believe the train could end up travelling at more than one hundred and twenty miles an hour in the event of a brake failure.'

As he spoke, he pointed at the simple graphs and diagrams he had prepared to bring his argument to life.

'Not only might this cause the train to derail, it could even lead to asphyxiation of the passengers,' he finished, dramatically thumping his fist on the boards like an auctioneer's gavel.

A few members of the audience gasped and I thought he was nothing if not a showman and a master of theatre. Still, I found myself wondering rather anxiously if he could be right about the danger, although the chances of a train reaching one hundred and twenty miles an hour sounded far-fetched.

In front of me I could see Brunel scribbling furiously on his pad. He stood up.

'If I might be allowed to comment, Mr Chairman, before Dr Lardner goes any further?'

The sarcastic tone with which he said *'Doctor'* caused heads to turn and Lardner to give him a most malevolent look. The chairman frowned but ignoring the murmurings in the audience, asked Brunel to proceed.

'I believe the good doctor's calculations are flawed. He has assumed the train will gain in speed as a result of the downward slope and loss of braking, but he hasn't taken full account of rolling friction or air resistance. If you include these factors, my preliminary calculations – and I would stress that they are preliminary – suggests the maximum speed attained in such a situation would be around fifty-five miles per hour.' He finished by saying, 'Perhaps Dr Lardner would be kind enough to check his calculations.'

Lardner stared at Brunel. He seemed at a loss for words, one might almost say aghast. He reminded me of walruses I had seen beached on a rock at the zoological gardens, looking like they weren't quite sure how it had happened. I suppose that he was used to simple populist messages that found favour with unsophisticated audiences. He must be realising too late that this was a discussion bound to be grounded in careful scientific and mathematical analysis. As Brunel retook his seat, we caught each other's eye and he smiled, his face suddenly lit up.

'Of course I will,' said Lardner seeking to recover his poise as he noticed the journalists in the room scribbling away for tomorrow's edition.

I sensed that little mattered more to Dr Lardner than how he was perceived by the public and the press. He took out his handkerchief and dabbed at his now moist brow. Taking a deep breath and puffing out his chest, like a peacock seeking to dominate its surroundings, he continued.

'Even if – for the time being – we use Mr Brunel's assertion of a maximum speed of fifty-five miles an hour, this could still lead to devastating consequences. A derailment with loss of life and injuries would very likely occur. Passengers may be starved of air and – even without a runaway train – the psychological effects on passengers of such an unprecedentedly long time inside a small tunnel are unknown. The whole design is foolhardy, to say the least.'

I looked around. Brunel's sense of relief had been premature. The audience were worried, their imaginations running riot as they envisaged themselves entering that long, dark abyss.

That evening, Brunel's father strolled back with us to Brunel's offices. He had attended to offer his moral support to his son I suppose.

As I walked along behind them, I noticed that they looked an obvious father and son pair, both shorter than average, with heads slightly larger than perfect proportions would dictate. Marc was stockier now, Brunel still wiry in keeping with his youth.

Although they were ahead of me, I could hear them quite clearly as they conducted a fiercely whispered debate.

'Father, you chose the wider gauge for the railway tracks you laid down in Chatham dockyard and now you are arguing that I should use a narrower one!'

'I agree with you that technically the wider gauge is superior.'

'Hah,' said Brunel, as if the argument were over.

'But,' continued Brunel senior, 'railways have already been built using the narrower gauge so surely it would be better to use the same to allow easy passage of trains and freight between operating companies.'

'Why should we be forced to make do with the gauge Stephenson has used?' exclaimed Brunel. 'We both know he chose it to match the rails used for horse-drawn wagons in a coal mine. And now we are to be stuck with it? Because of a horse? It makes no sense!'

Brunel senior replied wearily, 'My dear Isambard, it's not just about what the best engineering solution might be. Having the same width across the country will make life easier for everyone. Commercially speaking—'

'Commercial speaking, Father,' interrupted Brunel, 'if I use a broader gauge I can make the carriages wider, giving more room; the engines can be bigger and more powerful and at speed the train and carriages will be more stable.'

He struck a loose paving stone with his cane. I knew that he had enormous respect for his father, but I could see he was getting increasingly frustrated.

'But you have the northern shareholders ranged against you. Wouldn't it be a lot easier to compromise and get them on our side?' Marc sighed as he stopped for a moment and stared at his son.

'But we don't even know if that will pacify them. They want control. They want to see Bristol's days as a port finished and Liverpool triumph. I am not going to give up on the better engineered solution on a hope and a prayer and because others have already opted for second best,' declared Brunel, now swiping with his cane at a stray branch of a rose bush poking out through the railings of small square we were passing through.

They walked the rest of the way in stony silence. When we reached the steps up to Brunel's offices, Brunel senior said little as he took his leave.

While waiting for the doorbell to be answered, Brunel turned to me.

'Not even my father understands what we are doing here. We are creating a whole new communications infrastructure between major cities and it has to be the best. It will be the lifeblood of Bristol and the towns and cities along the way. I am not prepared to compromise.'

Men have died for their religious beliefs. Perhaps to Brunel this was something similar. Maybe it was an article of faith on which he would not, could not, yield. I worried that we were doomed to failure.

A sense of claustrophobia was beginning to overwhelm me as I sat for yet another day's proceedings in the low-ceilinged room. I felt an almost uncontrollable desire to push my way past the rest of the people sitting in my row, charge out the door, and run out into the fresh air.

Merewether was asking yet more detailed questions about the differences between the southern route via Basingstoke and the northern one chosen by Brunel.

'If you could imagine that the towns and populations on your northern route were in fact to the south, might you have chosen that route?'

'I suppose if that were the case, I might have,' Brunel replied. 'Although, as I have already stated, the topography to the south is nowhere near so well suited to the construction of a railway.'

He went on to demonstrate with the map, as he had done with Mr Peters in that field so many weeks ago, how the best southern route would likely wind its way down to Salisbury and then along the Avon valley. Lowther interrupted him.

'Mr Chairman, surely Mr Brunel isn't expecting us to believe that he would produce the best possible route for a competing scheme.'

Charles Russell had been as good as his word in being scrupulous in avoiding any show of bias, his position as the MP for Reading – a constituency which could benefit from the proposed northern route – making him a natural target for such claims.

'Mr Brunel, it seems a fair question. What's your response?' he said as Lowther sat back, hands folded across his richly brocaded waistcoat, smiling with a self-satisfied look.

'Engineering might be a new discipline but I think you will find that our members are focused on finding the best solutions, not deploying subterfuge for commercial gain,' Brunel replied.

'You say that,' responded Lowther tartly as he leant across the table, 'but there are very significant matters at stake here. We can't trust your profession's ethics.'

Someone called out, 'Hear! hear!' and another 'Shame on you!'. The chairman rapped his gavel, called for quiet and indicated to Brunel that he should continue.

'It would hardly do my reputation any good if I proposed a route which subsequently turned out to be a sham. However, may I suggest that, rather than take my word for it, the supporters of the Southampton Railway show us their proposed route,' he said, peering at the audience with a theatrical look of enquiry.

An older, nervous-looking man seated a few rows in front of me and to my right turned to his colleagues and, after a brief discussion, reluctantly got to his feet.

'I am afraid that we have not yet conducted a detailed survey so are unable to provide a proposed route, or indeed comment upon the merits of Mr Brunel's.'

There was silence for a moment followed by an eruption of noise. Multiple conversations broke out in the audience and the clamour only grew worse as MPs on the committee tripped over each other to shout questions at the beleaguered London and Southampton Railway representative.

As the chairman called for order, I smiled to myself. Brunel had been right. His diligence had made the opposition look foolish. Once calm had been restored, one of the other committee members spoke up, eager to share his point.

'I note the southern route is through rolling hills and – forgive my layman's terms – if you add all the ups and downs of the southerly route, you end up with a more-or-less neutral position. Surely then, the trains can speed up on the downward sections and use that speed to help them climb the inclines?'

'On that basis we should run a railway across the Lake District!' shouted a wag in the audience.

Brunel explained why that wouldn't work, and thankfully the chair called a halt to proceedings for the day.

On our way back to the office that evening, Brunel turned to me as we waited to cross a street.

'Well, Bennett, how do you feel it's going?'

'Sentiment is definitely moving in our direction, sir, but I worry that we haven't resolved the Box Tunnel questions raised by Lardner. Our northern route depends upon it.'

'Yes, you are right,' said Brunel thoughtfully. 'Let me think about how we might cross that bridge… or rather tunnel!' he laughed.

It was getting late and I left him at the corner of Whitehall and headed home. The sun was sinking behind St Paul's Cathedral, lighting up the dome like an angel's halo. I passed through the shadows and stopped in the pool of sunlight on the other side; resting my bag on the wall, I looked over the cloisters beyond. I smiled to myself. Joining Brunel was starting to feel like the best decision I had ever taken.

A small figure darted past my knees and made a grab for my bag.

'Not so fast, you scamp,' I cried as I grabbed hold of the urchin's arm, holding fast as he squirmed, desperately trying to shed his coat and get away.

His cloth cap fell off and a tumble of dirty blond curls fell out. I couldn't believe it. It was the same boy that I had come across weeks ago on the way to Brunel's club.

'Hold still. You're not going anywhere.'

'Sir, please let me go. I promise not to—'

'Promise not to what? Not to steal my bag now I've got a hold of you?'

He stopped squirming and dropped his head. I could hear the snuffling sound of crying. I found myself wanting to comfort him with a 'There, there', but reminded myself that he and my bag would have disappeared if I hadn't acted quickly. Instead I gruffly told him that we had met before, asked him what his name was and where his family now lived.

'James,' he snivelled. 'It's just Ma and my two sisters now. Dad's gone. We live south of the river.'

Holding him firmly by the sleeve, I told him to take me to them.

We crossed London Bridge and entered the hinterland of narrow alleys on the south bank. He looked up at me from time to time and then around, searching for an escape route, I suppose, but I ignored him and tightened my grip. Finally we turned down a narrow cul-de-sac. I found myself gagging as I was hit by the rich, ripe smell of decay from a pile of rotting garbage at the end of the alley. We ascended a short flight of rickety stairs to a flimsy, half broken door. Lying on a straw bolster in the corner of the small bare room, looking thin and wan, was a woman in her late twenties or early thirties. Her other two children squatted in the corner, playing a listless game with a couple of marbles and a small wooden cup.

'I am sorry to disturb you, madam,' I offered, as she struggled slowly to her feet, looking anxiously from me to her son.

'You must wonder why I am here,' I said gently. 'I came across your son, James, a few weeks ago and then again today.'

I decided not to mention his attempt to steal my bag. Either his mother didn't know what he was up to, or she did. It wouldn't help matters to mention it. I just knew I wanted to try and improve the lot of this family.

'I'd like to offer him a job as a runner for Mr Brunel over in Parliament Street. Here's a small advance for his services,' I said, putting a couple of coins on the table.

'Please make sure he's at number eighteen tomorrow morning at seven-thirty sharp, ready to work.'

'But…' stuttered his mother.

'No ifs or buts,' I said. 'You and he will be doing me a favour. We need someone with a bit of spirit.'

As I headed home I wondered whether I had indeed taken leave of my senses. What would happen to me if my new recruit was found stealing from us? And how was I to tell Brunel that I had offered a job to someone I had found on the street?

I arrived at the office early the next morning and went to see Bourton to inform him that a new recruit would be starting that day.

'New recruit, sir?' he replied, looking down his nose at me as usual.

'Yes, I've hired an extra runner given the volume of work we are now transacting.'

'I see, sir. Well, it's most irregular. As you know, I usually hire the domestic staff. I assume Mr Brunel has signed this off?'

I sighed. I should have anticipated that Bourton would be difficult. Our relationship was no better than it had ever been. His ability to sneer at me while hardly moving his features would be impressive if it weren't so infuriating.

James arrived before I had a chance to respond.

'Set him to work,' I said, hoping Bourton would let the matter rest.

Two days later as the committee was reaching the end of its deliberations, Brunel called me over at the lunch break. He handed me carefully drawn sketches and gave me precise instructions for the making of a model.

'Joseph, we need to get this made immediately, ready for tomorrow. I want to use it in my closing arguments. The hillside at each end of the tunnel needs to be exactly as I have drawn it to the dimensions I have specified. Similarly, the track-bed needs to be at the correct incline. Have them fit wooden rails and make a small model wagon that will run easily through the tunnel. Maudslay's will do it for you, I am sure.'

It was like the old days, standing in the corner of the workshop watching the men shaping wood and plaster. Maudslay had sent my messenger straight back to say that Frederick Patmore and Jonathan Roberts had agreed to stay as late as needed. I was grateful, they were his best craftsmen. I arrived late in the evening to find the work on the model well advanced. I stayed with them, checking that Brunel's instructions were followed to the letter, but also enjoying being with my old friends and colleagues. Life with Brunel had given me little time for socialising.

'Surprised to see you here,' said Patmore looking up briefly from sanding a piece of timber and grinning to take the sting out of his words. 'Haven't seen you in ages. Thought you must be too high and mighty to spend time with us nowadays.'

'Hah! Just found better company,' I replied, smiling in return.

'Looks like it's coming together well,' I said, running my hand over the side of the model.

They had set the baseboard at the angle Brunel had specified and then built up the hillside using pieces of timber, wire and plaster of Paris. I held a candelabra high overhead as they used various shades of green paint to complete the effect.

Brunel had agreed with Charles that the model would be displayed first thing the next day. Although we were late to bed,

I arrived early to watch over the workmen bringing it in by cart before the start of proceedings and made sure it was carefully placed on a table at the front of the room.

Brunel gathered the committee members around the model and asked them which way they thought the track sloped. I had looked at it myself and it was hard to tell. The hillside at each end was of a different height, matching the site itself, and this confused the eye.

While they talked amongst themselves and gathered around the end that by common agreement they thought the higher, Brunel placed the model wagon full of chalk at the other end. The wagon gained speed, ran through the tunnel in the opposite direction to that which they had expected, hit the buffers, and launched pieces of chalk into the faces of the surprised onlookers. I struggled to suppress a smile as chuckles broke out in the audience at the sight of our distinguished Members of Parliament being sprayed with chalk.

Brunel had made his point. Despite the optical illusion that he had fooled them with, they realised that the incline couldn't be that severe if they had misread its direction. Lardner was famous for using model steam engines to illustrate his lectures and I felt immense pleasure in seeing him undone through his own methods, hoist on his own petard.

Brunel summed up: 'As you can see, the tunnel isn't as steep as might first appear. Also, you might recall that Dr Lardner commented on how a lack of fresh air and light might affect passengers. The tunnel will have ventilation shafts at every six hundred yards and I believe this will be more than adequate.'

Committee members nodded in appreciation as Brunel showed them his plans for the shafts, and I could see that he had won the day. Years later, though, when the tunnel was being built, I did wonder if Brunel was being disingenuous that day. If you walked a few feet from the base of one of the shafts, it was pitch black.

Charles Russell summed up from the chair, approving Brunel's route, but my wide grin disappeared when I heard the sting in the tail. Brunel's initial plan had been to terminate the railway in Vauxhall, taking a southerly route via Fulham and Brompton, but the wealthy and well-connected burghers of Brompton had arrived in force at the hearings, and one after the other explained why driving a railway line through their leafy suburb made no sense.

A terminus had already been set aside at Euston for the London and Birmingham Railway and Brunel was forced to agree that he would, with the committee's blessing, seek to negotiate joint use. He turned to me and whispered, 'That's not going to be an easy conversation, but we have no choice.'

Burke jumped up and hugged Brunel as Russell called the hearings to an end, exclaiming, 'Wonderful! Wonderful to see all your hard work brought to life.'

'Old chap, your help was invaluable,' Brunel replied graciously. 'Not only in navigating the legal complexities, but as my companion on those many days and nights we spent out on the road.' Looking at me, he added, 'Joseph, you too. I am so pleased that you made the decision to join me.'

'It's been a pleasure and a privilege, sir,' I said. And despite feeling that since I had joined him I had been swept out from a quiet river into a maelstrom in the ocean, I meant it. I was surprised at the warm feeling of pleasure that spread through me, like the glow of contentment after a glass of sherry. The success of Brunel and the GWR had quickly become central to my life, I realised.

'The model turned the tide,' Brunel smiled. 'Thank you for seeing to it. I know I can rely on you.'

Before I had a chance to say anything further in reply, he was tapped on the shoulder and the all too brief a moment was over as he turned away to receive congratulations from the many other supporters that always emerge when success is assured.

I returned to the office and tried to concentrate on prioritising the matters that had been put aside during the hearings. I found it hard to settle, the room too quiet in the early evening and my head still full of the events of the last few days. There was a knock on the door, and Hortense came in to light the fire.

As she carefully tipped the coal scuttle, I chuckled and said, 'that's a steady hand you have there.'

She gave me a sly smile.

'You know what I like about the English sense of humour?'

'No,' I said, knowing I was setting myself up but content to let it play out to her advantage.

'Nothing!' she replied triumphantly.

Hortense and I were slowly getting to know each other. I liked her sense of humour, even if she pretended she didn't like mine. She said little and sometimes I wasn't sure if she had understood, but then she would make a pithy remark which displayed a glimpse of her love of fun and mischief.

She had told me a little more about herself and how she had ended up in our household. When Isambard was a teenager, Marc Brunel had arranged for his son to spend time with Breguet, a famous Parisian watchmaker, as part of his technical education. The Breguet family had written to Brunel a year or so ago to say that the son of one of their most loyal employees was to be apprenticed to a London watchmaker, John Arnold. The parents wished their eldest daughter to accompany him and the Breguets had written asking if he might know of some work for her.

'So here I am. I don't know whether Mr Brunel felt obliged to offer me a place, or it was a happy coincidence that he had an opening I could fill. Either way, I want to do a good job. But what about you? You told me before how you came to work for Brunel, but how did you end up at Maudslay's?' she asked.

'I was fascinated by all the talk about a new industrial revolution and had read about a special lock called the Bramah after its inventor Joseph Bramah. The article said it was of such a complicated design that no one had been able to pick it. It was on display in his shop window in Denmark Street and I was determined to go and see it. One day I was nearby, running an errand for my father – I worked in his ironmongers – and went to have a look.

The lock was larger than I had imagined, about twice the size of one of the big cakes of laundry soap we stocked in the shop. Its bronze metal face glowed, lit by candlelight to brighten up the shopfront as the evening drew in. The workings were partly obscured, I suppose to avoid people seeing the secrets of its construction, but I could see it was finely made, with a complex key hung on hooks below it.

There was a sign that said: *Two hundred guineas to the man that can pick this lock, many have tried and none have succeeded.* I stood there yearning to pick it up and examine the elaborate mechanism. I could see that each component was meticulously crafted and I wondered how many hours and what machinery could produce such finely worked parts.

It was funny that you mentioned Breguet, because the quality of the workmanship reminded me of the illustrations I had seen of chronometers – beautifully detailed, a testament to man's ingenuity.'

'How did that lead to Maudslay's?' asked Hortense, looking slightly impatient.

'I'm getting to that part. Are all French women as impatient as you?' I said laughing. 'Well, leaning against the wall beside the shop was a runner – one of the young boys who hang around the streets hoping to earn a ha'penny for carrying out a small errand for the shopkeepers. He told me that the real genius behind the lock wasn't Bramah but Maudslay. He said that Bramah may have designed the mechanism but that only Maudsley was a good enough craftsman to actually make it. So next time I was in the area, I ended up wandering past his factory and he invited me to look around.'

'Maudslay invited you in to look around?' she asked quizzically.

'It was either that or have me arrested. I was loitering and he caught me, but when I explained about the Bramah lock he could see I had a genuine interest.'

'How did that lead to a job?'

'That's a story for another time,' I replied. 'More importantly, how has your brother settled in?'

'Julien's doing well, thankfully. He's working with Arnold's new partner, Edward Dent. They are working on marine chronometers, actually. Some of Arnold's were taken on board HMS *Beagle* on Darwin's five-year voyage to chart the oceans and wildlife of the world. My brother tells me that he is assisting Dent to improve their inner workings based on what they learned.'

She knelt down to light the fire. When she had finished, I told her about our success with the committee but also the challenge we now had of negotiating with the London and Birmingham Railway Company.

She listened carefully, even though it was a world far removed from her own, and then with a woman's unerring instinct for getting to the heart of what really matters, changed the subject.

'How are you finding it, working for Mr Brunel?'

The question took me aback. I had been so busy that I hadn't really paused for reflection. I took a moment to think, swivelling my chair to gaze at the fire, the kindling crackling and the flames gently licking the coal. I was tempted to answer with a few platitudes but I realised I wanted – perhaps even needed – to say how I felt, and it was easier to be honest when I wasn't facing her.

'It's been daunting,' I admitted. 'The workload is high and Mr Brunel is impatient. As you know, he doesn't suffer fools gladly.'

'I know,' she said behind me, and I could hear the smile in her voice. I assumed she was remembering the episode with the coal scuttle.

'I'm getting to know how he likes to work. He is very driven but very charismatic, too. It's extraordinary watching him at work.' I turned back to her. 'He's exceedingly good at the mathematical calculations but also fascinated by the aesthetics. He produces beautifully detailed drawings.'

'Is it what you expected?' she asked as she bent down to the fire, prodding the coals to even out the heat.

'I suppose so. I don't know what I expected. At times he can be friendly and very short at others.'

'But has he told you that you are doing a good job? Have you been given any cause for concern?'

She stood up, brushing her hands on her smock.

'No, he has praised me for what I have done. But he wants absolutely everything to be taken account of and is always in a hurry. I sometimes worry that I won't be able to keep up or will make a mistake.'

This was the first time I had admitted my fears to anyone. I wondered if I was being wise to say so much, but looking at Hortense as she in turn looked at me with real concern in her eyes, I felt reassured.

'Do you wish you had stayed at Maudslay's?'

I reflected for a moment, catching the warm breath of the newly lit fire.

'No. It may be scary but it's also exciting.'

'That's how I feel, too,' she replied, fiddling with the crucifix around her neck. 'It wasn't my choice to come here, but I am glad I did.'

As I gathered up my things a little later to leave for the evening, I thought about Hortense and the other people I had met since I started working for Brunel. Why did they... *we*... continue working with him when he could be so difficult and frustrating? I realised the answer lay in something Burke had said to me while we stood together one morning waiting for Brunel to arrive at the hearings.

'He might be a difficult bugger, but no one could accuse him of being one of life's dullards. Everything seems more interesting when he's around.'

Chapter 6

A week later formal parliamentary approval was received and early the following day Brunel and I sat down to work through what could be done to accelerate our progress now we could move forward at full speed. We often met like this first thing in the morning when it was still quiet and we were less likely to be interrupted by the constant stream of messengers that marked out the passage of a typical day. The cook was familiar with what we liked to eat. Brunel was partial to anchovy paste spread liberally on his hot rolls, while I preferred toast and a couple of rashers of well-cooked bacon.

To check he hadn't forgotten anything, Brunel was flicking slowly through the handwritten notes in his workbook. He carried a dark-blue folio-sized hardback notebook with him at all times. Volumes of completed books filled the shelves behind us. He told me that his father had always kept a notebook and had advised him to do the same. I took the hint but it was some time before I found the ideal size, large enough to allow me to take copious notes at the many meetings I had to attend each week, but small enough to fit snugly in the pocket of my frock coat.

Each of Brunel's books was filled with his notes from meetings, reminders to himself of things to be done, and on many a page, closely crafted drawings of engineering problems he was in the midst of solving. It was these drawings I had mentioned to Hortense. He really was an outstanding draftsman. Even better than his father. Occasionally there was a beautifully rendered sketch of a decorative feature that had caught his eye: the ornamentation around a fireplace, the shape of a streetlamp or bench, the design of the cornice above a front door. He was particularly fond of the Italianate and Gothic. He told me that he liked to capture anything that might one day feature as adornments to the various railway stations and buildings that he would need to design.

As we worked our way through the long list of tasks, now work could finally begin in earnest, there was a knock on the front door. Moments later the footman brought a package into the room. Brunel frowned. His household knew that he didn't like to be interrupted in this brief oasis at the start of the day.

'My apologies for disturbing you, sir, but the messenger was most insistent this was given to you immediately.'

The man handed over the package and retreated rapidly.

There was a handwritten note clipped to a sheaf of papers held within thick grey cardboard covers. The note, from one of the investors in the GWR, merely said: *I have received the enclosed and thought you might find it of interest.* The title on the cover of the enclosure was 'Prospectus for a Steamship Packet Route between Liverpool and New York'.

Brunel flipped open the cover and glanced through it. 'Interesting,' he murmured. He paused for a moment, then closed it and passed it to me. 'I need to leave now to meet with Saunders.' Saunders was one of the directors of the GWR and a close confidant of Brunel's. 'But perhaps you can read it through, Joseph, and find out what you can about what status the proposal has reached. Let's talk about it when you have completed your enquiries.'

The prospectus had been produced by a chap called Junius Smith. I knew nothing of him, but this was the first time that Brunel had entrusted me with something of this sort so I went out of my way to do the required research. Hammond gave me some names to follow up and I soon ascertained that Junius was something of a buccaneering trader, who with his New York-based nephew ran a small import-export business between the continents: French lace, wrought iron, garments, hosiery and so on sent out by Junius from England in return for apples, cotton, timber and maize sent back from the Americas by his nephew.

Junius had been agitating to start a shipping line for a number of years but with limited success. He had little relevant experience, had never raised substantial money for such a venture and knew nothing of shipbuilding. However, he had experienced all the frustrations, delays and unreliability of sailing ships, both as a trader and as a passenger. He had himself been becalmed on his return from a visit to New York, and often his shipments of perishables had been ruined by a slow passage.

The plan, according to Junius' document, was to build four ships so as to be able to ply the route with a regular service. Further discreet enquiries suggested that he was finally making headway. A shipbuilder in Glasgow had become interested and was prepared to build the ships as well as provide much of the capital needed.

Two weeks later I took Brunel through my notes. He leant forward in his chair, listening intently, cigar for once forgotten and unlit in the ashtray by his side.

'What do you think?' he asked.

It felt good to be asked my opinion by someone who respected the views of so few of his contemporaries. I told him what I had concluded: 'It does look as if he has momentum. As best as I can judge, the shipyard in Glasgow is serious about it and has started to prepare a bigger slipway that could accommodate the ships. The feeling is that the merchants based in Liverpool will get involved as soon as they believe it's viable.'

'That makes sense,' said Brunel. 'The Liverpudlians will only back something once they believe it will happen. But if it does, Liverpool is an obvious port from which to operate such a service. The thing that's hard to judge is whether they will be able to build ships of that size and design engines strong enough to power them.'

In a fortnight's time, Brunel was due to update the GWR directors on progress on construction of the railway since parliamentary approval had been received. They were going to meet for dinner at Radley's hotel in Blackfriars.

'I might bring this up if the opportunity presents itself,' he said. 'If nothing else it might distract the directors representing the Liverpool shareholders from yet more tedious moaning about the broad gauge.'

After returning from his club on the afternoon of the dinner, Brunel came across to my desk and placed the folder in front of me, saying, 'I would like you to come this evening and present what you have learned about Junius Smith's proposals.'

I wasn't sure I had heard him correctly but knew that asking him to repeat himself would earn me a sharp retort. I spent the rest of the day in a nervous funk. I wanted to tell him that my role was as a supporter, a scene shifter in the wings, not an actor on the main stage, but I knew I would receive short shrift. Brunel was always ready to take on a new challenge and expected those around him to do the same.

I dressed with great care that evening. Now I know why women take so long to get ready. I had little to choose between – three dark suits and half a dozen plain cravats – and yet it still took me an hour to decide what to wear. My mother found it amusing when I asked her if I looked satisfactory. 'As always, dear,' wasn't quite the reassurance that I was looking for.

The GWR board were a mixed bag, some had been appointed for their connections and influence, others to represent particular shareholder interests. I could usually guess what their view would be on a topic. Anything which might improve the position of Bristol as a city would gain favour with those representing the Bristol merchants. Similarly, the representatives of Liverpool money could be relied upon to object to anything that didn't favour Liverpool, the north, and the construction of a national railway network emanating from there. Like a seam of coal, every debate was carefully mined for nuggets that might improve or reduce the relative position of the Liverpool and Bristol ports.

We arrived at the hotel and were directed to an ornate room, its walls decorated with purple satin and large gold candelabras lighting up each corner. Some of the directors were already present, mingling over pre-dinner drinks. Brunel made his way over to have a quiet word with the chairman, Benjamin Shaw; he wanted to understand what topics might be at the forefront of the directors' minds, about which they might be most sensitive or vocal. Shaw told him that the broad gauge issue was bound to get another airing, but that they were mainly interested in how things would progress now parliamentary approval had been obtained.

When dinner was called, I stayed in the anteroom as the directors made their way into the dining room beyond. The double doors were closed, a footman standing guard either side, and I sat nervously outside. As the doors were ceremoniously opened and closed for each course and the footmen marched past with laden trays wafting the smell of rich sauces, I felt the saliva gather in my mouth. I had been far too nervous to eat beforehand and now regretted it as my stomach churned. As dessert was served, I was called in and Shaw brought the room to order.

'If I could have your attention, please, Mr Brunel has an interesting idea for us to discuss and his assistant Mr Bennett, who will provide the background, has joined us. He is seated at the back of the room.'

He gestured in my direction. People turned for a quick look but soon lost interest as he went on to say that first Brunel would update the board on progress on the railway since parliamentary approval had been received. Brunel stood and, moving to the end of the table, began his report. It was a masterful performance. He recalled a myriad of facts without notes: how much each contract had been let for (and there were dozens), how many men and horses each contractor was using, the last time he had had a report from each of the many worksites, how much soil had been shifted, and so on. He finished with a grand flourish.

'I am pleased to report that, although it is early days, we are making good progress on almost all fronts and I am confident that we will achieve the objective of the company within the time and budget allocated.'

It's an old metaphor, but I was reminded of a swan sliding serenely across the surface of a lake while back in the office all the under-the-water leg kicking was going on, as we worked to get specifications agreed and work underway. We already knew we had serious problems at Hanwell where the unseasonably wet weather was causing the new embankments to slip.

Harold Simpson, one of the northern directors, looked like he might burst at the seams. He kept leaning forward as if to interrupt, but then remembering his manners, contented himself with a mild 'harrumph' as he waited for Brunel to draw to a close.

'Mr Chairman, if I may,' he called out at the moment Brunel had finished speaking.

After Shaw rather wearily nodded his assent, Simpson continued, 'Thank you for the update, Isambard. You didn't mention it but I assume common sense has prevailed and we will be using the same gauge as the rest of the country.'

There were a few 'Hear! hears!'. It was clear to me that he had been canvassing support before the meeting. Brunel stood once more – he had barely regained his seat before Simpson's question had come flying across the table – and said that of course it wasn't yet decided and that he would bring a full paper to the board in due course. I was inwardly congratulating him on his diplomacy when he couldn't resist adding, 'I must say, though, that I do still feel there is strong merit in the use of a broader gauge. It will allow us to use larger wheels, wider carriages and so provide a smoother ride for our passengers.'

It didn't surprise me when Simpson took advantage of the opportunity to indulge in a monologue about the advantages of an interconnected railway. Most of it was the usual stuff, repeated several times in different ways: livestock could be moved between different parts of the country with ease; passengers would not have to disembark; engines and carriages could be produced more cheaply to one design.

'I don't believe we as directors would be fulfilling our duty if we didn't ensure we created a railway that interconnected with the others,' he said, looking at each director in turn. 'What would our shareholders say if we wish to buy another railway company in the future to expand our network and they are using the standard gauge? Think of the cost and disruption of operating two gauges or changing one to the other.'

He stared briefly at me, too, as he slowly scanned the room. I looked quickly away, telling myself I shouldn't antagonise him, but in reality wanting to hide my sense of guilt. I had caught myself thinking that his arguments had a powerful logic, even if they were at odds with the views of my employer.

Brunel stood once more. 'I understand your point of view, Harold, but I think you overestimate the complexity of interoperability between networks. It would simply require us to have well-organised terminuses at a couple of key stations.

At the moment that would just be Euston, and perhaps in the future another in Birmingham or somewhere like Cheltenham or Gloucester. The option of the broad gauge would allow us to create the fastest, smoothest, most appealing railway in the country. In time, others may come to see the wisdom of our choice as speeds increase and comfort becomes ever more important to our passengers. But as I said at the beginning, I have not yet finished examining the advantages or otherwise of the broad gauge in terms of engine and carriage design. When I have, I will of course come to the board with a recommendation for a full debate.'

Shaw jumped in to say that the board would of course reflect further on this important topic when Brunel was ready with the report to which he had alluded, but in the meantime Brunel had an interesting idea for them to consider.

Rising briefly, Brunel explained that we had received a prospectus for a proposed transatlantic steamship service. Looking at me, he raised his voice slightly and announced, 'my assistant, Joseph Bennett, has carried out some research on the idea, which I have asked him to present to you.'

Mr Shaw indicated that I should come to the head of the table. I had become increasingly nervous as I sat waiting for the moment to arrive when I would have to speak. Harold Simpson's intervention had provided some breathing space, but rather than giving me a chance to calm myself, it had simply created more time for anxiety to spread through my body.

Over the last few minutes I had felt sweat seeping through my shirt, firstly across my back and then slowly spreading around my waist. Breathing slowly and deeply had helped for a few moments, but then the fear of what was to come had overwhelmed me. Even though the room wasn't particularly hot, my shirt was now drenched under my suit, as if I had stayed out in the blazing sunshine on an airless summer's day.

I slowly made my way to the end of the table, but the extra time afforded by my measured progress didn't help. I still couldn't remember a word of what I was to say as the figures around the table stared expectantly at me.

'Junius Smith...' I started, then came to a halt.

In front of me was an expanse of table, silver candlesticks, glasses and the remnants of cutlery scattered across it. The directors were staring at me and I couldn't bring myself to meet their eyes as I began again.

'Junius Smith is proposing to run a steamship service to New York,' I said, with a shaking hand holding up a copy of the prospectus, now slightly damp where my sweaty palm had been clutching its edge.

'Who is Junius Smith and what's this got to do with us?' grumbled Simpson, still unhappy about the broad gauge debate.

'Let Mr Bennett finish,' said Shaw. 'We can then discuss what, if anything, it has to do with us.'

I took a deep breath, steadied myself against the edge of the table and began my explanation.

'Junius Smith is involved in the transatlantic import and export of goods and has been trying to raise money for a set of four steamships to offer a regular packet service between Liverpool and New York.'

I knew I didn't need to explain to this audience that a packet service meant a regularly timetabled set of departures. My voice was still somewhat squeaky with nerves but I managed to keep going, frequently glancing at the piece of card in my hand where I had noted the points I needed to cover.

'I heard about these proposals some time ago,' interrupted one of the directors, despite the chairman's request to let me finish, 'but they were seen as ill-considered and unlikely to get backing.'

I agreed that Junius Smith's previous efforts had failed to get any support, but I described how I had found out that this time he did seem to be making progress, having found a shipbuilder in Glasgow willing to build the ships in return for a stake in the new shipping line.

'Junius Smith has been working away at this for a number of years,' I concluded. 'Those who have more experience and knowledge than me are saying that this time it looks as if his plan has real momentum.'

Brunel stood up and thanked me, adding, 'Of course, if it comes to fruition, it will cement Liverpool's position as the leading port for Atlantic trade.'

He knew full well such an outcome would please the northern contingent but would irritate the majority of the directors who wanted to see the Bristol docks regain their leading position.

'What I have heard from the people who know their stuff, is that steam engines aren't efficient enough to be viable for ocean voyages,' Simpson interjected.

'It's true that coal consumption will be critical,' said Brunel, 'but unlike a locomotive I believe a ship can be built as big as is necessary to carry sufficient coal and a large enough engine.'

'Dr Lardner has already proved that a steamship can't carry enough coal to cross the Atlantic without stopping,' Simpson responded irritably.

Brunel rose to the bait, perhaps as Simpson intended. Maybe the man genuinely thought it wasn't possible and was Machiavellian enough to think that he could antagonise the Bristol merchants and investors into backing a project that was doomed to fail.

'Dr Lardner has all sorts of theories, most of which have little basis in science,' Brunel snapped.

Simpson rose from the table.

'Mr Chairman, I will take my leave, if I may. The business of the company seems to have concluded and I have no interest in spending time on frivolous and speculative ideas. In my part of the world, we would call Junius and his followers 'claht'eads', as we would be if we pursued this idiotic idea. We have more than enough to do without pursuing this speculative adventure.'

Not waiting for a response, he stomped from the room calling out: 'You haven't heard the last from me on the topic of the broad gauge either, Mr Brunel!'

Although several of the others followed Simpson out the door, a small group remained. Brunel indicated that I should leave as they settled down to chat over a glass of brandy. Mr Shaw stood up and shook my hand.

'You did a good job, thank you, Bennett. Sorry about the heckling. Strong feelings around the table. Not always a bad thing, that. At least people feel they have had their say.'

As I departed, the remaining directors were huddled deep in conversation around Brunel at the end of the table and Shaw pulled up a chair to join them. I found myself grinning and tipping my hat to strangers as I made my way home. I didn't know how good a job I had really done, but I was certainly relieved it was over.

I didn't see Brunel until lunch the next day. He told the table that there had been real enthusiasm amongst this group for a Bristol to New York steam service. His new catchphrase, 'extending the GWR to the other side of the ocean', had struck a chord. They wanted to beat Junius and his Liverpudlian backers to the punch.

'Harold Simpson's intervention helped sway the other directors to back the idea,' chuckled Brunel.

Had that been Simpson's intention? I wondered again. Did he believe that coal consumption would be the ship's downfall and wanted to incite Brunel and the other directors into backing the project anyway?

'We have decided to set up a new company and build two ships that will eventually interconnect with the GWR railway and provide a seamless passage from London to New York.'

I felt a familiar sinking feeling as I began to contemplate what this might mean in terms of additional work.

'By the way, Bennett, you did a very good job of your presentation,' Brunel added.

I was taken by surprise. Brunel didn't hand out compliments readily.

'Thank you, sir. I have to say that it didn't feel that way,' I said. 'I was very nervous and the questioning seemed rather aggressive.'

'It's easy to see where Harold is coming from and how to head him off at the pass. The ones to worry about are the ones that don't say anything,' replied Brunel, picking up his fish knife and carefully stripping the flesh from the bones of the sole on his plate. In a few seconds, a single fillet sat in front of him, the bones off to one side. Trying to carry out the same operation usually left me with a pile of broken flesh with the odd piece of bone poking through. I wouldn't make much of a surgeon.

'Why is that?' I asked.

'The ones who don't say anything are the ones who plot behind your back. They are like scorpions, reaching behind you and stinging you when you don't expect it. This morning they will be up early assembling factions to stop us.'

He gesticulated at me with his knife.

'We can't let them win. First they took the lead with railways, now they are looking to do the same with ships.'

For a moment I wondered who he meant by 'they', but then he continued, 'The Northerners are already too influential. I have been trying for years to take on the likes of Hudson and that old goat Telford and have finally got the backing to do it. We have to seize the moment. Carpe diem and all that.'

I picked up my cutlery and had a go at filleting my fish. Success for once! Feeling enthused by our joint mission to conquer the north, and setting aside my apprehension, I spoke up.

'Sir, I for one will do everything in my power to help.'

'Good man, good man,' Brunel said as he pushed his plate away. 'Bourton, please serve the coffee in the office. We need to get on.'

I quickly finished my fish and followed him. Brunel's vigorous defence of the broad gauge and his new-found interest in shipping made more sense now, I thought. I too didn't like the bullying ways of Brunel's opponents and despite my worries, I wanted to do all I could to help see them off.

Over supper that evening, I recounted the day's events to my parents. My mother was most interested in how Brunel thought the presentation had gone.

'Sounds as if you did yourself proud,' she glowed.

'I don't know about that,' I replied honestly. 'But I do want to help Brunel bring all this to fruition.'

That night the moonlight flooded through my small window, picking out soft pillars of amber light on the wall at the end of my bed as it shone through streaks left by the rain earlier in the day. As I waited for sleep to come, I allowed myself to imagine the great ships and railways I would have a hand in building. I could see myself standing on the quayside watching the passengers arrive by train before boarding our ship. Before long the ship's horn would be blasting, flags flying, passengers waving, everyone excited to be on their way to America.

Chapter 7

1836

The front door banged and Brunel stomped in, barking at Bourton: 'No, I don't want coffee. I am worked up enough already. Bring me some tea.'

He entered the office and gave me a brief nod as he took his chair. It was two months after my presentation and I had been revelling in every moment of the project as it took shape. Brunel had just returned from a meeting at the newly formed Royal Society, and without raising my head I casually asked how it had gone.

'Fine. Apart from having to listen to the likes of Telford and old man Stephenson banging on about the regulations and qualifications that should be put in place for people wishing to call themselves engineers,' he grumbled.

He pulled out his notebook and drawings and laid them on the desk before dropping his battered leather satchel on the floor.

'They are arguing that we need these rules to avoid charlatans and amateurs destroying the reputation of our profession, but all they are really trying to do is to get everyone to stay within boundaries they feel comfortable with. Telford wants the institute to come up with a set of rules for almost everything: how long a bridge span can be, what the specifications for the underpinnings of a road should be, etcetera, etcetera.'

Bourton entered quietly with a tray. Trust him to come himself rather than send a footman when he scented trouble.

'But wouldn't it be a good idea to have minimum guidelines for some of these things to avoid substandard work?' I asked, without really thinking but with my liking for a natural order to things coming to the fore.

'Who are you to know what's best?' Brunel snapped at me. I tried to apologise but he carried on, feeding his rage. 'Your job is to see my instructions are carried out, not to query my line of thinking. I don't need any more people, least of all my clerk, telling me what to do.'

I gazed unseeingly at the documents on my desk, hoping not to provoke him but he continued, warming to his theme.

'Your job is merely to do what I ask. Talking of which, have you set up the meeting I asked you to arrange with Robert Stephenson to discuss the sharing of the Euston terminus?'

I felt my face burn as Bourton gazed on impassively, but nonetheless managed to catch my eye with a superior glance.

'Thank you, Bourton, that will do,' said Brunel.

Bourton was closing the door as I started to explain.

'He has proven very hard to pin down to a particular date.'

'I don't care. Your job is to sort it out, otherwise what purpose do you have?'

I was shocked. Of course I had seen Brunel lose his temper before. I had also seen his need to defend himself vehemently when he felt he wasn't being shown due respect, but this was the first time he had been truly angry with me rather than merely irritated. And I knew Bourton would have heard Brunel's words.

I felt wounded. I had thought of us as a strong team, working together to tackle the challenges in the many projects we were working on. Now he was staring at me belligerently, almost willing me to take him on.

I apologised – what choice did I have? – and promised to get a meeting set up as soon as I could. It didn't feel good. I felt mistreated, but I had seen him dismiss employees for less, and was unwilling to risk angering him further.

We made our way to Euston a few days later. I looked at him seated across from me in the carriage, busy making notes in his workbook, occasionally looking out the window as things caught his eye.

'There is one of those new hansom cabs,' he exclaimed. 'They look very light and manoeuvrable. I must get a look at how they are sprung and how the steering works.'

After our argument Brunel behaved as if nothing had happened. I call it an argument, but perhaps to him it wasn't. He carried on as he always did, treating me partly as a colleague and partly as an employee. No explanation, no apology. I didn't know whether this was ignorance of the impact it had had on me or wilful disregard for my sensibilities. It seemed as if I would have no choice but to put it behind me.

After his admonition I had quickly drafted and sent a note to the chief engineer at Euston and then gone out to the park for half an hour. I sat on a bench and stared at the lake, watching the ducks drift past as if they didn't have a care in the world and willing myself to feel the same. To move on. To roll with the punches. I returned to work, wondering anxiously whether Brunel would have calmed down or would still be in a foul mood. The room was empty, a pile of papers he had annotated sat on my desk awaiting my attention. It was hard to achieve much that afternoon after what had happened. However, over the next few days it had become clear that for Brunel nothing really had.

As the carriage drew closer to Euston, the enormous amount of work underway on the terminus and railway approaches became obvious. In the distance smoke streamed from chimney stacks where the huge quantity of bricks needed to line the embankments and build the viaducts were being made. But it was the noise and stench close by that was overpowering. There was the constant ringing sound of picks on stone, punctuated with insults and instructions yelled back and forth. Underpinning it all, like the brass section of an orchestra, was the constant rumble of horses and carts removing the spoil. The odour of sweaty unwashed bodies mingled with the smell of burning coal drifting from the brickworks, over-riding it all the pungent perfume of rotting garbage, excrement and urine that permeated the metropolis.

Before the meeting, Brunel wanted to walk the first part of the line. A few years ago, I read Charles Dickens' novel *Dombey and Son*. There is no one who could give a better description of the scene that unfolded in front of us:

> *The first shock of a great earthquake had, just at that period, rent the whole neighbourhood to its centre. Traces of its course were visible on every side. Houses were knocked down; streets broken through and stopped; deep pits and trenches dug in the ground; enormous heaps of earth and clay thrown up; buildings that were undermined and shaking, propped by great beams of wood.*

> *Here, a chaos of carts, overthrown and jumbled together, lay topsy-turvy at the bottom of a steep unnatural hill; there, confused treasures of iron soaked and rusted in something that had accidentally become a pond. Everywhere were bridges that led nowhere; thoroughfares that were wholly impassable; Babel towers of chimneys, wanting half their height; temporary wooden houses and enclosures, in the most unlikely situations; carcases of ragged tenements, and fragments of unfinished walls and arches, and piles of scaffolding,*

and wildernesses of bricks, and giant forms of cranes, and tripods straddling above nothing.

There were 100,000 shapes and substances of incompleteness, wildly mingled out of their places, upside down, burrowing in the earth, aspiring in the air, mouldering in the water, and unintelligible as any dream. Hot springs and fiery eruptions, the usual attendants upon earthquakes, lent their contributions of confusion to the scene.

Boiling water hissed and heaved within dilapidated walls; whence, also, the glare and roar of flames came issuing forth; and mounds of ashes blocked up rights of way, and wholly changed the law and custom of the neighbourhood. In short, the yet unfinished and unopened railroad was in progress; and, from the very core of all this dire disorder, trailed smoothly away, upon its mighty course of civilisation and improvement.

In front of us stood the enormous banks of earth where hundreds if not thousands of labourers were working away with picks and shovels to clear a level route into London. Houses that had stood for decades had been knocked down, and others to the side of the forthcoming track were now looking out at the dark brick retaining walls of high-sided embankments, viaducts and cuttings. It was as if Hadrian's Wall had been rebuilt in brick and dropped into the centre of London to keep apart the teeming hordes of western and eastern city dwellers.

Children scampered about the mounds of earth, carrying bricks, bringing food and drink to the workers and begging for scraps. To the right of the works, from which a steady stream of people were coming and going, was a group of buildings around a courtyard. A wooden sign on a post hammered into the earth beside the roadway stated that this was the temporary headquarters of the newly formed London and Birmingham

Railway. It was where its chief engineer, Robert Stephenson, had his office.

A long queue snaked around the courtyard, out the gate and beyond. We reached the high-arched entrance where the gatekeeper (there to keep out people begging for work and children on the scrounge) asked our business. Once he had heard our explanation, he directed us to Stephenson's office across the other side of the courtyard. In turn, I asked about the queue. He said that the building of the railway had generated many rumours about the risk to health associated with living alongside it – the likelihood that coals from the locomotives would set houses on fire, and so on. The queue was of people waiting to air their grievances and make their requests for compensation.

We made our way to Stephenson's office, passing other doorways around the courtyard yielding glimpses of people sitting at desks and drawing boards, presumably creating and updating plans and schedules, issuing instructions and generally dealing with the plethora of matters with which I was most familiar when it came to bringing a project of this scale to fruition. We reached the end of the courtyard and entered a small antechamber.

'It will be interesting to see Stephenson's reaction,' Brunel murmured while we waited. 'His father George is very prickly. Always had a chip on his shoulder because of his lack of formal training, I think. Just like Telford.'

I was wondering what Brunel might say behind my back about my lack of formal training when we were ushered in. Stephenson jumped up from his desk to greet us. I had read much about the Stephensons. They fascinated me because of the parallels with the Brunels, father and son working closely together. However, Brunel senior was well educated and had friends in society, whereas George Stephenson was self-taught. He and the establishment viewed each other with mutual suspicion, particularly after the controversy over whether he or Davy invented the mining safety lamp.

George Stephenson had made sure his son had a good education, and the man before us appeared at ease, offering Brunel a cigar, which he politely declined, drawing out one of his own. Robert was a good foot taller than my employer and broader of shoulder. He had the ease of manner of a young man with a good education and prospects, and confidence in his own ability and future.

One wall of his office was dominated by a painting of the famous locomotive, the Rocket, winning the Rainhill trials on the Liverpool to Manchester line. A scale model of it stood on a sideboard below. Brunel walked over and peered at it.

'Lovely model, Stephenson. You and your father's work paved the way for all of us.'

'Thank you,' he replied. 'Please, take a seat. I gather you are here to discuss sharing the Euston terminus.'

'That's right.'

Brunel waved his cigar expansively, as if the two of them were sitting, a brandy apiece, in armchairs at their club.

'Parliament has requested that we do.'

'I would like to be able to help,' Stephenson said smoothly, 'but we need all of the space on the land that we have purchased.'

'I am sorry to say we have little choice,' Brunel replied. 'Parliament has demanded that we share the terminus.'

The amiable expression left Stephenson's face, although he remained scrupulously polite as he leant forward.

'It's not for Parliament to tell a private company what it can do with its land and buildings.'

Brunel held up his hand, as if to still a child charging towards him.

'Let me show you how it could work. It may not be as difficult as you might at first imagine.'

'Bennett, pass the plans please,' said Brunel.

He took them from me and carefully unrolled them on the

desk. Pointing at the drawings, Brunel indicated where an area could be created between GWR lines coming in from the west and the London and Birmingham Railway from the north. Luggage and freight space could be shared for goods brought from outside the station or that needed to be moved between the lines.

'I am afraid I don't have the authority to agree to anything without my directors' approval,' said Stephenson at last. Sitting back, he continued, 'I can consult with them but I must warn you that this won't feature high on their list of priorities.'

'Now look here, Stephenson,' said Brunel, a little testily, 'it's your investors who are always arguing for common standards. Here is a chance to work together.'

'If you really wanted to work with us, you would adopt the same gauge,' responded Stephenson, the atmosphere rapidly shifting away from that of a friendly chat in the club smoking room.

'What? Adopt a coalmine tramway as the standard for intercity travel?' snorted Brunel.

'I think we are finished here,' replied Stephenson icily, starting to get up from his seat to show us out.

Struggling to keep his temper in check, Brunel took his time lighting another of his ever-present cigars. He pulled it out of the case, carefully tapped it on the box, took a cutter out of his waistcoat pocket and snipped the end. He carefully examined the cut, grunted in satisfaction and placed the cigar in his mouth. He then lit a match and brought it gently to the cigar end, taking a few sharp puffs to get it glowing.

Stephenson retook his seat, but throughout this performance looked increasingly frustrated. He was obviously keen to be rid of us, and once Brunel was finished with his cigar-lighting ritual, he ushered us out of his office.

'I will consult with my board about your proposal, but I have to tell you I will make it clear I am not supportive.'

'Nevertheless, I would be grateful if you would,' replied Brunel frostily. He shook Stephenson's hand and took his leave.

As we walked out, I couldn't help but reflect with amusement that an English gentleman will always pride himself on maintaining social niceties, even when in the midst of a vehement disagreement.

Back on the main road, Brunel stopped and turned to me. 'He might have better manners, but to me he seems just as difficult as his father.'

But it was only a moment later that he spied another of the hansom cabs across the street and immediately hailed it, Stephenson instantly forgotten. Brunel insisted on walking around the vehicle with its proud new driver, like a child excited by a friend's new toy.

'It can turn on a thrupenny bit,' the driver said, 'and the horse is much less tired at the end of the day. Best thing I ever did was getting this.'

We got in and the cab set off, Brunel admiring its advantages over the traditional slow four-wheel hackney carriages and commenting on how the method of suspending the carriage on its springs might be of benefit for his railway carriages. At last he returned to the topic of the terminus.

'We can't let them dictate to us, Joseph,' he said softly. 'It's taken years to get back on my feet after the Thames Tunnel saga. I thought things were looking up when I won the competition to design the Clifton Suspension Bridge, but then the money ran out to build it. The GWR has finally given me the platform to show my talents. We can't be held hostage by those that have only their own interests at heart.'

I wasn't sure what to say. I felt deeply uncomfortable in the face of his disclosures. He had always seemed so certain of everything. He had clearly decided to make me his confidant again but I was finding it difficult to keep up with the changes in his attitude towards me. He was looking at me questioningly. I avoided his gaze and stared out the window for a moment. I realised that above all I still wanted to help bring his ideas to life.

'I understand,' I finally said. 'I will do everything I can to support you, sir.'

Brunel sighed deeply and seemed to shake himself, like a dog throwing off water after a swim.

'Thank you, Bennett. What would I do without you?' After a pause, he continued to ponder: 'What do you think? Should we marshal Members of Parliament to try and force the London and Birmingham Railway into working with us, or should we find an alternative home for the GWR's London terminus?'

'Either option risks endless delays and a return to yet more parliamentary committee meetings,' I replied. 'Perhaps we need to pursue both in parallel, if only to show Parliament that we have sought to do their bidding.'

Slightly to my surprise Brunel immediately agreed – often he liked to examine things from all angles. However, he did have one caveat, stating, 'But we need to find an alternative to the Nine Elms site. I don't want to spend years wrangling with the wealthy homeowners in Fulham and Brompton over the best route through their suburbs.'

Hammond and I set off early the next morning. The weather was fine and sunny as we made our way across St James's, Green and Hyde parks, following gravel paths bordered by fresh daffodils.

'It's strange to think that Constitution Hill is named after the walks Charles the Second used to take,' I said, as we made our way past Buckingham Palace towards Hyde Park Corner. 'I mean strange in that we don't have a constitution.'

'It's as strange as Brunel sending us off to look for the ideal site for a railway terminus,' replied Hammond. 'This is the first time I can think of in all the years I have worked for him when he has been prepared to let someone else take the lead.'

'Although I suppose that he will have the final say.'

'True, but usually he would want to see all the options himself.'

As we continued on our way towards the north side of Hyde Park – Brunel had asked us to survey that area of town for possible sites for the final part of the GWR route into London – I asked Hammond to tell me what had happened next with the Thames Tunnel.

'Where did we get to?' he asked.

'Pinkerley had slipped and fallen in.'

'Ah yes. Well, the morning after was a hive of activity. Marc had calculated that we would need 15,000 bags to fill the hole. But before we could drop bags into the breach, we had to lay metal rods to provide a base for the clay to sit on. It took days to create a lattice frame – like a giant portcullis laid on its side – using the diving bell to guide the cranes. Once the hole was filled, we started the pumps. In a few days, we had drained enough of the water to enable us to punt our way down the tunnel in a small skiff to have a look at the damaged section. With myself, Brunel, and two of the company directors on board, we launched the boat from the access tunnel slope.'

Hammond shook his head at the memory, then continued.

'I can still remember the stench. Muddy water dripped from the ceiling and echoed around the tunnel walls. Although I knew the pumps had been holding the water levels steady for a week, I was nervous. It felt like the dam of clay bags could burst at any minute. Everyone on the boat was quiet, we must have all felt the same way.'

'Wasn't the shaft blocked up?'

'Yes, we hadn't gone far when we found a mound of silt blocking our way. The entire end of the tunnel, including all the frames, scaffolding and brickwork, was buried in the mud. As we beached the boat on the silt bank in front of us, Brunel stood up to check how well the rods were embedded in the roof of the tunnel. As he stretched up, the boat rocked. One of the directors panicked and leant hard the other way. The next minute the boat had capsized and we were all in the water.'

'But you told me before that you couldn't swim.'

'You're right. Neither could our distinguished guests. One of them was yelling – well, more like screeching – something along the lines of "Help me, help me, I'm drowning!"'

Hammond chuckled as he remembered the scene.

'He was terrified. It wasn't that deep because of all the mud. Brunel stood up and said, "For God's sake, stop yelling and stand up, man!" Once we were all standing, albeit up to our knees in thick black mud, we were able to right the boat and get everyone back on board.'

Our route had taken us to the shore of the Serpentine. There were a few skiffs scattered about, rowers enjoying the cloudless day, occasionally languidly dipping their oars in the water. A bench nestled under a tree facing the lake and on it a small plaque was inscribed: *Harold loved to sit and watch the world go by. Rest in peace 1780-1830.* Who was Harold and had he frequented this spot in retirement or all his life? I wondered. Who had he left behind who cared enough to put a bench here? Would anyone care that much about me when I was gone?

As we paused to watch, shielding our eyes from the glare from the water, I could see why Harold had loved this place. I suggested we sit for a few moments.

'Have you ever brought anyone boating here, Hammond?' I asked.

He shook his head. 'No, I haven't but it looks fun. One day maybe.'

He continued his story.

'It must have been about this time that Gravatt proposed we dredge the riverbed in front of the tunnel workings and drop bags of clay in, so we would know we were mining through a thick clay seam we had artificially created, but Marc wasn't prepared to countenance it. And to be fair to him, although ultimately it might have saved time and money, it would have been very expensive. He probably would never have got investor approval.'

'Did things improve?'

'No, they got worse,' Hammond grimaced. 'Flash fires occurred frequently as methane gas exuding from the gloop was set alight by our candles. The men wore dampened bandanas to protect their hair, but within days most of them had lost their eyebrows, singed off by the flames.'

'Good Lord! But how did Brunel react to all this?'

'I think I told you that when he was first appointed engineer he spent days at a time down in the tunnel driving the work on, taking catnaps on a cot tucked in a corner a few yards back from the tunnel face. He ended up looking like the workers – dirty and dishevelled and giving off that fruity vinegary whiff of drains and swamps.'

Hammond laughed at the memory.

'After the tunnel breach, though, he seemed less committed. He still worked hard but slept less at the tunnel face and made a conscious effort to restart his social life.'

'I heard that you and he used to go to musical evenings together.'

'That's right. He was keen on music and drama. Before being appointed chief engineer on the tunnel he had been a regular at musical evenings, and had even taken comedy parts in his sisters' homegrown plays, acted out in their living room in front of a handful of guests.'

A few people walked by, and after a pause to let them pass Hammond continued.

'We started going to concerts again. There was one night when we went to a soiree just down the road from here in Kensington. I remember it vividly because I saw my first monkey. He was outside, performing with an organ grinder.'

I remembered my first monkey, too. It hadn't been that long ago and I had been with Brunel on our way to a meeting. A man had been standing across the street, his battered instrument balanced on a long pole in front of him, ready for a quick getaway if the police arrived and caught him busking. A small monkey leapt from his shoulder to the organ and back again. The creature's movement seemed sometimes to be in time with the music and sometimes not, it was hard to tell. Then it started to clap along with the music, and looking intently at the pair of us, waved us over to join him. He seemed almost human as he beckoned energetically, clapped a few times in time with the music, and beckoned again.

Brunel had surprised me by pausing and saying, 'I know they're doing it for the money and we can't stay for long, but let's stop for a couple of minutes, it reminds me of my younger days.'

Organ grinders and their monkeys had still been quite rare in London then. They hadn't yet become so numerous as to be seen as a nuisance. Nowadays they are ignored and moved on by the police. Everything has its day, I suppose.

Brunel and I had clapped along with the monkey as the organ grinder cranked out a lively tune. In a few minutes there were ten or fifteen people who had stopped to enjoy the impromptu concert, clapping and singing along with the lyrics of a popular bawdy music hall number called 'The Rat Catcher's Daughter'. The first verse sticks in my mind.

Not long ago in Vestminster
There lived a rat-catcher's daughter,
But she didn't quite live in Vestminster
Cos she lived t'other side of the water.
Her father caught rats and she sold sprats
All round and about that quarter,
And the gentlefolk all took off their hats
To the pretty little rat-catcher's daughter.

Brunel sang along as lustily and loudly as anyone when it came to the nonsensical chorus: '*Doodle dee, doodle dum, di dum doodle da.*'

'Isn't it remarkable to think of the journey that monkey has had by land and sea from Africa here to England?' Brunel had said as we turned to go. 'I wonder what it makes of it all, particularly the weather!'

I relayed this story to Hammond, who told me how Brunel had arranged for an organ grinder and his monkey to perform as people dismounted from their carriages on the night of the great banquet. I had heard about the famous banquet under the Thames and had tried to imagine the scene when I had visited the tunnel before I started with Brunel.

'Was it as amazing as the papers described?'

'It was the most extraordinary sight. The brickwork of the tunnel glowed amber in the candlelight, like a medieval church. There were candles everywhere, in holders fixed to the brick arches disappearing off into the distance, and set out along the entire length of the dining table, which was long enough to provide fifty places per side. A simple round-backed chair with a loose deep-red velvet cover stood at each place setting and the candelabras along the table lit the glassware and silver cutlery marking out each place.'

Hammond reached down, picked up a stone from beneath our bench and skimmed it out across the water before continuing.

'It was all Brunel's idea. He said we needed a landmark event to rebuild confidence. Marc didn't seem too sure. I suppose he was worried that something might go wrong. I think it was because at the time no one had any other suggestions to give the project a boost and we all knew we needed more money to complete the works. But eventually he agreed.'

'The evening was a triumph. As people arrived, a military band played lively marching tunes in one tunnel, while in the parallel tunnel a party was underway for the workmen. Brunel had arranged for a pig to be roasted for a dinner for them while the formal banquet was underway next door. Relations with the workers had suffered as the conditions worsened and many of them ended up sick. The dinner helped heal some of those wounds.'

I smiled as I gazed out at the ripple-dappled water while imagining that glorious night beneath the river.

'So how did it go from that to a closed-up tunnel only open to sightseers?'

Hammond rubbed his face with his hands as he shuddered at the memory.

'It was at the end of January 1828 that things came to a disastrous end. As always water was leaking in steadily, but in one area of the frames the soil started to break up and become almost liquid. I can remember two tunnellers rushing forward to try and put in extra wooden shoring to stop the flow, but it was impossible. Foamy, glutinous water sprayed from around the wooden boards like some hellish form of quicksand. It kept on coming, increasing all the time. Then the pressure of the water started to undermine the frames of the tunnel shield and the scaffolding behind it. The men were still working away but I could see the panic in their faces.

'Brunel was alongside me directing the effort to shore up the shield and even diving in himself to help. We called for the tunnellers to escape but it was too late. The wooden scaffolding started to creak and groan, then it began to bend, and finally collapsed. Wood and debris fell on Brunel and the two tunnellers alongside him and held them down as the water continued to pour into the tunnel.

'I tried to go forward and help, but the force of the water was too great and I was washed back towards the access shaft. I could see and hear little above the roar of the water and the debris and bricks flying around. I tried to hold on to the remains of the scaffolding poles and see what I could do to help the others but the water tore me away.'

Hammond turned to face me, speaking quietly as he recalled the scene.

'I made it to the access shaft and crawled up the slope clear of the water. There was no sign of Brunel or the other workers. I called out for help. We stood there scanning the water, feeling helpless. Then one of the engineers had an idea. He lifted the lid on the access shaft for the parallel tunnel and found Brunel floating there face down, unconscious. A few moments later and he would have drowned.'

I had a vision of Brunel floating face down in the Serpentine in front of me and was glad when Hammond sighed, breaking the spell.

'Six tunnellers died that day including the two that had been trying to secure the shoring with Brunel. That was the end of it. Work on the tunnel ceased. Sufficient funds were released to allow for the filling of the breach and the building of a temporary brick end-wall so that the tunnel could be opened to visitors to earn a little money to pay for its ongoing maintenance. Hopefully the works now underway will see it completed, but I am very glad I am not involved this time.'

I looked out over the calm lake and thought how boats on the Thames must have passed overhead with no idea what appalling conditions were being suffered beneath their feet. All sunny and serene on the surface and like a scene from a Greek or Roman battle below.

Hammond and I rather reluctantly agreed it was time to get going. As we got up, I thanked him for sharing the story with me.

'I can see why Brunel is so anxious to make his mark. He must have felt he had given years of his life without much to show for it.'

'He is certainly more single-minded these days,' replied Hammond. 'There was a time when he and I would set off in the dark after work to row a skiff by the light of the moon, from

Battersea up to Richmond for breakfast before heading back for another day at the tunnel. Those days are long gone.'

More's the pity, I thought. Brunel would benefit from some distractions from his work. If I was honest with myself, I also envied the relationship their shared memories had forged.

We set off again and reached the main road at the north end of the park. It was a busy thoroughfare with a steady stream of wagons heading in and out of London to the orchards, market gardens, and further out the arable and meat farms to the west. In front of us were fields and to our left the gravel pits of Kensington. To our right was Portman Square and its environs, already built up with terraces of grand houses.

As we walked along the side of the fields, it was clear that if we wanted a terminus in this part of London, this would be the place to build it. There was a natural route in from the west, a branch of the Grand Union Canal nearby, and the impact on landowners would be limited.

I turned to Hammond. 'Perhaps Brunel didn't come with us because he knew the answer would be obvious.'

Chapter 8

The men driving the Briska headed off at dawn so they could set up Brunel's mobile office ready for our arrival. At Hanwell to the west of London earthen embankments were being created to keep the railway line level as it bridged a wide, bowl-shaped valley, like a giant saucer pressed into the ground.

Brunel had designed what I can only describe as a horse-drawn cabin on wheels, although it looked more like a hearse than a summerhouse at the end of a garden. He was very fond of it and nicknamed it Briska, or in other words his baby. It was fitted out in rich dark mahogany. There was a desk to the right as you climbed the steps up to the rear door, and cupboards and drawers filled every spare inch of space, except where windows provided a little light. In the middle was a stove and at the far end a cot berth which afforded Brunel some luxury on the road, while we made do with tents pitched nearby.

Brunel and I followed on horseback a few hours later, after he had finished drawing up an alternative route into London to finish at the site Hammond and I had recommended. Although we were quicker than the Briska, it was still a slow business making our way through the crowds. The street was a meeting and living space for many of what I suppose one would call the flotsam and jetsam of society. All manner of things were bought and sold, and people who had little else to do loitered, waiting for who knows what.

Pedestrians plodded onwards making little effort to keep out of the way of the traffic, except everyone knew to steer clear of the thundering mail coaches – they didn't stop for anyone. An old man caught my eye and briefly held my gaze. He was gaunt, dressed in torn trousers and a ragged waistcoat with scraps of cloth wrapped around whatever was left of his boots. He stared at me, blinking slowly once, before turning away, his eyes dulled by years of misery. I wondered how I would fare out on the streets. Would my wits be honed by the need to stay alert to uncertain dangers, or blunted by a sense of hopelessness?

As if the pedestrians weren't frustrating enough, we had to thread our way past omnibuses stopping frequently to collect people from their new houses in the outer reaches of London, and slow-moving wagons bringing goods into town or heading out to the farms and nurseries spread around the edges of the city.

Wending through this welter of human flotsam were others on horseback, hackney carriages, the newfangled hansom cabs, and for those who could afford it, privately-owned carriages in varied states of repair and luxuriousness.

After rain, the roads became muddy and deep-rutted. When a heavily laden cart or wagon became stuck it wasn't long before everyone was caught in a seemingly unbreakable logjam. Frustrated queues built up as the wagoner, his assistant and anyone else they could persuade worked hard to get it underway once more.

It had been raining heavily over the past few weeks, and we were anticipating a slow journey. But although the roads were still in a poor state – the ruts had not yet been patched up by the toll companies – the rain had switched to a light drizzle and we had a quicker trip than we might have expected, reaching Ealing in a couple of hours.

We had received a letter from one of John Hammond's on-site assistants, Robert Archibald, only a few days before. He wrote that the unseasonal summer rain had severely affected the earthworks being carried out by our contractor, the McIntoshes, and that 'the embankment at Acton has settled very unequally. At Church's culvert it has gone down three feet, at various other places from fifteen to twenty-two inches and in other places it has gone down like deep potholes.'

We rounded a bend and came to the works. Thousands of tons of earth from cuttings at Ealing, where there was a rise in the ground, were being moved to Hanwell and Acton to create embankments to cross the shallow valley. We reached the edge of the cutting and looked down on hundreds of men working away with picks and spades to fill a long line of horse-drawn wagons waiting to take the earth a few miles further out of town. We could see that stones had been laid in the track the wagons were using to make their passage easier, but the soft ground had given way in places, leaving the ground uneven like a footpath across a rocky moor.

As we watched, we could see sodden earth clinging to the men's picks, trapping them firmly in the ground each time they were swung in, like corks in bottles. Cursing, they scraped off clumps of heavy mud that clung to their spades and paused every few moments to ease their backs. The wagons were setting off half-filled to avoid becoming bogged down.

We made our way further out of town, following the wagons along the track. We reached the point where they were being unloaded to build the embankments. Water oozed slowly out from large cracks in the stacks of earth, and just as Archibald had described we could see that the slopes were sinking at different rates into the sodden ground beneath. Deep ditches had been dug along the foot of the bank to drain the water away to streams nearby, but it was unclear to me whether they were helping or making matters worse.

I assumed it must have been the contractor's son, David McIntosh, who was standing in the clearing by the Briska when we arrived. It was hard to see his face or judge his expression, buried as he was within his oilcloth raincoat and hat. Beside the Briska was pitched a tented awning with a cook working away over an open fire. We shed our outer garments under cover of the tent and as we climbed the steps into the Briska, Brunel called out for tea.

McIntosh was taller than Brunel. Both were thin but Brunel looked gaunt and walked with a slight limp as a result of his injuries. McIntosh by contrast was lean and wiry with a tautness about him like a wild animal prowling and ready to pounce. We sat down in the warm fug created by the stove, wrapping our hands around the hot mugs brought in by the cook. McIntosh started by explaining the difficulties caused by the terrible weather.

'We've tried bringing in additional men and wagons to speed things up, but they just get bogged down and make the problem worse. We've had to take it slowly.'

'I understand,' said Brunel. 'I saw the problems for myself as we rode along the side of the cutting on our way here. It's clear to me that you will need to do more to secure the banks.'

'What do you suggest? We have been adding more earth and further drainage without success.'

Brunel sat back, a surprised look on his face. I wasn't sure if it was for theatrical effect or he was genuinely bemused as, adopting a rather patronising tone, he went on to say, 'It's really not my role to tell you how to do it. You took on the works and you must complete them to the specifications.'

McIntosh frowned – Brunel's tone would certainly have irritated me if I had been McIntosh – then took a deep breath and replied calmly, 'Well, it's impossible in the current conditions. We will have to wait until the soil has dried out.'

'But that may well not be until next year. The railway can't wait that long. And from your point of view I would imagine you want to be paid before then.'

Brunel took a slow gulp from his mug, making sure to hold McIntosh's gaze over the rim as he did so.

McIntosh frowned and leaned forward. He radiated tension as he gripped the edge of the desk and spat out his reply between tightly pursed lips.

'What do you mean, won't be paid?' His Scottish accent became noticeably stronger as the meaning of Brunel's words sunk in. 'You can't reasonably expect us to carry on without being paid any extra.'

Brunel paused, carefully putting down his mug.

'Evidently the current approach isn't working. Perhaps you would be better going about it a different way, for example, replacing the embankments with brick arches.'

'Of course we *could* do it that way,' McIntosh said, making what was clearly quite an effort to remain composed, 'but it will be a lot more expensive and, as I said before, how will the extra cost be dealt with?'

'If we don't get these works completed, then we won't be able to raise further funds to finish the railway. Once it's done we can discuss a settlement covering all the work you are contracted to complete for the GWR,' replied Brunel calmly.

I was wedged into the corner out of their line of sight but still I felt acutely uncomfortable. McIntosh was doing his best to achieve a fair settlement but I knew that the contract gave Brunel control over how costs would be apportioned for any overruns or changes and that McIntosh would have little choice but to do his bidding.

As McIntosh continued to try to reach an agreement, Brunel finally lost patience, holding up his hand to stop him speaking.

'I don't know whether you want to continue or not, but there are many other contractors who would love to be involved in the building of the line if you do not wish to carry on.'

McIntosh stared across at me as he fought some inner battle to keep his temper in check. I shifted uncomfortably under his gaze. Eventually he looked back at Brunel and sighed deeply.

'I warned my father something like this might happen when he took on the contract.'

Brunel's eyes narrowed as he held McIntosh's gaze. 'I am not sure what you mean by that, but whatever was said between you and your father is irrelevant to our discussion.'

Whether Brunel really did know what McIntosh meant, I don't know. I did though. The McIntoshes were an experienced firm with a good reputation for their work on other railway projects, such as the Dutton viaduct in Cheshire and many miles of heavy earthworks on the London and Southampton Railway. The father had built the business up from scratch and had a simple creed: trust in the people you work with, do a good job, and success will follow. His son was from a new generation, technically trained and more focused on the minutiae of the contract.

Hammond had told me that McIntosh's father, Hugh, had been the driving force for bidding for work on the GWR. He had been charmed by Brunel. According to Hammond, his son had been unconvinced and had warned his father to steer clear.

Brunel pulled out his battered leather wallet and carefully picked out a cigar. He took his time lighting it, as he always did when he wanted to give himself time to think. Drawing on it, he continued quietly but firmly, 'Your company has signed a contract to complete these works within an agreed time and budget. Are you going to abide by the terms or not?'

'As you know, I have little choice,' said McIntosh.

He banged his mug on the table and stood up to leave. At the open door he stopped and turned around.

'At least my father and I are clear with everyone that we are in business together. Everyone knows your father helps you, but his name isn't attached to anything.'

'I advise you to watch your words carefully,' Brunel answered. 'Nothing you are saying is in the remotest bit relevant to the work you are contracted to carry out here.'

McIntosh was now too angry to exercise any caution over what he said next.

'People know how much your father helped you with the Clifton Suspension Bridge. Who knows the extent to which he is advising you here. He always seemed a reasonable man. Maybe it would be better for all concerned if he were more formally involved and could help reconcile our differences.'

Brunel turned bright red. Standing up, he shouted: 'How dare you!'

Figures passing outside, indistinct in the misty rain, stopped to see what the commotion was about. Brunel lowered his voice to a fierce whisper.

'I am in charge here. The contract is clear. Get the work done or stand aside and we will find others to complete it.'

McIntosh gazed at him for a moment before walking over to the mess tent to reclaim his overcoat and hat. He marched off without looking back.

Hammond rode into the clearing in the early evening having spent the day out at the cutting looking at the problems with the drainage. We were due to share a tent that night, pitched alongside the Briska where Brunel had spent the afternoon undisturbed before retiring to bed.

We ate some sort of stew from tin plates as we sat by the cooking fire, chatting quietly as dusk fell and the sounds of the men at work died away.

'Thank God the weather has finally cleared up,' I said, handing the cook my empty plate.

'Yes, although it's going to be hard to make up the lost time, particularly as they will have to dig down to create solid foundations for the brick arches. The arches themselves will take more time still.'

Hammond sighed as he handed over his plate. He shook his head when offered tea, asking for a glass of whisky.

'It's been a long day,' he said.

I told him about Brunel's disagreement with McIntosh.

Hammond took a small sip from his whisky.

'That explains why Leishman was in such a foul mood when he came over this afternoon to tell me they had started work on building arches.' Leishman was the foreman and usually known for his equanimity.

'I am not sure how I feel about today,' I said in a low voice. Brunel had only just put his light out and I didn't want our conversation to be overheard.

Hammond leant towards me.

'You mean Brunel refusing to agree to pay extra?'

'Yes, I get quite a few letters from contractors requesting overdue payments. Brunel generally tells me to ignore them. He says we will sort it out when the work is done, and in any event, the contracts give him the final say.'

Hammond drained the rest of his whisky.

'On the tunnel he used to hold back the workers' wages if they refused to work extra shifts or wanted to quit. It caused a lot of unrest but in the end they had no option but to fall in line.'

'You mean he has always used it as a tool for getting people to do what he wants?'

'I suppose so. It was always hard to get the investors to release funds when we were behind schedule on the tunnel so perhaps Brunel did it in order to keep costs in line with progress. Maybe it's become a habit.'

The tent flap lifted gently in the dying breeze and rattled against the wooden pole. The sun had disappeared but the horizon was blood red as night fell.

'Is there any truth in what he said about Marc Brunel helping with the suspension bridge?'

'I don't know exactly,' whispered Hammond. 'Years ago I spied some drawings and calculations he had done, so he was definitely involved to some extent. And of course he provided the initial introductions to the Guppy family in Bristol who helped Brunel get the job in the first place.'

The tent's canvas was lit up by the rising moon and the last flickerings of the fire. At the edge of the clearing the trees were thick with leaf, like a stockade keeping out the mysterious creatures of the forest.

Hammond shifted in his camp chair, trying to find a more comfortable position. 'Both McIntosh and Brunel have been helped by their parents, though. I am not sure I would draw much of a distinction. It sounds like McIntosh was angry and just looking for a means to attack.'

It was time to turn in. I lay down on the narrow cot but the conversation I had just had with Hammond kept me awake. Did the end justify the means? Would Brunel really allow contractors to become bankrupt if it led to delays and might affect his reputation? A restless mind and camping do not mix well. I hardly slept, what with questions fizzing around in my head, the rustling of animals and birds in the woods close by and the sound of the workmen chatting by their fires in the distance.

I rose early, saddled up my horse and returned to the office, feeling tired and fretful. I saw James lurking by the basement door and stopped to ask after his family. All was well, and to my relief so was James's tenure at Parliament Street. He had shown himself a willing and able employee, and thankfully nothing had disappeared. Bourton, for whatever reason, had chosen not to raise his employment with Brunel, so for now all was good.

I went into work feeling a little better about things, but later that morning a short note arrived from Mr Maudslay.

My dear Bennett,

I trust that you are well. Perhaps you could come and see me at your earliest convenience. A matter has arisen upon which I would very much like to consult you.

Yours as always

I sat at my desk facing a large stack of paperwork, finding it hard to get started as Maudslay's letter played on my mind. On what topic might he find my counsel remotely useful? Might there be some dispute between him and Brunel that he would try and draw me into? Eventually I dashed a note off to him to say how pleased I had been to hear from him and that I would stop by that evening on my way home.

After working rather desultorily at the easier tasks in the pile for a few hours, I made my way over to Maudslay's.

'My dear fellow,' he said, jumping up from his desk as I was shown into his office. He shook my hand and invited me to take a seat in the chair on the other side of his desk.

'How are you? How are things going?' he asked.

'It seems a lifetime ago that I worked here, Mr Maudslay, even though it's less than two years.'

It felt strange to be sitting in this office again. My life had changed so much, yet everything here was exactly as it had always been. Mr Maudslay leant forward.

'I won't beat about the bush. Mr Purley is not well and I would like you to return as chief clerk.'

'I am so sorry to hear that. Will he be away from work for long?'

'Unfortunately he won't be coming back. He has cancer,' said Mr Maudslay, looking grave.

I was shocked. Mr Purley had been chief clerk at Maudslay's

for many years. He had never looked well, his skin grey and his cheeks sunken, but I thought this was the result of endless hours hunched over ledgers in the office rather than anything more sinister.

'That's awful,' I spluttered, conscious of how inadequate my words were to describe the situation facing Purley and his family.

Maudslay nodded sombrely. 'You can see how important it is for us to have you back. You would be able to pick up the reins immediately.'

I paused. Mr Purley had always felt to me like a part of the fixtures and fittings at Maudslay's, as if his dry and dusty demeanour had rubbed off from the whitewashed walls, but even if I could have imagined a world without him, I would have assumed one of the under clerks, almost as old as Purley himself, would have taken charge.

'Despite the circumstances, I am flattered by your offer, Mr Maudslay, but surely the other clerks with more seniority than I would be natural successors?'

'They may think that, but I want a change of guard – young blood to shake things up. What do you say?' he asked with a wide, confident smile.

'I know this may sound ungrateful, but may I think about it for a day or so?' Seeing his puzzled expression, I added, 'It's just that it is all a bit of a shock and I have been so busy with the GWR that I have had hardly a moment to think these last few weeks.'

'Of course, dear boy,' he answered, shuffling the papers on his desk to hide his disappointment. 'Take your time. Let me know by the end of the week, if you would.'

He walked me to the factory gates and as I shook his hand and took my leave he held onto mine for a few moments.

'Things are going very well here at the moment – machinery for all the new railways being built, steam engines needed for all sorts of purposes, new devices being invented. Interesting times. I think you would enjoy it.'

'I am so glad business is flourishing, sir. And thank you again for your offer. I will be back in touch shortly.'

I walked home wondering why I had not accepted Maudslay's offer there and then. It would involve managing many more people than in my current role and would be seen by others as a significant promotion. The factory was familiar to me. Working there had been a formative time in my life alongside other young men Maudslay had taken on and I still saw many of them socially. But however frustrating Brunel might be, my time with him had been exciting and I wasn't sure I was ready to leave.

I arrived home late and went straight to bed. I slept poorly for the second night in a row and arrived the next morning at the office with that feeling you get when dog tired. You want the world to slow down to your pace, but it just keeps on going while you struggle to keep up. I couldn't concentrate. An image of myself sat at Mr Purley's tall desk looking out over the rows of assistants kept popping unbidden into my mind. Here I was, drowning in papers, with one assistant and no time to recruit another.

I rang for some tea. Hortense answered the bell, as I had hoped she would.

'Would you fancy a turn around the park when you finish work?' I asked.

'Are you asking me out alone? That doesn't seem very seemly,' she said, raising an eyebrow.

'No, no. I wanted your opinion on something,' I stammered, my cheeks burning.

'I am just teasing you,' she replied with a laugh. 'I can meet you by the lake at six.'

We stood looking at the ducks as the church bells over in St James's rang out with the call to evensong. I closed my eyes and for the first time that day felt a moment of calm.

'There are lakes in Paris,' said Hortense, interrupting my reverie with her slow accented English – but gently, as if taking me by the hand and slowly leading me out of the woods, 'but they are all much more formal than this. Parks like the Tuileries and Jardin de Luxembourg are made up of square gardens and long, straight avenues. I love the sense of being out in the natural world that you get here.'

'Do you miss Paris?'

'I miss my friends and family. With all the troubles over there, I worry about them. My father wrote to say that my younger brother was almost shot the other day. He happened to be passing nearby when the conspirators opened fire on the King's procession. They had created what they are calling 'an infernal machine' which can fire twenty-five guns at once. It was like a Chinese firecracker going off, he said, as if an entire regiment had been assembled rather than a few ragged *terroristes*. Troops loyal to the King rounded up everyone in the area and he was arrested. They were threatening to shoot them all when my father intervened. Luckily, General Denys De Damrémont loves watches and was one of his regular customers. He went to see him and managed to negotiate his release.'

I thought of the Chartists here – imprisoned for demanding the right to vote.

'Can it be right to use any means even if it's to achieve a just end?'

I was startled when Hortense replied to my whispered words, 'I suppose if all other avenues are exhausted, there may be no option. In France, the King is pandering to the wealthy to maintain his reign. Even though my brother was innocently caught up in it, the rights of ordinary people like my family are being taken away.'

She paused for a moment, saying that she would like to follow the path around the lake. We walked in companionable silence as others strolled alongside us, but we angled off across the lawn and sat on the steps of the bandstand, set up temporarily each summer.

A notice announced when concerts were due to be played, weather permitting, but today it was deserted.

'It's always in the back of my mind, the worry. Things aren't getting any easier for them there.'

As she talked about her concern for her family she played with the thin silver bracelet on her wrist. We were sitting side by side and I wanted to reach my arm around to give her a hug but I told myself that would go well beyond the bounds of propriety. The truth, of course, was that I was too shy.

The air was warm and musty with the smell of grass recently cut and mouldering in the evening stillness. We set off again around the lake, passing an old man engrossed in his newspaper, folding it open to a new page with the sharp crackle of a fresh crease.

A young child flitted by, running in and out of the trees pursued by a friend. St James's Park with its colourful flowerbeds and footpaths meandering around the lake had become one of my favourite places to walk and take time for quiet reflection,. Hortense was right, it was extraordinary how artfully John Nash had designed the man-made hollows and hillocks, more natural to the eye than nature itself.

I told Hortense about Brunel's fracas with McIntosh and the job offer from Maudslay.

'I am sorry to be burdening you with this. It seems a trivial matter to be worrying about when your concerns are so much greater.'

'No, no. It's good to have something else to talk about.'

'Please keep it to yourself. Brunel wouldn't take kindly to me even contemplating Maudslay's offer.'

'Of course. You needn't worry.'

'Thank you, Hortense. I know I can trust you.'

'I am not sure what to do,' I continued. 'With all this going on I haven't slept properly for days.'

The lawns to the side of the path were full of buttercups and a little further along three girls were giggling quietly while they assembled necklaces of green and yellow. Without the benefit of the latest books on manufacturing techniques, they had created a specialised production line. The first roved about, carefully selecting flowers and bringing them back a few at a time. The second used her teeth to carve a thin cut along the stem of the flower. The third carefully poked each new buttercup through the hole created in the stem of the last. Two necklaces already lay on the ground and they were working away at a third, the evening sun reflecting off their white petticoats as they worked.

Hortense reached down to pick one of the flowers for herself as we stopped, enjoying for a moment the bucolic scene.

'It would be nice to be so carefree,' she said rather wistfully, spinning the flower daintily back and forth between her thumb and first finger as we watched the girls complete their third necklace and start on a fourth. I wondered if another friend was on their way or if they were simply enjoying their collective efforts.

'Maybe we should get them on our staff, although I am not sure how they would take to Brunel's manner. At least they would realise school isn't so bad after all,' I laughed.

'He is having to deal with rather more than a schoolmaster does,' replied Hortense a little sharply.

'Yes, but is that pressure an excuse for treating people badly?'

'No, not an excuse. An explanation perhaps.'

We walked on in silence and paused when we reached the little ornamental island at the southern edge of the park where we would go our separate ways.

'I will miss you if you decide to go,' she said. 'But of course that shouldn't be how you make a decision.'

She laughed, then kissed me on the cheek as she took her leave.

I made my way home wondering what I should do.

We had a maid, of course, but my mother liked to cook and I enjoyed sitting at the kitchen table while she prepared the evening meal. She asked how the trip had gone and I explained about the altercation with McIntosh.

'Your father has always said it takes a strong man to change the world,' she said, beginning to chop onions with her favourite bone-handled knife.

'It's more than that. It's bullying really,' I replied.

'Do you wish you had stayed at Maudslay's?'

She took the onions and some potatoes she had peeled and added them to the pot on the range. I had been avoiding telling her about the dilemma I faced but now I had no option, and taking a deep breath steeled myself to tell her about the letter and my visit to Maudslay's.

She paused to listen carefully to what I had to say, her head cocked to one side, the wooden spoon she was using to stir the pot held lightly in her hand, just as when I had come home as a little boy excitedly launching myself into the kitchen with my latest news.

'If you are finding it stressful at Brunel's and you don't like the way he treats his suppliers, why don't you return to Maudslay's?'

'I don't know. It would be a big promotion. It's the obvious thing to do.'

'Well, what's causing you to hesitate?'

She had turned her back to me, busy again at the range.

'There's something about the excitement, the sheer enormity of what we... he is trying to achieve that makes it hard to step away.'

Finished with preparing the food, she spooned a small portion of tea into our old enamelled pot and filled it from the kettle on the range.

'You can always come back here to the shop,' she said as she poured the tea. 'It would please your father.'

I didn't reply. Gazing at the stew bubbling away on the range and carefully blowing across the top of my cup to cool the steaming liquid, I wasn't sure I knew what I wanted any longer.

Chapter 9

We leant over the map-table placed in the centre of Patterson's office. The room reminded me of a shipmaster's cabin, the table and Patterson's desk crafted in polished mahogany, with a patina the colour of a well-aged port. A large bay window along the length of one wall gave views across the shipyard to the harbour and City of Bristol beyond.

Before we gathered around the table, I had stood at the window, taking in the scene. There were ships stacked two or three abreast along the wharfs and opposite was a repair yard with boats crammed on the slipway, crawling with men at work. To the right was a coal wharf, black mounds piled up against retaining walls, dark dust clouds blowing gently away, like mist on a hilltop.

Either side of us stretched woodyards stacked high with timber from all over the world: oak brought from around the British Isles by local coasters, tall pines from Scandinavia, exotic hardwoods from Africa and the Americas. The tide was high in the gorge and ships were queuing at the dock entrance, waiting to clear the lock and take advantage of the outgoing stream to hasten their passage to the sea.

Above the docks were sweeping terraces of brightly painted houses following the contours of the hills. Patterson had earlier pointed out the recently completed Royal York Crescent, its imposing half-moon façade of tall merchants' homes dominating those around it.

Below us was the yard itself and the stern of a ship under construction reared up a few feet from the window. At the far end her bow hung out over the water, like a dog pulling at its lead, ready to head to sea as soon as she was finished.

To the left, under long, overhanging roofs, we could see stacks of timber running along the full length of the ship. Tucked in every spare space on the slipway were smaller boats being constructed or in for repair. It was hard to imagine how so many had been crammed in, or even how the workmen avoided getting in each other's way as they scurried around.

The noise of hammering and sawing filtered through the closed windows in a not unpleasant orchestra of sound. The smell of newly cut wood and the melted pine pitch used to caulk the decks was overpowering, even up here above the fray. The aroma reminded me powerfully of my youth, when I would hang around the gates of the yards along the River Thames, watching ships slowly emerge from a forest of wooden scaffolding.

There were four of us, heads bent over the table studying Brunel's drawings: Patterson, Brunel, Claxton and myself. Claxton and Brunel had got to know each other a few years before when Brunel had been laid up in Bristol after his Thames Tunnel injuries. Now the Great Western Steamship Company had been formed, he had asked Claxton for advice on how best to proceed. Claxton had been a ship's captain but had become the Bristol dock warden once he had a young family so that he wouldn't be at sea for weeks on end.

Claxton in turn knew William Patterson. Patterson had recently taken over Scott's long-established but moribund yard and had quickly earned a reputation for innovation and open-mindedness in an industry renowned for sticking to a particular way of doing things, developed slowly over many decades. The effectiveness of his designs had rapidly made him the leading shipbuilder in Bristol. Claxton had promised that Patterson was the best in Bristol and that he would be open to Brunel's new ideas.

Brunel asked me to summarise Junius' prospectus, as I had done for the GWR directors. I warmed to the task and this time found myself enjoying it. Of course, things are easier when repeated, but speaking to two people keen to learn what was afoot was a very different experience to standing formally in front of an audience, at least some of whom I knew to be hostile. Brunel let me finish and then added his view.

'What Junius is trying to achieve makes sense to me, even though people are laughing it off as fanciful. Delays due to lack of wind ruin perishable cargos and merchants often disappoint their customers when shipments arrive late. Some people are claiming it can't be done, but I have done some calculations and I believe it can. My problem is that to carry enough coal to make it across it would need to be two hundred and fifty feet long – the largest ship ever built – and that's why I need your advice.'

Patterson was a sinewy, mild-mannered, but straight-talking Scot. When Brunel said two hundred and fifty feet, I had heard his sharp intake of breath but now he was quite still, tapping his pencil against his teeth as he frowned in concentration.

'Building ships longer than two hundred feet has proved difficult. They are flexing more than any of us would like, despite heavy reinforcement in the hull.'

'Aha,' said Brunel, pointing his cigar at him and grinning like a schoolboy who knows the answer to a teacher's question, 'that's where I believe my engineering experience can help. Railway bridges bend far more than road bridges when heavy locomotives pass over them. To avoid the possibility of derailment, we now use box girders and iron strapping to reduce the flexing. I believe the same approach can be applied to ships, but I need your help to work out how it can best be done. Let me show you some sketches I have drawn up.'

I could see that Patterson was both worried and intrigued. On the one hand he was excited by the project but on the other concerned about his reputation if it all went awry.

Brunel unrolled the drawings we had brought with us. They illustrated how longitudinal beams and iron strapping could be used to strengthen the hull, just as he had done with his railway bridges. I had watched when he had sat at his desk, smiling to himself, deftly using his pencil to bring the structures to life with differing shades of grey. He had depicted placing wide strips of iron around the beams to lock them together, using their combined strength to support each other. I felt that I could reach into the drawing and pick up the metal bars and retaining bolts he had carefully drawn, brought to life by the delicate shadowing.

Claxton and Patterson leant forward to peruse them. It's hard to put into words the exquisiteness of Brunel's sketches. Even those in the margins of his notebook were small masterpieces of precision. Straight lines and hand-drawn curves looked as if they had been produced with a ruler or set of compasses. When he drew a component – a shaft or a lever perhaps – it was with the meticulousness of an engineer, but to me the extraordinary thing was the beauty. Of course, I am biased but others said that his work reminded them of the sketches of great artists such as Leonardo da Vinci.

I tried to imagine a forest full of trees so long and straight that they could be hewn to produce the large gently curved beams that Brunel had drawn. As you stood at the base of a tree, you would be able to see little but the bark of a mighty trunk stretching endlessly up above you. It would take the arms of several men to reach around the girth of these trees. It was difficult to picture how such a tree could be felled, brought out of the forest and transported to the shipyard.

'I see what you are suggesting but it's untried,' said Patterson thoughtfully. 'Perhaps we should build a smaller ship as a test?'

'We don't have time if we are to beat Junius. Locomotives bend wooden bridges just as the sea does ships. I am sure it will work.'

Patterson looked over at Claxton. 'What do you think?' he asked.

I sat back, aware that I had little to add to the conversation. I was struck by how much more relaxed Brunel was than usual. He was smiling, listening carefully to Patterson's questions and answering without the formality and prickliness I often saw him display – even when Patterson appeared to be questioning his judgement by asking Claxton's opinion. I wondered why; and why hadn't he responded to McIntosh in the same way? Perhaps he was taking pleasure in working on a bold new idea, or financial pressures had yet to impinge on this project. I wasn't sure. Either way I admit that I was enjoying being at the birth of something so new and exciting.

'As long as you can build it, I don't see why it wouldn't work,' said Claxton.

Patterson chewed on his pencil as he slowly scanned the drawings. After what felt like an age, while the world seemed to pause despite the evidence of the noises from the shipyard below, he looked up at Brunel.

'Alright. I may come to regret it but I agree. It should work.'

'Excellent!' replied Brunel, rubbing his hands together and smiling broadly like the cat that has got the cream. 'How quickly can you let me have your detailed designs and costings?'

'Give me two weeks then I will send them to you in London. If you are content, we can meet again to finalise things.'

We were due to visit Brunel's family friends, the Guppys, so took our leave. We shook hands at the gates of the yard and then Brunel dismissed the waiting curricle.

'Let's walk, it's good to get some fresh air.'

We headed off along the wharfs, weaving our way through the horse- and hand-drawn carts stationed every few feet along the dock waiting their turn to load or unload goods from the ships moored along the harbour wall. Out on the water, men were shifting packages and bundles from larger ships onto smaller boats.

Set back thirty or forty feet from the quayside were rows of warehouses and storage yards. Most of the warehouses had enormous wooden doors facing directly onto the wharfs to allow cargo to be moved about easily, but the doors of the tobacco warehouses were small and iron-clad, their red-brick walls peppered with small barred windows, all designed to keep the valuable cargo safe from thieves. They looked as if they might be prisons holding thousands of inmates.

Brunel was in a good mood as we left Patterson's.

'Someone I can do business with,' he said rather jauntily as we crossed the swing bridge and headed alongside the dockside to College Green.

Thomas Guppy and his family were old friends of the Brunels. Marc Brunel had met Thomas's father when both were working in New York many years before. Thomas's family had started out as sugar merchants, but Thomas had always been interested in scientific progress and had been one of the Bristol merchants who had argued most forcibly that they should invest in a railway to London.

The Guppys lived at the top of Whiteladies Road away from the noises and smells (I suppose if you were being honest you would say the stench) of the city and the docks. I was worried that Brunel would find the walk arduous, but I knew better than to argue. I found the climb up Park Street from College Green hard enough and I couldn't help but admire him as he ignored his limp and powered up the hill, chattering as he went.

'Extraordinary woman, Mrs Guppy. She has six children and is a devoted housewife, but she never stops inventing things.'

'What kind of things?' I puffed, struggling to speak and stay at his side.

'Household improvements as you might expect, such as a method of steaming eggs and of reducing the risk of kitchen fires, but also things you would imagine were well beyond her natural sphere of knowledge.'

'Such as?' I asked, sucking in a big lungful of air.

'A way to reduce barnacle infestations on ships, which she sold to the navy for the princely sum of £40,000,' he said rather wistfully.

I wondered how she had gained the experience to come up with something like that, but before I could ask, Brunel continued, 'She also designed a new method of securing foundations with wooden piles. She let Telford use it without charge for his Menai Straits bridge because she believed it would be good for the citizens of Anglesey to get across to the mainland more easily.'

'That was very good of her,' I wheezed.

'She let me use it for the Clifton Suspension Bridge, as well. Although of course the lack of funds to finish it mean that the people of Bristol aren't yet getting the benefit!'

At last we arrived at an imposing house on Richmond Hill, set in its own gardens. We passed through the large wrought-iron gates and walked up the sweeping gravel drive.

Mrs Guppy greeted us at the door.

'Hello! Welcome back, my dear Isambard, and you must be Mr Bennett.'

'Please call me Joseph.'

She was dressed in a long, flowing dress with a light shawl over her shoulders, her greying hair held back in a bun. She had a lovely, rather carefree smile which made me feel immediately welcome. If Brunel hadn't told me about her accomplishments, I would have taken her as no more than a rather scatty, warm-hearted matriarch.

She guided us into her drawing room, painted in pale grey and filled with light from the wide sash windows that rose from below my knee to approaching twice my height. They offered stunning views back down the drive, the chimneys of the houses on Blackboy Hill peeking over the trees. She sat me beside her and busied herself pouring us tea and handing out delicately cut sandwiches and small cakes.

'I make these myself,' she said, offering me a cake. 'It drives our cook quite mad, but I enjoy it, so why shouldn't I?'

As Thomas Guppy and Brunel moved to the other side of the room to discuss the new steamship, she turned to me. 'So, tell me, Mr Bennett… Joseph. How is it that I haven't met you before? How long have you been working for Isambard?'

'It's about two years,' I replied, 'although so much has happened it seems a lot longer.'

Mrs Guppy – she asked me to call her Sarah but I couldn't bring myself to do so – went on to ask me about my circumstances and upbringing. I answered dutifully but found it hard to concentrate. My eye was constantly drawn to the glass cabinets placed on tables around the walls of the room. Inside each were fine models of sailing ships, bridges, steam engines and the like. When I could do so without appearing rude, I asked her about them.

'Oh,' she said, 'a little hobby of mine. My father was always interested in science and it was one of my great pleasures growing up to sit with him and build models. I have kept it up as a respite from the rigours of family life.'

'How do you have time for all of this, as well as your family and your various inventions?' I exclaimed.

I turned red as I realised that my question might well have come across as rather impertinent. She laughed, putting me at ease.

'Many of my ideas come to mind watching things done every day around the house. For example, I came up with the idea of a fireguard when seeing our cook almost burn herself.'

'But what about your ideas for ships and foundations?'

'That's where the models come in. A new method of piling came to me while building a model of London Bridge. I realised that better ways could have been employed to build it.' She paused, taking a dainty sip of her tea. 'I am very fortunate to be surrounded by people like my son Thomas and Isambard who are always telling me about the latest innovations.'

It seemed such a huge leap to go from building a model to coming up with a new method of driving in piles to secure foundations that I found myself at a loss for words. To fill the awkward silence, I asked how long she had known Mr Brunel.

'You mean Isambard?'

I realised that of course she knew his father too. 'Yes,' I replied.

'Marc, his father, whom my husband had known for many years, sent Isambard to Bristol to convalesce. As you probably know, he was badly injured when the Thames Tunnel flooded.'

'I can't imagine him quietly convalescing.'

'You are right, of course,' she said, grinning broadly. 'Thomas got Isambard involved in suggesting some solutions to a problem we have had for years here with the docks. They are a long way from the sea and as ships have got larger, we have struggled to keep up with other ports like Liverpool. A few years ago, the river was dammed and a new cut created to allow the river to bypass the city. This meant that ships could stay afloat alongside the wharfs at all states of the tide, but the docks steadily silted up, making navigation more difficult.'

She explained that Brunel had told them that the long-term solution was to build a new dock at the mouth of the river at Avonmouth but money was tight and they wanted a cheaper answer.

'That's when Isambard designed a steam dredger that uses a system of wire ropes to pull itself around the docks and to scrape the silt off the bottom with a large scoop. It had the merit of being both cheap and effective – and we're still using it! Claxton, the dock warden, was heavily involved and became a firm friend.'

She went on to describe how Brunel was then persuaded to enter a competition for the design of a bridge to span the Avon Gorge to join Clifton with the Leigh Woods area of the city: 'In 1753 a Bristol merchant called William Vick left a sum of money to grow with interest to the point it could be used to construct a bridge across the River Avon. By 1829 it had grown to £8,000, and a competition was held to find a design for the bridge.'

She insisted I had another cake.

'Those yellow ones might not quite look the part but I assure you they are very tasty.'

They were a curious bright lemon colour but I dutifully took one and through a mouthful nodded my appreciation – they did indeed taste good – and urged her to continue.

'Twenty designers submitted entries, including Brunel. The judging committee rejected most of them, either on cost or aesthetic grounds. They then called in Thomas Telford – you know, the famous Scottish bridge and road builder – to help them make a final selection from the five remaining entries. Telford rejected all the designs, arguing that the five hundred and seventy-seven feet span of his Menai Straits bridge was the maximum that anyone should use. He then produced a design proposing a one hundred and ten-feet-wide suspension bridge, supported on enormously tall Gothic towers from the base of the gorge, which would have cost around £52,000.'

'But didn't you say that the budget was £8,000?'

I put down my cake as a few crumbs went down the wrong way and set me choking.

'Are you alright?' she exclaimed, patting me gently on the back before continuing.

'That's correct. None of us could believe that the committee might be prepared to accept a design which so manifestly didn't meet the project brief, but they did. However, after a public outcry, two new judges were appointed and eventually Brunel's design was accepted.'

'So that explains why Brunel isn't a big devotee of Telford?'

'Yes. It's a bit unfair because Telford isn't as backward-looking as Brunel would have you believe, but it is true that he tends to think his way is the only way. You could say they are somewhat alike in that regard,' she said with a smile. 'Anyway, the connections he had made in improving the docks and bidding for the bridge design work put him in a good position when a surveyor and engineer for the GWR was needed.'

I had been so engrossed in listening to Mrs Guppy that I had failed to notice that Thomas Guppy and Brunel had finished their conversation.

'Dearest Sarah,' said Brunel, 'we must take our leave if we are to catch the mail coach back to London. I am sorry you and I didn't have much chance to talk.'

'Not to worry,' said Mrs Guppy. 'I very much enjoyed talking to your clerk. It's a bright young man you have there.'

As we settled in under blankets for the long journey home, Brunel asked me what Mrs Guppy and I had talked about. I said that she'd asked about my background and I'd asked her about her models and her inventions.

'But didn't I also hear her telling you about the Clifton bridge?'

'Yes, she did. She mentioned the role Telford played in the selection process.'

'Old fool,' muttered Brunel. 'Did good things in his time but became reluctant to take risks and not prepared to push the boundaries. You can shoot me if I end up like that.'

He held two fingers to his temple in mock execution, then paused for a moment before continuing quietly, 'You know, that was a low time for me. The Thames Tunnel work had stopped; my contemporaries were all busy building railways, roads and bridges and I couldn't see where my future was heading.'

He sighed and stretched out his legs, taking care not to knock against the passenger opposite.

'I owe the Guppy family a lot. They introduced me to the right people in Bristol. I still don't know exactly how much influence they exerted behind the scenes when it came to winning the bridge design competition and the work on the GWR.'

I looked out the window at the black night rushing by. Beside the door was my favourite place in a carriage. I disliked being wedged tightly between sharp-elbowed fellow passengers as the coach bumped and rolled along. I was usually able to sit here, others didn't like the draught but I enjoyed the breeze ruffling my hair.

I wasn't sure what to say. Brunel hadn't been this open with me before. I didn't want to take his having confided in me for granted but neither did I wish to appear presumptuous.

'Whatever assistance they may have given you, it seems to me it's what you made of it that really matters,' I replied.

'Hah! A good riposte,' he said rather impishly, his mood brightening. 'But there's still plenty we need to make of it yet. The others are pressing ahead and there's always someone trying to hold us back.'

The coach lurched, throwing my head forward, the door frame bringing it to an abrupt stop. Brunel laughed, saying it served me right for taking the window seat.

I smiled in reply and suddenly realised that I couldn't take the job at Maudslay's. It might involve more seniority, and it might make for an easier life, but I would miss all this. I would miss being there to see the new steamship brought to life, the arrival of the first train in Bristol and who knows what other projects which might come to pass over the coming years.

Feeling a sense of relief at a decision made, I tucked a fold of the blanket between my forehead and the door and settled down to rest. I knew that after we arrived back in London Brunel would want to be straight back in the office, pausing only for a quick wash and some breakfast

Sleep didn't come easily. The greys of a new day infused the blackness around me but the world outside remained distant. It could have been another era, the two of us comrades in arms setting out on a crusade, each of us driven on by our own dreams.

Chapter 10

It was a Monday morning about a month later when Brunel called the whole household together. As we waited in the dining room for him to join us, I could hear the maids whispering to each other anxiously. I, too, was worried about why we had been assembled – had Brunel over-reached himself and needed to pare things back? I kept my concerns to myself, and it wasn't long before Brunel joined us and broke the unexpected but happy news that he was to be married.

Hammond led us all in a rousing 'Hear! hear!' then as we left the room he took my arm and steered me into a side room.

'This is a surprise, isn't it?' he said with a chuckle.

'Yes, I thought he was married to his work.'

I was still struggling to absorb the news. Naively I had thought that Brunel's requirement of a promise from me not to get married meant that he wouldn't either.

'When we were working on the tunnel together he was sweet on a lady called Ellen Hulme. He was tying himself up in knots about it. One minute he felt he couldn't live without her and the next he didn't feel his prospects were yet certain enough to marry. Good for him that he has finally crossed the Rubicon.'

As we returned to our desks, Hammond leant in close and whispered, 'Luckily he told us his bride to be was Mary Horsley before I blurted something out about him finally realising that he had made a mistake letting Ellen go!'

Hammond, Gravatt and myself had been invited to the party that was to follow the family-only church service. I sat in my favourite seat in our rented carriage as we rattled along on our way to the Horsleys' house at Kensington Gravel Pits. It was about a mile further west than the new site for the GWR terminus at Paddington – thankfully the land had been bought before the owners found out that we weren't able to agree a plan to share Euston and tried to extract a higher price.

A garland of flowers was woven around the wrought-iron gate that opened onto a small paved courtyard at the front of the house. We made our way through the house towards the gardens beyond. Large vases lined the hallway and the sweet smell of freshly cut flowers filled the air. As we approached the large French doors at the back, we could see the lawns stretching out in front of us, with views over the gravel pits to the city in the distance. The trees were hung with paper lanterns, glowing in the summer twilight. Lamps hung on metal crooks were planted around the edges of the garden, lighting up flowerbeds that looked like an artist's palette, dazzling with pigment.

In the carriage we had been supping from a small flask of whisky, laughing at Hammond's jokes and teasing Gravatt for his serious manner, but as we stepped into the gardens we fell silent, overawed by the spectacle in front of us. Silver-haired gentlemen stood conversing in small groups, dressed in the most formal of evening clothes, many of their jackets marked out with glittering ranks of medals. Some of the older guests looked as if the weight of their metalware might overwhelm them, toppling them inexorably into the shrubbery, to be lost in a riot of colour.

Elsewhere young women, beautifully clothed, chatted animatedly. Their elders decked out in old-fashioned finery, whispered confidences. Feathers on hats bobbed above fine lace collars, like a flock of multi-coloured swans. We glanced at each other. Even Hammond, who was the most used to society amongst us, was unsettled by the yawning gulf between our backgrounds and circumstances and those in front of us.

As we stood quietly, feeling rather ill at ease, Mrs Guppy detached herself from the group gathered around her and made her way over to join us, accompanied by a young woman who had been standing by her side.

'It's so lovely to see you again, Mr Bennett,' she said. 'Who is this you have with you?'

Smiling gratefully at Mrs Guppy for her thoughtfulness, I introduced the others. Mrs Guppy in turn introduced us to her companion, Mary's sister, Fanny Horsley. Gravatt and I were left talking to Fanny, as Mrs Guppy turned to talk to Hammond.

I found it hard to warm to Gravatt. Hammond said that their early days working together on the tunnel had been difficult. Gravatt became a member of the Institute of Civil Engineers earlier than Brunel and his high opinion of his own technical prowess often made him argumentative. I found him to be quarrelsome – highly sensitive to how he was being treated and quick to take offence if I, a mere clerk, did not formally address him as a professional engineer.

We asked Fanny Horsley how long she had known Brunel and she replied that he had been a family friend for many years.

'But I had no inkling that he had an interest in my sister Mary. He had been acting a little strangely of late, often coming to the house. Good company as always, yet a little distant, as if he had something on his mind. Which he obviously did!' she exclaimed, laughing delightfully.

'We've had such fun over the years,' she continued. 'We often put on plays and musical evenings at home, and Isambard needed little encouragement to join in. Before he became too busy with his work, he used to love playing the swashbuckling hero or even the hapless fool.'

I planted what I hoped was an interested yet benign expression on my face as I struggled to absorb these different sides of a man I had thought I knew well. I found it hard to imagine him willing to play the clown.

The dancing was about to begin and Miss Horsley took her leave. Gravatt and I stood awkwardly alongside each other. I scanned the crowd, hoping to find something that I could remark upon. I rather hoped I would see someone I knew and find an excuse to take my leave without offending him. Thankfully, Hammond rejoined us and slightly slurring his words introduced his companion.

'Bennett, this is Joseph Locke. Joseph, meet another Joseph.'

'I think you already know each other?' Hammond said to Gravatt.

'Yes, we do,' said Gravatt rather brusquely. He turned to me and said, 'Joseph and I are members of the Royal Society together.'

'It's good to meet you,' I said politely.

'And you. I have heard about you. Your presentation about the Atlantic steamship opportunity was very well received by some members – although not by all,' said Locke, smiling.

I reddened. 'Oh yes, that. I am afraid that it was my first time addressing a group like that and I found it all rather overwhelming.'

'I only heard good things,' he replied. 'Your—'

Before he could finish, someone grabbed his elbow and spun him around.

'I can't believe how you let my father be treated after all he has done for you,' said the newcomer, his furious whisper carrying easily to the rest of our small group.

It was Robert Stephenson, who I had last seen nine months ago in his office at Euston. He stared at Locke fiercely, his previous urbane manner cast aside.

'It wasn't my decision, Robert,' replied Locke, prising the fingers from his arm.

'You could have refused to take on his duties. That would have been the gentlemanly thing to do,' replied Stephenson, visibly angry but keeping his voice low.

'I owe a great deal to your father but I felt I had no option from a professional point of view. I couldn't leave the investors in the lurch.'

Locke's calm and professional response seemed to further enrage Stephenson whose rising voice caused people to glance in their direction.

'There we disagree. It wouldn't have left the investors in the lurch if my father had continued. He would have done a good job. And they would have been forced to retain him if you had refused to take over his duties.'

The two of them now stood in a small empty circle, like pugilists facing off against each other. The crowd had moved slowly back, shifting away, as it became apparent that a heated debate was underway.

I saw Brunel appear on the fringe of the circle. He looked the perfect groom, wearing spotless white trousers rather than the usual dark, creased and stained material of his working clothes, and a beautifully brocaded waistcoat under a new frockcoat in the latest style.

He stepped forward as soon as he realised what was going on.

'Gentlemen,' he said. 'I invited you both here to celebrate my wedding rather than to quarrel. Can I suggest you leave this for another day?'

Stephenson took a deep breath, nodded brusquely to Brunel and walked away. The air seemed to lighten, the hubbub restarting and people turning back to their small groups with a sense of relief.

'If a man's not up to a job then what's the alternative?' said Gravatt.

'Life's rarely that simple,' replied Locke. 'It's true that things were falling behind but they often do. Unfortunately, old man Stephenson had ruffled feathers along the way. There were those who wanted their pound of flesh.'

Hammond and I exchanged looks and I imagined we were both thinking the same thing: this wasn't the kind of life lesson that Gravatt was likely to absorb. As their talk turned to the intricacies of railway-sleeper design, we took our leave and wandered over to watch the dancing.

On coir mats laid out on the lawns, couples flew past to the sound of the string quartet. Hammond told me about this exotic new dance, the waltz, where couples danced close together as they made their way around the dance floor. It was easier to follow than the complex dances I had seen glimpses of earlier in the evening, with sets of couples moving in and out and around each other, as if making their way through a complex maze invisible to a bystander.

I noticed most of the waltzers were young. The older generation apparently thought the waltz showed far too much familiarity in public, even for married couples.

I asked Hammond about what had just transpired.

'Locke and George Stephenson were originally jointly tasked with building the Grand Junction Railway from Birmingham to Manchester, but last autumn Stephenson was removed by the board and Locke put in sole charge. Robert Stephenson, George's son, was the one who accosted Locke.'

'Yes, I met him at Euston when I went with Brunel to discuss sharing the terminus. Why does he blame Locke?'

'I think he is just very protective of his father. I am not sure Locke could have done much about it really, but who knows what went on behind closed doors.'

At that moment, Brunel and his new bride danced their

way past us. He grinned broadly and called out, 'Find yourselves partners and join us!'

As Hammond took the cue and asked a young lady to his right, I stood watching, reflecting ruefully that I would need to learn to dance and have the courage to ask someone to be my partner before I ever got anywhere near a dance floor.

Hortense was hungry for all the details when we sat the next day, taking a few moments over a cup of tea at the kitchen table. The clumsy performance with the coal scuttle had masked her quick wittedness. She had rapidly learned how to express herself in English, even though she still spoke with a strong French accent, sometimes emphasised I think to give herself a touch more continental glamour. As she settled into the household, a smile appeared to be lurking just behind her eyes, her dimples ready to be exchanged for a full-blooded laugh at any moment. She and John Hammond often indulged in witty banter, leaving me at my most clumsy and tongue-tied. Nevertheless, she always seemed to make time to talk to me and I began to look forward to those occasions when we had a brief chat at the end of a meal or some other snatched minute in the day.

'It was a lovely evening. I have never seen anything like it. Such gorgeous dresses. And the gardens lit up like a magical playground.'

'Did the bride look beautiful?' asked Hortense, a little wistfully.

'Yes, she did. Stunning.' I went on to do my best to describe how Mary had looked in her long flowing off-white dress, her veil folded back over her hair and held up in intricate knots and garlanded with flowers. I had only seen her at a distance and was painfully conscious that my ability to describe a lady's dress was woefully insufficient to provide the detail Hortense craved.

'Everyone was so elegantly turned out,' I continued. 'I felt a bit plainly dressed to be honest. Hammond was the best attired amongst us. He wore a lovely frock coat – made of velvet, I think.'

'Did you enjoy it?'

'I did. It was more formal than I am used to, but there was music and dancing and everyone seemed very jolly – although there was a strange altercation early on.'

'Altercation?'

'I mean there was an argument.' I told her what happened. 'Stephenson behaved so differently to the first time I met him. He almost lost control. For whatever reason, he is clearly very sensitive about his father.'

'Did it ruin the party?'

'No, it was like a pebble thrown in a pond. The ripples quickly subsided. And Brunel was in fine form. Dancing. Chatting with friends. He looked really happy.'

'Doesn't sound too much like the Brunel we see every day,' snorted Hortense, hunching her shoulders as if pretending to creep around a room anxious not to disturb a sleeping giant.

'John Hammond has recounted tales of the two of them having all sorts of fun on the river and going out to musical and theatrical evenings together,' I replied, 'so perhaps that sense of mischief is still in there somewhere.'

'Well, he doesn't seem to have a lot of time for that sort of thing now,' said Hortense. 'It's incredible that he managed to find the time to win her hand.'

I laughed. 'Exactly. Now we know where he has been disappearing off to in the last few weeks.'

'Did you dance?'

'You are joking, aren't you? I never learned to dance. But I loved watching them. It looks so intricate, like butterflies fluttering around each other.'

'Perhaps I will teach you to dance one day. Don't look so surprised. I learned to dance when I was young. We Parisians aren't... what do you call it... heathens, like you English.'

'I would like it very much if one day you taught me. I would love to dance at my wedding.'

Just then, Bourton appeared. He moved so quietly that he could easily have had an alternative career as an assassin.

'Your wedding?' he repeated. 'Is that something we should be looking forward to shortly, sir?'

Although dressed up as a polite enquiry, his voice dripped with sarcasm.

I hated myself for rising to the bait, but found myself babbling, 'Actually, I promised Brunel I wouldn't marry as long as I worked for him.'

Bourton looked from one of us to the other, smiled, and said, 'I see, sir,' then turned and walked out.

After he had gone, looking at me rather oddly, Hortense asked, 'Why did you promise Brunel that?'

'It was a condition of being employed. At the time Mr Maudslay was pushing me hard to get the job, as he wanted to be helpful to Brunel. I felt I had little choice.'

'We always have a choice,' she said, getting up rather abruptly, leaving me alone at the table.

I stared after her wondering what on earth I had done to upset her.

Chapter 11

B runel and his new wife spent just a few days on honeymoon, travelling by stagecoach to North Wales and the West Country. Mary Horsley, now Brunel, was then installed in the upper rooms above our office. She quickly took control of domestic matters and often joined Brunel for lunch, so the midday gatherings of the team, which I had slowly come to enjoy, became less frequent.

Mary stormed into the office one Tuesday morning three weeks after they returned, followed closely by Bourton.

'I'm so sorry to disturb you, Isambard, but I wanted to tell you that I have had to fire that lad Bennett brought here,' she said, switching her gaze between us, looking as if she was waiting for me to challenge her. All I felt was a sense of dread. What had James done?

She paused before continuing, 'I came into the kitchen to find Bourton with a box full of the silver we were given for our wedding and that young rascal skulking behind him. When I asked what was going on, he started to explain that he had caught your young man with it. Next moment, the scoundrel bolted for the door. Bourton only just managed to catch him. I insisted Bourton see him off the premises immediately. I wanted to call the peelers but Bourton insisted we didn't. He said the loss of his job was enough punishment. It was so helpful to have you there, Bourton,' she said, smiling at him gratefully over her shoulder.

She sat down heavily in the chair in front of Brunel's desk.

'How could he? How could he abuse our trust like that?'

She turned to me.

'What possessed you to offer him a position, Bennett? Bourton tells me you caught him trying to steal from you but decided that you could rehabilitate him.'

I stumbled to my feet and bowed my head. I was aghast at the turn of events and feared for my own job. How could I have misjudged James so badly?

'I'm terribly sorry, madam. I really thought that all he and his family needed was the chance of a fresh start.'

'Once a thief, always a thief, I say,' she responded with a disdainful flick of her head. Bourton lurked behind her, trying to hide a thin grim smile of satisfaction.

Brunel finally spoke. 'Well he's gone now. A bit of a lesson for you, Bennett. People generally don't change their spots.'

He got up and escorted his new wife to the door, saying, 'I am so sorry you had to deal with it, my dear. It must have been quite a shock. Now you will forgive me, won't you, if we get back to work?' He gave her a quick kiss, and closed the door behind her.

'Bennett, don't ever do anything like that again without my say so. We've got enough on our hands without dealing with self-inflicted wounds.'

I mumbled my assent, still reeling from the news. How could I have got it so wrong?

A week later, we were back in Bristol for a meeting of the British Association for the Advancement of Science, which was gathering to discuss the future – or otherwise – of ocean-crossing steamships.

The association had been formed in 1831 by Reverend William Harcourt and Sir David Brewster who felt that the Royal Society was too elitist. They wanted to popularise science. At their first meeting in York there were doctors, philosophers, clergymen and nobility alongside the engineers and scientists you would expect.

We entered the great hall of Bristol's Horticultural Society and took our reserved seats near the front. Brunel had been up since dawn, writing and rewriting his speech.

'This needs to go well,' he muttered.

The outcome of the meeting wouldn't affect the building of the SS *Great Western*, which was well underway, so I asked him rather tentatively why he was so concerned.

'We want to build more ships, and any problems with our first will be seized upon by our enemies with glee. We need to use this meeting to reassure and gain people's confidence.'

He spoke sharply, not for the first time assuming anyone was an idiot who didn't immediately understand a line of thinking which to him seemed self-evident.

Proceedings began with the chairman Lord Lansdowne reminding the audience that the society had been set up to promote the cause of science and its role in improving people's lives and furthering economic prosperity.

'It is for debates such as the one we are about to have that the society was established. Will steamships become the way of the future, and sailing ships disappear from the high seas, or are they a technological dead end?'

He finished by saying who better to argue the case for and against than the learned Dr Lardner and the famous engineer Isambard Kingdom Brunel.

Since we had last crossed swords with Lardner at the GWR parliamentary hearings, more rumours of his colourful personal life had started to swirl. Eventually, he would divorce his wife with claims and counterclaims circulating about drunkenness, amoral behaviour and wife-beating, but the scandal was only just breaking. In the meantime, his lectures and articles remained popular with the general public and despite the Box Tunnel saga he was still seen as a scientific expert.

He made his way to the lectern soberly dressed in a dark frock coat, artfully cut to hide his large stout frame. His wild red Irish hair was cut shorter than usual, I suppose to minimise its potential to detract from the thoughtful and conservative demeanour he was cultivating.

Mrs Guppy slipped in beside me, murmured a greeting, and then retrieved something from her bag. As Lardner prepared to speak, I could hear a quiet clacking beside me and looked down to see her deftly working a pair of knitting needles through some burgundy coloured wool.

'It helps me concentrate,' she said. 'I hope I am not disturbing you.' I smiled and shook my head as Lardner began his speech.

'Thank you for your kind words, Lord Lansdowne. It's always a delight to be invited to speak to such an august group of scientists and select members of the press who are interested in scientific progress.'

Lardner was always good at sprinkling water liberally on the egos of the press. He was well aware of how his reputation had been built and enhanced by them, but also how easily they can turn against their protégées.

'As you know, I have made the study of steam and steam engines my life's work. As such, their use for transportation, whether that be in locomotives or ships, has held a particular interest for me.'

Lardner went on to explain why he believed that a steamship could never carry enough coal to cross the Atlantic carrying a decent payload of passengers and freight.

'As a ship gets bigger it needs proportionately more energy to drive it and hence consumes more coal. This increase in resistance means that a larger ship will still carry insufficient coal to complete an Atlantic crossing.'

Although I had read his articles and knew his line of argument well, I took out my pencil and began to write down the key points.

'I am not sure what notes you have been taking. You could have just written 'poppycock' in your little book,' Mrs Guppy whispered to me, as Lardner finished.

I stifled a laugh as the chairman thanked Dr Lardner and, in introducing Brunel to the stage, alluded to the fact that he was sure that he would be offering a different perspective to Dr Lardner.

'That's a very diplomatic way of putting it,' the indefatigable Mrs Guppy whispered as Brunel rose from his seat and made his way to the front.

'Is he looking after himself?' she asked me. 'He seems a little tired.'

I didn't have a chance to answer before Brunel began.

'It always gives me great pleasure to follow Dr Lardner,' he started with a chuckle, aiming I suppose to be both sardonic and a touch patronising. 'Dr Lardner is very good at explaining things simply, but that doesn't mean that his simple explanation is the right one!'

Ripples of laughter drifted from the audience, and out of the corner of my eye I caught Lardner turning from the front row to look back down the hall with an angry stare.

Brunel smiled at his audience and continued.

'Let me try and put my viewpoint across simply, also. Let's say you double the length of a ship and increase its width and height proportionally. By doing this, you create an internal volume not *twice* as large but *four times greater*, giving plenty of room for the required coal, passengers and freight.'

The italics are mine, because these were the words emphasised by Brunel as he held up the appropriate number of fingers each time.

'Dr Lardner might argue, "Ah yes, but you also double the water resistance and hence the speed at which you burn coal." But there is no evidence whatsoever that water resistance will be doubled and I don't believe for a moment that it will. And we shall soon prove it when we launch our new transatlantic steamship, the SS *Great Western*.'

'However,' he continued, 'even supposing for a moment that Dr Lardner's completely untested claim about water resistance did prove to be true, the SS *Great Western* will be able to carry far more than double the amount of coal of a ship half her size.'

Brunel carried on in much the same vein, carefully seeking to demolish Lardner's arguments step by step. As he finished, he looked down at Lardner while wagging his finger in his direction as he made his points.

'Unlike Dr Lardner, my investors and I have committed our time, our money and our reputations in support of our views. Dr Lardner has merely consumed a few column inches of paper and ink in pursuit of his! If he is wrong, his only cost is the consumption of a few more inches to apologise and rationalise his change of perspective.'

Open laughter rang out from the audience now, while Lardner sat rigidly, looking straight ahead.

Mrs Guppy turned to me as Brunel finished his speech and murmured, 'Well said. He knows his stuff, does our Brunel. Now, if you will excuse me, I must be off.'

She carefully put her knitting back in her bag and quietly left.

I waited patiently for Brunel as his supporters clustered around to praise his speech. When we eventually emerged from the hall, Lardner was waiting for us under the portico. As the crowds flowed past us, the conversation began civilly enough.

'My dear Brunel, I always try to keep my comments about our professional disagreements just that – professional. Engineering and science are both new disciplines, and in my view we must avoid arguing like fishwives about our respective theories. The key is to get the general public to understand that science and technological progress are not to be feared but embraced.'

Both men spoke quietly at first, aware of glances from fellow members of the association as they brushed past, apologising for having disturbed them.

'Dr Lardner, to you these may be interesting abstract arguments as part of your efforts to educate the common man, but to me and my investors, these are the bread and butter of our business.'

Brunel was stoking his sense of outrage as I had seen him do before. He jabbed his finger at Lardner.

'In fact, not only are your comments ill-conceived but they raise doubts about our whole profession in the minds of parliamentarians and investors, and as such they are foolhardy and dangerous.'

He jabbed at Lardner again, now genuinely angry.

'I can only assume that you make them either through ignorance or self-aggrandisement.'

The two of them had stepped into the shadows behind the pillars as the debate became more heated. Nevertheless, their raised voices carried clearly to me as I waited at the top of the steps. I avoided catching people's eyes as they looked curiously for the source of the quarrel.

I could see Brunel's point but I didn't understand the benefit of antagonising Lardner in this way. I would have preferred to follow the advice of the old proverb 'revenge is a dish best served cold'. In my view, we would be best showing Lardner to be wrong through our actions – that is, a successful Atlantic crossing with the SS *Great Western* – rather than engaging in a fruitless argument on the fringes of a scientific meeting.

Lardner was furious, his usually florid face now puce, like a piece of ripe fruit ready to burst. However, he still sought to keep his temper in check and maintain an air of professionalism as passers-by on the busy street looked inquisitively in our direction.

'Unfortunately, your investors are about to find out that you and they have made a terrible mistake,' Lardner said, with a clipped voice that still carried further than he realised or would have liked. 'I have tried my best to warn you but to no avail.'

'No, you will be shown to have been mistaken, but as I said in the hall, your only cost will be a few words of explanation or the retraction that you will be forced to make in the near future.'

Brunel almost shouted these last few words. He turned on his heel, called me to follow him and we left, marching rapidly down Park Street towards the docks. He strode on as fast as his limp would allow, saying nothing, his anger still burning strongly. I lengthened my stride to keep pace, reflecting that for both men it was their reputations that were at stake, and there is little more precious in life than that.

The following morning I spied the day's papers laid out on a table by the breakfast room at the hotel. I could see the letters 'Brun—' poking out and hesitantly pulled the paper clear of the stack, fearing the worst: 'Brunel risks all on behalf of his investors'. Revealed below was another: 'Brunel says he is confident but Lardner casts doubt'.

I picked them all up and sped off to find Brunel, nervous about his reaction but knowing I could not delay. He was finishing his coffee when I arrived and silently handed them over. He was furious, and his mood was not improved when we received urgent requests for a meeting with the Great Western Steamship Company directors.

At eleven we made our way under dark blustery skies to the Merchant Venturers' Hall. Thomas Guppy was there to greet us when we arrived. He urged Brunel to remain composed.

'My dear Brunel, they just need to give vent to their anxieties. Please do not take it personally or as in any way impugning your engineering skills and knowledge. It would be best if you could calmly explain why Lardner is wrong. After all, the ship is now being built, the money is committed, and we will soon show Lardner to be a mistaken fool... again.'

The directors were waiting for us, seated around the table looking like a group of undertakers in their old-fashioned black frock coats. One had his handkerchief flopping out of his top pocket in a style I imagine he hoped gave off the appearance of a London dandy, except that he didn't have the athletic good looks to carry it off and instead brought to mind an image of clothing spilling out of an over-stuffed chest of drawers.

I perched on one of the simple wood and cane seats placed around the walls, as the questions flowed thick and fast. The foppish one was first.

'You talked us into this, Guppy. You said that the project was sound and would help Bristol regain its rightful position as the leading port for international trade.'

He slapped a copy of the morning paper on the table.

'Now we hear that there is significant doubt about the basis of the whole enterprise.'

Another chimed in, 'Mr Brunel, how certain are you that the *Great Western* will make it across?'

'Quite certain,' said Brunel. 'I have considered each element of the design carefully and employed the best in the country to assist: Patterson's to build the ship and Maudslay's the engines.'

He spoke with authority, although I thought Mrs Guppy was right, he did look tired. I saw a slight tick – an involuntary flicker – in his right eyelid that I hadn't noticed before and realised that he must be feeling the strain.

'But it's never been done before, so how can you be so sure?' asked another.

'It's a matter of scientific calculation. The newspapers chose a sensationalist headline, but as most of the audience understood at the meeting, building a bigger ship allows lots of room for coal, the engines, and plenty of fare-paying passengers and cargo space.'

The mood in the room remained funereal; the directors stayed unsmiling, only Guppy nodding in agreement with Brunel's answers. There was some way to go before this audience would be satisfied, I reflected anxiously.

'How can you be confident that such a large ship can be built successfully?' asked the man with the handkerchief.

'The building of the ship is going well. Claxton has been keeping a close eye on the works and I will be visiting her again this afternoon to ensure all is as it should be.'

'And the engines. How sure are you about them?'

'Maudslay's have assured me that they will be able to build the engines to my specifications. As you know, there is no better firm in the country, and they have lots of experience with the side-lever type that we intend to use.'

I had heard from my old colleagues that Maudslay's had been struggling to get their design to fit within the dimensions of the ship's engine room, so I was relieved to hear that good progress must have been made for Brunel to be able to give this assurance.

More questions followed, and although tiresome, for once Brunel listened to the advice he had received from Guppy and managed to avoid getting on his high horse. He dealt coolly with their concerns and within a couple of hours we were able to leave.

Guppy escorted us out, wreathed in smiles.

'That's a relief. Well worth the effort. We had them back on board by the end.'

'Not at all, dear fellow. Needed to be done,' Brunel said.

'Shouldn't we publish some sort of rebuttal in the press?' I asked, fed up with the impact Lardner was having on my life.

Although we had won the battle over the Box Tunnel at the parliamentary hearings, his theories – presented as immutable facts – had caused me endless amounts of extra work. I was beginning to dislike him with a passion. I thought of him as a blustering Irish windbag. Like a politician, he advanced opinions as confidently on subjects he knew little about as those upon which he was an expert. He didn't let the truth get in the way of playing to his constituency, but the problem for us was that many in his audience were also in ours.

Brunel waved his hand dismissively.

'No, no. It will just give his theories oxygen to continue to burn brightly. Best to let the story die.'

'I agree,' said Guppy as he shook Brunel's hand.

We climbed into the carriage that Claxton had sent to take us down to Patterson's. We passed below Royal York Crescent and lurched our way down Granby Hill, the coachman pulling hard on the brake to slow our progress down the steep incline.

'That went well, sir. But I wish there was more we could do to curb Dr Lardner's propensity to spout his hypotheses as if they were facts.'

I knew Brunel didn't like Lardner and was surprised he didn't take the opportunity to express his feelings too. He sat quietly, gazing out the window while massaging his neck.

Claxton met us at the entrance to the shipyard and we walked around the end of the new ship – its topsides emerging slowly from a chrysalis of scaffolding – to reach the steps to Patterson's office. She stood tall and stately above us, dominating the yard. The bow projected out over the dock wall and the stern was hard up against the sheds that surrounded the slipway on which the ship was being built. It reminded me of the viaduct at Euston, the sides looming over us, cutting out the light. She looked like a foot being squeezed into too small a shoe, as even a large, modern yard like Patterson's struggled to keep up with the ever-growing size of ships.

There were piles of oak planks and lengths of iron strapping stacked around her. The buildings surrounding the ship were filled with all manner of machinery for shaping and cutting the oak and working the iron. Their great doors stood wide open so that while the machinery in the sheds was protected from the elements the men could easily pass between machine and ship as they trial-fitted parts before taking them back for further shaving or shaping.

Men swarmed everywhere carrying materials to and fro, while others clustered around the machines, fashioning wooden blocks with buzzing bandsaws, or hand-finishing with planes, sandpaper and files. Foremen marched back and forth, directing the piecing-together of the mighty jigsaw. Three men walked past us weighed down by a smooth curved section of oak, the wood as thick as a man's thigh, destined I assumed to provide vital strengthening deep in the hull. Beyond them, others were heating and hammering metal, the machine pounding the thick bar until a long strap emerged, as thick as a man's finger and as wide as his hand, like a giant's belt.

Claxton was pointing at something while yelling in Brunel's ear, but I couldn't hear a word. Hell's own orchestra would struggle to compete with the banshee wail of the saws, the roar of the blacksmith's furnace and the ringing of the iron hammers. The air was full of the smell of cut oak and sawdust, the aroma reminding me of a fresh hardwood log being cast on a fire, pungent smells filling the room. When the world changed to working in iron, a pervasive vinegary tang of cut and worked metal hung in the air, never again the deeply satisfying aroma of burning wood.

Patterson was at the top of the stairs saying farewell to a harassed-looking man.

'Don't worry, your repair work will be completed by the twelfth as agreed,' he said as he shook the man's hand. The visitor gave us a quick smile as he left, but I could see his eyes remained anxious.

Patterson invited us into his office, the sounds from the yard now muffled behind glass and brick.

'Some of my customers are worrying that the *Great Western* is taking up all my time and resources,' he said, gesturing in the direction of the departed visitor.

'I would be disappointed if it wasn't,' replied Brunel with a brief smile. 'It looks busy out there. How is the work coming along?'

'Good, good,' replied Patterson. 'We are making excellent progress with the hull, and Claxton has designed a rig which I think will work well.'

Although Brunel had calculated the overall dimensions necessary for the ship – how big she would need to be to carry sufficient coal to make a transatlantic crossing, and the power of engines required to drive her paddle wheels – he had allowed Patterson and Claxton, given their much greater maritime experience, to take the lead on the detailed design and construction.

Nevertheless, he hadn't been able to stop himself from writing regularly with suggestions for improvements on established practice. And of course he had been intimately involved in the design of the metal strapping to reinforce the wooden hull so that she would be able to cope with the buffeting of an Atlantic storm.

Claxton reached past Patterson and plucked a scale model off the shelf. I briefly wondered whether it was one of Mrs Guppy's, but I could see it was too primitive to meet her lofty standards.

'I have designed the rig and sails such that they will power her in light winds, but also so that we can set reduced canvas in rough seas to keep her steady enough so her paddle wheels keep working.'

'Why four masts?' asked Brunel, peering closely at the model.

'Fishing boats have long used small mizzen sails at the stern to keep the boat steady while casting and retrieving nets. I have employed a similar principle for rough weather to reduce rolling, hence the short stern mast next to the rudder post. The other three masts have tall top sections so that we can set plenty of sail when conditions are favourable.'

'Makes sense, makes sense,' said Brunel almost to himself as he stared at the model. After a pause, he looked up.

'Now she is coming together, how confident are you that she will have the strength and capacity to make it across the Atlantic?'

Brunel's voice was low and I leant forward to make sure that I could catch their replies. Patterson spoke first.

'May I enquire if you are asking because you want to see if we have doubts, or because you have some concerns yourself?'

I thought Brunel might think him presumptuous but to my surprise he didn't take offence. I realised that he must value Patterson's opinion highly not to have taken exception. He often did in such circumstances.

'I continue to believe that all will be well, but now that the construction is progressing I thought I should ask your opinion.'

'The combination of the longitudinal strengthening we are using and your iron strapping will be strong enough, I believe,' replied Patterson.

'I also think the rig will work well,' Claxton added. 'The area where we are both less qualified to judge is the engines.'

Brunel paused, stroking his chin, then with hunched shoulders he detonated his bombshell.

'There's the rub. While I have enormous faith in Maudslay's, they are struggling to design powerful enough engines to fit within the hull.'

There was a sharp intake of breath, I am not sure whether from Claxton or Patterson, followed by silence. It had suddenly become clear to me why Brunel had wanted to come here today. He usually believed he could solve any engineering problem with enough effort, but he must be increasingly concerned about whether he would be able to with this one. It was obvious to me now that he had painted far too optimistic a picture for the directors. No wonder he looked under undue strain.

'Can we have a look at the plans, to see if we could make more space?' he asked.

Patterson looked stunned.

'My dear fellow, the ship is almost finished. We can't redesign her now.'

'We might have to. My investors are hardly going to accept a sailing vessel when they commissioned a steamship.'

173

Patterson, about to reply, stopped himself, and instead turned and pulled a large-scale drawing of the ship from a shelf and laid it on the table.

'Couldn't we widen her midships?' asked Brunel, after scanning the plans for a few moments.

'You are joking, aren't you?' exclaimed Patterson. 'We would have to cut her in half to do that. She would never be strong enough for Atlantic crossings after we had finished. The only option is to finish her and start again.'

'That's never going to happen. It's not possible,' replied Brunel, beginning to get angry as he often did when things weren't going his way. 'How about you help with some solutions rather than pointing out the problems?'

Patterson was taken aback. His look reminded me of McIntosh when he and Brunel had argued about the embankments. The difference this time was that this truly was Brunel's issue to resolve. Patterson stared at Brunel for a moment and then said icily, 'I will do whatever I can to assist, but this is your problem, not mine.'

Claxton looked at each in turn and then reached out to take Brunel's arm.

'Perhaps a stroll along the dockside would be a good idea. We can all calm down and meet again in twenty minutes.'

Brunel allowed himself to be led out, telling me to stay while he and Claxton took some air.

'Brunel is under a lot of pressure,' I said apologetically to Patterson once we were alone. 'You heard Lardner at the association meeting.'

'I thought Brunel did a pretty good job of demolishing his arguments,' said Patterson, rubbing his forehead and staring a little vacantly at the drawings on the table, as if seeking divine inspiration.

'Yes, but nevertheless he has managed to sow some seeds of doubt. We have just come from a difficult meeting with the directors. The newspaper articles have got them worried – it took two hours to calm them down.'

I didn't think it wise to mention Brunel's assurances about the design of the ship; Patterson would hear about it soon enough. News travels fast around a small city like Bristol.

Patterson continued to stare at the plans and I moved over to join him.

'Wouldn't it be possible to move those frames back two or three feet until they abut the main bulkhead there?' I asked tentatively, pointing at the cross-sectional drawing of the ship.

Patterson leant in for a closer look.

'You know, you may be right. Do you think it would create enough space? It doesn't add that much.'

'I am not sure. But anything you can do will help.'

Patterson straightened up and stretched with a long sigh.

'I thought it was all going too well. Leave it with me for a few days.'

'Thank you,' I said gratefully.

I thought quickly. I knew if Brunel returned he would want to pore over the plans looking for solutions and that Patterson would most likely quickly become defensive again.

'It may be best if I catch the other two as they return and let them know you will write within a day or so with your conclusions,' I said hastily, and headed down the stairs to catch Brunel and Claxton at the entrance.

Brunel reluctantly agreed to go back to London after I assured him that Patterson would be reviewing all the options and writing as soon as he could. As we left Bristol and reached the open countryside, he was preoccupied, gazing out the window and chewing on the end of an unlit cigar. I held on tightly as the coach hit a bump. I asked if there was anything I could do to help – I had no idea what, but was keen to offer whatever support I could.

'Thank you. No, I don't think so,' said Brunel. 'Once we hear from Patterson we will just have to work closely with Maudslay's and work out how to fit the engines into whatever space we have.'

He said nothing for what seemed an age before murmuring, 'I would hate us to fail for other reasons and he still claim victory.'

Who was 'he'? I wondered, before realising it could only be Lardner.

I suppose I should have been pleased. If we had done as I suggested and publicly rebutted Lardner's arguments, we would have been ridiculed if we couldn't make the engines fit, even though it wouldn't have proven anything about the ability of a ship to carry enough coal to cross the ocean. I must have been tired. I wasn't thinking clearly. Of course, we would still be a laughing stock if we couldn't get sufficiently large engines into the ship.

Brunel rubbed his face. 'Time for some sleep,' he said. 'Things always seem better in the morning.'

That depends on whether you get any sleep, I thought. I still hadn't got over James's abrupt departure. I hadn't heard from him and even if he did make contact I didn't know what I would say. And now I had the ship's engine problems rattling around in my head, too. Restless, I stayed awake as the stage coach continued to sway and lurch its way towards London.

Early the next morning when we reached Parliament Street at the end of a long night's journey, I headed downstairs for a quick wash before starting the day. As I reached the bottom of the stairs, Hortense rushed up to me, dragging one of the maids along behind her.

'Thank God you are back,' she cried. 'This is Anna. She has something to tell you that you must hear.'

Anna seemed to shrink back, as if she wanted to carry out a vanishing trick and disappear before my eyes.

'Just tell Mr Bennett what you told me,' said Hortense.

'Mr Bennett, sir,' Anna stammered in her broad West Country accent.

I rubbed my eyes. I was tired and dirty from the journey and wondered what could be of such importance as to keep me from a bowl of hot water and some soap.

'Mr Bennett, sir,' she repeated. 'I saw him – Mr Bourton that is – taking the silver.'

'Taking the silver?' I repeated. 'I know. Mrs Brunel said that he caught James with it and took it off him.'

'No sir,' she said more loudly and with a firmer voice. 'I saw Mr Bourton putting the silver in the box.'

'You saw what?' I cried, astonished.

'He had his back to me, sir, so didn't see me. He was picking out some of the wedding presents from the back of the storeroom and loading them into the box. He was heading for the door when Mrs Brunel caught him. He must have seen James in the background and realised he could blame him.'

I rubbed my eyes again, struggling to take it all in.

'Why didn't you say all this before?'

She wrung her hands, looking close to tears. 'Mr Bourton rules the roost here. I thought I would lose my job. My family can't afford not to have me working, sir.'

Hortense spoke up. 'She confided in me, Joseph. Her conscience wouldn't let her leave things be.' I took a deep breath.

'Come with me, young lady. You too, Hortense.'

I knocked on the office door and we all trooped in. I made Anna recount her story to Brunel, Hortense nodding in agreement when Anna described herself as being afraid of Bourton ('He's a bully, sir') when Brunel, like me, asked why she hadn't spoken up before.

Brunel sighed. 'Leave it with me, I will speak to Mrs Brunel.'

By the end of the day, Bourton had packed his bags and left.

I couldn't persuade Brunel to have James back.

'What's done is done,' he said, shaking his head. 'I'm sorry, I know you had a soft spot for the lad.'

I explained things to my father and asked if he would take James on. Slightly to my surprise, he agreed.

'Well, I need someone trustworthy to help around here,' he said pointedly.

Chapter 12

1838

I stood at the edge of the deck just below the wheelhouse. The sun rose slowly, the sky still clear as it so often is early in the morning before the clouds move in. At last the ship was ready and the stokers had been busy since dawn building the fires and raising the temperature in the boilers. The river was still quiet, the tide near full, but the ship creaked and groaned as the heat fanned out through the new boilers and pipework.

It had felt like a race against time since the meeting with Claxton and Patterson eighteen months ago. Patterson had written to me within twenty-four hours to say that he could indeed move the frames a few feet to create a little more space. Brunel grunted, 'Knew he was a good man,' when I told him, their heated words quickly forgotten. I had too much sense to attempt to explain my role in resolving the crisis, Brunel wouldn't take kindly to an amateur's involvement.

The ship was finished and launched six months later, before being sailed around to the Thames. Weeks were spent at Maudslay's working out how best to squeeze the engines into the ship. Finally we thought we had a solution, although the tolerances would be tight. The engines were built and assembled in the workshop and then taken apart to be reconstructed on board.

It took hours of careful handling with crane and ropes to get the boilers and the other large castings over the side and down through holes cut in the deck. In the confines of the ship, parts didn't fit as they had ashore. The engineers spent day after day buried in the bowels of the ship, fitting, adjusting and refitting the pieces.

Brunel had been bad-tempered throughout, at his worst in a situation like this when obstacles stood in his way, about which he could do little but fume. As Christmas drew near, things took a turn for the worse. It was late in the evening and the daily report we had just received from Maudslay's was not good. The engineers had spent another frustrating day on the ship. The cold weather was making a difficult task even harder. Even Brunel appeared to be losing heart as he sat at his desk, staring out the window, deep in thought.

The bell rang and as the footman went to answer, the sounds of carol singers drifted in. Wouldn't it be wonderful to just relax and enjoy Christmas, I thought? *God rest you merry gentlemen*, indeed.

There was a commotion outside and Claxton burst in without warning, *May nothing you dismay* accompanying him as he came through the door.

'Bad news, I am afraid,' he gasped.

The sound of carols faded as the footman reached around and pulled the door closed.

'What is it, man?' asked Brunel, sitting up in his chair.

Claxton was standing in front of Brunel's desk, the frost on his hat and coat puddling slowly at his feet.

'Junius' British and American Company have procured an Irish packet steamer, the *Sirius*, to try and beat us across.' He took a deep breath to regain his composure and continued, 'They say that she has been completely stripped out so that she can carry far more coal than usual. It's a travesty. We must go to the press and tell them it's a sham.'

Brunel's scowled and got up, savagely stubbing out his cigar as he rose.

'No. Enough of the press. Even though it's not a fair fight they won't care. They'll just write the headline. There will be no prizes for coming second. The only way to deal with this is to beat the *Sirius*.'

He pointed his dead cigar at Claxton.

'Get down to Maudslay's and see what can be done to get her ready sooner. I want you sleeping there if you have to.'

'Bennett,' he said, turning to me, 'work on the assumption that her sea trials will be carried out on the way back to Bristol to pick up the passengers for the Atlantic crossing. Change whatever needs changing to make that happen.

'Let's get going. We have work to do,' he said, rubbing his hands together, the familiar steely glint back in his eye, reinvigorated by the challenge we had been set.

Here we were, three hectic months later at the end of March 1838, making ready for her maiden voyage under power. The engineers had worked ceaselessly every day and through most nights since the news about the *Sirius*. There had been no time for celebrations when the engines were finally complete and working. All attention was focused on getting her ready for sea.

I had gone down below a week ago to watch the final tests. When the engine turned over, the long beam which took the power from the engines to the paddle wheels rocked back and forth like a child's seesaw. It swung alarmingly close to the ship's sides and each time looked as if it might scrape a few inches from the wood. But it defied my senses and swung freely, the engine emitting a comforting blast of steam with each rotation. I hoped it would stay that way as the ship twisted and turned in the ocean swells.

'Make ready to slip the lines,' Claxton called from the bridge.

The river, stationary in that brief moment at the top of the tide, was about to turn. I looked over the side to see small rowboats being expertly manoeuvred alongside, men calling out to each other as lines were thrown between ship and boat. The river started to move, slowly at first, as if a carpet were being dragged steadily downstream, then within minutes rushing and tumbling towards the sea, like a large crowd making for the exits at the end of a long day's races.

Behind me up on the bridge Claxton gave the order to cast off and the men in the boats to begin rowing. The outer paddle wheel was put into reverse and the inner set to forward. The ship slowly swung out into the Thames as I watched the oarsmen pull hard, like beetles scrabbling for a grip on a smooth floor, as they heaved her out into the tidal stream.

I could hear the pistons thumping up and down, each stroke finishing with a wheeze as the steam was expelled from the cylinder. A bell rang on deck and was answered below. The paddle wheel on my right slowed to a halt and then began thrashing the water as it joined its twin on the left in driving the ship forward. At the same time, the sailors clustered at the bow cast free the rowboats. Bending over their oars, they pulled away from the ship before stopping to raise their caps, cheering us on our way. I looked back to the wharf to see well-wishers there too, raising their hats. Dotted amongst them I recognised the weary faces of the engineers, relieved to see the ship underway and their work complete.

We set off down the river, making our way slowly round the tight bend at Rotherhithe. Ahead of us stood the naval hospital at Greenwich, its green lawns and shining grey stone colonnades standing out against the dirty brown wharfs and shipyards lining the banks before it. Men and women busy at work along the riverbanks stopped for a few moments; some waved while others just shielded their eyes to watch the extraordinary sight: a ship travelling down the river without sail or oar to help her on her way.

The river was in full flow now, carrying us swiftly on towards the flat marshes beyond. Claxton ordered more power, concerned to maintain steerage as we headed rapidly towards the open sea. Gulls wheeled overhead, their shadows flitting across the deck as they clustered around the ship, calling out, hoping for scraps. The cloying London smell of burning wood and coal fell away and was replaced by the seaweed-infused tang of the sea. I took in a deep lungful of the fresh air and was turning to make my way to some shelter away from the stiffening breeze when I heard a shout from the bridge.

Did he really say 'Fire!'? I looked over my shoulder to where the man was pointing. I could see nothing amiss at first, but then a few wisps of smoke blew out of the forward hatch like puffs from one of Brunel's cigars, then disappeared, blown away by the fresh breeze as if they had never existed. More smoke followed, thickening rapidly, leaving no room for doubt. It was as if a change in the weather had arrived, heralded by billowing dark grey thunder clouds.

The bell on the bridge clanged again and the sound of churning water quietened as the engines were stopped. Claxton rushed past me, looking anxious, Brunel just behind, his limp holding him back. Three of the crew – Harold, Tom and John – ran out on deck as a klaxon high up above the bridge hooted repeatedly like a demented foghorn. Claxton stopped at the edge of the hold.

'Get the hose from the foredeck! Quickly!'

Brunel was hurrying across the deck towards him, made awkward by his limp. Claxton held up his hand.

'Wait here, sir. Let me see what has happened.'

He stepped backwards over the edge of the coaming, clambered down the ladder and disappeared from view. I stood feeling helpless as I watched Brunel pace back and forth, shielding his eyes as he tried to peer down into the hold, the smoke continuing to thicken and pour out. With the ship slowed, the acrid smoke hung over the deck, driving away the smell of the fresh sea breeze.

Tom and Harold were struggling to free the hose from its drum, and I – eager to have something to do and to help in any way I could – ran over to help. It was wound over itself and their efforts to free it were making things worse. I pushed them aside, and having got some slack in the hose pulled at the coil underneath and managed to free it. Choking in the thickening smoke, John and I dragged it to the edge of the hold while Tom and Harold grabbed either end of the stirrup pump. They worked the long handle up and down and soon the hose filled and seawater started to gush out. I angled the flow down into the hold and the air filled with a furious hissing sound as great clouds of steam billowed out.

'Pump harder!' I called out.

Harold started the chant: 'One, two; one, two.'

He and Tom redoubled their efforts, the handle going up and down like the beam of the engine down below, as they pumped like demons. We plied the hose back and forth across the flames, and although the smoke remained thick, the fire seemed to be dying back.

'That's it. Keep at it. You're doing a great job!' Claxton called from below.

I felt Brunel's hand on my shoulder.

'I'm going down to help,' he shouted in my ear.

'Wait, sir,' I gasped, and tried to grab his arm, but the hose jumped and twisted in my hands like a wild snake and when I looked up again he was gone. A loud crack sounded from down below, like a gunshot. Then nothing. I strained to listen but all I could hear was the bellows of the pump and the gushing of water from the hose.

'Stop pumping,' called Claxton tremulously from down below.

'Stop pumping!' I yelled to the men. 'Something's happened.'

The silence was sudden, all we could hear was the sound of the gulls circling overhead, calling to each other, oblivious to the turmoil below. I dropped the hose to one side, fell to my knees and peered over the edge of the hatch. A small gust of wind blew some smoke into my face and I wiped the tears from my eyes with the back of my hand. The ladder was black and charred and still smouldering. About halfway down, the rungs had gone. The crack I had heard must have been the sound of snapping wood.

'Are you alright, sir?' I shouted, my voice breaking with fear. There was no reply.

Through the haze I saw a crumpled figure twenty feet below on the floor of the hold. I felt sick. It was Claxton. He was lying on the ground buried under something, a fallen piece of cargo perhaps. As the smoke cleared, I realised it was a body he was underneath. He squirmed free, and I groaned inwardly, maybe even out loud, as it dawned on me he must be pinned down by Brunel. Even from this distance, I could see that Brunel's right leg was at an unnatural angle, twisted across and underneath his body.

'Claxton, are you alright? I yelled.

Claxton looked up and croaked, 'Yes, I am alright, a bit winded, that's all.'

Brunel was as still as a waxwork.

'What about Brunel? For God's sake, is he breathing?'

He leant over Brunel for what seemed an age.

'Yes, he's breathing!'

My heart was thudding as I watched Claxton feel around Brunel's head.

'I can't find any damage to his skull but he really doesn't look good. He's still unconscious, his face is white and his leg is badly broken.'

I turned to the crew waiting beside me.

'Go and find another ladder. Quick. Bring a stretcher, and ropes too.'

'Get the crew to launch a boat,' Claxton shouted up to me. 'One of my stokers is seriously burnt and we need to get them both ashore.'

Harold and John swung one of the ship's derricks over the hold, lowered a stretcher, and brought up the stoker, whose name was Philip. The men below had wrapped him in a sheet, but one arm had been laid carefully on top, the skin blistered and burnt like a slab of raw meat charred on a red-hot spit. He lay on deck, muttering and groaning.

'Find him a tot of rum,' I instructed one of the crew as I turned back to see Brunel being winched from the hold.

His face lined with pain, Claxton slowly made his way up the replacement ladder and stiffly climbed out of the hold. He looked dreadful – as if he had been badly beaten. His face was covered in soot and his hands deeply scratched, with bright red patches where he must have been burnt as he fought the fire.

Refusing offers of help from the crew, he said 'Don't worry about me. I've suffered worse. How's Philip?'

'Not in a good way. We need to get him ashore.'

I helped guide Brunel's stretcher down onto the deck.

He stirred and I gripped his hand and asked, 'Sir, are you alright, sir?'

He turned to me, his eyes glassy and unfocused.

'Should have heeded what you said, Bennett,' he whispered.

'We need to get you ashore, sir, so that your injuries can be properly treated,' said Claxton. 'The fire is under control – thank God the damage wasn't too serious. The lagging caught light. It had been taken too far up the funnel and got too hot.'

Brunel reached out, grasped my coat and pulled me in close.

'I can't go, Bennett. I must make sure that the ship sets sail for America on time.'

His skin was clammy with sweat and his face distorted with pain.

'Sir, Claxton and I can handle it between us. Your leg needs to be set straight and you need to rest.'

Brunel tried to push himself up, but groaning with the effort, let out a cry of pain and sank back down again.

'The whole thing needs to be orchestrated, Bennett. There's so much to do. I can't just trust it to happen.'

I took a deep breath.

'Sir, if you want, I will go with the ship to America and make sure everything is pushed forward and dealt with as you would have done.'

Brunel looked at me, confusion and doubt showing through the pain.

'Trust in me, sir. I will see it through.'

He nodded once, then turned his head away.

I watched with a heavy heart as John and Harold started to lower him into the boat. He called out feebly to Claxton, 'Make haste: *Audentes fortuna adiuvat* – make sure you beat the *Sirius*!'

News of the accident travelled fast and cancellations flooded in. While Claxton made sure the ship was ready, I wrote to every passenger to reassure them that the ship was safe and that we would depart on time. I even wrote to the press and provided them with a full summary of the causes of the fire. It was simply a fault in the finishing work, not a fundamental flaw of any kind. Brunel wrote regularly from his lodgings on Canvey Island asking for updates on progress and I in turn asked after his health. His leg was mending slowly. To his evident frustration there was little he could do other than to rest.

Despite my efforts, I had to write to Brunel on the morning of 7th April, prior to our departure from Avonmouth, to inform him that sadly only seven passengers were aboard. More than fifty had cancelled. I told him that we had heard that the *Sirius* had departed in late March, but we knew she would be stopping at Cork to refuel en route, so we still had a chance if we made good time.

We steamed down the Bristol Channel and into the Irish Sea, the weather calm, with Claxton driving the ship as fast as he dared. There was nothing more I could do other than enjoy being a passenger. She was beautifully fitted out with a promenade deck forward of the belching funnels, and below deck the first-class passenger cabins clustered around a large saloon decorated with elaborate cornicing, lemon-coloured panelling and velvet drapes around the windows and portholes. Brunel had asked Mrs Guppy for her advice; I remember sitting in her drawing room when she had proposed the yellow theme. Brunel wasn't sure. 'Wouldn't purple be more statesmanlike?' he'd queried.

'In my experience, ships can be dark, gloomy places. Let's lighten it up, make people feel it's modern and airy,' she replied, and so yellow it was.

The sun streamed in through the large stern windows and through light-boxes built into the deck, whose frames could be opened wide when the weather was good, like glass-topped vegetable frames in a kitchen garden. Mrs Guppy had been right, the saloon was a light, airy place where the few passengers lingered, whiling away the days chatting, playing card games and reading.

Pillars ran the length of the room in two rows like elm trees lining a country house drive. I ran my hand down one of them, feeling its smooth curves. I had watched the master craftsmen at work carving soft bulbous spirals into these pillars one by one, but making sure they matched each other so closely that the eye could not see that each was unique.

The ship was making good progress, and I only wished I could relax and enjoy the experience as I anxiously scanned the horizon for signs of the *Sirius*. Although Claxton was the seafarer, I felt the full burden of our endeavour and must have driven him mad as I asked every few hours about the performance of the engines.

After clearing the north-east coast of Ireland, we met the full force of the Atlantic swell. I had felt queasy since we had started the voyage. The smell of the animal fat used to lubricate the bearings would have been obnoxious enough ashore but was far worse when pitching and rolling at sea. Now I was physically sick until I had nothing left to give up. I lay in my cabin retching bile into a bucket by the bed. For four days I did not think of Brunel or the *Sirius* at all. If the ship's doctor, a cheery chap also called Bennett, had offered me arsenic I would have gladly taken it.

On the 15th April, eight days after we had set off, I began to feel better; life might be worth living after all. I emerged from my cabin to find that wooden frames had been fitted to the table tops to stop the china flying around. The stewards served plain food to the few of the passengers and ship's officers who felt able to eat, adeptly swaying in time to the ship's movement to prevent their fully loaded plates from spilling.

The days slipped by accompanied by the steady thrumming of the engines. It was cosseting, keeping the mighty sea at a distance, like a plate-glass window placed between us and the elements. But when the engines stopped without warning – when the boilers were being cleaned or the bearings greased – the ship rolled mightily in the swell. Each time this happened I worried that there was a problem with the ship and that the race might be lost. I gripped tightly to the arms of my chair, or the guardrail if I was on deck, relaxing only when the thump-thump resumed as we got underway once more.

Claxton invited me up on the bridge.

'How are you feeling, Bennett? Got your sea legs now?'

'Yes thanks,' I replied, ignoring his amused glance.

I scanned the horizon, but could see nothing beyond the endless rolling blue fields of the ocean.

'Any news on the *Sirius*?'

'No. We think she is still in front of us and we are going as fast as we dare.'

The crew drove the ship on. We had no idea how far behind we were, or what speed the *Sirius* was making. Fifteen days after leaving Avonmouth, on the 23rd April, we finally sighted land in the distance and within hours were entering the Hudson River and approaching Manhattan. I stood on the bridge with Claxton, scanning the docks through eyeglasses for signs of the *Sirius*.

I focused on the ships one by one, hoping against hope that none of them would have '*Sirius*' picked out on the bow or stern. Then I saw an 'S', and tightening my grip, hoped against hope that it wouldn't be her. It was, moored alongside the wharfs on the Lower East side. My last drops of hope drained away. All that work and she had beaten us.

I didn't say anything, but frowned as I pointed and handed Claxton the glasses to look for himself. I couldn't speak, but went to my cabin. I lay down on the cot feeling a deep sense of despair, its cheery comfort – it had come to feel like home after two weeks at sea – seemed to mock me. All that hard work. All that hope. 'She has beaten us', echoed in my head.

It felt like an age until there was a banging on the cabin door.

'Bennett, it's Claxton. You must come at once.'

I opened the door to find Claxton standing next to a thin, wiry man with a moustache.

'Bennett, this is Rudy Thompson, a reporter from the *New York Times*. He wants to write about the race.'

My heart sank further. An article in the *New York Times* lauding the *Sirius* for a great victory over the *Great Western*. What would Brunel say?

Claxton asked one of the stewards, to make Thompson a coffee and seat him in the saloon. As he was led away, Claxton came into the cabin and shut the door.

'Bennett, when the pilot boat came alongside, one of the crew told me that *Sirius* arrived only a few hours before us.'

'That almost makes it worse,' I said miserably.

'No, listen. He said that she was missing her yardarms. They ran out of coal and had to burn anything they could lay their hands on.'

I stared at him, not sure why Claxton thought this mattered. Then I realised what he was thinking and I saw a glimmer of hope. If we could get the paper to tell the story in the right way, then maybe we could still achieve the publicity Brunel... all of us... wanted.

'I see what you mean.'

I felt a rush of excitement and grabbed my coat from the end of the bunk.

Thompson was sitting in one of the little round-backed armchairs in the stern, one of my favourite places on the ship. He stood as I approached him.

'Apologies for bothering you before you are berthed, but I need to meet the deadline for tomorrow's papers. It's a story our readers will love, a steam race across the Atlantic.'

'I am pleased to talk to you, Mr Thompson,' I replied, gesturing for him to retake his seat, while I sat opposite. Between us was a small table on which rested two fine china cups.

I thought quickly. What would Brunel do? He was good at this sort of thing. Desperately casting about for the best way to start, and conscious that the saloon was likely to be far more impressive than the *Sirius*, I politely asked if he had had a chance to visit the other ship.

'Yes, lovely little steamer.' He looked around him. 'Not quite as grand as this, though.'

'Mr Brunel took great care to see that this ship was equipped with the finest fittings and furniture: Waterford china, Dalton glass, Wilton carpets.' I leant back and gestured at the breadth and length of the saloon. 'Not only that, but he also made sure that she was big enough to carry sufficient coal for the trip.'

I was hoping that the newspaperman would take my hint but he didn't appear to, asking me how I felt about losing by such a small margin. My heart sank again. A headline describing our narrow loss would not be what Brunel would want to read.

'Of course, we would have loved to have come first,' I said, 'but we did start over a week later. And we didn't have to burn all this fine furniture to get here.'

'What do you mean, burn the furniture?' asked Thompson, finally swallowing the bait.

'Oh, I thought perhaps you knew,' I replied. 'The *Sirius* wasn't designed for crossing the Atlantic so they had to strip her out to make room for more coal. Despite that, I understand that they were forced to put almost everything into the furnaces to get here.'

'Hmm,' said Thompson, rising to leave now that we had reached our berth four ships down the dock from the *Sirius*. 'Thank you for that. Interesting twist to the story.'

After an anxious night I woke early and went ashore to find a newspaper. The quayside seemed to stretch to eternity as I walked on and on until eventually I found a small store at the dock gates. I stood by an empty packing case and unfolded the paper with shaking hands.

'The *Great Western*, the first 'proper' steamship to cross the Atlantic,' stated the headline. I read on. 'The *Sirius* might have got here to New York first – by just a few hours – but the real honours belong to the *Great Western*. The *Sirius* was stripped out and had to burn her own spars and furniture to complete the crossing. The *Great Western*, by contrast, will be capable of crossing the Atlantic time and again with a full complement of passengers and cargo...'

I let out a cheer, causing a few passing dock workers to give me an anxious look, and hurried back to the ship. Running up the gangplank I waved the paper madly at Claxton up in the wheelhouse.

'We've done it!' I shouted, jumping up and down on the deck.

Later that morning I sat at a table in the saloon and completed my report for Brunel:

We have just arrived in New York and I must finish this so that I can place it on the first ship heading back to England. I am afraid to report that the Sirius *arrived before us. However, she was only six hours ahead and I enclose the morning's papers, which make much of the close-run race, despite the Great Western starting out more than a week behind. As you will see, they also make it clear that the* Sirius, *unlike our ship, is incapable of providing a regular service. They have highlighted the fact that she only just made it notwithstanding the extra coal on board and the burning of every last bit of wood that they could lay their hands on.*

In summary, our ship has performed most satisfactorily. We arrived with some 200 tons of coal left on board. Claxton is very pleased with her seaworthiness. The engines were a little troublesome to begin with, but the engineers seem to have worked out how often they need cleaning and oiling. A particular issue has been the accumulation of salt water deposits in the engine, necessitating a proper clean out every few days. A full report will follow from the engineers and from Claxton.

She is as luxurious, seaworthy and efficient as you could have hoped and I confess to looking forward, now I have my sea legs, to embarking on her for the return journey.

Yours sincerely
Joseph Bennett

It was the 22nd May when we dropped anchor off Avonmouth on our return trip, taking just fourteen days with sixty-six passengers on board. I returned to the office the next morning, the flowers in the park in full bloom. Brunel was back at work. He looked tired and his face was pale, but he was as energetic as ever.

'Come on in, come in. Sit down. Make yourself at home. We've missed you.'

'It's a pleasure to be back, sir. It was an unforgettable trip, although I regret that it was your accident that made it possible. How are you?'

'Fine, fine. Thank you for your report, and for all your efforts. Made very interesting reading. The papers here have made much of the fact that Lardner has been proved wrong. It has been really most gratifying.'

'I am pleased, sir.'

'Yes, well. Excellent. But I think there are things we can do to make the next ship better still. I have made some notes which I have put on your desk. See what you think.'

'Of course, sir.' I looked across at my desk to see papers piled high in stacks covering every spare inch. My heart sank.

He saw my expression and shook his head slightly.

'The clerks have been getting sloppy while you have been gallivanting around. Well, at least you know there is always a job for you! Now, if you will excuse me, I must run. All sorts of people are asking my opinion about the best method of building steamships now.'

I sat down and drew the first pile towards me. My part in the success seemed to have been quickly forgotten. I felt a headache coming on as I contemplated the work before me.

There's nothing like the smell of slowly roasting pork, I thought, as I sat in my mother's kitchen that evening. It was odd to be sitting at a table getting ready to eat without the smell of sea in the air or the steady beat of the engines. I told my mother about my trip. She was less interested in the voyage – which she had read about in the papers – but asked lots of questions about America.

'In some ways it's not that different from here,' I said. 'Almost everybody in New York is from Ireland or Scotland it seems, although there are quite a few Italians around as well.'

'The shops were a sight to behold. They seem to stock everything.'

I was about to tell them how delicious the food was, but stopped myself. My mother wouldn't appreciate me heaping praise on someone else's cooking. When she passed me my plate, I breathed in the familiar smells.

'Nothing like home cooking,' I said smiling. 'It's so good to be back.' I reached across for more of my mother's homemade bread. 'Returning to work has been a bit of a shock, though. Brunel is already onto his next challenge and I have a mountain of work waiting for me.'

'Surely he was pleased with how you managed things while he was bedridden? You put so much effort into it. Didn't he realise what a strain it was?'

'I think so. It's hard to tell with him. He is always onto the next thing.'

She passed me a second helping.

'I am just glad to have you back.'

As I helped clear the plates away after dinner, she said, 'I hope you get some time for yourself. Won't Mr Brunel need to finish the railway before he starts something else?'

'I think he worries he will be left behind if he doesn't keep pushing on.'

'Well, I worry about you. You won't be much use to him if you are worn out, will you?'

'I'll be fine. I enjoy a challenge, too.'

'Don't forget we all need time for ourselves.'

I laughed as I started to head off up the stairs to bed.

'Very well. I will tell Mr Brunel that I would like a regular day off. Shall we meet each Thursday afternoon for tea?'

'Very funny, dear. Sleep well.'

I lay in bed looking around me at the familiar room: the threadbare curtains, the old wardrobe in the corner, the tarnished mirror above the washstand, the cheap poster of a steam engine's workings on the wall. But it didn't feel as comforting as it should. I missed the rocking of the ship and the cosiness of my little cabin. It was hard to get to sleep. My head was full of all that I had garnered from the papers I had skimmed through that afternoon: problems with progress on the GWR, requests for tenders for other railways, his initial thoughts on a second steamship.

The single concern that I had lived with for weeks had been replaced by a multitude of issues bouncing around in my head as I waited for dawn, the sound of gulls replaced with the groans and mutterings of people living cheek by jowl in the narrow streets.

Chapter 13

The next few months were the busiest since I joined Brunel. My voyage on the *Great Western* seemed a distant memory. Brunel was anxious to begin work on his second ship, but had been forced to concentrate on the railway. The first section from London to Maidenhead had finally opened, but that had not been without incident. Brunel's method of bedding down the rails caused the trains to lurch up and down as they passed over each piling, like a hopping rabbit or leaping deer. Eventually he admitted defeat and adopted Locke's transverse wooden sleepers.

Hudson continued to be a thorn in our side. He and his cronies used every avenue to argue against the use of the broad gauge. All summer and into the autumn Hudson kept up his relentless harrying. He caused reports to be commissioned on Brunel's approach to track-laying, on the costs and the advantages and disadvantages of the broad gauge, and on the performance of the engines.

Brunel's old nemesis, Dr Lardner, was asked to examine the latter, looking at the efficiency of the broad gauge engines versus the standard – or narrow, as Brunel insisted on calling it. Lardner asked Stephenson for help but he refused. He wasn't prepared to cast judgement on a fellow professional he admired, even if he didn't always agree with him. Even so, the directors of the London and Manchester Railway lent Lardner one of Stephenson's locomotives so that he could compare it with Brunel's.

After he had completed his tests with that engine, the day came to examine ours. As dawn broke, Lardner met us at the doors to the engine shed. He was accompanied by Hudson. Four men in overalls followed a pace or two behind them. Brunel ignored Lardner's outstretched hand.

'Who are all these men you have with you?'

Lardner cannot have expected a warm greeting, but nevertheless looked surprised at Brunel's tone.

'I've brought them to operate the locomotive. They are the same men that I used for the standard gauge tests.'

Brunel gestured at the men.

'I won't have our train driven by men from rival railways. They are bound to be biased.'

'Parliament has authorised these tests,' interjected Hudson. 'They will take a dim view of your failure to cooperate.'

'I won't permit it. The tests will be compromised. How do I know if these men know how to correctly operate these advanced engines?'

Hudson stared angrily at Brunel before turning to confer with Lardner.

I secretly applauded Brunel for being difficult, but I also thought he must be worried. He knew already that the engines had problems which he and his new locomotive assistant had been working on. His own designs had proven wanting, the boilers being too small, meaning that additional water towers now needed to be constructed along the route. What other mistakes might be exposed by Lardner's tests?

Hudson and Lardner emerged from their whispered conversation and suggested that the engine be operated by Lardner's men but with a representative of the GWR on board.

'No. My men will operate the engine. That way I know she will be handled properly. It's either that or abandon the tests.'

I grinned inwardly but worked to keep the smile from my face. I knew that they faced a stark choice: agree to Brunel's conditions or return to Parliament to seek more specific authorisation.

'We agree, but you will regret this,' said Hudson, his northern accent more pronounced as he spat out the words. He was a man who wasn't used to being bested and would cultivate his resentment until the time was right for retaliation, like a housewife carefully tending her vegetable patch until the crop was ripe.

Brunel signalled for the *North Star* to be readied and she puffed slowly out of the engine shed as we stood and watched. Over the next three hours, Lardner had the engine run back and forth at various speeds while monitoring the consumption of coal.

I peered down the track, waiting for the locomotive to reappear for its final run. It was still early, and mist was rising in tendrils from the grass as the sun started to burn off the early morning haze. The locals had told me it was a bad omen, frost on the ground in August. In the Wheatsheaf Inn the previous evening, the farmers had grumbled about the weather, as they always did, but for once their complaints rang true, since the wet start to the year had been followed by unheard of overnight freezes in mid-summer. Some claimed it was the effect of the new industrial engines and factories belching smoke into the sky, others an act of God, punishment for men's sins. To me, it was merely an obstacle to progress, making the completion of the line more challenging.

The engine hove into view. She swept past us at full speed but a few seconds later sparks flew from her wheels as the brakes were applied hard. Her whistle blew forlornly, like a bugle signalling the last post.

We rushed along the track towards the engine, now stopped a couple of hundred yards down the line, with the engine shed another quarter of a mile beyond. The occupants had jumped down from the footplate and were standing by the right-hand front wheel, looking down at the ground. I arrived as one of them took off his old woollen jacket, stained with grease, and laid it carefully down. I caught a glimpse of something I never want to see again. A man's head had been crushed by the front of the train.

No one knows why one of Lardner's railwaymen had chosen to walk close by the edge of the track, failing to pay attention to the oncoming locomotive. Perhaps he was on his way to the engine shed to greet them on their return. The driver, busy with the tests, didn't see him. The man, later named as Peter Tanner, was killed instantly, his skull split open by the impact.

Brunel shook his head sadly, saying to Lardner, 'What a waste, and for what?'

Lardner nodded grimly to Brunel but said nothing. A wagon was brought up and the remains of their fallen comrade loaded carefully aboard. They set off slowly, Lardner up front beside the driver, gripping tightly his notebook with its carefully tabulated columns of figures.

It was a few days after Christmas and I couldn't quite believe that I was sitting in yet another hall listening to Lardner pontificate. It was a shame that I didn't have the indefatigable Mrs Guppy alongside me. She had wanted to attend but had been feeling unwell and a journey to London by coach in the winter, particularly with her advancing years, was a significant undertaking.

The meeting was the last in a series of bad-tempered gatherings to discuss reports on different aspects of the construction work. It was well attended with thirty to forty of the shareholders present. The Bristol directors, led by Guppy and another director loyal to Brunel's cause, Gibbs, had done all they could to fend off the northern contingent, but even they acknowledged there were teething problems with the line for which Brunel needed to be held to account.

Three weeks ago Saunders and Gibbs had come to Brunel with a proposal that they appoint another engineer alongside him.

'The northern shareholders smell blood. They are arguing that you are too young and inexperienced. They have suggested that you either work alongside, or are replaced by Locke.'

Not as well-known as either Brunel or Stephenson, Locke was quietly and successfully completing lines to Birmingham and Southampton. I hardly knew him, but at Brunel's wedding I had been impressed by his composure when under fire from Stephenson.

'They are pointing out to anyone that will listen that his design for holding rails in place is working rather better than yours. And his trains haven't had the problems we have had.'

Even I, who had now worked with Brunel for several years, found it hard to work out whether he was bluffing as he replied calmly and with a touch of humility, 'If the board has lost faith in me, and my approach, then I should step aside.'

'Would there not be merit in getting advice and guidance from a man with Locke's experience?' asked Gibbs. 'It doesn't call into question your general abilities, but he does have more railway experience than you.'

'If the board want someone else, that is of course their right,' said Brunel, 'but I have found working with another does not work. There can only be one principal engineer.'

Saunders sighed and looked at Gibbs.

'Nothing for it but to brave it out with a formal vote. I will arrange a final meeting where all this can be aired once and for all.'

Lardner had been asked to present his findings and was in full flow.

'I ran a series of tests comparing the two engines at different speeds. I have found that the broad gauge *North Star* uses significantly more coal.'

He droned on, pointing to the tables of figures he had pinned up on the walls.

'I believe this is due to increased wind resistance arising from the wider body of a broad gauge locomotive,' he concluded, to rousing cries of 'Hear! hear!' from the northern shareholders, as if we were in the Houses of Parliament.

I sat up, realising that this was the opportunity Brunel had been hoping for to spike Lardner's guns once and for all. Charles Babbage rose to his feet but couldn't be heard against the hubbub. Babbage was a controversial figure. Although admired for his mathematical prowess and his work on industrial processes, he had failed to achieve acceptance as a traditional academic and now tended to make his arguments forcefully, alienating many. He was seen as an ally of Brunel's – he too was a believer in pushing the boundaries – but even Babbage's opponents respected his scientific views.

Saunders banged his gavel and called for order, as if he were the Speaker in the Commons. Babbage started again.

'Dr Lardner's postulations are fundamentally flawed. His instruments aren't accurate enough to produce such firm conclusions as he has offered up.'

'Hear! hear!' responded the Bristol shareholders, pleased to find a cause to rally behind.

'Why don't we ask Brunel to give his perspective?' suggested Babbage.

Brunel was called upon by Saunders. He stood up, straightened his coat, and walked slowly to the front.

'I hadn't intended to speak today. Others, like the learned Dr Lardner, have more than enough to say for all of us.'

Laughter broke out in some sections of the room while others looked irritated, no doubt annoyed by Brunel's uncanny ability to capture and entertain an audience.

'Dr Lardner's work has highlighted the issue of coal consumption of which we were already well aware. However, his conclusion that it is due to increased wind resistance is completely erroneous – as erroneous as his previous failure to take account of it when calculating the speed with which a runaway locomotive might pass through Box Tunnel!'

I could hear laughter around me as people turned to their neighbours to reminisce over Lardner's previous failings. Lardner sat uncannily still in the front row. I couldn't imagine how he would be taking Brunel's quips.

'Since Dr Lardner's tests, we have been working on the performance of the *North Star*. I am pleased to say that we can now achieve 0.95 pounds of coal burnt per ton per mile versus the 2.76 measured by Dr Lardner. A threefold improvement! The problem was with the design of the internal exhaust systems and blast pipes – nothing to do with wind resistance or the width of the engine.'

This was true. In August Brunel had hired as his locomotive assistant Daniel Gooch, who had previously worked at Robert Stephenson's famous locomotive works. Although he would never have admitted it, he must have had grave concerns about the performance of the engines to have done so. He didn't usually take on staff with prior experience with railways. He liked his own 'original' views to prevail.

Gooch was the perfect foil to Brunel. He had been brought up at the Tredegar ironworks where his father was a manager and had been involved with steam engines since his early teens. He avoided arguing with Brunel, instead stating his view together with a rational explanation of why he held that perspective. It won Brunel around more often than I would have guessed would be the case, although by that time Brunel must have realised that his own locomotive designs were poor, making him more receptive to another's view than would usually be the case.

After Lardner's tests, Gooch and Brunel had spent a day at the locomotive shed with the engine stripped down, the pieces scattered around them, happy as pigs in mud as they contentedly discussed what the problem might be: the design of the fireboxes? The way the air was being drawn into and out of the combustion chamber? Or perhaps, though less likely, greater rolling resistance from the larger wheels?

Eventually they decided that the design of the funnel and blast pipes was flawed. They were too narrow and incorrectly positioned, stopping the coal burning as efficiently as it should. Gooch had new parts fabricated and after reassembling the engine took it out to rerun the coal consumption tests. The figures were dramatically better.

Brunel had decided not to forewarn Lardner or Hudson about the improvement they had achieved. Saunders had agreed to plead ignorance if challenged. As chairman he needed to appear impartial, but he couldn't resist the idea of watching Brunel publicly dismantle those who continued to be a thorn in his side.

'So Dr Lardner, I am afraid that yet again you have espoused an erroneous theory. I wonder when you will stop making wild guesses and employ more considered science in your work?'

There were gasps from the audience. I felt uncomfortable. It was one thing to gently mock Lardner, another to attack his professional integrity so directly. Brunel, sensing that the audience may have felt he had gone too far, sought to justify his attack.

'You may feel my comments do Dr Lardner an injustice, but as I have said before, his assertions come cheaply to him. To us they cause untold extra work, unproductive debate and delay.'

I sighed when Brunel, unable to resist a final flourish, finished by pointing at Lardner and posing a rhetorical question: 'Surely, he can never again be called upon as an expert given his history of errors?'

Even Saunders looked aghast. Brunel had allowed himself to get carried away. The frustrations that Lardner had caused him over the years had bubbled up and he had thrown caution to the wind.

Lardner pulled himself to his feet.

'In times gone by I would have called you out for this.'

Brunel stared at him, a thin sardonic smile on his face, as if he were indeed waiting to be challenged to a duel. Lardner stared back for a moment, then realising what a fool he was making of himself turned and stumbled towards the exit. He tried to hold his head high but the fight had gone out of him. He passed me, his face ashen. I suppose it was dawning on him that he was finished. I recalled all the extra work that his postulations had caused me and felt a guilty pleasure in seeing him vanquished.

Brunel looked over to the chairman.

'Perhaps I could now address myself to some of the other criticisms that have been levelled against our efforts?'

Saunders indicated that he could continue.

'With regard to the method of holding down the track, I freely admit that the approach I have adopted has not worked as well as I would have hoped. We are already converting the track to a similar system to that used on the London and Birmingham Railway.'

'Why didn't you use that system before?' called out one of the northern shareholders, a thin, pinched-looking man with an old-fashioned string cravat. 'It feels like you must design everything from scratch, having no interest in using what's already available, tried and tested.'

'Not at all,' replied Brunel. 'I closely watch developments with the express intent of using the best of whatever new methods may emerge. However, in this case I knew already that Stephenson's design – using large concrete blocks – was causing a bumpy ride, and the design utilised on the London and Birmingham was also untested at the time.'

Brunel might say that, I thought, but I knew better. He loved nothing more than to come up with his own ideas, seeking out what he always hoped would be a more innovative solution.

'Finally,' he continued, 'with regard to the earthen works, then this is Mother Nature at work. The contractors are doing their best in difficult circumstances and it is hard to see what alternative approach could be adopted, or indeed could have been considered.'

Brunel and I were asked to leave the room while the shareholders debated what course of action they wished to take. We sat in the anteroom, Brunel puffing on a cigar. He seemed remarkably calm. I asked him if he felt that we would win the day.

'I don't know,' he replied. 'Saunders is confident, but I am not so sure. The northern shareholders have a lot of the votes and wouldn't need many others to change their allegiance to carry the day.'

'You don't seem unduly concerned,' I ventured. I by contrast felt sick, thinking that all the hard work of the last few years would come to nothing if the vote went against us.

'I have done my best to explain my position and can do no more,' replied Brunel. 'I… we… are now in the lap of the gods. The time for regrets will be if we don't carry the day.'

The doors opened and Saunders emerged smiling. He and the Bristol-based directors surrounded Brunel as the others left as a group, all long faces, frowns and quiet mutterings, like a murder of crows looking angrily over their shoulders as they took flight.

'We carried the day by over 1600 votes: 7790 to 6145,' declared Saunders. 'Your honesty won over the waverers.'

As we headed back to the office, Brunel asked me to make arrangements for the Briska to set out for Box in the morning.

'Enough talking. We have work to do.'

A year later, the newspapers were full of salacious articles about Lardner eloping to Paris with a Mrs Mary Heaviside and being chased down and whipped by her jilted husband, a captain in the Dragoons. He ended his days scratching a living in America. I was surprised I didn't take more pleasure in his downfall. Revenge might be a dish best served cold, but time had passed and all I felt was pity.

Chapter 14

1839

We climbed down from the train to the temporary wooden platform at the end of the line, and waited for the horses to be brought around from the stables. It was almost five years since I had last stood here, grateful to have completed our survey of the southern route but apprehensive about the challenge ahead.

Back then, we had rounded the final bend and I had stopped and stared. How could a tunnel be driven through this huge obstacle? The tall grassy hillside had reared up in front of us, tracks cut in its steep sides by ambling sheep, bushes scattered over the slope interspersed with clumps of rocks. Now a deep hollow had been dug out at the base, marking the beginning of the tunnel; the earth and rock were exposed like a giant scar defacing the bucolic scene.

We rode around the hill and down to the village that had sprung up where the railway line from Bristol terminated, awaiting completion of the tunnel. As we arrived, we heard a rumble, like the muted noise of thunder. A cloud of grey smoke gently drifted over us as one of the main contractors, George Burge, greeted us.

'Good to see you, sir.' He gestured towards the plume. 'Rock's turning out to be tougher than we thought. We are having to constantly blast it to make decent progress.'

I had listened to Brunel assure both investors and the members of the parliamentary committee that the tunnel was to be driven through soft limestone and would present little impediment to hardworking men. I was beginning to see why progress had been slow.

The lane beside us was filled with carts waiting their turn to pick up the tunnel spoil for use elsewhere on the line. Across the road wooden shacks lined the street with narrow thoroughfares leading to yet more ramshackle dwellings climbing the hillside beyond. A shanty town had been swiftly built on the slopes and would as quickly disappear when the work was done, carted away to the next construction site or purloined by locals.

A woman dressed in shapeless brown garments approached me.

'Would you like some fresh produce from my garden, sir?' she said, holding up the grubby, torn straw basket she was carrying, lined with a few rotting carrots for sale. Hawkers were making their way up the line of carts, their faces desperate yet resigned, again and again offering up their goods.

Burge was briefing Brunel and I caught snatches of their conversation: 'difficulties', 'doing our best', 'will try to catch up time'.

I watched small children running around between the houses, hollow-eyed and dressed in rags, yet still finding the energy to play a game of hide and seek, the flicker of youthful vigour impossible to extinguish. Women huddled around cooking pots, slowly stirring the thin gruel that would form their family's meal.

The smell given off by people living in close quarters was overpowering, like overripe fruit or the sickliest of perfumes. I was grateful for the wood smoke that drifted our way, a balm to the noisome odours.

I realised that Brunel was talking to me.

'I have agreed that I will address the workers when they change shifts at six o'clock this evening,' he said. 'We can return to London immediately afterwards.'

As we had a little time, I asked if I could visit the works. A young lad, slouched nearby against a wall with his hands in his pockets, was assigned to take me around. He didn't look like someone who could give me an informed perspective and I wondered whether to request a different guide, before deciding I didn't want to cause a fuss.

He brought over his horse, a magnificent chestnut specimen, and suggested we set off. His voice betrayed his breeding and I realised that I might have jumped to the wrong conclusion. As we rode along the side of the gulley being dug out for the entrance to the Bristol end of the tunnel, he introduced himself as Henry Thompson and explained that he was the son of a local landowner and had pushed hard to become involved with the works.

'As second son it was the army or the church for me,' he said. 'Neither really captured my imagination and then this came along. As part of giving up some land, my father negotiated my position.'

'Was he happy to see you abandon the other professions?' I asked.

'I think he hopes I will see sense. Engineering is not yet seen as an honourable calling in the same way as the others, but on the other hand he does believe in the march of progress. He's not a Luddite.'

As we started to climb up the hill towards the ventilation shafts, people out in the fields acknowledged our passing with a slight tip of the head. I envied him as he smiled or waved back, putting people at ease with his confident and easy manner. He pointed ahead of us at a group of people working around what looked like the top of a large well.

'Mr Brunel specified that first of all ventilation shafts should be dug at regular intervals so that tunnelling work can be carried on simultaneously from each shaft, thereby making the completion that much quicker.'

I knew this of course, but was too polite to interrupt his flow. If I am honest, I enjoyed listening to him extol the virtues of my employer's methods.

As we weaved our way up the wide muddy track, I remembered how different the landscape had been when I had first visited. There had been barely a soul for miles around then, the fields quiet as the farmers waited for the seasons to change, the hillside a haven of woods, fields and hedgerows, the only sounds the rustle of the trees and the call of birdsong. Now there were men, horses, carts and donkeys on the move everywhere.

I realised with a jolt that Henry was talking to me.

'The shafts are twenty-eight feet in diameter and between seventy and three-hundred feet deep. Within each one, they are tunnelling in both directions towards the adjacent shafts. We will find out soon enough if Mr Brunel has got the calculations right so that they meet up!' he laughed.

I wondered if I should be taking offence at his devil-may-care attitude, but I sensed that underneath his levity he was as worried as I was about whether Brunel's approach was going to work.

We reached the top of the hill and approached the deepest of the access shafts. On one side was the usual line of carts waiting to pick up their loads of rubble, and on the other a large wooden drum with long wooden spokes stretching out from it. Attached to each spoke was a pit pony, four in total. They slowly made their way round and round, steadily winding the long rope around the drum as they hauled up the load from below. A huge wooden tripod stood over the hole, the edges of which were guarded by a low brick wall. As we arrived, a bucket appeared and the men swung into action, hauling it off to the side so that it could be tipped into a waiting cart.

'You can see how long it takes to get the spoil out,' said Henry. 'The rock is also proving pretty tough to break up. I think you heard that we have had to blast a lot more than we thought we would.'

I asked if I could descend to the tunnel face at the bottom of the shaft: 'Only if it doesn't hold things up, of course.'

Henry assured me it would cause no delay and I was winched down, clinging on as the bucket swayed and spun round. It was made from thick planks of oak strapped together with metal bands, resembling a giant barrel of beer sawn in two around the centre. I got to the bottom to find the air thick with dust, lanterns glowing eerily in the half-light. Over the cacophony of the men hammering and bashing the rock, then loaded it into the bucket using spades and their bare hands, the foreman explained how each foot of tunnel had to be created by the blasting of the rock with gunpowder, followed by the use of sledgehammers and pickaxes to break up the stone. The stone was then loaded into the bucket and pulled slowly to the surface by the horses working away at their endless circular task. It was slow, filthy work. Each time the tunnel face was blasted, the men had to be winched up in the bucket out of the way, the dust had to settle and the men descend to dig out the spoil from the explosion. There was water everywhere, leaking out of the rock face and pooling at our feet. The stone dust and clods of earth that fell from the shaft had formed a quagmire through which the men were forced to wade back and forth.

I knew that accidents happened often – men hit on the head by falling rock, pickaxes deflecting off rock and spearing men in the arm or leg. Contractors often decided to speed things up by keeping the men in the access shafts when blasting and they could be struck by rocks careening out from the explosion. While hacking at the face, sharp stones had cut the men's clothing, and bruises, gashes and grazes could be seen wherever I glimpsed their exposed flesh. I couldn't imagine working in these conditions for a few hours, let alone days on end.

When I got back to the surface, Henry was waiting, looking uncharacteristically anxious.

'We need to hurry. Mr Brunel is about to speak and I would like to hear him.'

We arrived back to find a crowd of hundreds. As Brunel climbed onto the back of a cart, the gathering fell quiet. His voice carried clearly, amplified by the natural amphitheatre of the cutting leading up to the tunnel entrance. It was as if he were speaking to each of them personally.

'Thank you for giving me your time today, and more to the point, thank you for coming here to help bring this immense project to life. I recognise the sacrifices it has entailed, bringing you miles from your own communities and friends, living in makeshift dwellings for months on end.'

I could see groups of women whispering to each other and nodding. I don't imagine they were often praised for their fortitude. It was clear the crowd was warming to him. He raised his voice a level, his oratory soaring across the valley, his arms spread wide to embrace them all.

'I assure you it will be worth it. You are part of an extraordinary endeavour. You are creating the longest tunnel in the world. People will come from far and wide to see it when it is open. We are bringing progress to communities throughout the south west. Food will be shipped easily and quickly from where it is grown to where it is needed. Companies will be able to produce their goods and transport them across the country and the world. This tunnel is the last piece in the jigsaw in creating a seamless journey from London via Bristol to America. Just imagine, when the tunnel is complete someone will be able to board a train in London, change to a ship in Bristol and arrive in New York, all within a month!'

Scattered applause broke out around me and spread across the audience. I couldn't see if someone – one of the contractors perhaps – had started it off, but it didn't matter; within seconds everyone had joined in, clapping enthusiastically. Brunel paused for a few moments, waiting for it to die down. He starting speaking again, his voice quieter and more intimate. It was as if he was talking to his own family, telling them how grateful he was for their support.

'I want to thank each and every one of you for the part you are playing in this. Whether you are hard at work in the bowels of the tunnel digging out the stone or standing over a fire preparing the evening meal for the family, you are doing your bit to bring this vision to life. The company and I are grateful to you and wish you well for a speedy finish to your endeavours.'

As I scanned the crowd, I could see that his words had captured their imaginations. He had temporarily lifted them from the struggles of their daily lives to see that the work they were doing mattered. Maybe their sacrifices were worth it, I thought, when you considered what we were achieving.

As the train clattered its way back to London that evening, I told Brunel about my visit to the tunnel face.

'Sounds as if you had a more productive time than I did,' he replied. 'I have spent all afternoon listening to one contractor after another explaining how difficult the work is. What am I supposed to do about it if they made overly optimistic assumptions to win the work in the first place?'

I stopped myself from blurting out what I was thinking: these men are living through hell. Yes, their bosses may have made optimistic assumptions, but Brunel too had thought the limestone would be soft and easily hacked out. Did he not care about what was happening here? Was his only interest in getting the work finished irrespective of the impact on the workers? Was all he had just said a sham?

That night I dreamt of shrouded figures, worn down, stumbling through dimly lit corridors but I am ashamed to say that the memories quickly faded, driven out by pressure of work and the passage of time.

We didn't receive many unannounced callers at our offices, and usually turned away anyone without an appointment, but a few weeks later Hortense came to me to say that a woman in a great state of distress was waiting outside, refusing to come in but wanting to talk to someone in authority at the GWR.

With a sense of misgiving, I made my way to the front entrance. A woman, looking tired and dusty, and wrapped in a dirty grey shawl, was waiting there. Her hands were tightly gripped together, almost in supplication.

'How can I help you?' I asked.

'I beg your pardon for the intrusion, sir, but I don't know where else to turn. I have walked here from the other side of Chippenham. My husband can't work because of an accident building the GWR and we now have no money and I don't know what to do. I wouldn't have thought of coming here but I heard Mr Brunel speak at Box and I thought perhaps he might be able to help. He spoke so well about what he is trying to do and we... my husband, I mean... was just doing his part to bring it to pass.'

She had come here from the other side of Chippenham! I could hardly believe it, it was such a great distance to have walked. I looked down to see that the remains of her boots were held together with bailing twine. I shook my head in disbelief and then smiled gently at her when I saw her look of alarm as she assumed I was about to turn her away.

'Please do come inside,' I said.

The footman, Alfred, gave me a look of alarm. 'I am not sure Mr Brunel would appreciate us letting in waifs and strays who happen to turn up at the door, sir.'

'She's walked getting on a hundred miles. The least we can do is to offer her some refreshment and a listening ear.'

The woman refused to cross the threshold. I could see she was uncomfortable, and Alfred remained a frowning presence at my side. I wasn't sure how to proceed. I certainly wasn't prepared to discuss her business on the doorstep. Hortense came to our rescue by pushing past me.

'Come with me, let me show you the way,' she said kindly as she led her down the steep steps beside the front door to the servants' quarters below, as I followed close behind.

Hortense sat her down at the kitchen table with a cup of tea. Once we were settled, I asked her to give me some background.

'Please tell me your name, and the name of your husband and where was he working.'

'Martha Abbott, sir. My husband's name is Joseph. He was an assistant foreman working down number two shaft when a rock broke away and crushed his foot.'

She told me that he had been working fourteen hours a day because the tunnel was behind schedule. The contractors and foremen were driving things forward as hard as they could but they had to stop frequently to blast the face with gunpowder.

She repeated what I had learned for myself on my visit. As the pressure had increased to get the tunnel finished, the men had sheltered behind piles of rocks at the far end of the shaft instead of being winched up out of harm's way. After each explosion, they went forward with their sledgehammers and broke the rock up into smaller pieces to be carried on wheelbarrows to the access shaft and taken to the surface.

'The day of the accident the rock didn't break away fully where it had been blasted. Joseph told me that they didn't want to waste time setting another set of charges, and so he volunteered to climb up and use metal wedges to break up the face.'

Martha's husband had driven two metal wedges into cracks above a lump of rock and was driving a third into the side when the rock came away. He couldn't move back quickly enough and a large rock landed on his leg.

'He was stuck for more than three hours before they managed

to get some wooden beams under the rock and lever it far enough off the floor to slide him out.'

My eyes were stinging as I thought about the agony that Joseph must have endured and I watched Martha's eyes fill with tears as she recounted the story. She took a sip of her tea, and gave Hortense a grateful look when she pushed a plate of biscuits towards her.

Although liquor was banned on site, they had given him swigs of gin to dull the pain. Joseph was laid out on a wooden table in the front room of the doctor's small house in the village just beyond the workers' makeshift huts. The hundreds of men working on site, and the regular occurrences of accidents of one sort or another, meant that a doctor was more or less fully employed by the railway contractors.

'He wanted to amputate, but Joseph refused. How could he earn a living with only one leg? he said. The doctor took me to one side and told me that if he didn't do it, he would almost certainly die from blood poisoning.'

Tears were spilling down Martha's cheeks.

'What choice did I have? He wouldn't have been much use to me dead, but Joseph still pleaded with me not to let the doctor do it.'

She stopped, unable to continue, her shoulders shaking as she wept.

'Excuse me, sir. I am so sorry,' she stammered.

Hortense lent her a handkerchief and held her hand tightly.

'Don't worry. Please take your time,' I said.

In any event I didn't need Martha to describe the scene I could too easily imagine: Joseph screaming as he was held down by several helpers while the doctor took a saw to his shattered leg.

Martha handed back the handkerchief with a grateful smile and continued her story. Joseph was lucky that infection didn't set in. The doctor must have been well-versed in the latest techniques for avoiding sepsis, the table thoroughly scrubbed and treated with iodine.

Joseph was a good worker and the contractor gave them some money to pay for rent and food while he recuperated. Most workers who had suffered an accident were laid off immediately and left to fend for themselves with whatever help they could get from friends or family, or were reduced to begging around the entrance to the tunnel works. People gave what they could, knowing that next week it could so easily be them holding out a tin mug at the gates, unable to earn a living for themselves.

The wound was healing, but Joseph suffered from endless aches and cramps from his missing leg. It kept him awake at night and he couldn't bear anything to touch the end of the stump. The pain meant he couldn't concentrate or as he put it 'do anything'. They had two children, aged five and seven, and now that he had been off work for six weeks, they had no money. Martha had left her little family in the care of her sister and walked to London in order to plead for help.

'I am so sorry for taking up your time,' she finished, 'but I heard tell of new jobs on the railway – guards and ticket-sellers at stations and suchlike – which I thought perhaps, when he is better, might allow him to be of service?'

It was a remarkable story but not because of Joseph's injury. I knew that was commonplace. I had seen the statistics for the number injured or killed on the Thames and Box tunnels and on other major engineering works. No, it was remarkable because Martha had taken it upon herself to try and do something about it. She had arrived exhausted and hungry at the door, but still desperate to avoid our pity as she asked for help.

Hortense gave her something more substantial to eat and I went to see Brunel. He was in the thick of designing his new ship, the SS *Great Britain*, and wasn't best pleased to be disturbed. I explained that the wife of one of the workers on the Box tunnel had turned up unexpectedly and she and her family were close to destitute as a result of an accident from when they were blasting.

Brunel sighed, threw down his pencil and looked at me.

'Why are you bothering me with this? It's the responsibility of the contractor to sort it out and do whatever they feel is right for their injured worker. We can't afford to set a precedent by helping out one family that happens to have arrived at our doorstep. If we do that, we will have a queue of them down the street making all sorts of claims and requests for assistance.'

We both knew that the contractors were under severe cost pressure and would likely do little or nothing to help, and although I knew it wasn't my place to continue to plead her situation, I couldn't stop myself from trying.

'I understand what you are saying, sir, but this woman has walked almost a hundred miles to make her case. Her family will be destitute as a result of an accident that happened on our site. She has young children, just as you have.'

Brunel's son, Isambard junior, had been born two years earlier. He was a sweet little boy, who occasionally came into the office in the early evening to see his dada. Brunel always made time for him, dropping down to the carpet to roar like a lion or give him a quick ride around the room. I thought mention of children might elicit a change of heart but I was disappointed.

'I have told you once, and I don't intend to repeat myself, tell her to apply to the company that employed her husband.'

Brunel bent his head back down to his work and dismissed me with a wave of his hand. I knew the discussion was over and quietly left the room. It was just one case, and hundreds of workmen had been injured or killed during construction of the GWR, but this one was on our doorstep asking for our help.

I went downstairs and asked Hortense to step outside for a few moments so we could have a word. The two of us left Martha in the kitchen, and in the pantry I explained what Brunel had said.

Hortense looked crestfallen. I too felt miserable. We both knew we had little option but to send her away.

'I am sorry, Martha. I have spoken to Mr Brunel, and much as he would like to be of assistance, the railway isn't at a stage where there are jobs available that might suit Joseph.'

I couldn't bring myself to look either Martha or Hortense in the eye as I made my little speech. Already worn down by her long trip, Martha seemed to shrink back inside herself. Her eyes became flat and colourless, hope draining from them.

We tried to give her a little money and some food for the return journey but she would take nothing.

'I didn't come here for charity, sir. We will find a way. Please don't worry.'

She slowly climbed the steps and set off down the street.

In the days after Martha left, Hortense became withdrawn, dropping her eyes and busying herself with her work whenever we came across each other around the house. I too was consumed with guilt, haunted by Martha's quiet dignity in the face of her family's ruin.

I had made a promise to accompany Hortense and one of the other housemaids, Sarah, to an art exhibition at the British Institute. Nowadays – since the Great Exhibition, I suppose – it no longer seems strange for anyone to wish to visit a gallery or museum, but back then it was considered unusual for all but the wealthiest to show an interest in the arts. Hortense, though, had always loved the paintings scattered around the house. Brunel was an avid collector and a few years later went even further and commissioned various artists to paint a series of scenes from Shakespearean plays for the dining room.

I knew that Hortense was unlikely to relish indulging in frivolous activity while Martha continued to prey on her mind, but I assumed she wouldn't want to let Sarah down. I was also keen to go, hoping we might be able to snatch a few quiet moments together to clear the air. So on the day in question, I tentatively asked Hortense whether it would be convenient to meet her and Sarah in the kitchen at five o'clock, which should give us plenty of time to get there. Even to my ears it sounded oddly formal.

Sarah was ready first. I rarely notice such things but even I could tell that she had taken the greatest care over her costume. Most days she wore a fawn dress, made of strong material and scrupulously clean, but dotted with faded stains despite the protection of the crisply starched aprons the housemaids always wore. Today she wore a dress in muted tartan, a discreet but pleasant pattern. Over her shoulders she had placed a dark shawl, and a pretty if plain bonnet was tied under her chin.

Hortense arrived soon after and looked simply stunning. I had seen her dressed for church, of course, but today she was wearing an elaborate blue dress I hadn't seen before. I could glimpse her dark flowing hair peeking out from under her bonnet and she had applied powder to her face and something around her eyes that seemed to bring them alive despite her melancholy air.

I complimented them both on their attire and held open the kitchen door leading to the steps up to the street. We caught the omnibus from the end of the road. The bus was busy as they almost always were. The conductor apologised and said that I would have to go up on the roof, but he would try and find space for the ladies inside.

'Come along now. Which gentleman is prepared to make way for these lovely ladies?' he called into the cramped interior.

Two young men clambered out and the three of us made our way up the iron rungs to the roof. A bench ran its full length and we grabbed the handle running along the top as the driver cracked his whip and the horses set off with a lurch. We made our apologies to the passengers already seated and, taking care not to be pitched over the side of the roof as the bus weaved its way through the crowds, slid gingerly into our places.

We reached Pall Mall and I climbed down from the roof and helped Sarah and Hortense disembark. We stood before the gallery, taking in the grand entrance built of stone in the classical style, and the steady flow of impeccably dressed ladies and gentlemen entering and leaving, or simply passing by along the street. Before we all lost the courage to continue, I bundled my companions across the street and we entered the building.

My heart sank. In front of us were Brunel and his wife, Mary. I knew that Hortense found Mary difficult. From the beginning, she had been keen to establish her authority but was unversed in the ways to best manage a household. She admonished the servants for trivial matters but allowed the cook to over-order and pilfer the excess with impunity. She took exception at the smallest perceived slight.

She stared at us open-mouthed. For a brief moment I was at a loss as to what to do. I could hardly introduce her to her own servants. Quickly I gathered my wits about me, smiled politely at Mary but addressed myself to Brunel.

'Hortense and Sarah have developed a love of painting from those on your walls, sir. They asked if they might view the Vermeer of which they have heard so much.'

It could have been worse. Although it was the most awkward of moments, the Brunels had already visited the exhibition and were on their way out. Brunel finished helping his wife on with her coat.

'Capital, capital. You will enjoy it. Wonderful pictures.'

'Yes, do enjoy it,' added Mary, smiling weakly but still looking at us most oddly. It must have been chastening to find herself in attendance at the same event as her housemaids.

We made our way into the gallery to find small groups huddled around each picture. Snatches of conversation drifted our way: 'Wonderful, just wonderful. Look how Vermeer has caught the light entering through the window, such a contrast...', 'Of course,

I have always loved the Italian masters. You can see their influence in all the other paintings, just look at how…'

I glanced at Hortense and Sarah. They were staring at the pictures, engrossed, but I wondered if they felt as inadequate as I did, listening to all these people able to expound at length about what they saw before them.

We came at last to the Vermeer. I loved the thoughtful look on the woman's face as she looked down and prepared to pour water from the jug, but I had no idea how to express my feelings in the kind of language those around me were using.

Hortense turned to me and smiled wistfully. 'This is beautiful. Thank you for bringing us. Those other people made such intellectual comments but I just like the feelings the paintings bring out in me. It lets me… how do you say it in English… lose myself, to forget the day to day.'

I smiled back gratefully. I had been scrabbling around for something sensible to say, and her words had removed the need.

'I am so sorry about Martha,' I whispered. 'It preys on my mind. Have you heard anything?'

She shook her head and sadly turned back to gaze at the pictures.

I was about to talk about all the good Brunel – and by extension we – were bringing to our fellow human beings: enabling prosperity, allowing people to sell their goods to a bigger market, permitting visitors from the provinces to come to exhibitions such as this, but I stopped myself. I was suddenly reminded of an old story that my mother had told me.

A boy comes across many starfish stranded on a beach and starts to pick them up and throw them back into the water one by one. His father asks what he is doing, saying 'We don't have time, you can only save a few. You really can't make a difference.'

'I am making a difference to the ones I throw back,' replied the boy, continuing to return them to the sea until they had to leave.

Hortense was concerned with the one she could have rescued, not all the others she might not be able to help, or the ones struggling out at sea. It was no different from what I had done with the boy, James. I realised that I was deeply troubled by Brunel's lack of interest in the fate of his workers, and by extension my role in their suffering.

I pulled Hortense gently to one side. Sarah stayed a little way away, diplomatically burying herself in the careful inspection of a picture.

'Hortense, I want you to know I am greatly concerned about what has happened.'

Hortense said nothing, looking down at her feet.

'Look,' I said, reaching out for one of her hands. 'I know that Brunel pretends to care about his workers, but he doesn't. He doesn't really care about anyone apart from his family and his position in society.'

She still said nothing, her hand limp in mine. I reached out and lifted her chin so that she was forced to look at me.

'I know how unhappy you are about this and I want you to know that I am too.'

Finally she spoke, wiping a tear from her eye.

'What can we do? I hate not being able to do anything.'

'I don't know,' I replied. 'But at least we know we both feel the same way.'

We exited the gallery and stood rather awkwardly on the pavement outside, saying little, Sarah waiting patiently. I didn't want the evening to end. I had so much I wanted to say: how Hortense had brought peace and fun into my life; how she was so easy to talk to, to share my thoughts and concerns with, but I didn't know how to begin to speak about any of this. So instead, as we parted company I reached across and squeezed her hand as I said my goodbyes. She smiled softly at me and I left, feeling like I truly was the cow that had just jumped over the moon.

Chapter 15

I was sitting at my desk, distracted by the midday sun streaming in through the window. It was hard to concentrate. Infused by a warm glow I kept thinking back to the previous evening with Hortense at the exhibition. Could I ask her to marry me, I wondered? How would she react? Was there any chance she might accept?

The doorbell rang and I tried to ignore it, endeavouring instead to reconcile the supplier's request for payment set out in front of me. There was a knock at the door.

'Come in!' I called out, sighing deeply. I couldn't work out why the supplier thought the amount he was claiming was in any way accurate given the job was only partly complete. The footman poked his head around.

'A messenger for you, sir.'

The messenger must have known that he was the bearer of bad tidings. As he stood at the doorway holding out the folded note he seemed to radiate sadness and compassion. Many were ex-military service personnel, and I suppose they must have seen terrible things in their time, but I doubt they were trained to deal with the trials and tribulations of everyday life.

The short letter from my father said that my mother had been taken ill. I scribbled a note for Brunel, grabbed my coat and called for a cab. My mother has a strong constitution and would never make a fuss. For my father to write – and to spend money on a messenger – things must be serious.

I sat in the cab, chewing my fingernail. Not a pleasant habit, but I was worried. Epidemics of typhoid, typhus and cholera had swept through parts of London in the last few months. The authorities had conducted various clean-up campaigns but as one outbreak seemed to wane, a fresh wave would hit the city. My mother often helped out at local missions, providing food and spare clothing to the poor of the neighbourhood. I had always worried that she might become exposed to a serious illness but my entreaties to stop were met with a polite, 'But they are less fortunate than us, dear, and who else will help?'

My father opened the door of the shop as I arrived.

'Thank God you're here.'

He looked anxiously up and down the street and beckoned me in as if he had committed a crime.

'She's in a bad way,' he said, his face crumpled like an old paper bag. 'I have tried to cool her with damp cloths but she remains feverish.'

'Have you called for a doctor or asked the neighbours for help?'

'I daren't. If news gets out, no one will come to the shop. Things are quiet as they are.'

I briefly wondered what he meant by that. I thought my contributions were enough when combined with the takings from the shop to make our lives comfortable. It was true that dinners had been sparse recently, tough old mutton and a few vegetables stewed for hours and served up each day from a large pot. I cast the thought aside for the moment and followed my father upstairs.

There wasn't much room up there. Just a couple of bedrooms. The kitchen and parlour were on the ground floor behind the shop. Wooden boxes stacked up to the ceiling lined one side of the corridor, the only available space for extra stock.

As I walked to my parents' room, I could smell her illness, that unmistakable mix of warm fetid sweat combined with the sweet vinegar of sick itself. There was something else too. Dear God, I thought miserably. She has lost control of her bowels. I knew what that might mean and approached her bedside with dread.

My mother lay still, her breathing laboured, and although her eyes lit up when she saw me and she attempted a smile, her face was pale and glistening with sweat, and her hair lay matted and stringy on the pillow. She looked exhausted, worn out by the struggle. I always thought of her as indomitable but I realised that she would know as well as I that there was a good chance she had cholera. I wondered if she was as frightened as I was – the word rattled around in my head, the thought making me feel sick.

I went to kiss her, but she was having none of it. She waved me away saying that she didn't know what illness she had, but she definitely didn't want to give it to me. I sat on the small wooden chair beside the bed and she slowly grew calm and shut her eyes, but she wasn't at peace. She grimaced each time her body was racked by stomach cramps.

I glanced across at my father. He stood by the door, seeming uncertain as to whether to stay there or head back downstairs. On the surface he was the master of the house but it was my mother who often took the difficult decisions. When customers didn't pay what was due on their account, he would agonise over what he should do. She would quietly advise him whether he should extend credit or not. She had her ear to the ground and knew whether a family was in real financial trouble and needed help, or just living beyond their means. She had been my rock, too. She had realised that I needed to follow my dreams away from the shop, had encouraged me and eventually persuaded my father.

She groaned and tried to swallow. Quickly I took the water glass beside the bed and, putting my hand gently behind her neck, tilted the glass to let a few drops flow in. She smiled again, as weakly as before.

'Thank you,' she whispered. 'It's so nice of you to have come, but don't you need to get back to work?'

I smiled back, squeezing my eyes to stop the tears.

'I'll stay a while if you don't mind, Ma,' I said, then added a lie. 'Mr Brunel has said it's fine.'

I didn't think he would miss me today, but how long he would tolerate my absence would depend on whether something came up and he needed me by his side, I thought.

'I remember you as such an inquisitive boy,' she murmured. 'Always asking how things worked and why something was as it was.'

I didn't say anything, but reached out and took her hand.

'I am sorry you never had a brother or a sister. We tried but it wasn't to be.'

'I was happy with you and Dad, Ma,' I said as my eyes stung and I wiped away the tear rolling down my cheek.

My mother closed her eyes and I quietly got up and crossed to my father by the door.

'I don't know what to do,' he whispered. 'We can't afford a doctor and business will dry up immediately if people suspect anything.'

Neither of us mentioned the word 'cholera'. There was no cure and we both knew from the epidemic in 1831 that sufferers could die within hours.

'If the authorities find out they will close us down anyway,' I said. 'I think it's better if we shut the shop now.'

My father's shoulders sagged. He nodded his assent and headed back down the stairs. I returned to the chair by my mother's bedside. I was finding it hard to breathe and unfastened my collar, oppressed by the stuffiness in the room and the feeling of powerlessness that threatened to overwhelm me.

'Please don't die,' I muttered under my breath.

I heard my father climbing the stairs, the sound of his voice floating up ahead of him.

'He's talking to himself now,' I thought.

'Mr Brunel has sent his doctor!' he announced as he reached the bedroom door, stepping aside to let Dr Hansworth into the room.

I must have looked puzzled, I am sure, as I quickly got up and went to shake his hand.

'Brunel sent me over. He was worried about the note you left and thought I might be able to help. Let's see the patient.' He made his way to the bed. 'How are you feeling, my dear?' he asked in an avuncular tone. It's a tone that I remember from my illnesses as a child, when the doctor had been called and his melodious, baritone voice always seemed to make me feel a little better.

Dr Hansworth was tall and thin, with wispy grey hair and a permanently worried look on his face, creases etched into his forehead. He placed his battered brown holdall on the floor and leant over the bed, examining her gently, although taking care not to touch her, I noticed. He thanked her for her patience and suggested we might speak downstairs.

'I am not sure what it is yet, but it's best to keep her cool and make sure she keeps drinking to replace the lost fluids. I'll give you a sedative to keep her comfortable. That's all we can do other than wait for the fever to pass.'

He opened his bag and handed my father a little bottle.

'This will ward off the pain. Administer five drops every four hours.'

My father thanked him and I showed him out.

'Send a messenger if things take a turn for the worse, otherwise I will return in the morning to see how things are,' he said, before hurrying off down the street, the clacking of his cane marking his rapid progress.

My father and I took turns by my mother's bedside. As I sat there in the early hours and fretted, I wondered why I hadn't asked Dr Hansworth if it was cholera. Deep down I knew it was because I didn't want to hear the worst.

The hours passed slowly by with her murmuring and muttering in her sleep. I must have been dozing when she reached out and grasped my arm. I jerked awake.

'Look after your father,' she said, staring at me, then collapsed back on the bed.

'Don't worry, you will still be around to do that,' I began my reply, when I realised that she had been talking in her sleep and would be oblivious to anything I might say.

My father and I replaced each other every few hours at her bedside, neither of us saying what was on our minds, which was how could he possibly cope without her. Near dawn, as grey shadows slowly crept across the bedroom floor and the sounds of the city waking up reached in through the windows, my mother seemed more serene. She took little sips of water and smiled her thanks. Was it the calm before the end? I wondered, trying desperately to keep my anxiety under control.

Dr Hansworth returned, and after a brief examination appeared much cheerier as we gathered again downstairs.

'I think the fever is starting to break,' he said. 'It looks to me like your mother may be through the worst.'

My father fumbled behind him to find the top of a nearby chair and sat down, giddy with relief.

I showed the doctor to the door, and as we stood together on the threshold, he added, 'We are not completely out of the woods yet, my dear fellow. Make sure she keeps drinking. I will return again tomorrow.'

'Thank you, thank you, doctor.'

Not knowing quite how to broach the subject, I went on to say how very kind it was of him to have come and Brunel to have sent for him, but I wasn't sure we would have enough money to pay his fees.

'My dear chap! Not to worry. Brunel was quite insistent that he would pay for any treatment required.'

I closed the door and leant against it. I wondered how I would ever be able to thank Brunel for his kindness. I took a deep breath and went to find my father. He was still sitting where I had left him and I could see he was close to tears. I rather awkwardly reached down and hugged him. We didn't show much emotion as a family but somehow it seemed right in the circumstances. As we broke apart, he looked away and straightened his shoulders. 'Get a grip,' I would guess he was saying to himself, and as I left to go back upstairs he pulled himself wearily to his feet.

I spent the day by my mother's bedside, but could see that she was improving all the time. The next morning I caught her out of bed, a little wobbly on her feet but slowly making her way around tidying and dusting the room. I chided her as I tucked her back in.

'You must take yourself back to work, dear,' she said, leaning over to straighten the blanket. 'I will be up and about in no time.'

I did as she asked and returned to work, leaving a little vase of fresh flowers on her bedside table to cheer her up. I tried to thank Brunel and discuss how I might repay the money over time but he would have none of it.

'I have come to rely on you, Bennett, and you having a sick mother isn't helping anyone, so consider it selfishness!' he said, waving me back to my desk and bending his head back to the papers on his.

I had been back at work a few days, when Hortense took me to one side and asked if we could meet in the park later that afternoon. As we took our usual route, I told her about my mother.

'It was so kind of Brunel to help without being asked,' I said.

'Yes,' said Hortense, turning to face me, 'but don't you suppose he was also wondering how he would manage without you if you were absent for a long time?'

'Maybe, but I am still in his debt.'

'Surely you are not in his debt if he did it for his own ends?'

I looked out over the water at a couple picnicking with their young boy. The father stood up and took hold of his son's hands, heaving him off the ground and spinning him round, his feet whizzing just off the ground like a miniature fairground ride. He squealed with delight. It brought back a memory of Brunel playing with his young son; I had been passing the door to the sitting room when I had spied Brunel on his hands and knees, tickling him, the young lad screaming with laughter.

'I don't think it's that simple, Hortense. Of course he is full of self-interest, but he does care, at least about those close to him.'

She looked at me searchingly, and then turned away and spoke quietly.

'I am sorry, Joseph. I don't feel the same way.'

She took a deep breath and I felt a sense of dread. I started to raise my hand, as if to stop her, but she carried on speaking, slowly but firmly.

'I have decided to leave.'

I sank down on the nearest bench and put my head in my hands. I couldn't think of what to say without sounding pathetic. Hortense perched beside me and took one of my hands in hers.

'I am sorry, Hortense,' I said, looking up and taking her other hand in mine. 'I must be tired. It feels like the world is crashing down around my ears.'

'No, I am sorry,' said Hortense. 'I know it's not a good time but a job has come up with my brother's employer and I don't feel I am able to stay in Brunel's house any longer.'

A couple walked past us and we sat silently until they were gone.

She reached across and took my hand.

'Why don't you ask Maudslay if he would offer you a position? I know you feel as I do.'

'I can't. Whatever the reason, without a moment's hesitation Brunel reached out unasked to help me and my family. Maybe it was only his self-interest, but nevertheless I owe him my loyalty now.'

Hortense got up and stood facing me, looking sad.

'Well, it's goodbye then,' she smiled gently, 'although I hope it's *à bientôt*.'

She held out her hand for a kiss, trying to keep the atmosphere light, I suppose. I stared at her. The thought of not seeing her every day filled me with misery. It was hard to believe that it was only a few days ago that I had been working out how I might ask her to be my wife. I stood up, pulled her in and held her tightly, breathing deeply to capture the smell of her.

She headed off along the path, and as I watched her leave I wondered whether I was making a huge mistake. Had Brunel acted solely to buy my loyalty as Hortense had suggested?

Chapter 16

1841

I t was hard to believe how much time had passed since my mother, now fully recovered and still visiting the poor of the parish, had been struck down with cholera. It was two years since Hortense had given her notice and moved out, her absence leaving me with a dull constant ache, reminding me of Martha's description of the pain of Joseph's missing limb. I threw myself into my work. There was plenty to do and I wanted no time to think of anything else.

The SS *Great Western* had been hailed as a triumph, concerns about the fire on her maiden voyage now a distant memory. Passengers flocked to use this fast, reliable and luxurious new way to cross the Atlantic. The Great Western Steamship Company wanted another constructed as soon as possible, but Brunel being Brunel, to simply build a sister ship to the *Great Western* was never going to be enough. He persuaded the directors that their second should be bigger again – around one and a half times as long – and should be built solely of iron to deal with the stresses such a large ship would face in an Atlantic storm.

The project was already over a year behind schedule. After the keel had been laid and work on the hull was well underway, Brunel heard about a new means of propulsion: the propeller, which reportedly was far more efficient than paddle wheels. After sending Claxton on a voyage on an experimental ship, the *Archimedes*, Brunel changed the design to accommodate a propeller, requiring all sorts of changes to the internal layout.

The switch to a propeller required a different type of engine, capable of running at faster speeds. Brunel drafted in his father to help and the resulting engines did prove to work well – much better than Brunel's designs for the GWR locomotives – but the changes led to further delays. It was two days before Christmas when Brunel lost patience and asked me if I would go to Bristol to determine the true state of affairs. He would have gone himself but was inundated with work, including the completion of the line to Exeter, numerous requests to extend in other directions, and even a suggestion from Italy that he supervise the building of a railway network around Turin.

The Box Tunnel had opened six months before, and trains now ran all the way from Bristol to London. Some passengers still refused to go through the tunnel, travelling by coach to the other end and catching a later train. I understood their concern. I could still recall my apprehension as I watched Daniel Gooch drive the first locomotive through it. He had climbed up onto the footplate and smiled, saying that he was looking forward to proving Lardner wrong. However, as he leant his elbow out of the window waiting for the signal to proceed, I noticed him nervously fingering something at his throat. The green flag was waved, and he reached to pull the steam lever, the crucifix he had been holding swinging back in place around his neck.

He was grinning broadly though when he returned. Despite his nervousness and Lardner's dire prognostications, all was well. No one fainted or was asphyxiated, and neither did the train run out of control. Gooch descended from the engine to be greeted by Brunel like his long-lost prodigal son.

The quickest and easiest way to see the ship for myself was to catch the train to Bristol. I decided to catch the first, the 4.30 a.m., in the hope I could return that evening to celebrate Christmas with my parents. I only just made it, finding it hard to leave the comfort of my bed. I rushed down the platform, past the goods wagons to the third-class carriages. They were basic, just low-sided open carriages with seats nailed across their width, but there was no other option on this early a train. Four young men and women sat around me and were talkative, even at this time on a chilly December morning.

'I wonder whether Molly will say yes this time?' asked one, nudging his companion.

'Hah,' his friend replied. 'Are you sure your Agnes won't have run off with someone else by now?'

'Would you like a piece of pie?' the first speaker asked me. 'Makes for a grand breakfast. Sets you up for the day.'

I shook my head and politely declined.

'I'm Tom and this is John. We are off home for Christmas. This here's Joan and the other one's Liz. We all live in the same village. They work in one of them grand houses – we just build them!' he said, showing off his massive calloused hands.

I just had time to introduce myself before the whistle blew and we pulled out of the station. It was soon too windy to talk and as the countryside raced by I marvelled at the speed at which we were travelling. True, the carriage lurched around a little, but compared to bouncing up and down all night in a mail coach it felt like a miracle. I couldn't stop myself grinning. We truly had changed the world.

We stopped at Twyford to take on a few more passengers. Good-natured insults were traded as we shuffled along the benches so that the new arrivals could squeeze in. With a plume of steam and smoke we set off. We rounded the bend and entered the cutting at Sonning, the train travelling at full speed now as we passed under a wooden footbridge and waved to a labourer looking down at us.

People say that an accident happens in slow motion and so it seemed to me. I still recall it vividly. Firstly, my confusion on seeing an earth bank that seemed to stretch across the track; then the locomotive tilting in front of us as it hit the landslide, like a ship pulled up and left to dry out on a beach. The back of our wagon reared up, the weight of the goods vans behind us pushed it into the air.

I don't remember any more. Whether I shut my eyes or blacked out as I was propelled out of my seat like a cannon ball, I don't know. I came to lying face down on the ground, my mouth full of dirt. I moved my head to the side to see my old brown satchel a few inches from my nose, and beyond that a workman's tools spilling out of a canvas bag. I rolled over and sat up. Liquid was running down my face, and when I felt my head there was a long gash above my right eye. My hand came away sticky and wet, streaked with blood. I was lucky, though, nothing seemed broken.

Around me, some lay unnaturally still while others sat up silently or groaned quietly, looking as stunned as I felt. A few feet further up the cutting, I could hear the steam engine panting and sighing as it cooled, like an ageing animal calmly reaching the end of its natural life. Men came hurtling down the embankment, drawn by the noise of the crash.

'Are you alright?' they asked, helplessly.

'Where's Joan, where's Joan?' called out the woman who had been introduced to me as Liz. She staggered across to one of the figures and dropped down to her knees.

'No, no,' she whispered, and began to sob.

The rest of the morning passed in a blur. I helped as best I could. Sixteen of the most seriously injured were taken to the hospital at Reading. Those that had died were laid out in a hut at the top of the embankment. Each broken and bloodied body bore ever heavier on my conscience. My earlier thoughts felt like mindless arrogance. Oh yes, we had definitely changed the world for these people who had simply wanted to get home to spend time with their families, but not for the better.

I sat by the footbridge, dog tired, and with no more that I could usefully do. I stared down at the scene below – the train was part buried in the bank, the second of its carriages thrown upside down against the side of the cutting with a line of heavier goods wagons remaining upright on the rails behind. Earth and boulders were strewn across the track. I felt as if I might faint and took a deep breath. All the problems we'd had with land slippage had come to this.

It was midday when Brunel arrived, the relief train steaming to a halt a few yards down the track. I stumbled to my feet and scrambled down the embankment to meet him. He peered at me anxiously.

'My dear fellow, are you alright? I got here as fast as I could after I received the telegram.'

'Yes sir, but I am sorry to say that the embankment has given way. Eight people have been killed and many others injured.'

Brunel said something under his breath – 'Oh my God!' perhaps – and then started to bark out orders. Men that he had commandeered from GWR works across London streamed from the train to begin to clear the line and prepare to right the carriages. I stood, shoulders sagging, finding it hard to find the willpower to offer my assistance. Brunel returned to my side.

'Are you sure you are alright, Bennett? You look in a bad way.'

He frowned as he looked up the line at the men starting to dig.

'I don't understand. The cutting was only inspected a few days ago.'

'Does it matter, sir?' I replied wearily. 'The fact is that the passengers had no protection whatsoever. They... we... were all herded into cattle trucks. When we crashed, there was nothing to hold onto. We were all thrown clear. I was lucky, I didn't hit anything hard.'

I could hear my voice breaking, overwhelmed by shock.

'Well, we will have to investigate all that, of course. But we mustn't jump to any conclusions.'

'I can assure you, sir, that the design of the carriages made it worse.'

A wave of anger surged over me.

'You're not yourself, Bennett. We need to get you back to London to get some rest.'

I felt the blood rushing to my face, a burst of adrenalin. 'We must admit blame, sir, and help these people.'

Before Brunel could reply, we heard a loud voice call out: 'Let me through! Out of my way!'

We both looked further down the line to where half a dozen GWR employees were holding back curious onlookers. A self-important looking man dressed in black was striding towards us, accompanied by a couple of lackeys.

'I'm Palmer, the local Member of Parliament. It's my constituents who have been killed or hurt.'

He pointed at Brunel's men.

'You mustn't touch anything without the coroner's permission. What are they doing?'

'We need to get the track cleared and the line back up and running,' replied Brunel.

'You can't do that. All this will be needed as evidence for the inquest.'

'I am afraid they must. We can't have the railway closed for any longer than is needed to get it cleared and safe again.'

Brunel nodded to one of the foremen, Jones, who was standing nearby watching, ready to act if needed.

'Please escort Mr Palmer away so that he is in no danger.'

Palmer looked as if he might argue, but when he saw that he was surrounded by a group of Brunel's workers, he made the best of a bad job and retreated with as much dignity as he could muster.

'I'll see you at the inquest tomorrow. Nine a.m. sharp, mind. We'll see how things go when you have to testify in front of a jury.'

Brunel called Hammond over from where he was supervising the work and whispered to the two of us: 'I don't know how tomorrow will go. Judging by the local mood there is a chance I will be arrested. Hammond, you will need to take over here. Bennett, Hammond will get you on the train and back to London so that you can take to your bed and rest.'

I was about to remonstrate, but feeling overwhelmed with tiredness and realising it would be useless to protest, instead allowed myself to be steered by Hammond back to the relief train to lie across a cushioned seat in Brunel's private carriage.

I stayed in bed for twenty-four hours, worn down and restlessly dreaming of bodies flung into the air. When I awoke, my mother fed me chicken broth and handed me a note from Hammond.

'My dear Bennett,

Forgive the brevity of my update but I am still working hard to make secure the embankment. All is well. There were different views at the inquest as to whether the slip should have been foreseen or not. Brunel argued strongly that it couldn't but local witnesses claimed they had seen several slides in the area over previous days. The company needs to pay £1000 in compensation to the victims and for the costs of recovering the engine and carriages, but no further action. Brunel returning to London later today. I trust that you are recovering well.

With best wishes,
Hammond'

Despite feeling that the company was more to blame than had been judged, I breathed a sigh of relief. I had convinced myself that Brunel would be tried for manslaughter.

It was with a heavy heart that I returned to work. Less than a week later, Parliament ruled that open third-class carriages should be outlawed. Why couldn't Brunel have taken the initiative, I thought, instead of being dragged to the altar like an unwilling bride?

I didn't want anything more to do with the construction of railways and asked Brunel if I might instead concentrate on helping push forward work on the SS *Great Britain*. He looked at me askance, but brusquely nodded and grunted his agreement. Of course, the train was by far the quickest way to get to Bristol, and for many months afterwards I looked anxiously ahead as we steamed along, anticipating an accident around every bend.

Chapter 17

1843

P reparations for the launch ceremony for the SS *Great Britain* were disrupted by the 'coin incident', as it came to be known. Brunel had run upstairs to be with his children. He didn't see them as much as he would like, but his face lit up when he did. Isambard junior was now six and the new arrival, Marc, one. Peals of laughter echoed down the stairs as his attempt at a magic trick went wrong. He swallowed the coin that was meant to be plucked from his mouth after he had pretended to push it into his ear.

Two days later he consulted Sir Benjamin Brodie, the eminent surgeon, after his endless coughing made him realise that the coin had deposited itself in his lungs. Sir Benjamin attempted to use forceps to retrieve it, but Brunel suffered such a fit that he had to desist. Brunel's father then suggested, and designed, a rig to turn Brunel upside down and retrieve the coin that way. The first attempt ended in yet more violent coughing, but the second, utilising a tracheotomy to help him breathe, saw the coin tinkle to the floor. When the coin hit the back of his teeth, Brunel said it was the most exquisite sound he had ever heard in his whole life!

While he was convalescing, it was left to me to oversee the arrangements for the naming ceremony and the launch. Prince Albert had agreed to come and a special royal carriage had been designed, its interior lavish with hand-painted ceilings, velvet drapes at the windows, and plush armchairs instead of the usual thinly upholstered benches. Third-class passengers might not receive this kind of luxury, I thought, but at least they now had a roof over their heads and proper compartments to protect them.

Brunel – now recovered – and I waited as the train stood ready, steam pressure up but held tightly by its brakes, like a dog straining at the leash. My anxiety at travelling by train had started to ease and I inhaled the clean sharp tang of burning coal wafted across the platform by clouds of steam.

I watched a young couple rushing to catch a train on the platform alongside ours, the girl hanging onto her partner's arm. The way she threw her head back and laughed as they got on board, the door slamming shut as the train pulled out, reminded me painfully of Hortense. Two years ago, Hortense had been called back to France when her father had become seriously unwell. I felt as if a part of me had gone with her, my life somehow less complete. You don't realise that you aren't whole until you find someone that you can share anything with, knowing that they will support you, respond in a way which makes you think differently, make more of who you are. Once you have, even if you rarely see them, their spirit lives on within you. Something will happen – like the girl running to catch the train – that brings them back into sharp focus. Or you think to yourself, 'What would she have said? How would she have dealt with this?'

But slowly it fades; your memory of what they would say, the things that you yearned to share with them. It withers softly away. Hortense had written a little at first but then less and less.

Eventually I stopped too, feeling that the relationship had become unbalanced. It was over a year since I had last heard from her.

Prince Albert finally arrived surrounded by his entourage, stirring me from my sad reflections. He was tall and thin, conservatively dressed in black with a plain dark waistcoat but sporting a luxurious moustache. We clambered quickly aboard and with a blast of the whistle we were off.

We reached Bristol to find an honour guard awaiting us incorporating the local police force, soldiers from the Gloucestershire Regiment, and the Prince's personal bodyguard. As the Prince alighted from the train, the band struck up a rousing tune. I kept to the edge of proceedings. I felt like an imposter, as if I had been dropped into the corner of one of the ceremonial paintings I had seen hung at the institute.

Long tables had been set out under the immense hammer-beamed roof of Brunel's new station. I stood at the end of the room, watching a sumptuous breakfast being served to the local gentry and what I suppose you would call 'people of influence'. The ladies' dresses and the colourful uniforms of the gentlemen made it look as if flags and bunting had been laid out along the tables instead of adorning the walls and ceilings of the magnificent wooden building.

Horse-drawn carts resplendent in newly painted GWR livery made their way along a route lined with boys and girls from the City and Redmaids' schools, the streets garlanded with flowers and ivy. Thousands of people had turned out to see the Prince go by. Patterson had already launched the ship to avoid any last minute embarrassment, and she was lying alongside the quay waiting for the Prince to christen her.

They say that a failure to break the bottle on a ship's bows is a sign of trouble to come, and when the Prince's first attempt bounded unbroken off the ironwork, I wondered what it might portend, little knowing that eighteen months later the ship would not yet be plying the world's oceans. He swung the bottle much harder the second time and the SS *Great Britain* was duly christened. After a quick tour of the ship, the Prince left for London.

She was so much larger than any other ship yet built that the lock gates at the exit to the docks needed to be widened to allow her to leave. Unfortunately, the harbour authorities had failed to carry out the modifications they had promised and so she sat alongside the quay for months after her official launch, looking forlorn and unloved, like a debutante ready to dance but with no suitable partners in sight.

Brunel found it hard to contain his growing frustration. He had been far more involved in the design and construction than her predecessor, the *Great Western*, and was very keen to see how she performed. He decided to take matters into his own hands. Now here we were at the dock entrance eighteen months after Prince Albert had christened her, desperately trying to get the ship out before we missed yet another tide.

An army of workmen had spent the previous day removing the coping stones from around the lock. Brunel drove them on, although he was savvy enough to make sure that there was a steady supply of beer available to keep their spirits up. As night fell, there was much left to do. Brunel ordered the setting-up of lanterns along the line of the docks so that the men could still see well enough to work. It was back-breaking. Each stone weighed several tons and they could only be shifted one at a time. If one or more dropped into the lock, all our efforts would have been in vain.

The lantern flame flickered in the wind, the night so dark that its light served only to cast quivering shadows across the open page of my notebook. I stood, feet frozen beyond the warm reach of my thick travelling coat, watching the silhouetted figures bent over, hard at work along the dockside in front of me. If the work wasn't completed in time, we would miss the spring tide.

I stamped my feet as the cold seeped in. Time was marching on. I could make out the first glimmers of dawn as the sky began to lighten over the hills beyond Bristol. The dark grey flow of the rising tide was eddying around the wooden posts at the mouth of the dock and creeping up the gates. It wouldn't be long before the day was with us and the tide at its highest. Brunel was calling out to the men to redouble their efforts as he too saw we had only a few hours left.

Late morning and the top of the tide was with us. The water in the river was still, quiet in those few minutes before the ebb began and the waters flowed fast back out to sea. The steam tug *Samson* under Claxton's command slowly pulled the great hull forward. A crowd of several hundred had gathered; a few of the directors and employees of the company were watching, quietly anxious, while others with less at stake swigged beer and yelled encouragement.

The exhausted navvies, exhorted to one final effort, hauled on ropes to guide the great ship into the middle of the lock. Wooden poles were jammed into the narrow gap between ship and wall to protect the iron sides from the raw, exposed stone.

There was a cry. The ship had been blown towards the far side of the dock and a workman had lost his footing and fallen into the water. Brunel and I rushed to the edge to see him desperately grabbing at the side of the ship. I realised he probably couldn't swim. Even worse, the ship could float back towards us at any moment, crushing him against the dockside.

'Drop your poles into the gap!' Brunel ordered the workmen standing helplessly beside us, unsure how they could help their friend. 'As many as you can. Quickly. Before she drifts back this way.'

'But, sir, if we fill the dock with wood, we will miss the tide,' I said without thinking.

'We've got to try and help him,' replied Brunel. 'Quickly, quickly!' he called out. 'Drop them down either side of him. Watch out, don't hit him. That's it. More. Quick as you can.'

The men rolled lengths of timber into the water as fast as they could. Brunel looked down at the man, now desperately holding onto the end of one of the logs.

'Who knows his name?'

'Jeremy Long, sir,' gasped one of the workmen as he and a colleague tipped a large lump of timber over the side to fall with a mighty splash.

Brunel grabbed a coil of rope and threw the end over the side, putting a turn around a nearby bollard.

'Jeremy, catch the rope!' he called out. 'Quickly man, we don't have much time.'

The timbers were creaking and groaning as the ship pressed against them. The gap was narrowing fast.

'Grab this, you men. Pull up as soon as I say.' He peered over the side to check that Jeremy had a firm grip on the rope, then yelled, 'Pull away!'

Jeremy came flying up and landed dripping on the paving slabs beside us, like a fish whipped up out of the water on the end of a rod.

There was the sound of logs splintering and breaking, as the ship swung hard back in our direction.

'Thank you, sir. Thank you,' he gasped.

'Couldn't leave you down there, could we?' replied Brunel kindly, before turning back to call for a final effort to get the ship out before it was too late.

The navvies hauled on the ropes, the crowd cheered, and then suddenly she was on her way. She slipped silently past me, the tug *Samson* pulling her through the dock. All I could see was a slow-moving black wall, her sides towering above me turning daylight back to dusk. But within minutes she was like a toy boat in the distance, dwarfed by the gorge, as the *Samson* towed her down the river towards the sea and a safe anchorage off Portishead.

I stood watching her, embarrassed that I had been worrying about the ship while Brunel was trying to save Jeremy. I wondered what had made Brunel react the way he had this time, when he so often seemed not to care. He had shown little or no interest in looking after an injured worker like Joseph, or redesigning dangerous third-class carriages. I suppose for better or worse, he was a man of action. If something helped him meet his objective, then he would seize it with both hands, whether that was helping my mother, saving someone from drowning or getting the railway line reopened after a landslip.

After the ship had disappeared around the bend, I turned and walked back towards Patterson's yard. Bristol wouldn't be seeing a ship the size of the SS *Great Britain* again, I reflected. Certainly not one built by Brunel. The docks just weren't large enough to cope with the size of ships that were now being built. Even after a ship had left the city, it was miles down the narrow twisting gorge to the sea. The city's days as a major port were surely over. Liverpool offered deep water and a straightforward passage into its harbour. Could it be that nature would ultimately hand victory to the Liverpudlians?

Chapter 18

1847

O ver the next two years, the SS *Great Britain* successfully plied back and forth across the Atlantic, proving the worth of a propeller-driven ship. But then we received word that she had been blown ashore in Dundrum Bay near Belfast. Brunel was devastated, reliving all the effort that had gone into her launch.

It was still unclear why the ship had run aground so far off course. Was it, as Captain James Hosken had said, a problem with the compass being affected by the iron of the ship? If so, how had he been able to successfully cross the ocean so many times? Or perhaps an error on the charts? Unlikely, given how busy these shipping lanes were. Or perhaps most probably, simply a navigational failure by the captain in poor weather.

Whatever the cause, Brunel was adamant that she must be saved, and sent me out to oversee the building of a palisade to protect her from the winter storms. Crossing the Irish Sea was a nightmare. The ship pitched and corkscrewed her way through the steep short waves, the tops of the crests cut off, as if by a giant machete. If I had not felt so ill, I might have enjoyed watching a practical demonstration of the shortcomings of paddle wheels as the violent rolling caused them to creak and groan, throwing up great plumes of spray as they struggled for purchase against a churning sea.

It had been a shock, utterly different to my Atlantic crossing. Back then, like an undulating pasture, the waves had been spread out across the ocean, making the ship rise and fall as if in a well-sprung carriage. Crossing the Irish Sea was like riding in an overladen donkey cart as it banged and crashed its way through the ruts of an ancient byway.

It was now six months after she had been stranded and I was returning with Claxton to oversee the attempt to refloat her now the weather was benign. I stared out of the porthole; the sea was grey and glassy smooth and the ship barely moved beneath me. All I could hear was the quiet thrum of the engines as she steadily ploughed her way across. What a contrast with my last crossing.

We chugged up the estuary, the paddle wheels fighting the river current, and came alongside at Belfast docks. Mr Bremner was waiting for us, just as he had been six months ago. He owned a local shipyard and had experience of refloating many ships run aground along this treacherous coast.

It took us the rest of the day to reach Dundrum. Although I was anxious to see how the ship had fared after the long winter, I couldn't help but admire the green rolling hills as our horses picked their way along the rutted road. It was good to get away from the London smog and breathe fresh sea air.

We arrived in the early evening, crossing the low dunes to reach the beach. The sand was wet, grey against an overcast sky. Small ripples scudded across the wide pools of water scattered across the flat, unforgiving landscape. The vast dark shape of the wrecked ship stood out against the skyline, its masts poking up towards the clouds, like the old prison hulks moored in the Thames estuary.

We circled the ship once before dark. The tree trunks remained firmly lashed in place on her seaward side. We had been lucky the weather had held just long enough for us to build the protective barrier; when the tide was out, we had dug a trench around the base of the ship, hauling tree trunks up against the side of the hull with block and tackle, and lashing them together with ropes passed through the portholes in the ship's side. Each day the trench, filled with sand by the incoming tide, had to be dug out once more and new trees added until we had finished the job. It took five days of back-breaking work and even then I had wondered if it would do any good.

'How has she weathered the winter?' I asked.

'The hull is more or less intact,' said Bremner, 'but she's badly damaged below the waterline and her engines have been totally destroyed by the sand and salt.'

I felt sick. Even though I dreaded the answer I felt I had to ask: 'What do you think the chances are of getting her off?'

'There's a very high tide due in two weeks' time, at the next full moon.'

I looked up to see a pale moon floating above the horizon. It was still indistinct, the sky not yet dark enough for it to shine, but I could make out that it was almost completely round, with just a thin edge lopped off, like the first slice taken from a round of cheese.

'If the weather is good, that will give us the best chance of refloating the ship,' he continued, 'but it's not going to be easy. She's sitting on a rocky outcrop that has punctured her midships. We will need to lift her clear, otherwise she will be ripped open from stem to stern like a tin can.'

I watched labourers crawling over the hull, fixing in place chains and getting ready for the mighty lift. Pits were dug and giant levers, fashioned from pine trees a foot and a half thick, inserted under the hull. The ship's lifeboats were placed on the far end of the levers and filled with sand. I understood the principles of what we were trying to do – the lifeboats were intended to act as counter-ballast, exerting pressure alongside the incoming tide to lift the ship up – but so much could go wrong. The levers could penetrate or bend the hull, the lifeboats could capsize or be dislodged. Or perhaps the immense force would still not be enough.

Claxton strode up, looking cross.

'This lot, they are just like the Africans.'

'What do you mean?' I asked, knowing that I would probably regret asking.

'Look at them leaning against the lifeboats, having a smoke. You've got to work them hard otherwise they'll take to drink and idleness, just like the blacks.'

Claxton had been captain of a slave trader in his seafaring days, and it didn't look like his views had changed much.

'Well,' I replied, 'there isn't much to do until the tide comes in, is there? I'm not sure they are doing much harm.'

'I suppose not.' Claxton took out his pipe, knocked it against the heel of his boot, then pointed at the men with it. 'Look at them though, standing around like they own the world. Things are changing too fast if you ask me, mostly for the worse. The riots last year up in the Potteries, the clamour for everyone to be able to vote, where will it all end?'

'I don't think we can have it both ways,' I replied, keeping my voice low. 'The scientific progress we are helping bring about is allowing people to travel, to learn, to communicate. Expectations are bound to change.'

He was right, the world was changing fast. Almost two million had signed the People's Charter, arguing for Parliament to extend the vote to all. The riots Claxton had mentioned had led to 1,500 being brought to trial for sedition when arguably all they had been doing was asking for fair wages and conditions. It all pointed to the perspectives and aspirations of the common man – people like me, in other words – changing as fast as the new methods of transport and communication.

Claxton shook his head.

'I don't agree with you at all. I was involved with Brunel in quelling those riots in Bristol back in '31 because I didn't believe it was right that every man should have the vote, and I still feel that way.'

He continued, now jabbing his pipe at me to reinforce his argument.

'I remember very well Brunel saying where will we all end up if everyone has the right to determine our future path as a country? It will be the rule of the mob. Short-term populist policies will be the order of the day with no reasoned debate over the long-term interests of the country. Politicians will vote based on what they think their electors want, rather than what they need.'

I felt myself getting steadily more agitated at what I saw to be Claxton's – or rather Brunel's – hypocrisy. He had managed to get himself appointed as chief engineer for the GWR through a combination of hard work and chutzpah – weeks spent surveying the route on horseback, a refusal to be considered inferior to the much more established surveyor, Harrison. He was happy to upset the status quo when it suited him and to aspire to a higher position in society, yet he and people like Claxton would deny others the same opportunity.

I knew it would be better to leave it be, but couldn't stop myself.

'I met a family on the train to London a few weeks ago, all dressed up in what was clearly their Sunday best. They had three young children, just like you.'

'What's your point exactly?' said Claxton, looking at me impatiently.

'They had a whole tour planned. Their father took me through it all: Westminster Abbey, the burnt-out Houses of Parliament, London Bridge, the Burlington Arcade, Buckingham Palace, the Royal Parks… They had even booked a show at a theatre for Saturday evening.'

'I am afraid that I still don't see what your point is,' said Claxton, looking bored.

'My point is that most of these people are little different from you and me. They just want to better themselves. What's so wrong with that?'

Claxton didn't have a chance to reply before a wavelet washed across his boots. He jumped back and swore, then said as he shook his wet foot, 'Looks like we are getting close.'

We watched anxiously as the tide crept up the sides of the ship. Feeling helpless, I stood silently beside him, willing the ship to lift. The minutes ticked by. One of the lifeboats groaned and shifted and the men rushed to stabilise it. A log moved, swinging another lifeboat around, men hanging on like cowboys at a rodeo. A cry went up. The ship was moving. She was lifting! Claxton and I grinned at each other, our argument forgotten.

Bremner was yelling instructions to his men, working hard to get the ship stabilised.

'More sand in the boats! Haul on the ropes! Push the wedges in!'

He waded around the base of the ship, water up past his waist, peering around, trying to understand why she wouldn't float free. Half an hour passed. Then an hour. My sense of elation drained slowly away as the tide receded. The ship had lifted around fifteen inches but then sank back. Bremner looked shattered, his men dispirited.

We trudged back to our lodgings – a cottage on the edge of the harbour – took an early supper and went to bed. I spent a restless night wondering how it would be possible for us to move forward.

Early the next morning Claxton and I were sitting opposite each other eating breakfast, with little to say to one another and not much appetite, when Bremner burst into the room.

'The wooden wedges were crushed,' he announced. 'They weren't strong enough to hold her off the rocks. We will try again tonight.'

Bremner's men spent all day hacking and chopping at the trunks of huge oak trees. Time was slipping by and he exhorted them to work harder still.

'Come on, men! We need to finish as many as we can. We've only got a few hours left to get them in place.'

I grabbed an axe and joined in, sweat pouring from me as I desperately worked at the unfamiliar task. The tide was up now, lapping around the bottom of the ship. Once again the weight of the lifeboats did their magic and the ship lifted. However, when the tide receded this time, she sat proudly above the rocks, resting on our newly fashioned supports. She looked as if she were back in the yard where she had been built, ready to be sent down the slipway and into the water.

Just offshore waited HMS *Birkenhead*. Brunel had managed to persuade the Admiralty that helping pull a stricken ship off a beach was a worthwhile training exercise. As I watched the tide come in for what I hoped would be the last time, boats were used to run warps out to the *Birkenhead* sitting half a mile out to sea.

Bremner had placed small boats along either side of the *Great Britain* to act as floats, attached by chains running under the hull. As the tide came in, the weight of the great ship was taken by the boats. They sank so low in the water that I feared that they would be overwhelmed by the rising water.

We were ready. As the tide hit its highest point, the *Birkenhead* built up a full head of steam and her paddle wheels strained and threshed as she attempted to pull the SS *Great Britain* out to sea. Slowly, very slowly, the ship eased along the wedges under her hull. The stern was now fully in the water, and to a great cheer from the watching crowd it started to rise, showing she was finally free of the clutches of the land. Men placed in the boats stretched along either side of the hull bailed furiously, the success of the launch giving them new impetus.

A few more feet and she was clear. The warps were quickly adjusted so that the *Birkenhead* could pull her from the bow, and soon she was off, steaming round to Belfast so that the *Great Britain* could be grounded on a mudbank for further repairs before the long tow to Liverpool for a full refit.

I found myself smiling as I trudged up the beach to begin the long trip home. What a ship! I thought. She should have been named *Lazarus* or *Phoenix*. Nothing could destroy her.

I got back to the office to find Brunel immersed in drawing up bridge designs for the extension of the GWR railway down into Cornwall.

'Good work, Bennett. Excellent. So glad my barrier worked. The thing is, the company can't afford to carry out the refit so she will have to be sold. Never mind, though. Onwards and upwards!'

He bent his head back down to his bridge drawings.

'This is such a nightmare, Bennett. They have given me so little budget that I am going to have to build these out of wood.'

I couldn't quite believe my ears. All those weeks spent in Ireland and Brunel was almost as dismissive of my efforts as when I had returned from crossing the Atlantic on the SS *Great Western* all those years ago. I thought the rescue of the SS *Great Britain* was something that really mattered to him. Perhaps it did, but he had an odd way of showing it.

Chapter 19

1848

It was a year later when Mary Brunel stormed in with the morning paper and, ignoring me, slammed it down in front of Brunel saying, 'The press are making fools out of us. It's got to stop. We will be the laughing stock of London society.'

Brunel sought to calm her down. He gestured for me to leave the room but Mary stopped him.

'Why shouldn't he stay? You and he discuss everything so he has had as much a part in this as you have.'

Although I felt momentary pleasure at being lumped together with Brunel in this way, it was a somewhat inaccurate description of our relationship. I flattered myself that after all these years I could influence how he went about presenting his proposals or dealing with issues, but the final say was always his. And in any case he would never ask my opinion about matters of engineering design, or if he did, it would be more to air the arguments than to seriously consider my views. It was only his father, and one or two others, that he truly respected.

I felt the best thing to do was to bury myself in the papers on my desk as Mary read out the headline: 'Atmospheric railway proves to be an expensive shambles.'

I had seen the paper earlier in the day, and alongside the article a cartoon, the caricature unmistakably Brunel, who was puffing a cigar while attempting with his other hand to chase rats away from the rails.

At the time, it had appeared a sensible, if bold, decision. On the south Devon extension of the GWR beyond Exeter, Brunel had decided to use a new approach utilising atmospheric pressure. A piston attached to the bottom of the train was drawn through a fifteen-inch cast-iron tube running alongside the rails. Large steam engines positioned at intervals along the line created the vacuum pressure to suck the trains along.

The trains could be much lighter. Brunel had visited a railway utilising the same principle in Croydon and had realised how the approach might cope with the hillier landscape beyond Exeter better than conventional locomotives. Unfortunately, in practical use we had suffered all sorts of problems: poor signalling meant the steam pressure wasn't up at the right time, or more coal was burnt than needed; the seals had frozen in the winter and dried out in the summer, causing the leather to crack and rip, hence losing vacuum pressure. A myth had spread that rats had eaten the leather, hence the cartoon that was so exercising Mary.

'What are you going to do about this?' she asked, slapping the paper down on the table.

'Well, we have been applying a new type of grease to the leather—' started Brunel.

'No, you fool. I mean what are you going to do about this article?'

Although his position in society was something Brunel cared about more than he would admit and perhaps had led in a great part to the mutual attraction, for Mary it seemed it was all that mattered. I could see she was only interested in an end to the public embarrassment.

Foolishly, I stepped in. I had yet to learn never to come between a husband and wife circling each other ready for battle, like deer about to clash antlers.

'It's usually better not to make a comment. It avoids adding fuel to the flames. Let it get overtaken by the next bits of news they turn to.'

Since our battles with Lardner, I had determined that the press were best avoided.

'What?' she cried. 'Firstly, I didn't ask your opinion, Bennett, and secondly, that's ridiculous. "Leave it" indeed!'

She strode up and down the room. I couldn't stop myself thinking that her frown and pinched face were at odds with her matronly figure and plump décolletage, gained from spending too long at the richly laid tables of her new friends.

'Now, now,' said Brunel, rather feebly.

'Don't "now, now" me. I am not one of your minions who do what they are told or face the consequences. This makes us a laughing stock. What are you going to do?'

There was a hesitant knock on the door. No doubt the servants had heard the fracas and would have rather stayed away, but Mrs Brunel had a visitor. She swept out, glaring at both of us.

'You got us into this mess. I suggest you work out how to get us out.'

Brunel took in a deep breath, then let it out slowly.

'This will take some careful thought. As you know, generally I believe in just pushing on harder in the face of difficulties, but perhaps in this instance I have been misguided and we should cut our losses.'

Within a week, he had made up his mind. He went to the GWR board and recommended that the system be abandoned. He admitted that there had been problems he hadn't foreseen, that locomotives were getting ever more powerful and that it wouldn't be long before they could cope easily with the inclines on the coastal line.

The press did indeed have a field day, ably fuelled by our old enemies up north, but I was relieved to be proved correct when the noise quickly died down as other news took over.

Brunel did what I expected, which was to bury himself in his work and wait for the storm to blow over. It helped that someone as respected as Stephenson publicly stood by him. Despite their professional rivalry and differences of view over the broad gauge, they had become firm friends. Stephenson was struggling with the building of a railway bridge across the wide and fast-flowing Menai Straits and the two worked closely together on the tricky matter of floating out the bridge sections in the face of the strong tides.

Brunel's mood was further improved when he heard that Hudson had been caught defrauding his investors, paying out capital as dividends.

'Couldn't have happened to a nicer fellow,' he chuckled.

Eighteen months later, in December 1849, we were in Chepstow working on another difficult bridge – spanning the Wye to carry the South Wales Railway from Gloucester to Swansea – when news came that Brunel's father had died.

I was working my way through the latest costings, seated at a bare wooden trestle table inside one of the large tents we had pitched alongside the river, when a messenger arrived with a telegram. I opened it and slumped back down into the canvas chair, knowing what a shock it was going to be to my employer.

Marc Brunel was eighty. He had suffered a stroke four years before, that had paralysed his right side but he had taught himself to write with his left hand and carried on as best as he could. I had seen him briefly ten days ago and although he had been frail he had looked well enough, out in the park in his Bath wheelchair, wrapped up tight in a large blanket to protect him from the winter chill.

I crossed over to Brunel's Briska drawn up beside the footings for the bridge foundations. I didn't know how to break the news, so I silently handed over the telegram.

He took a deep breath, rested his chin on the palm of his hand and stared at the piece of paper. Eventually, he looked up at me.

'I am so sorry, sir. I know you and your father were very close,' I stammered.

'Thank you, Bennett. I will miss him.'

I tried to think of some words of comfort, conscious of how bereft Brunel looked.

'I recall well, sir, your visit to Watcombe with all of your family. Your father looked very happy, he was so much enjoying the company of his grandchildren.'

'And they his,' he said, smiling at the memory. 'I remember him showing them the little black insects inside a blue convolvulus, telling them all about how the insects spent their whole lives inhabiting their blooms. It reminded me of how he used to show me all manner of things when I was young, sparking my interest in the world around me.'

Brunel had bought fifty-five acres on the coast just north of Torquay and had spent the last two years meticulously designing a country house and landscaped gardens. Just after he bought it, the entire Brunel family had taken a trip down there to view the new purchase. I had arrived from Dawlish and ridden slowly up the drive, marvelling at the views over the sea sparkling in the distance. We were in the midst of the problems with the atmospheric railway and I was bringing the latest test results. They weren't good.

I have to admit I was walking my horse very slowly. I wasn't looking forward to Brunel's state of mind when he saw the figures. It was quiet, just the warbles and tweets of birds in the trees, when suddenly I heard the tinkling laughter of young children running around in the undergrowth. They burst out in front of me: Isambard junior – about ten then I suppose – and Henry who must have been five. Baby Florence was just a few weeks old.

They shot off into the bushes and when I arrived at the clearing where the family were gathered, I could see the children beside Mr Brunel's wheelchair buried deep in the flowerbed. They were peering through a large magnifying glass into the centre of the blue convolvulus as Mr Brunel talked animatedly. It was a lovely family scene and the memory brought a lump to my throat. He had lived beyond his three score and ten, but it still felt strange that he was gone.

I envied Brunel's close working relationship with his father. I remember the old man scarcely able to contain his beaming smile at the launch of the SS *Great Britain*. He was always prepared to help his son, working away in the background and taking no credit for his contribution.

To the outside world, Brunel continued as normal, busy as ever. He had told me that he thought Hudson's arrest for fraud would end the railway mania amongst investors, and so it proved. As a result, he was anxious to complete as much of the railway network as he could before the money ran out.

Every now and then though when we were alone in the office, he would stare vacantly at some complex problem he was working away at, and mutter, 'what would Father have suggested, I wonder?'

Chapter 20

1851

The invitation arrived with the morning mail. Mary Brunel picked it up off the post tray, examined it briefly and handed it to me.

'So sorry, didn't realise it was for you. I didn't know you knew Mrs Guppy so well.'

She was looking at me askance. I assumed she was wondering what had led to my invitation. It was twelve years since they had married and she had moved in, and she continued to treat me as the hired help. Our relationship hadn't really recovered after the atmospheric railway episode and it suited us both to keep our distance.

The invitation was to a private viewing at the Great Exhibition, which was due to open shortly in Hyde Park.

Even though I was nervous about attending such a grand occasion, I decided I would go. I arrived early and lingered outside by one of the large oaks that marched off, line abreast, into the distance, like a row of soldiers guarding the exhibition. How fitting, I thought, that at the end of the line stood Apsley House, a gift from a grateful nation to the Duke of Wellington, commander of our troops at the Battle of Waterloo.

I fingered my new cravat as I waited, watching the steady stream of immaculately dressed gentlefolk arrive, descending elegantly from gleaming carriages or strolling in on foot, seemingly without a care in the world. I looked out towards the Serpentine, and despite my nervousness thought that heaven must feel a little like this, as a soft breeze ruffled the trees and the sunlight sparkled and danced, reflecting the lake in the hundreds of panes of glass facing me.

I rounded the end of the building to find the main entrance and could see why it had earned the sobriquet 'the Crystal Palace', a term first used by a writer for *Punch* magazine. It might be made of glass, but elements of its design and its scale really did echo the recently remodelled Buckingham Palace a short distance down the road. As I approached, I spied the cast-iron water towers high up on stilts at the far end that represented Brunel's small contribution to the edifice.

I had thought the new glasshouse at Kew botanical gardens an extraordinary engineering marvel, but this was so much larger and more imposing. The airiness and grace put me more in mind of the delicate tracery of a cathedral window than the grand facade of a palace.

I made my way into the entrance hall. A twenty-four ton lump of coal more than twice my height faced me, its black sooty bulk causing visitors to stop and stare. The board alongside explained that it was this coal, fuelling steam-powered machines, that enabled the manufacture of the range of fabrics, domestic items and *objets d'art* displayed within.

Prince Albert had agreed to sponsor the exhibition and had also provided its theme: tracing the production of goods from the mining of raw materials through their conversion into useful components to their final form as manufactured objects. He was keen to show how mankind's ingenuity and technological progress were changing the world for the better. However, the aim of many of the exhibitors and their financial backers was to display their wares and increase sales. They wanted a marketplace where they would be able to promote their goods to new customers.

The debate had raged over many months. The organising committee had been torn. On the one hand they agreed that the exhibition should be primarily educational, but they were also responsible for making it a financial success. They knew from other exhibitions that manufacturers would not participate if they could see no commercial benefit in attending. Eventually, clear rules had been set down. No prices were to be displayed and nothing could be sold, except souvenirs. Exhibitors could treat the event as an opportunity to promote themselves, but not to sell their goods and services. To my surprise, Brunel, who usually hated compromises, thought it an elegant solution.

Lost amongst the vast array of exhibits around me, I asked a steward where I might find Mrs Guppy's party. I was directed further into the building. The hall reached way up above me and was topped with a rounded arch made from laminated wood. The whole area was filled with light and a large fountain made from pink glass was set up in the centre, like the gateway to some magical kingdom. Just before the fountain stood one of the great trees of Hyde Park, left intact as the building was erected around it. Leading off the main hall were long corridors extending to the length of the enormous building. Each corridor was overlooked by galleries hosting smaller exhibits.

I can't say I had visited it often, unlike my pious mother, but the layout of the building reminded me of St Paul's Cathedral. However, the sense of airiness could not be more different from that dark, shadowy building. While the cathedral was built to honour the mystery of the Being that created mankind and the natural world we live in, this building was a testament to something else: the work of man in adapting and improving upon the natural world we had been gifted.

In an alcove near the back, behind a thick satin rope, were clustered Mrs Guppy's guests. Quiet murmurings and the occasional loud laugh drifted across from the group. I hesitated. I was very fond of Mrs Guppy, but Mary Brunel was right. What did I have in common with these people? They were the pick of society and I was just a clerk living above my father's shop. I could see Mrs Guppy at the edge of the gathering, surrounded by well-wishers. She was bent over, supporting herself on a carved wooden stick. She looked smaller than I remembered and painfully thin, her skin the colour of alabaster and her face engraved with a network of deep lines. She was getting old, but she looked as alert as ever, laughing brightly at some anecdote.

I walked quietly away and headed for the exit, feeling miserable about my loss of nerve, but what would I find to say to these people in their finery?

'Joseph, Joseph!'

I looked around, vaguely conscious that someone was calling my name.

It was Hortense! I hadn't seen her for almost ten years but still found myself grinning like a demented monkey as she introduced her friends, Agatha and Ella, who were working as maids in other houses along her street.

'You are back in England?' I exclaimed, still not quite able to believe that it was her. A few small lines showed at the edges of her eyes but she really didn't look any different; she was as beautiful as ever.

'I returned a few months ago. I meant to let you know, but...' she tailed off, shrugged her shoulders and looked embarrassed.

She turned to her companions.

'Would you mind if...?'

The two maids giggled and gave us both a knowing look, flooding my face red. They linked arms and headed off, leaving us together.

'It's so good to see you,' I said, not knowing how to put into words how pleased I was to have bumped into her.

'And you. I am so sorry I didn't write more often. My father was dying and it was hard to put down on paper how I was feeling.'

I reached out and took one of her hands in mine. It felt oddly familiar.

'That is such sad news,' I said rather lamely.

I suddenly realised how obsessed I had been with my own feelings when I had stopped writing, rather than Hortense's situation.

'I wanted to write and tell you I was coming back, but after all these years it was hard to find the right words.'

I took a deep breath. The only woman I had ever loved. Did any of it matter now we were here together?

We sauntered through the exhibits arm in arm. I was amazed by the variety of objects on display, from Persian rugs to Chinese vases, and from model sailboats to Grecian statues. On the ground floor was an immense steam hammer and one of Stephenson's locomotives. To ease the moment, I took on the role of lecturer. Hortense, to her credit, maintained an interested – if amused – expression.

Off to the side were displays from faraway lands, each with a centrepiece to bring that country to life: for India, a stuffed elephant; for the Americas, an Indian canoe. The Maltese exhibit featured tall urns and vases engraved with elaborate silverwork. The stand for the Caribbean isles was bursting with birds artfully arranged to show off their colourful plumage.

'I would love to visit these places one day,' Hortense said wistfully.

I found myself indulging in wild dreams of us visiting them together.

As we wandered, we overheard people excitedly pointing out to each other some new marvel.

'Look at this knife with seventy-five blades! Over here – there's a two-wheeled machine that you push with your feet!'

Around a corner I was astonished to find Bramah's lock set up on a large table, with a man hard at work trying to pick it. He was an American named Hobbs, and I learned later that he finally managed to do it after fifty-two hours of hard labour spread over fourteen days, winning the two hundred guinea prize. After seventy years, Maudslay's craftsmanship and Bramah's ingenuity had been cracked.

The biggest queue was to view the Kohinoor diamond, but Hortense wasn't interested.

'Better to sell it and spend the money on food for the poor,' she said, looking rather self-righteous, I thought fondly.

We had seen our fill and stopped at one of the refreshment stalls to buy tea and a little cake-stand of treats.

'So, how are things with you?' I asked after we had found ourselves a little round table at which to sit.

She told me that she was enjoying being back at the watchmakers.

'I like the household, and my mother and I were getting under each other's feet.'

'And how about you?' she asked.

'Oh, more of the same.'

Hortense poured us both tea and offered me some cake.

'I don't know why you stay with them.'

My mouth was full of ginger cake, so I had a moment or two to reflect. Why had I stayed with the Brunels? Inertia? Loyalty? The work itself was no longer as appealing as it had been. Brunel spent his days building branch lines connecting to the GWR and overseeing railway projects in far-flung lands. When he had spare time, he drew up endless designs for the gardens and house near

Torquay. I rarely travelled with him nowadays, there was so much administration to do. The offices were now much larger and the lease had been acquired for number nineteen next door, to create more space for all the staff.

'I was going to tell him I was worn out when I got back from Ireland after the SS *Great Britain* was refloated, but he was in the midst of trying to sort out the atmospheric system and I didn't feel I could leave and let him down.'

I was startled. I couldn't quite believe that the truth of what had been lurking in the back of my mind had flowed out so easily. I stared at her, almost uneasy at the knowledge that the connection between us seemed as strong as it had ever been. She was wearing a light fawn coat with a fur collar, a pretty pink scarf wrapped artfully around her neck, her dark hair spilling over the top. Her eyes were dark brown but seemed to glow as she smiled gently at me.

'But you have to think about yourself as well.'

'I did think about leaving to help run the shop, but I've got used to being at the centre of these large projects. I couldn't see myself taking over from my father, sitting behind the counter for the next ten or twenty years.'

'So, which goes on first, the jam or the cream?'

'Sorry? Oh, I see. Always the jam. An ancient Devon tradition.' She took a bite and smiled.

'There are some things the English can cook.'

I wanted to ask whether there was anyone in her life, or even if there was a remote chance that we could have a future together, but didn't have a clue how I might raise the question. I went red again just thinking about it, so instead I asked her whether she had heard from Martha.

'Not for a long time. She got someone from the village to write when her husband died two or three years ago. He was never the same after his injuries.'

She shook her head sadly. After a pause, she brightened.

'But her children are grown up now, and she said they are doing well, one an apprentice to a builder and the other with a young child of her own.'

'What about you, are you happy?' I asked.

She cocked her head to one side, looking directly at me until I blinked, unable to hold her gaze.

'Why do you ask?'

She reached across and took my hand, forcing me to look back at her. I realised that 'I just wondered' would have sounded pathetic.

'Because I care,' I found myself saying.

She looked me in the eye and I felt my insides dissolving.

'I care too,' she said simply.

It might be a cliché, but the world did stop. I stared at her, finally realising that my feelings were reciprocated as she continued to hold my gaze. I stumbled to my feet before dropping to one knee.

'Would you marry me?' I blurted out.

She reached down and squeezed my hand. She smiled at me lovingly and for a moment I thought it was all going to be alright. Out of the corner of my eye, I could see people at the tables around us looking over and grinning. Then I saw the look in her eyes and felt I was about to be sick as she leant forward.

'I would love to,' she whispered, 'but you told me many years ago that you wouldn't be able to continue working with Brunel if you got married. In any event, I am not sure that I could share my husband with another mistress.'

My confusion must have been apparent, because she quickly added, 'His work, or in your case, his employer.'

'Are you really saying you wouldn't marry me if I stayed with Brunel?'

'No,' she replied, shaking her head sadly. 'I am saying I wouldn't want you to make that sacrifice. You are devoted to him and his work and I wouldn't want to get in the way of that. It would hardly be the basis for a successful marriage, forcing you to leave.'

She stood, the sound of her chair scraping back on the tiled floor hitting me like the screech of one of Maudslay's machines catching a strand of metal. I hauled myself to my feet too, self-consciously wiping the dust from my knees.

'It has been so good to see you again, Joseph. I wish you well.'

I am not sure how to describe the kiss she gave me. I suppose you could call it a peck on the cheek, but there must be a better description for the slow sad touch of her lips as she turned and left.

I wanted nothing more than to sink back into my chair unobserved. It felt though as if the eyes of all those in the café were still upon me, so instead I headed unseeingly towards the exit. I felt utterly bereft.

I arrived at work the next day feeling tired, my eyes sore. I had hardly slept.

Brunel was at his desk, head down, hard at work. I sat at mine, unable to concentrate through a fog of misery and unanswered questions spinning around in my head. Did Hortense really feel about me as I did about her? I was desperate to find a way to be with her, but she had said that she didn't see us being together even if I left Brunel's employ. Would she really not marry me if I decided to leave? Could I really bring myself to do so? I knew I was stuck in a rut. Maybe this was the catalyst for change.

When the maid brought in the morning coffee, I cleared my throat.

'Mr Brunel, sir. I have a dilemma.'

'Is this anything to do with your visit to the Great Exhibition yesterday?' he asked. 'Rumour has it that you ended up rather disappointed.'

I blushed deeply. Even Brunel had heard about my very public marriage proposal.

'You may not know, sir, but I have carried a torch for Hortense for many years. I mean, I have always been very fond of her. You may recall she used to work here.'

'I do, I do,' he chuckled. He pointed at the fire. 'I well remember the coal scuttle.'

'As I think you may have heard, I asked her to marry me but she refused. She thinks I am wedded to my work.'

'I see. Well, I suppose we all are. You know, Bennett, they say that people often marry as a refuge from loneliness.'

He paused, staring thoughtfully at me.

'Isn't it enough to be part of my extended family? That's how we think of you.'

I shifted uncomfortably under his gaze.

'Marrying Hortense would mean more than that to me, sir. It has just taken me rather a long time to realise it.'

'I see. So what's your dilemma?'

'She has refused to accept my offer but I wondered if there was any way I might persuade her. We talked about marriage when I joined, but it's been many years now and you seem to be able to combine work and marriage. I was wondering if you might have any hints and tips as to how I might do the same.'

'It's been a sacrifice, Bennett, so I am not sure I am the right person to give you advice. In any event, and more to the point, I couldn't contemplate my right-hand man, always there when I need you, having sufficient time to make a success of a marriage.'

He took his time lighting a cigar and taking a sip of coffee before continuing.

'I suppose I am saying I think you need to choose.'

I hated the wheedling note that crept into my voice, like a child begging for a treat.

'But, sir, I have seen children make you a happy and doting father and would like to think that I, too, God willing, could perhaps enjoy the same.'

'I am sure you would, Bennett, but as I made perfectly clear when you first joined, I require a chief clerk who is completely devoted to my work, with no distractions. Look, why don't you take a couple of days to think about it. I would hate you to act in haste and come to regret it.'

I dashed a note off to Hortense asking if she could join me that evening at our old meeting place alongside the lake. The rest of the day passed in a blur.

I left work early, unable to do anything useful, and took the long route around the lake, thinking the fresh air would soothe my chattering thoughts. It was cool now, the trees beginning to change colour. I sat on one of the benches that looked out across the grass to the lake beyond. Some youngsters were playing in the leaves, throwing them up so they fluttered down, twisting and turning in the gentle evening breeze.

I saw Hortense approaching, silhouetted against the setting sun. I stumbled to my feet.

It was my turn to peck her gently on the cheek and to ask her if she would sit with me for a while.

'Hortense, it was a shock seeing you yesterday, and frankly even more of a shock to find that you reciprocated my feelings.'

She drew her shawl more tightly around her shoulders.

'How so?' she replied. 'Hasn't it always been obvious I cared for you?'

'I know it might sound silly now, but I always thought you cared for me as a friend rather than anything more.'

'Much more,' she whispered, 'but our roads diverged.' After a moment she sighed, 'Sometimes life is like that.'

I looked out over the water. Wavelets on the lake were shimmering, flickering beads of light forcing me to narrow my eyes against the glare; it helped to have them half-closed as I sought to find the right words.

'I've been in a bit of a state all day,' I confessed. 'You made it clear that I shouldn't leave Brunel because of you, and he has made it clear that staying wouldn't be an option.'

'What do you mean?'

'I told him about us – actually, he and everyone else about town seems to know. Such news travels fast. And as my mother always says, the tastiest gossip travels the fastest.'

I stopped and cleared my throat, realising I had strayed away from answering her question.

'Anyway, he made it clear that his original condition about not marrying while in his employ still holds.'

I couldn't stop a note of bitterness creeping into my voice as I said this. I was still shocked that he would treat me this way. Hortense didn't say anything for a moment, just tilted her head back and allowed the last of the sun to play across her face.

I looked at her, really looked at her, realising that I finally had the right to stare without worrying that she might take offence. She was beautiful. It wasn't just her impish smile and lovely rounded face framed by her thick dark hair, she radiated an inner beauty, a serenity that I now knew was connected to me, and which caused me to relax and enjoy inner calm, too.

I suddenly knew what I wanted, needed, to do.

I got down on one knee again.

'Hortense, will you marry me?' I asked for the second time in as many days.

She looked at me with surprise but smiled slightly.

'I thought we had already discussed this?'

'I know that I want to make a life with you, for us to have children together. It's time I moved on from Brunel. You've helped me reach that conclusion but I've realised that it's what I want, not anything you are forcing me into.'

'Are you sure?'

'I am not sure I have the right to ask when my fate and financial situation are so uncertain, but I am sure about Brunel, yes.'

She laughed delightedly and reached out and squeezed my hand.

'I want to be with you, Joseph. I can keep working while you, while you... what's the English expression... land on your feet? I am sure you can find another job, or perhaps join your father in the shop?'

I pulled her to her feet, looked deep into those dark brown eyes and kissed her. Why had I been in such a state of agitation all day? This felt so obviously right. We walked around the lake arm in arm, nodding to other couples out for an evening stroll. It felt perfect as we turned the corner to see the gas lights on the Mall being lit one by one, throwing out a warming glow like a string of lighthouses guiding us home. Perhaps Hortense was right, maybe it was time to get involved in my father's business.

Brunel merely nodded and returned to his work when I told him of my decision the next morning. I became increasingly excited by the thought of a new life away from him, but I had worked there a long time and resented the choice he had forced upon me. I found it hard to remain civil to him for the remaining few weeks we spent together, although my terse responses did not seem to affect him in the slightest.

It was with mixed feelings that I packed my things on my last day, in the same old battered satchel with which I had arrived seventeen years before. When it was time to leave, Brunel asked me to join him in the dining room. I crossed the hall, reminding myself that no good would come of being rude to my employer. I might need a reference one day, even though my intention was to settle in my father's shop with my new bride.

I pushed open the door to find all the staff assembled. Brunel smiled at me, then produced a small ribbon-wrapped box from behind his back and handed it over.

'I will miss you, Bennett. We have been through much together, and when I have felt under attack you have been like a rock, helping protect me from the crashing waves and siren calls of my opponents. This is a small token of my appreciation for all your hard work.'

I didn't know how to react so instead busied myself with unwrapping the little box. Inside, nestled in a dark-blue silk cocoon, lay an intricately engraved gold pocket watch. Carefully I pulled it out. I was speechless. I had never contemplated owning such a fine object. I turned it over. Inscribed on the back was: *Onwards and upwards! My thanks for your years of service. IKB.*

I didn't know what to think, let alone say, but managed to mumble my way through some sort of thanks.

That evening, when I showed the watch to Hortense, her first comment was: 'Just a watch?' Then she laughed. 'It is beautiful, but it's only what you deserve.'

Chapter 21

1854

I found it hard to adapt to my new life. Time seemed to slow, like watching snowflakes drift by on a winter's evening. Hortense left early and returned late, my hours in the shop punctuated only by a slow stream of customers.

The shop was crammed full of goods, piled high on shelves running up to the ceiling, stacked in the corners or hanging off hooks screwed in wherever there was space. It could take an age to serve a customer. There was little room at the counter and I regularly had to ferret around to find what someone wanted. My father was elderly now, mostly content to while away his days sitting on a stool and chatting to customers. When I asked where something might be, he often couldn't remember.

If there was one thing I had learned from Brunel, it was to strive for something better. I started to search for larger premises, somewhere I could employ more people and let the business grow. A place three times the size came up around the corner. My mother and father fretted about the risks but Hortense urged me to go ahead.

The day before we opened, I stood in the doorway and looked around. It had swallowed the contents of our old shop and still looked empty. I stood there, looking at the gaps in the shelves, my stomach churning. Had I made the most awful mistake? Did Brunel ever feel like this or was he always as certain as he appeared?

Trading the first day was slow. I tried not to think about what would happen if it didn't pick up. Steadily, though, more customers started to come. Now people could see what we stocked, and the extra space enabled me to take on an assistant. Business started to boom.

I was relieved. Hortense had announced she was pregnant a month after we had opened the shop. She had known a few weeks before that but hadn't wanted to worry or deflect me in the midst of setting up the new store. With the arrival of our baby boy, Alexander, I felt more keenly than ever the need to provide for my little family.

I couldn't quite believe it when I looked around the shop now. The shelves were full and goods were stacked in every available corner. We offered all manner of cleaning products, from the old-fashioned tried and tested to the latest formulations. Tin buckets and basins were arranged out front, the largest big enough for bathing. We carried a wide range of pots, pans and kettles, from the largest jam-making saucepans to the smallest milk pans, available in the usual cast iron or the more expensive copper. Hanging from the ceiling and ranged along the top shelves were different types of candelabra, from simple one- or two-candle cast-iron candlesticks to ornate brass chandeliers holding six, eight or even ten candles. Towards the back of the shop were our tools and ironmongery: forks, spades, hammers and saws; nails, hooks, hinges and latches, handles and knobs. Sometimes it felt as if Aladdin – whose adventures I had devoured as a child – had brought his cave to life in my shop.

Once things were on a more even keel, I would meet Hammond from time to time in one of our old drinking haunts to get an update on Brunel's goings-on. Despite her grounding, the SS *Great Britain* had been seen as a success and Brunel had been asked to design two sister ships for the Australian run. He chose to use a chap called Scott Russell to build them at his yard on the Thames because he had heard him speak at the British Association about his new hull shape, the wave line. As always Brunel admired anything – or anybody – innovative.

Even as the ships slid down the slipways, Brunel's imagination, ever fertile, was dreaming of bigger things. The coal en route to Australia was poor so he pondered the building of a giant ship, able to reach the other side of the world without refuelling. Nicknamed the 'Leviathan', and eventually christened the *Great Eastern*, she had begun to take shape on the banks of the river at Millwall. Every now and then I caught a glimpse of her over the roofs of the nearby factories and warehouses, shrouded in scaffolding.

Inevitably, perhaps, the work ended up way behind schedule. Scott Russell had underbid to win the job and went bankrupt. Hammond told me that the relationship between Brunel and Scott Russell had broken down irretrievably when Brunel found out that Scott Russell had lied about how much progress had been made. Work stopped while the receivers and the shipowners argued it out. Rumour had it that Brunel had put almost all of his money into the project, but still more funds were needed before they could recommence. It didn't sound good. I was torn between relief at not being involved and a sense of guilt that I wasn't there to help. I thought about investing from our savings, but Hortense persuaded me to reconsider.

Eventually the money was raised and the day scheduled for the launch arrived. It was to be open to the public, so I bought a ticket and made my way there early in the day, joining the stream of others attracted by the spectacle.

The area alongside the river seemed a magnet for all humanity: dock workers queuing by the gates for work, cart drivers and their boys waiting patiently to pick up loads, purveyors of all manner of items hawking along the sides of the road, and ladies of ill-repute standing quietly in shady side streets, their long dresses and extravagant headgear advertising their trade. The odour of unwashed people, stagnant water and rotting fruit and vegetables was almost overwhelming.

As I drew close to the shipyard, stalls offering snacks and treats to the crowds lined the path, the aroma of roasting chestnuts and caramelised nuts and apples temporarily banishing the underlying stench. Tall warehouses with barred windows designed to protect the goods offloaded from the wharfs nearby lined either side of the street. The crowds were heading through an arched gateway on the left, *Scott Russell's Yard* picked out in iron fretwork above the gate. I joined them and headed across the cobbles, past the tall ships' plate-making house towards the river.

The Leviathan sat lengthways just above high tide, its bulk blocking out the sun. At the far end I could see the vast rudder, its shaft as thick as a full-grown oak. In front of it was the propeller, more than twenty feet tall from tip to tip, painted dark red. She had paddle wheels to make her more manoeuvrable and capable of operating in shallow waters; I could see men carrying out last-minute adjustments inside the enormous paddle box, which was affixed to the side like a giant carnival wheel. Smoke drifted across the yard from the braziers used to heat the rivets until they glowed red; boys as young as six or seven scrambled along the side of the ship carrying them in tongs, ready to be placed and hammered over by the waiting riveters. I had read that she had a double-skinned hull for extra security and that some of the ship's workers believed that a rivet boy had fallen to his death and was encased inside. I thought it more likely that he had simply become fed up and quietly bunked off.

The scaffolding was gone, replaced with chains and hydraulic rams. The Leviathan was finally ready. A sideways launch of such a large ship had never been attempted before. A dry dock had been deemed too expensive and Brunel believed that the river wasn't wide enough to handle a normal launch. In any event, construction would have been almost impossible with the stern having to be built forty feet or more up in the air to achieve the correct slope.

The yard was packed with sightseers. Youngsters, unable or unwilling to afford a ticket, climbed on the walls to get a view over the heads of the crowds. Hammond told me that Brunel was aghast when he discovered that thousands of tickets had been sold to onlookers to help defray the cost overruns. I felt momentarily guilty. It hadn't stopped me buying one.

Large capstans had been secured up the slope from the ship to steady her progress in case she started to run out of control. I knew there was a risk she would roll over if she hit the water too fast. Each capstan was some twenty feet across, with four men manning each of its eight spokes, ready to slow the descent of the ship.

I carefully scanned the scene to see if I could spy Brunel. I saw a huddle of men standing beside one of the capstans, Brunel's diminutive figure facing away from me as he pointed to various parts of the ship and gave his final instructions to the waiting crew. I watched the photographer lead him over to a large winch to take the famous photograph of him standing before the holding chains looking confident. But photographs can be deceptive. Moments later I watched him as he toured the launch equipment, head down and chewing on his cigar in the way he did when anxious. I guessed he must be agonising over whether all was in place for a successful launch by this untried method.

My involvement with ships had always seemed to involve high tides and prayer. This time I was just a bystander, so I could do no more than watch and pray, for Brunel's sake, that things would go smoothly. The chocks were knocked out one by one. The stern of the ship started to move, quickly gathering pace, the timbers groaning as she moved down the ramp. A mournful groaning rang out from the ship herself as her metal plates twisted under the load. A gasp of wonder rippled through the watching crowd, as thousands of tons of iron slid towards the river.

Even from where I was standing, I could hear Brunel, as he yelled: 'Lean in, slow her down!'

It was too late. The capstan nearest me was rotating at speed, the men leaping clear. One man slipped and fell. He tried to get up, but a spinning bar came around and with a ghastly smack he dropped back down. I instinctively moved to help, but the crowd had surged forward and there was no way through.

The ship had come to a grinding, shuddering halt. When the stern slid down, the bow hadn't moved and now she lay canted at an angle, seized solid on the ramp. There was a moment's silence, then screams from the people standing nearest the winch. I shifted position and climbed upon a stack of timber to gain a better vantage point. The man was lying beneath one of the poles, not moving and with his head at an unnatural angle.

'Quickly, chock her back up!' called out Brunel, gesturing to the workmen to hammer the retaining chocks back in under the hull.

He called out urgently to others who were advancing on their fallen comrade.

'Hold back, hold back. We need to know the ship is held firm before we go near.'

I prayed that the ship wouldn't move again as the workmen worked to get the chocks back in. Two stood over each of the giant wooden wedges, taking turns with their sledgehammers, in a rhythmic but frenzied attack. The thuds reverberated around the yard, like a platoon's rifle fire as they sought to hold back the enemy's advance.

I breathed a sigh of relief when I could see that the ship was safely secured, the men no longer in danger of being crushed. Finally they were able to gently lay the injured man on a piece of tarpaulin and fold it carefully over his body. As they covered his head, I heard someone near me whisper, 'He's dead. That madman has got a lot to answer for.' I thought it unfair to blame Brunel. Without the crowds, it would have been easier for him to direct operations.

Brunel's old friend Stephenson had come along to provide support and I saw the two of them huddled in conversation under the dark stern of the ship. Brunel called over one of his assistants and soon after the marshals begun to usher us out. I guessed that he must need some time to work out how best to proceed.

I stood there for a moment, reflecting that if only the man had stayed down on the ground when he first fell, he would have survived. I shook my head, sad at the loss of yet another life.

I headed home feeling sorry for my former employer but also relieved that this time someone else would have to deal with his mood when he got back to the office. As I passed through the archway and into the street, I could hear a pair beside me laughing as one said to the other, 'Jinxed from start to finish, that ship.'

I wanted to chastise them but couldn't find the words. Then the moment was gone. I walked slowly back to the shop thinking that maybe they were right, perhaps he had pushed the boundaries too far. On the other hand, wasn't it the case that man's ability to open up new frontiers depended on men like Brunel?

I heard afterwards that Stephenson's suggestion was simple: apply more power. Over the four weeks before the next spring tide was due, Brunel sourced hydraulic rams from all over the country and fastened them to the timber work, ready to push the reluctant ship the rest of the way down the slope and into the water.

On the chosen day, I decided to stay in the shop and await the news. However, after an hour or two I could stand it no longer and hurried down to the riverbank opposite the launch site. Although Brunel had forbidden the sale of tickets, the river was crowded with boats of all shapes and sizes. Against the backdrop of the vast ship, they looked like toys bobbing around in a bath. It was extraordinary that so many people had time to spare to watch the spectacle. Why did humankind so enjoy the possibility of a disaster, I wondered.

As I arrived, there was a tremendous cheer. Those watching around me told me that the first attempt had been abandoned when one of the rams burst, spraying water everywhere; they had heard the debris ricocheting off the ship's sides and clattering down the workshop roofs. Another pump had been quickly installed in its place and now they were trying again. The ship had just begun to slide down the ramp when I turned up. A few minutes later, a mighty cry from the men manning the boats in the river in front of us indicated that the ship was no longer bound to the land but instead bobbing gently up and down in the tidal stream. She might not yet be kitted out with her masts and rigging, but she still looked like she was at last where she belonged, in the water.

I turned for home, finding it impossible to wipe the grin from my face.

Six months later, and almost three years to the day since I had left Brunel's employment, I received a short note from him asking if I would kindly meet with him down at Scott Russell's. I was surprised – I had not heard from him since I had left – but intrigued. Hortense was not best pleased but even though the shop was busy I arranged to meet with him the following day.

Brunel was waiting for me when I entered the yard and greeted me warmly. He looked tired. The events of the past few months must have taken their toll. The endless delays and cost overruns of the launch and days spent arguing with Scott Russell's lawyers, negotiating extra funds and overseeing the minutiae of the build were wearing him out. He suggested we walked across the cobbles to the riverside so that we could see the ship.

The sun beamed in from the east, lighting up the tidal ripples and sending a myriad of tiny rainbows dancing across the river. The ship sat calmly at anchor, the river traffic passing by as if she had always been there. She was an extraordinary sight, as tall and wide as one of the new apartments blocks springing up all over London. I wasn't surprised to see that little appeared to have been done since I had last seen her. I had heard that the cost of the launch had exhausted the remainder of the company's funds and the last six months had been spent raising more.

'Thank you for coming, Bennett. I won't beat about the bush. I need your help,' Brunel admitted, leaning heavily on his cane in a way which reminded me uncomfortably of Mrs Guppy at the Great Exhibition.

She had died six months later. I regretted the briefest of notes that I had dashed off to her after missing her reception, more interested in the fact that by doing so, I had chanced upon Hortense.

I shook my head clear of thoughts of Mrs Guppy and replied, 'Of course, I will assist you in any way I can.' I was flattered that he wanted my help and assumed he must need some paperwork sorting, or some such.

'The damn doctor has told me that I must take some time off. He insists that I get away completely. Mary and I are booked to go to Egypt, of all places.'

I was shocked. The longest holiday I could recall Brunel ever taking was his honeymoon in Wales, and even then he had stopped off en route to visit the site proposed for a new dock.

'Oh,' I said lamely.

'I was wondering if you would be able to mind the shop and see the ship finished – like you did back when I was laid up after the fire on the SS *Great Western*.'

'Oh,' I said again, somewhat at a loss for words.

'I know it's asking a lot, Bennett, but I don't know what else I can do. Scott Russell has left us all in a hell of a mess and I need someone I can trust to oversee things.'

He looked abject. I am not sure whether it was because he hated the idea of leaving his pet project or having to go down on bended knee to ask for my help.

I stared over Brunel's shoulder at the ship. I still felt keenly the sense of betrayal when he had let me go, but it would be exciting to be involved with the project, particularly with Brunel absent and unable to issue endless detailed instructions.

'I may be able to assist, sir, but it depends on when you need me to start and for how long. I have the family shop to consider. Business is booming.'

'The ship to Egypt leaves next week,' he sighed. I realised that he hadn't been able to bring himself to write to me until now, reluctant to give it all up until a few days before his departure.

I told him I needed to reflect on how the shop could be managed in my absence and that I would get back to him as quickly as I could.

I returned home to find Hortense sitting at the little upright piano I had bought her, playing something by her compatriot Bizet. She had told me she had learned as a child and so I had acquired the piano as a surprise. It seemed to take no time for her to pick it up again, and to my ears she sounded like a natural. She paused, her hands resting delicately on the keys.

'So, what did he want?'

I explained about Brunel's state of health and what he had asked of me.

'You aren't seriously contemplating it, are you?'

I knew what she meant. A year ago we had handed over the running of the first shop to James and opened our second. It had been Hortense's idea to have a business focused solely on tradesmen.

There were new houses and apartments going up everywhere, but few were offering a dedicated service to the builders.

We had been busy from the outset. Margins were lower but volumes good. Our customers could have purchased what they needed more cheaply from specialist suppliers, but mostly they wanted to get on with the job in hand and were prepared to pay a little extra for the convenience of having everything in one place.

Just then, Alexander came running in pursued by my mother. Now two years old, he was a happy little boy, doted on by all of us. He liked nothing better than to perch on a stool beside his grandfather in one of the shops, watching the comings and goings, his hand resting on my father's knee. When I looked across, I wasn't sure who was looking after whom.

Why was I even thinking about helping Brunel? We were happy. They say a newly-wed and her mother-in-law never really see eye to eye but maybe mine were the exception that proved the rule. Hortense and my mother were as thick as thieves, sharing the household chores and care of our child. If I took on the work Brunel had asked me to do, they would inevitably have to take on more, Hortense in the shop and my mother with Alexander and around the house. It really wasn't practical to offer Brunel any assistance.

'I don't think so, no. But despite the nature of our parting, I still feel a sense of loyalty. I know it doesn't make any sense.'

'Of course it doesn't make any sense. You would be mad to do it!'

I watched Alexander as he sat with my mother, picking up each finger of bread and contemplating it carefully before popping it into his mouth.

'His reputation is falling apart before his eyes. I feel sorry for him.'

'But it's not your concern any more. It's his legacy, not yours. Yours will be our business and our family.'

I had a restless night. Hortense was right of course but I still wasn't happy leaving my old employer in the lurch. We didn't speak of it again that day, but in the evening as we sat by the fire she laid her hand on my arm.

'I know you too well, Joseph, that's my problem. I can see you are troubled. If you feel you have to do this then do so.'

I looked across at her. How lucky I had been to find her again. It was still a little hard to believe that she had chosen to share her life with me.

'Thank you, Hortense. I don't know why, but I feel I owe him this.'

I juggled ship and shop as best as I could. It was odd at first to find myself back on familiar territory. I wished that Brunel were there to bat them away when I received what seemed like never-ending requests from the directors to justify the monies spent to date. 'They have managed to raise the funds that are needed to finish the job so why spend so much time raking over the past?' I said to Hortense, exasperated. Slowly, though, I began to find my feet. The directors asked for a proposal for whom to use to complete the fitting out, and despite my misgivings I eventually recommended Scott Russell.

Brunel had told me not to trust him, and I found him a difficult man. Thin with grey wavy hair, he was of average height but held himself tall; he was a dour man of few words and when he did speak had an almost impenetrably thick Scottish accent. Outwardly he maintained a certainty of demeanour that belied the failure of his business.

'I have heard tell that you ended up way behind schedule but always protested that things were on track,' I said when we met to discuss his bid.

'Well, sir, first of all you have to understand that Brunel kept interfering. He seemed to want to manage every detail and yet kept changing his mind.'

I couldn't help but recognise my old employer in the description I was hearing, and worked hard to avoid nodding my understanding.

He continued, 'I have studied ship design all my life, and when I built the first two ships he just let me get on with it. With the Leviathan it was a different story.'

'That doesn't justify misleading him over progress, though, does it?' I asked.

'No sir. I admit I am a proud man, and I am proud of the work I have done on that ship,' he said gesturing out the window at her vast bulk. 'I didn't want to risk not being allowed to finish her. Not that it did me much good in the end,' he finished, sighing.

It was a dilemma. He knew the ship better than anyone, but although he was the best qualified to carry out the work, he had provided the lowest quote and might again succumb financially and fail to complete it. I am not sure whether it was my endless requests for proof of progress or just that he was a difficult man to work with, but our relationship was frosty at best. I could see how he had worn Brunel down.

But it was true that he was committed to seeing the ship finished. Perhaps one of the reasons that he and Brunel clashed was that each had felt that the great ship was their baby. It was an odd term for something so large, built of iron, but it was often how Brunel used to describe her, his tone eerily similar to a parent eulogising over their newborn.

If Brunel had been dead, he would have turned in his grave at the decision to use Scott Russell after all the difficulties he had endured. Instead, he rushed back from Egypt as soon as he was able. His respite had done him little good, I thought. His eyes had not regained their familiar glint, and he looked tired and careworn. As I had done in numerous letters over the past weeks, I explained that things had progressed well under Scott Russell and that the ship was almost complete. He was anxious to inspect her as soon as possible and the next day we rowed out to where she was moored upstream of Greenwich Hospital, almost ready to put to sea.

She had been transformed since Brunel's last visit, six new masts each stretching up a hundred and fifty feet or more to touch the sky. As we drew near, I hoped it would lighten his spirits when he saw how luxuriously she had been fitted out. Claxton and I held his arms either side as Brunel stumbled across the bobbing gap between our boat and the ship's gangway. It must have taken fifteen minutes for us to make our way from the opening in the hull where the small boat docked to the deck high above. We climbed slowly up through the four levels from waterline to promenade deck, with Brunel pausing for breath at each and taking in his surroundings. He could scarcely fail to be impressed, despite her difficult birth.

Narrow stairs led from the entrance door at sea level to the deck above, but then we ascended a sweeping grand staircase that looked as if it had been borrowed from a stately home or high-class hotel. In the main saloon, ornate iron pillars lined the room, while in the centre a light and airy balcony overlooked the assembly rooms below. A magnificent piano stood against a mirrored wall at one end of the room, its lid covered in carvings that wouldn't seem out of place on the walls of a Roman temple. In front of us stretched a long mahogany dining table with elegant legs, chairs upholstered in red satin lining both sides. The ship looked more than ready to host a welcoming party for her well-heeled guests.

Brunel said little, conserving his energy, but every now and then allowed himself a little half-smile and a grunt of satisfaction. It would have been nice to have been complimented, but I knew that Brunel was unlikely to praise me for the appointment of Scott Russell, even though things had turned out well. We climbed the last set of stairs and reached the top deck. Brunel looked all in. He posed for another picture beside one of the funnels, his attempt at a brave face unable to mask his sickly pallor and emaciated frame.

Seconds later, his legs seem to fold beneath him and he collapsed onto the deck. I dashed to his side and propped him up against the side of the funnel. I waved the photographer away as he rushed to help, fearing – irrationally, I know – that he might take another picture.

'Bring a stretcher, quickly.'

Moments later Claxton was beside me and I was reminded powerfully of the last time we had stood over Brunel on the deck of the SS *Great Western* twenty years before.

'Don't worry, sir. We will get you home directly,' said Claxton.

'That's not what worries me,' replied Brunel, smiling weakly. 'It's what the doctors might do to me when I get there. I've had enough of their leeches and potions.'

Two sailors brought a stretcher and gently loaded Brunel on to it, just as he had been two decades earlier. Like last time, his face was white but now he seemed shrunken and his eyes had lost their sparkle. He really did look like a shadow of his former self.

He reached across and grasped my hand.

'You will see her finished and put to sea, won't you, Bennett?'

'Of course, sir.' I said, patting his hand, as you would a child.

I asked the sailors to carry him back down through the ship. It was like a funeral procession, I thought dismally, as we slowly descended in single file.

The sailors caught the stretcher on the handrail as they negotiated a turn in the stairs, causing Brunel to stifle a moan.

'Careful! Please take care!' I cried out.

He was drifting in and out of consciousness as we transferred him to the boat and rowed him ashore.

Chapter 22

1859

The room was quiet, the slow ticking of the small carriage clock on the mantelpiece marking the passage of time. I was reminded of those solitary lunches punctuated by the tick tock of the clock all those years ago when I first joined Brunel. So much time had passed. Now, instead of the sun streaming in through the large bay windows of his office, the bedroom was gloomy, lit only by a couple of candles on the mantelpiece and the light creeping around the side of the drawn curtains.

I could only just hear Brunel's breathing as he slept, a snuffling inhale followed by a long drawn-out sigh as he breathed out. It was four days since his collapse. The great ship was at last ready to put to sea and I had come to tell him that the final preparations were complete.

The door was thrown open and Mary bustled in with her children in tow. The eldest two were full-grown now: Isambard junior was twenty-two and Marc seventeen. Mary still treated them as if they were toddlers, shepherding and scolding them as they came into the room. Although the oldest, Isambard was training to become a lawyer, while it was Marc who was following his father into the engineering profession. Behind them was little Florence, still only twelve, and looking bereft. While her father was always quick to admonish his boys, he indulged her, chiding her without conviction when she ran into his study or left one of her dolls in the hallway.

Mary spied me on the far side of the bed and frowned.

'Bennett, if you would be so kind as to leave us, thank you,' she said rather brusquely.

Isambard turned to his mother. 'Let him stay. He chose to help Father out when he needed it.'

'That's as maybe,' said Mary, busy straightening the blankets, 'but although your father may confuse family with work, I don't.'

I didn't want to be at the centre of a family dispute and stood to leave, but awoken by the noise Brunel lifted his hand as if he was about to grant a benediction. He was merely seeking to arrest the clamour. He spoke so softly that we had to strain to hear.

'There are things I need to discuss with Bennett,' he whispered, coughing from the effort. Then, without lifting his head from the pillow, he turned in my direction.

'Please wait outside, Bennett. I will call you back in a few minutes and we can talk.'

I had only been waiting a minute or two when a messenger arrived and handed me a note. I could hardly believe it. The *Great Eastern* when setting out on her maiden voyage had suffered from an explosion. A valve had been left closed, a funnel had been blown off and several stokers killed. I was horrified. Must all that Brunel do with the sea come to grief? First the fire on the *Great Western*, then the grounding of the *Great Britain*, and now this. I didn't know how I was going to tell him.

The door flew open and Mary and her family swept out. As Mary passed by me, I reached out to stop her. She gave my hand on her arm such a fearsome and contemptuous look, that I withdrew it immediately.

'My apologies,' I said, 'but I have received some terrible news.'

I told her about the accident.

Mary waited for her children to move further away, then took my elbow in a firm grip and drew me into the corner. She whispered fiercely in my ear.

'We must all work together to avoid him becoming an object of pity or even worse a laughing stock. First we had the atmospheric railway and now this. You had better tell him. We can't afford for him to hear about it like he did about Scott Russell.'

I didn't need her sharp, knowing look to understand this was a barbed comment aimed at my failure to keep Scott Russell away from the SS *Great Eastern*.

I went back into the room and sat down, wondering how I might break the news. The room was quiet, smelling faintly of antiseptic, a few coals glowing in the grate. The clock ticked as I waited, not wishing to disturb Brunel if he was resting. The sheets rustled as he stirred and shifted in the bed.

'Bennett? Bennett, is that you?'

'Yes, sir,' I replied, and then after a pause. 'I have something I need to tell you.'

'Before you do, fetch me something, will you? In my writing desk there is a leather notebook with a small lock. Can you find it and bring it here?'

I lifted the lid of the desk and saw tucked to the right the book he must mean. It was old and battered, black and leatherbound, with one of those little metal clasps locking it shut. It could be easily forced but I suppose would deflect the casual finder.

'Open it,' whispered Brunel from his bed. 'The key is in one of the drawers.'

I rummaged around until I found the little brass key hidden at the bottom of an old snuff box.

I opened it and read the first few words.

'I had always intended that this book should perish with me…'

I flicked on a few pages.

'What a life, the life of a dreamer building castles in the air… what time I waste…'

I realised that it must be his journal, written when he was a younger man. Brunel said something I couldn't catch. I bent over close and he whispered very quietly, 'There is a page somewhere near the middle that I need you to find. It talks about Eleanor.'

I fumbled my way through the book, anxious to find the page, but ready to hide the book if Mary came in. As I flicked through the pages, scanning each rapidly, I realised that much of it had been written when Isambard was perhaps seventeen or eighteen, at a low ebb with the failure of so many of his dreams and ideas. The Thames Tunnel work had been stopped, the Gaz engine had come to nothing. He was injured, with no work, and what must have seemed to him poor prospects, while his rivals were busy designing railways and other major projects. He was worried that he would be left behind, cast aside as others built their reputations.

I found a page mentioning Eleanor, or EH, as he described her, and read it out to Brunel:

'What am I to do? I love her but what can I offer now my fortunes are at such a low ebb. We have become so intimate and yet I am unsure. It feels like we have travelled too far to turn back but what gentleman compromises a woman in this way…'

'Stop, stop! That's the page,' he said. 'Please rip it out. I don't want my family seeing it.'

Not wishing to damage the book by simply pulling out the page, I scanned the room for a knife or scissors. There was a dark wooden washstand in the corner, the rim of its wide china basin resting in a hole cut in its centre. Beside it was Brunel's shaving equipment. I quickly crossed over, picked up his razor and took it and the book across to the table by the window. Under the light, I carefully excised the page, cutting along the edge of the spine.

'Good,' said Brunel. 'Burn it.'

'The smell might cause suspicion,' I said. 'I can take it home and burn it in the range later.'

Brunel gave a deep sigh and nodded his assent.

'Thank you, Bennett. That's a weight off my mind.'

I folded the paper and tucked it in my jacket pocket. I felt an almost desperate desire to take the book, rush home and read it from cover to cover. Over the years I had seen only the smallest glimpses of doubt from Brunel, but from the extracts I had read he seemed to harbour the same kinds of worries and concerns as the rest of us. Maybe it was the angst of a young man at a low ebb, but he had committed his innermost thoughts and feelings to the journal and I was keen to read more. I reluctantly locked it and placed it back in the writing desk and the key in the drawer.

I resumed my seat in the pleasantly over-stuffed armchair beside his bed. It would be easy just to sit here quietly, I thought, but I knew that sooner or later I was going to have to break the news.

'I am sorry, sir, but you may remember when I came in there was something I said I needed to tell you.' I took a deep breath. 'There's been an explosion on the *Great Eastern*.'

'What?' Brunel tried to sit up.

'We don't know the full story yet but they believe steam pressure was somehow trapped in a funnel condenser and caused it to explode. The ship has suffered only minor damage but unfortunately five stokers were killed and one is seriously injured.'

Brunel hauled himself up on the pillows and stared at me. If it were possible, he grew even paler as he seemed to age in front of my eyes.

'God that ship!' He turned and stared at the wall. 'I will be humiliated.'

He looked so agitated I worried that this might hasten the end. He was convinced that it had all come to nothing, his youthful dreams. What could I say to help him? The press would probably have a field day, but surely it would wash over.

'No, sir,' I replied. 'There might be a few days of nonsense in the press but it will pass. People will see your work for what it is, visionary.'

I still wasn't sure that they would, but it was what Brunel needed to hear. I leant over the bed and held a cup of water to his lips, gently tipping it up so he could swallow. It would be wrong to say colour returned to his cheeks but he did look slightly less ashen.

'I've pushed the boundaries too far, Joseph,' he said as I wiped away a few spilled drops of water.

Maybe he was right, maybe if he had been more careful then some of the accidents wouldn't have happened – Martha's husband, the worker manning the capstan at the *Great Eastern* launch, so many others I didn't want to recall. I needed to find something more positive to say. I thought back to when I had first arrived, a youngster keen to make my mark.

'You probably don't remember, but when I first joined you I said I wanted to work with the people shaping the future, not those playing a supporting role. You have done that. People have seen the wonders of the modern world and their minds have been opened to the possibilities of scientific progress thanks to you. Your railway has brought thousands to London, to let them see beyond the narrow confines of their day-to-day lives.'

I helped him settle back down into the bed.

'But at what sacrifice?' he muttered as his eyes started to close. 'I have hardly seen my children grow up. I have been obsessed with work.'

'You are being too hard on yourself, sir. Your children are a credit to you.'

He smiled his thanks and drifted off to sleep.

He died six days later, his family at his side. I felt strangely numb. My life had been so inextricably linked with his for so many years and now he was gone.

I was surprised a week later to receive an invitation to the private family funeral. Isambard junior must be a stronger character than I had thought to have prevailed over what I imagine would have been Mary's preferences. I arrived as Brunel's coffin was brought out of the house to be loaded into the hearse. The small family group were waiting at the top of the steps clinging together like mussels on a rock. I joined them. Mary ignored my greeting, but Isambard and Henry shook me warmly by the hand.

The hearse was a large glass-sided carriage, its black bodywork gleaming. The horses, anxious to set off, stamped their feet, the tall black plumes attached to their harnesses waving in the air.

The streets had been deserted, but as we descended the steps to take up our positions behind the hearse, people started emerging from their houses. Soon the street was lined with folk, Brunel's peers standing on the steps while their servants climbed the stairs from basements and gathered quietly on the pavement.

The hearse set off, preceded by a featherman carrying yet more black plumes and two mutes wearing 'weepers' – black ribbons that hung down to their waists. Although nowadays it might be seen as excessive, back then funerals were more ornate, and by the standards of the day it was a simple cortege.

Mary choked back a sob, overwhelmed by the sight of so many of her neighbours showing their respect, silently removing their hats as we proceeded down the road. We turned the corner to find a mass of people lining both sides of the street, members of the Institute of Civil Engineers, managers and workers from the Great Western Railway and tradesmen and suppliers to the Brunels from around Westminster. I swallowed hard. He would be… would *have* been pleased to see how many people wanted to honour his memory.

I was shocked to spy Scott Russell in the crowd, and hoped to God that Mary didn't see him. A strangled cry dashed that hope. She rushed over to him before anyone could stop her. The procession slowed, coming to an uneasy halt.

'What are you doing here?' she hissed.

Isambard and I tried to usher her on but she shrugged us off.

'I have come to pay my respects to a great engineer,' he replied in his strong Scottish accent.

'The way you could show respect is to stop claiming his work as your own,' she spat.

In Brunel's obituaries the papers had been dismissive of the *Great Eastern*, calling it Brunel's Last Folly and the Great White Elephant. Worse, some had argued that Scott Russell had saved the day, getting the ship finished while Brunel was convalescing. Mary was clearly convinced that he had been briefing the press.

'Perhaps it would be best if you left, so that the family can grieve in peace,' I suggested.

'Just as you wish,' said Scott Russell, slowly removing his hat and bowing. 'But I want you to know that I wished Brunel no harm. Although we had our differences, he did indeed achieve great things.'

With that, he stepped backwards and disappeared into the crowd. Mary took a couple of deep breaths and placed her hand on Isambard's arm, indicating that we should rejoin the procession.

'Horrible man. How dare he show his face.'

She turned to me. 'Thank you, Bennett. I know that you will always protect my husband's reputation.'

I breathed a sigh of relief that we had escaped without further public embarrassment. As we walked slowly on, I wondered whether Mary's words had been a compliment or a warning.

We reached the cemetery at Kensal Green where Brunel was to be buried in the family plot. As we passed through the gates, I looked back. Behind us were hundreds of mourners, a top-hatted army stretching back as far as the eye could see. Each had decided to make the long journey out here. It might be a small family interment, but his friends and colleagues hadn't let that stand in the way of showing their appreciation for his life's work.

His work had exhausted him in the end and he died aged just 53, but Brunel should have been proud of what he had achieved. What a pity we aren't able to see how the world judges us after we are gone.

Chapter 23

1864

Although Brunel had been born in Portsmouth and lived most of his life in London, Bristol had clearly adopted him as one of their own, deciding to celebrate his life in style. Some get a mausoleum, others a plaque or an elegant tomb. Brunel was getting a bridge.

I was excited but nervous, like a child anxiously anticipating their first day at school. Would the engineers have done justice to his talent – his unique ability to create an aesthetically pleasing blend of the natural and man-made?

I walked slowly up the hill, past rows of grand Georgian terraces decked out with bunting. I could smell the sharp vinegary tang of the sea as gusts of wind eddied through the winding streets, the air filled with the snap and crack of the flags as they rattled and banged in the breeze.

It was five years since he had died but it felt like only months, and I had been unable to resist the temptation to come. The climb from the docks to the Downs had always been steep but now I was over fifty I thought it might be the end of me. My wheezing sounded far off, as if an old chain-smoking vagrant was toiling his way up beside me. Unlike the flat London thoroughfares, the roads in Bristol wound their way uphill like serpents twisting and turning under a snake-charmer's spell. I stopped, gripping the railings separating the houses from the pavement. I drew in lungfuls of air, bent over so that I might breathe more easily. I must have looked like a man who had spent his life lifting heavy loads rather than a quill pen. It had been hard enough working for Brunel for all those years; even from the heavens he seemed to be making my life difficult.

He wanted to be seen as the most accomplished, most successful member of his profession. He died thinking he had failed, destroyed by his own hubris and by the taunts of his enemies. As I drew in a deep breath and began to plough my way upwards once more, I hoped a much happier man was looking down now, watching people from across the kingdom come to celebrate his achievements.

A light horse-drawn carriage came up behind me, the driver yelling at me to get out of the way. As it swept past, I glimpsed inside a familiar face, even if it was somewhat more lined than when I had last seen it. John Lowther was on his way to join the great and the good at the top of the hill. He was looking out the side of the carriage and I turned my head to avoid catching his eye. The Yorkshireman might be considered part of society's great and good today, but Brunel wouldn't have welcomed him here.

Large crowds were passing now, heading towards the bridge as the time for the grand opening neared. I was overtaken by all manner of folk: young lads skipping about and chatting as they went; dock, rail and shipyard workers pleased to get a few hours off work, but also happy to pay homage to the man who had created jobs for them; merchants and craftsmen who worked around the dock area and city centre. Most were clothed in their Sunday best.

For the wealthier ladies, sating gowns poked out from under the thick capes protecting them against the December chill. The less well-off made do with threadbare, roughly made overcoats over their clean but tired suits or dresses. I paused every few minutes to catch my breath.

The crowds thickened and the carriage drivers with the gentry on board called out to be let through. Mostly people moved aside good-naturedly to let them pass. One of my earliest memories is stepping out of the way of thundering carriages. They probably weren't moving very quickly – everything is amplified when you are young – but my parents had constantly urged caution. Sometimes you heard them coming from way off, calling out the wares they had on offer to households as they slowly trundled past, others came upon you quietly and at speed, cursing you as they flew by. The rumble of carriage wheels always caused my heart to quicken. Although I was very young, I still have a vivid memory of playing in the street, absorbed with chasing a small piece of bright cotton blowing in the wind. There were shouts that I didn't realise had anything to do with me until I looked up to see a coach hurtling down the road towards me, the noise growing louder like a rapidly approaching storm. I had drifted into the main thoroughfare at the end of our road, and it was only the quick reactions of the driver hauling hard on the reins that kept me safe.

I reached Royal York Crescent and paused again. Brunel and I had often made a detour along this long, curved terrace to enjoy the views over the city and docks to the countryside beyond as we made our way up to the bridge or to the Merchant Venturers, the exclusive club for Bristol's wealthiest businessmen. I reached the rocky outcrop overlooking the gorge and finally caught sight of the newly completed bridge. I am not someone that shows a lot of emotion, and of course I was very familiar with the design drawings and illustrations that had been prepared to gain final approval, but the sight of the bridge in front of me made me gasp.

The last time I had been here, the money had run out long before and there had been just two great brick and stone towers isolated on either side of the gorge, looking forlorn and forever separate, like a young couple gazing at each other across a dance floor. But now Brunel's vision had been brought to life in front of me. Long chains draped in loops from one shore to the other between the simple arched towers, below them a slender roadway crossed over the gorge, supported from the chains by thin vertical links.

I realised that William Barlow and John Hawkshaw, the engineers appointed to finish the works as a mark of respect to Brunel, had produced something even more striking than he had originally sketched.

Standing in front of this wonderful bridge, I thought how ironic it was that controversy still raged over his legacy. Some still thought Brunel's ideas for a modern broad gauge railway extravagant and self-aggrandising, while many others saw them as far-sighted and forward-thinking. But it was the SS *Great Eastern* that had polarised opinions. It was an enormous beast, and many of his supporters – myself included – felt that he had pushed too far beyond the limits of what was practicable.

Perhaps every successful man makes his enemies along the way, some of whom are envious only of success itself. Others saw the ship, and by extension Brunel, as heroic, a sign of the future brought to life today. They were proved right in a way. She was the only ship large enough to lay the first transatlantic cables. Never mind that she had a difficult birth and had been a bad investment for her first owners, the ship's legacy was a telegraph communications network spanning the world.

Brunel would never know the efforts his family and his supporters would put into promoting his legacy. This bridge was a testament to their unceasing efforts. Although it was some way away from me so I could see little of the detail, I could still see that it was beautiful. The stonework glowed in the winter sunshine, the bands of sandstone encircling each pillar lit up honey-coloured against heavily shadowed granite blocks. Even the battleship-grey chains came alive as they shivered in the wind, joined to the roadway by gossamer thin threads.

As I reached the lawns atop Sion Hill, I found people milling around as if at a country fair. A brass band played lively tunes as children scurried in and out of the crowds. The smell of roasting chestnuts and charred meat filled the air. Many of the workmen were clustered around the beer tents. The ladies and gentlemen kept their distance, strolling through the stalls and amusements.

I made my way slowly along the path to get a closer view, keeping to one side to avoid the crowds and darting youths. The rows of stalls stocked all manner of things and I paused to look at lithographs of the newly completed bridge and celebratory mugs and plates printed with images of Brunel's great works – the Box Tunnel, railway engines, his ships and bridges.

Of course, there were pictures of Brunel himself. I particularly liked the famous one set against the launching chains of the *Great Eastern*, with him looking confident that all would be well, not yet knowing how difficult a process getting that leviathan into the water would be. I came close to buying one of the scarfs with a print of the bridge, but the finest were too expensive and the affordable a little tawdry.

People began making their way to a roped off area near the bridge where the cream of Bristol Society were gathered. I knew that Mary Brunel had refused to come, claiming that insufficient acknowledgement had been made of her husband's role in designing the bridge. Difficult to the last, I thought.

I have attended a lot of opening ceremonies over the years and knew the arrangements well. There would be long speeches from a variety of people who had had some role to play in the approval, financing, organisation or building of the new scheme. Most of the crowd wouldn't be able to hear, or if they could, wouldn't be that interested anyway, and would become increasingly restless and rowdy.

I had been travelling since early in the morning, making my way to Paddington Station, taking Brunel's Great Western Railway from London, and then walking across Bristol to be here for the opening, but the moment that I had set eyes on the completed bridge had been enough to make the day worthwhile. I didn't need to stay long, and after standing quietly for a few more minutes taking in the new bridge I turned to go.

As I reached the edge of the hill and began to descend once more towards the station, I turned back for one last look. The bridge looked as if it had always been there. Brunel's design blended perfectly with the contours of the landscape. The large towers echoed the rock faces along the edge of the gorge, and the bridge deck, high up above the gorge, created a wonderful symmetry as it joined the two sides.

I had a little time before the train back to London so I sat in the station waiting room. Brunel had had an intimate involvement in the design of every aspect of the railway and its station, and this room had been designed by him as an expansive but comfortable drawing room. It featured a dado rail running around the room, ornate plasterwork on the ceiling and heavy velvet drapes at the windows. A large carved stone fireplace with bright coals glowing to ward off the chill occupied one side of the room and gave off an intense but pleasant charcoal like aroma.

Above the fireplace was a large gilt-framed mirror in which it was hard to avoid your own reflection. My back and shoulders were rounded, compared with when I was a young man and I have to admit that I now did what my mother always told me not to do, which was to stoop, bent over from years spent hunched over desks.

My hair was well and truly grey and had become wispy with patches of scalp showing through. People talk about pink skin but mine was off-white with a few liver spots here and there, more the colour and texture of an old sheet than a baby's light pink blanket. I don't consider myself vain, but we all regret from time to time the passing of our youth.

Sitting in the waiting room was a young man, somewhat similar in build to me – that is to say, tall and thin. He carried a small moustache which seems an affectation of many a young man these days. Every minute or so, he followed a pattern. He sat up in his chair, looked around the room, checked his watch and reached inside his collar to release the tension.

I guessed the suit and tie were new and that he was on his way by train on a matter of some importance to his future prospects, given his air of nervousness and his new attire. Attempting to put him at ease and, if I am honest, my curiosity having been piqued, I engaged him in conversation.

I started by asking him if he had seen the opening of the new bridge and he said that he had not, on account of wanting to be sure to catch his train, but that he had of course seen it being completed over the last few weeks.

I suggested that the train journey must be of some importance if he was so keen not to miss his train. He told me he was off to London for an interview to join the offices of a renowned law firm as a clerk.

'Are there not good law firms in Bristol?' I asked.

'Of course, but London is where the most interesting legal work is conducted,' he replied, 'and I want to learn from the best.'

Before I had an opportunity to question him further, a porter, bringing in an icy blast as he opened the door to the waiting room, announced the train had arrived and passengers wanting to travel to London should embark.

As we parted ways to go and find our seats, I wished him all the best for his future. With the passengers aboard and the doors slammed shut, the train pulled out with a blast of steam, like a weightlifter's exhaled breath as he lets his heavy bar drop back to the ground.

We made our way through the outskirts of Bristol towards Bath. I gazed absent-mindedly out of the window at the passing countryside and thought how it might all have turned out for the better if I had had a clearer sense of my own future at his age. I judged him to be around eighteen or nineteen years old, a year or two younger than when I had first met Brunel.

The train stopped outside Swindon, I suppose to wait for a platform to be free or a signal to turn green. To my left stood the newly built workers' houses and locomotive sheds, already blackened with soot. The engine sheds ran on for what seemed like miles, giant temples to the railway and the age of steam. People often described their interior as like Dante's inferno, the darkness and flames, the endless crashing, banging and thumping of heavy machinery, and the men ceaselessly working the metal with their heavy lump hammers. To me, however, the smell of hot iron being forged and oil burning off as machines shaped metal formed a heady mixture that reminded me powerfully of man's ingenuity. I had smelt the same smell at shipyards, factories and mills. It was the smell of progress, of the creation of new technologies that would make people's lives easier or open up their horizons to new places.

Since Brunel's death five years ago, Mary and the family had worked tirelessly to protect and bolster his reputation. His extraordinary bridge across the River Tamar at Saltash had been completed just before he died. The magnificent bow-like structure sat atop an iron column three-quarters of the height of Nelson's in Trafalgar Square, the Admiralty blindly insisting that there be sufficient clearance for their sailing ships with the tallest masts – just as Brunel's steam-powered vessels were consigning them to the graveyard.

Brunel had appointed Robert Brereton as resident engineer, and due to Brunel's ill health, Brereton had overseen much of the work. The family heard that he was to present a paper to the Institute of Civil Engineers describing the way that the central column had been built – using air pressure to keep the caisson watertight. Isambard junior was immediately dispatched to ensure that Brereton would be in no doubt as to whom he should credit for all the key design decisions.

Scott Russell remained a thorn in the family's side, constantly claiming credit for the successful parts of the *Great Eastern* while insisting all the flawed decisions were Brunel's. They needn't have worried. Although appreciated by marine architects for his wave-line hull design, his reputation never recovered from the financial irregularities that surrounded the building of the SS *Great Eastern*.

After the *Great Eastern*'s funnel was repaired, she made the fastest transatlantic crossing yet seen at just over nine days, but she did seem to be cursed. Perhaps the rumour about the rivet boy lost in the hull was true. Her paddle wheels and rudder were broken in a storm and she was later holed on a rock off Long Island (when her double-skinned hull proved its worth by keeping her watertight). Passengers took fright and cancelled their bookings, and the company went bust.

Daniel Gooch, Brunel's old locomotive man, took the lead in seeing her converted to lay the first transatlantic telegraph cable. Brunel's creation was finally seen as a triumphant success, joining America and Great Britain in a way unimaginable before. Perhaps fate – or God – always had in mind a higher calling for Brunel's last great hurrah.

The train finally started to move and slowly rolled into Swindon station. While the locomotive took on fuel and water, myself and a few fellow passengers visited the station for refreshment. It had been some time since I had been inside. Brunel had refused to use it, sending them a pithy put-down which I well remember: 'I didn't believe you had such a thing as coffee in the place, I am certain I never tasted any.'

Perhaps it had new owners. The coffee was perfectly acceptable and the cakes were rather good. I found it very congenial to spend a few minutes at a little table beside the fire.

The young fellow I had met just before we left Bristol took a seat at a nearby table and when the guard called us back to the train, I introduced myself – his name was George Simpkins – and asked if he would care to join me for the remainder of the journey.

We clambered aboard and were off again, clacking along to the beat of wheels on the track and the heavy breathing of the locomotive.

'Forgive me, Mr Bennett,' said young Simpkins, 'I should have asked what brought you to Bristol.'

'Not at all, not at all. I went to see the opening of the bridge.'

'Do bridges interest you?' he asked politely.

'This particular one, yes. I used to work for Mr Brunel.'

George leant forward, his interest aroused.

'Really? What was he like?'

Where to start? I thought.

'Well, he was inspirational. Very driven. Always striving to push the limits.' I couldn't stop myself adding, 'But probably like all great figures, he could be a bit unreasonable at times.'

'I am sure you know, but he is seen as a hero in Bristol. How long did you work with him?'

'About twenty years – from the beginnings of this railway to the launch of the *Great Eastern*.' I felt a moment's guilt at omitting the four-year gap, but that would bring questions I wouldn't want to answer.

'Gosh, I would love to be at the centre of things like that. That's why I am off to London. The firm I am joining does a lot of legal work for Parliament.'

I sat back, remembering the endless parliamentary meetings it had been my misfortune to endure. I wondered if George had any idea what he was letting himself in for.

'How did that come about?'

'I have been working in the offices of Mr Gore-Langton, the Member of Parliament for Bristol. He helped me. My father is a merchant, but I have always been drawn to politics.'

I smiled, remembering my desire to break free as a young man. I almost asked him if he was prepared for the sacrifices he might have to make, but knew that I would probably come across as rather condescending.

He frowned and sat back.

'I see you smiling. What did you find amusing in what I said?'

'I am sorry. I wasn't belittling your aspirations. Quite the contrary. My father ran a shop and at your age I too wanted to do something different. I was drawn to engineering.'

'Do you have any advice for me?' George asked rather earnestly. He was clearly a thoughtful young man, inclined to take himself too seriously perhaps.

Advice for him? What would be the lessons from all my years spent working with Brunel?

'That's a difficult question,' I replied, giving myself time to reflect. 'I don't think anyone has ever asked me that before.'

I ran my hands through my thinning hair as I thought what I could usefully say to someone like George at the start of their career. What had I learned? I thought back to Brunel's treatment of his suppliers. Perhaps not to lose your moral compass? That sounded a little too much like what his parish priest might say. Possibly it was to stay open to new ideas and opportunities. Something Brunel was far more capable of than I. Maybe for me it was around having maintained a belief in what I was doing.

'I hesitate to offer any guidance. It seems such a long time ago when I was in your position. I was going to say make sure you are involved in things that you have a passion for, but I think that's a bit trite. You won't always have the luxury of doing what you fancy. There was a number of years when I wasn't sure why I was still doing what I was doing, but I couldn't see a way out. And in the end it was probably for the best that I did stay.'

I stopped talking, conscious I wasn't making a lot of sense and that I was beginning to reveal details about myself that I would rather not.

'I am not sure what to take from all that!' said George, laughing.

I laughed in turn.

'Well, I did tell you no one had asked me before.'

I tried again. I thought back to the small boy I had seen in the alley on the way to Brunel's club many years ago. He had little say in how his life turned out, and I suppose had been lucky that I had been there to give him a helping hand.

'Many people don't get to decide what they do with their lives, but you have the wits and attitude that mean you will have choices to make. I suppose I am saying to grab the opportunities when they arise, even if at the time it might feel somewhat alarming.'

I paused, wondering if I had followed my own advice. Hadn't I done that when I had got the job at Maudslay's and left my father's shop behind? After that, though, I had stuck with Brunel through thick and thin. How ironic, I realised with a shiver of surprise, that my decision to leave the comfort of Brunel's employment to marry Hortense was a direct result of me watching him over so many years, always ready to take on a new challenge. So in the end, I suppose he had taught me to make braver decisions than I might otherwise have made.

George interrupted my train of thought.

'What else did you learn from working with him?'

Feeling rather foolish, I saw that he was interested in what I had learned from Brunel rather than my life story. I thought for a moment.

'I suppose to stretch yourself as far or even beyond what you think you are capable of. I would never have expanded my business the way I have if it hadn't been for working for Brunel.'

'What do you mean "stretch yourself", if you don't mind me asking?'

'In my case, it was about opening new shops; in Brunel's case, it was about being willing – or even keen – to embrace new ways of doing things. He pushed things too far sometimes but he wasn't like some, content with the status quo however unsatisfactory it might be.'

George nodded enthusiastically.

'One of my father's favourite sayings is that you can't make an omelette without cracking a few eggs. I suppose you mean something similar.'

'Yes, I think so. My experience is that if you want to make your mark on the world, as Brunel did with his railways and ships, you have to take up what others see as unreasonable positions to have any chance of driving things through.'

'But how do you do that while avoiding falling out with everyone around you?'

It was a comment that to me revealed more about his feelings about his father than anything else, but nevertheless the same question could as well apply to Brunel.

'Maybe it's a price you have to pay if you really want to challenge the status quo,' I mused.

The train slowed as we reached the London suburbs. I looked out the window and saw half a dozen boys playing in the sidings outside Paddington, hopping back and forth to balance one-footed on a sleeper. They looked carefree and reminded me of my son, Alexander, about to turn nine, waiting back at home. He was a delight, a cheeky grin almost permanently planted on his face. Full of mischief, but kind too, always happy to help around the shop.

What would he do with his life, I wondered. Would he be satisfied working in the family business, or would he, like George and me, need to reach beyond the narrow confines of his early years? Whatever path through life he chose, I hoped my son wouldn't feel himself to be living in my shadow, as Brunel had lived in his father's, constantly striving to live up to, or even outperform, his deeds. Which is better? To have a father's reputation to live up to, like Brunel, or like me wanting to escape what you see as your parent's humdrum existence. Both put a yoke around your neck, a heavy burden that can take most of your life to lift.

With a final blast of her whistle, the train drew into the platform and came to a shuddering halt in a cloud of steam. George leapt up to open the carriage door and help me alight. To my surprise and pleasure, Hortense and Alexander were there to greet me. I introduced George and told him that he must come and visit us once he was settled. He took his leave and we stood and watched until he was lost in the crowds leaving the station.

Although a part of me envied him as he walked towards a new life bringing challenges and opportunities yet unknown, I was thankful that I had reached that stage in my life where I no longer had the inclination or time to change my destiny.

What a pity Brunel died feeling that he had failed, I thought. If he had been there today to see his bridge completed by his peers in homage to his life, perhaps he would be able to rest in peace. Yes, there were people who were wounded by the way he treated them or the money they lost, but his legacy was secure. He had set standards that others followed and everywhere there are railways, bridges and ships which incorporate his ideas and bear testament to his engineering genius.

I wouldn't have made the sacrifices he did as he sought to fulfil his ambitions. I am more than happy with what I have achieved and to have my loving family around me. Perhaps some people aren't destined to find their own peace. Their fate is to change the lives of others. Not many are able to say, as Brunel could, that they have truly transformed the world.

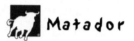Matador

For exclusive discounts on Matador titles,
sign up to our occasional newsletter at
troubador.co.uk/bookshop